ANTIDOTE

Don't... Book Two

JACK L. PYKE

CREDITS

Cover art: Adrienne Wilder https://authoradriennewilder.blogspot.com
Formatting: Joseph Lance Tonlet http://josephlancetonlet.com/
Proofreading: Archer Kay Leah https://archerkayleah.wordpress.com/

DEDICATIONS

TO ALL MY BETA READERS: I hope you make it through this one!!

TO MY BETA READERS: on this reedited edition: Kat, Vicki, Jane, Elaine, Debra… thank you sooo much, guys!!

Love always,
Jack

CONTENTS

	Acknowledgments	i
1	Edge Me	1
2	A Slice of Jack	11
3	Working Order	21
4	Ensuring Rank	33
5	Tempting the Devil	49
6	Thursday	61
7	Masters' Circle	69
8	Re-Mastered	81
9	Sleeping with the Pack	95
10	Don't…	107
11	Jan, Meet Cutter	117
12	Far from Okay	129
13	Collared	147
14	Trust, Respect	157
15	Feeling the Chill	167
16	Hiding	179
17	Straightening out the Kinks	191
18	Death-Play	199
19	Play in Session	209
20	The Taste of Things to Come	221
21	White Christmas	233
22	Cracker, Jack?	241
23	Christmas Blues	255

24	Vince	265
25	Escape	275
26	Home Away from Home	285
27	Keal	299
28	Main Street	313
29	Aftercare	323
30	Broken Pieces	333
31	Blame Games	341
32	State of Mind	353
33	OCD	365
34	Lost Within	383
35	Where I Want to Be	398
36	Watchers	407
37	Do You Miss Me?	417
38	The Devil You Don't Know	431
39	The Devil You Always Do	446
40	Missed Opportunity	457
41	Written in the Darkness	467
42	Lost Voices	479
43	Psych-Play	493
44	Head Games	504
45	Mercedes, Mercedes-Fucking-Benz	515
46	After Gray	527

HEARTFELT ACKNOWLEDGMENTS

TO MY CONSULTANTS:
I have the best with me:

Elaine (my computer and MI5 technical guru!),
Vicki (my dark content edit go-to lady!),
Katerina (my medical-and-everything-else stunner),
and Dilo Keith (as always, awesome conceptual guidance into Gray's
world!).

It wouldn't be the Don't… series without you guys!!

TO MY PRODUCTION TEAM:

Adrienne Wilder: your cover art is amazing!!
Joseph Lance Tonlet: thank you, thank you thank you!!
Archer: your proofreading is still so frickin' awesome!!

SHARED-WORLD NOTE

Introduction to The Society of Masters: two-worlds, one BDSM
universe.
Don't… series & Deliver Us series.

This novel introduces a cross-over world between my Don't series
and Lynn Kelling's Deliver Us series. Here you see mention of a trip
to America, where Jack, Jan, and Gray meet Dare, Trace, and Gabe.
These are Mrs. Kelling's characters from her Deliver Us series, and
what happens over in America is continued over in Lynn Kelling's
Forgive Us. I then borrow Dare, Gabe, and Trace for both Don't… 3
(*Breakdown*), and Don't 4 (*Backlash*).

Huge thanks to Lynn for allowing me to use her guys, and her skill
for portraying Jack, Jan, and Gray in hers!

If you want to see what happens over in America, please check out
Lynn Kelling's website at:

http://www.lynnkelling.com/

"Hell is empty
And all the devils are here"

Shakespeare. *The Tempest*

CHAPTER 1
EDGE ME

Jan Richards

I FOUGHT BACK a chuckle, and it was hard—so bloody hard not to let it go. Jack naked and in front of me? It wasn't usually something to chuckle at (and he'd probably swear enough to make even the devil cover his son's ears if I did), but the reason behind *why* Jack was standing naked in front of me? In Gray's bedroom?

No good, I wouldn't be able to keep it together much longer.

I could understand why Gray had done it. Mostly. He'd been away on government business for a few weeks, and me and Jack, we'd gotten to know each other in Gray's bedroom, study, garage, pool... well, just about everywhere. And Gray hadn't liked it. Considering he was the main aggressor behind our triad relationship, with all of his strong tastes of dominance, I could understand why being left out hadn't gone down too well with him.

"Your fucking fault," Jack had said just a few weeks back

as Gray had returned that first night. Jack had looked good, trying to hide in Gray's shadow. "Most normal people do the basic two-up, two-down with a small terraced house, but no, not you." Jack gave one of those tough-guy sniffs, wiping his nose on the arm of his blue garage coveralls, trying to look not in the least bit threatened by his MI5 intelligence officer, and failing miserably in the process. "You've been ponced up in a manor, all butlers, pool guys, and all that shit, with more rooms than an orphanage." He'd looked at me. "So give two poor, horny guys the order to 'get to know each other,' what *th'fuck* do you think we're gonna do? I mean," he said to Gray, "you don't hand someone a game of Snakes and Ladders and not expect them to ride a few lengths—"

"Snakes," I'd whispered quickly, nudging him. "You ride snakes in Snakes and Ladders. Although it's Chutes and Ladders over in America."

"Seriously? Chutes?" Jack glanced at me, then tried so hard to stop smirking at Gray. "Yeah, not shoot off riding a few snakes."

"*Jack,*" I whispered heatedly.

"What? I only mentioned the snakes. You—"

"Think you're funny?" Gray looked far from impressed, especially since he hadn't been able to get *in* on the Snakes and Ladders action. And as "Nottingham," or whatever code he used with Jack to indicate government work or whatever else he got up to had called Gray away for *another* three weeks, Gray hadn't gotten to see any action for a second time.

And, boy, had Jack caught the backlash. Starting the night he'd gone away for the second time, Gray left Jack in a state of lust that wasn't to be broken.

The order was clear: "By all means make Jan come, in fact, you ensure you fucking do, but you don't get off yourself." I'd enjoyed the attention, don't get me wrong, but poor Jack... this particular three-week lesson had left him somewhat worse for non-wear of some of his hardest attributes.

And tonight, Gray was back. Hence the whole cock-teasing point behind Jack's grin.

"Bet you I make Gray come first," said Jack in a hushed whisper, throwing me a wink as he stood opposite, occasionally edging closer to Gray's bed as if that would hurry the sex along.

"You think?" I whispered back, keeping my voice as low as possible so Gray didn't hear. Gray hadn't been laid in over six weeks, Jack only three, but if Gray said come, even sperm did a mass exodus for fear of going one-on-one with the man. Jack was going down, and he was going down, in Jack's words, hard-fucked style.

Giving a look back towards the bedroom door, Jack offered one of those *You're on* half-smiles. If it wasn't for the fact he was naked in front of me, trying his best to hide a blush that marked the beginning of his red-light district as he stroked his hard-on, looking so desperate to get laid, I would have chuckled. He just looked too goddamn sexy to laugh at. That and the fact I was busy fighting off stroking my own hard-on through the thickness of my jeans.

"So, hmmm, Gray." I swallowed a very high-pitched bite to my tone as I shouted back over my shoulder, finding it hard to look away from Jack. "What... what's this very—very—basic BDSM technique that Jack's been re-learning over the past three weeks since he forgot to read his contract with me all those weeks back?"

Jack groaned and covered his face as Gray came out

fresh from the shower. Gray graced us with a glance as cool air dried his toned nakedness, and lust hitched up a notch seeing him out of a suit.

With Jack, I swore he had that slight Italian hint to his look: black hair, dark tan, all offset by startling fight-night grey eyes; whereas Gray, his Spanish connection carried most of his finery. Despite being half Welsh, he had the "Raoul" element: dark hair, olive skin that had such a hard muscle tone to it, topped off by ice-cool blue eyes, and this gorgeous shiver of fine dark hair that measured the tempting distance between navel and pubic hairline.

"Edging," said Gray. "The ability to keep a sub in a heightened state of sexual arousal. Or in Jack terms: basic fucking self-control." All humour had gone from his voice. "Which my Master sub there seems to lack in excessive amounts when you're around him, Jan."

So I failed to hold back my chuckle as Jack wished for divine intervention in the shape of a shovel, gardening gloves, and two to three acres of *just leave me th' hell here to die alone* grassland. The past three weeks hadn't been helped by Gray spending phone time with Jack, leaving Jack so close to orgasm that the poor sod was reduced to cold showers and reciting engine parts to stop himself coming around me; I think even I could strip an engine by now with the mechanic's prayer code Jack always seemed to use to distract his mind from body. I wish to God I knew what Gray said to him, but Jack would get off the phone, looking torn between throwing me on the floor, tossing off, grabbing his mechanic's prayer manual, or just falling at Gray's virtual feet and pleading mercy. And I knew which one of those Gray was angling for. The phone talk was notched up with Jack having to strip, kneel on the floor at my feet, and bring himself to the point of orgasm, then stop, forcing him to go to bed more than frustrated, his dick dancing that *s'cuse me, problem here* code on my ass as he spooned up.

"And stop trying to wind Jack up, Jan," said Gray. "Get undressed."

I gave Jack a soft grin, and he only shook his head at me as I shifted and pulled my T-shirt over my head. "Can I blame the Master?" I said, winking at him and starting on my jeans. "The Master sub is, after all, a reflection of the Master Dom, isn't he?" I stepped out of them, then made sure I folded my jeans over by my T-shirt after seeing Jack's slight frown. "And if the Master Dom's sub can't last longer than five seconds with someone else, well," I added, giving a flash of eye at Jack's mumbled protest, "what can I say?"

The breath was stolen from me as hands snuck around my waist, a cool, damp body pressing into mine as my dick was grabbed.

"Any time you wish to test out my training skills as a Master Dom again, Jan, you just give the word." Gray's grip on my dick was hard, not painful, but hurting in the fact it never moved up my bloody shaft like my dick demanded. Jack, that wicked curl to his lips, he had that *let me at him* look lowering his eyes too.

"What's the word, Jan?"

My hand fell on Gray's, to how the thickness of my dick shaped his hand, then I offered Gray a tentative kiss, the thickness and length of his shaft pushing against my hip as he shifted and roughed the kiss up, forcing another groan from Jack and a secret smile from me.

"Get Jack to plead please," I mumbled pathetically, "and I'm all yours."

"Doubt it would take much," Gray muttered. "Poor pup's in a state. Only have to blow on his cock and he'd lose it."

Jack shifted for us with a growl, but a single shake of Gray's head held him in place.

"Oh come the fuck on," said Jack, half-pissed, half-desperate to get in on some action. "This isn't fucking funny anymore."

"No," said Gray. And Jack listened, barely, fidgeting like a teenager waiting for the go to fuel his car-thieving addiction. One thing Jack had managed to shake in maturity. I hoped, anyway.

Playing Gray's hand down my dick, I reached behind and fisted Gray's hair, much to Jack's growing frustration. "Any particular punishment you have in mind for him if he comes before you do?"

"Today's lesson is riding the thrill without coming," murmured Gray, playing his breath against my ear. "Stop trying to rile him or I'll fuck him first and leave you nothing to play with but yourself."

"I am here, you know," said Jack, folding his arms across his chest. "As much as a guy likes to see a pissing contest over who's going to fuck him, I'm actually off duty from the Masters' Circle for a few more weeks." In Jack's defence, he had been given time off to recover from Mark Shaw's vicious cut to his head; well, that and other things. "So," added Jack, "pack it in with the lurid remarks about me being fuck material." He gave the biggest puppy-dog eyes, held his arms out, and called us both over with an offer of a hug. "C'mon. Y'know you want one."

After a kiss at my neck, Gray pulled me back as I failed to ignore the pull, then he went over and stood shoulder to shoulder with Jack. "Being Master sub, it's you just being fuck material now, is it?" Christ, could you hear Gray's Welsh connection with that. Had Jack even caught on yet?

"Hmm." Jack's arms fell to his side and he shifted awkwardly, looking over at me like the devil caught out and needing backup from his wannabe incubus. Like heck would I help; I'd kind of come to get a kick out of seeing him stumble for words around Gray when Jack was usually such a hard-nosed thug to anyone else.

"Wouldn't say fuck material, per se," said Jack moodily before offering a nervous smile.

"Per se?" said Gray, and he let the back of his hand run under Jack's jaw. "What would you call it, stunner?"

Stunner? One day I'd find the balls to ask Gray why he called Jack that. From Jack's reaction, it had nothing to do with how he looked. He let his gaze drop to the floor, but as he looked at me, something very wicked played in his eyes. Sneaking an arm around Gray's neck, he slipped a foot behind Gray and took him down to the floor in one fluid movement. Gray landed with no wind knocked out of him, Jack controlling the fall so very carefully, ending things by straddling Gray's hips and holding him down at the wrists. Jack obviously loved the position, automatically sliding down on Gray, his body now flat, muscles tensing in his shoulders as he lifted his upper body so all pressure was on Gray's wrists, their hips.

"I'd call it opportunism," Jack breathed, looking down on Gray. "Speaking of which, when the hell are you going to let me fuck you?" It had been a question he'd asked like this countless times over the past four months, and then, like now, Gray simply gave that raised brow, the kind only found with an owner who was sick of the puppy caught constantly trying to hump his leg, which Jack hadn't grown out of doing yet.

I'd kind of come to understand why Gray hadn't touched Jack for two years. Even at twenty-nine, two years older than me, Jack still had that *I want it, give it* intensity when it came to Gray, especially since their formal Master Dom/sub boundaries had gone beyond the professional in the last five months, but Gray wasn't about to *give* anything. Not with knowing how easily Jack could lose himself in dangerous ways that had nothing to do with sex. Hooking a leg over Jack's, Gray used his hip to shift his weight, flipping Jack onto his back, and returning the compliment of pinning Jack down by his wrists.

"I haven't forgotten," he breathed, every muscle in Gray's ass given fine contours that moved and shifted as he kept Jack still. "Your refusal to use a safe word around Jan because you'd hit him…." Jack became very still. "Violation of a Masters' Circle contract… one you never fucking read… two hours punishment with me…." Gray shifted his hips against Jack's, just once but enough to cause Jack to groan softly. "Do I take your display of martial arts to mean you're well enough to *really* fuck around with me, Jack?"

"Ah…." Jack gave a nervous chuckle; then, the sweetest thing, a gentle rub of his nose came along Gray's cheek as he offered a very put-on wounded look. "You know my head still hurts, right?"

"Yeah," said Gray, smiling, almost answering Jack's quiet touch by allowing Jack to kiss at his throat, then gently kissing Jack's cheek in return. "That ass of yours too, huh?"

"Now hang on." Jack tried to backpedal as much as he could. "I never said anything about my ass. My ass is just fine. In fact, anytime you and Jan—"

Gray was up and pulling Jack with him. "Whoa, fuck,"

said Jack, connecting with the bed and going face-first into the covers. Within a moment, Gray had Jack's hands cuffed behind him and Jack almost flat on his back, the cuffs arching his position slightly. A pull on Jack's ankle had him lined up with me, legs open, and Jack rolling off a few curses at Gray's rough manhandling. Not that I minded; I was all up for getting a slice of Jack.

CHAPTER 2
A SLICE OF JACK

I'D HAVE SENT a note to my dick to pay attention to just how damn sexy Jack looked with Gray holding him down for me on the bed, but my dick, in theory, at least, was already there, going in balls deep without me.

"Be careful with the flower," said Gray over to me. "Not only does *she* apparently have another headache, but she tends to lose it with the slightest breath off you."

"Hey." Jack looked down at Gray as Gray knelt by his feet, that strong grip on Jack's ankle keeping him still. "You know that's not fucking funny, right? I've never been anyone's fucked-up flower."

"Over four months off from training Doms due to a headache?" Gray snorted. "You're a fucking white-pansied, vanilla-scented pussy of a delicate petal in the BDSM world."

Jack didn't look happy. "A new business on top of my garage to take care of, Gray," he griped. "It's not just because of a concussion. And like *fuck* am I coming before you tonight because of that vanilla comment, you twat."

Gray shifted, grabbing Jack by the throat, his body tensing, relaxing, tensing as he came in close and held his lips inches from Jack's. Jack stilled, the muscles in his throat strained as Gray forced his head back. Jack's breathing was so deep now, the pull on his taut stomach muscles suddenly screaming *thrill* at having Gray pinning him still on the bed. Even his dick wept a touch; hell, give it some tools and mortar, I'd swear it would build its own Gray memorial right there on the bed if Gray hinted at it.

And Christ, the smile that touched Gray's lips knowing it. "Watch that mouth, Jack." He brushed a thumb over Jack's lips. "It'll get you seriously fucked one of these days."

"Yeah?" Jack let this slight curl of a smile touch his lips. "Fuck you, Gray."

Gray came down with every hard-fuck signal going: all there in the threat of a rough kiss, how his body threatened to swamp Jack's completely as he started to move.

I coughed, deliberately breaking Gray's feast before he even touched down. "Right," I said to Jack and Gray, gaining their attention. "What's wrong with us vanillas all of a sudden?"

"Nothing." Jack shook off Gray's touch, backpedalling again, and very bloody quickly as Gray eased back with a smile. "It's just, well, you know vanillas, they—"

"You're digging a grave with two shovels, Jack. Shut the fuck up." Gray stroked at Jack's outer thigh as he spoke, and the gentleness of his touch was in direct conflict to his rough tone. "If it gets around the Masters' Circle I have a Master switch who loses it within three seconds of a vanilla fucking him, there'll be hell to pay."

"Seriously? With you? What're we talking?" Jack's head

was up off the bed. "Whips? Chains—you and Brennan?"

I suited myself up as I climbed on the bed, and Jack went quiet for a moment, then almost distracted, he was back with Gray. "Because, you—brought to heel by Brennan? All spread out on a bondage cross, typical X stance: whipped, chained, then leg-spread. Hooded, pegged an—*fuck me, Jan!*"

I wasn't as gentle as I should have been pushing into Jack, but then he needed shutting up. From how hard Gray was, I thought I'd better claim Jack quickly before Gray dragged him downstairs to his cellar. Yeah, I'd seen the sort of toys this Master had been sharpening recently down there, especially since he hadn't been able to use them until Jack was given the all clear from the Masters' Circle they both worked for outside of their other careers.

Jack eased back down, stretching his neck as he arched his body, and breathed out such a comfortable sigh that it made me shiver. Gray kept out of the way, now sat back onto his heels at Jack's side, analytical of every move he made.

Running my hands to Jack's inner thighs, I eased his knees up to his chest as I slid and filled him to the hilt.

"Mmmmm," murmured Jack. Now so quiet, relaxed, like he'd just lain down in a hot bath and every aching muscle had melted into the hot water. Christ, was he ready for this.

"Slow and gentle, Jan," whispered Gray, no doubt seeing the change in Jack and letting his hand find the root of Jack's dick. "You feel him tensing, you hold here. It's not a guarantee he'll stop, but I want his arousal maintained as you come."

Sounded easy—real easy. Right. Head down to my chest, controlling the shaking I felt with having Jack take me, loving the sight of being root-deep in him, I made my lengths long, deep—slow. Jack groaned, forcing me to look up, and an arch of Jack's body came, instantly tensing, the grip around my dick with his ass tightening to choking degrees.

"Jack, seriously?" Gray snorted. "Four strokes—you're his?"

"Huh?" Jack grunted, brought back down to reality as Gray gripped his dick again, stopping him from coming. Twisting his face away and hiding in the covers, he gave such a sheepish chuckle. "Jan fucking looked at me."

"All the Doms you've helped train, and it's a vanilla's cute look that brings you to your knees?"

"Jan's look," breathed Jack. "There's a big fucking difference." He couldn't stop chuckling, and his words pushed me so close to the edge. "May I be blindfolded, please?"

Gray snorted disgust. "No you can't; fucking sub up."

I couldn't join in Jack's chuckles—wanted to, but seeing Jack the way he was, it wasn't helping me much either. Pleasure knotted my stomach, and every nerve from balls up seemed to sweep with need. I took him a little harder, fingers digging into his thighs, pressure pulling my balls tight, my body crying out for release.

"Fuck, yeah." Jack was no longer hiding in the covers but looking up at me. "Come on, baby."

Gray ran a hand through Jack's hair, then took a hold, keeping his head back, body arched. "Maintain it."

"Do… hmph… do you want me to stop?" I groaned. Don't make me stop, please….

"This is basic control, Jan. He knows this. If anything, enjoy him, and let him fucking see it."

I let Jack take the force of my own need to come, sometimes stumbling with pace, and Jack sucked in a breath, now reduced to animalistic traits in order to not let his body react normally and come.

"Jan." Jack arched his body up to meet a deep grind of dick in him. "Fuck, baby, yes—"

Gray tightened the grip in his hair. "Maintain it."

"Christ." Jack's whole body tensed. "*Sir, fucking please,*" he snarled, his body struggling. The "Sir" tag fell so naturally from him. Maybe Jack hadn't realised he'd let it slip, but it darkened Gray's eyes as he pushed his thumb against Jack's slit. Jack cried out, maintaining the need in his body, barely, but it was too late for me. For those few precious seconds, there was nothing but the feel of Jack's ass and my dick held deep in him, stretching him to the full, then I came back down and made sure Jack took the last few ounces from me, a little careless with how Jack was struggling.

"Yes…." I doubled over Jack. "Just, Jesus, baby. What the hell do you do to me?"

"Jan, move," whispered Gray, and a gentle tug at my arm hinted that I should get out of the way. Gray settled between Jack's thighs, and as he undid the handcuffs keeping Jack still, there was an instant switch in Jack; a change in lover, in handler, that Jack's body recognised as he levelled his gaze on Gray.

"You're gonna make me come first, eh?" said Gray with a knowing smile, tracing a touch down Jack's side to find his hip, fingers constantly digging deep into the toned flesh.

"Heard that, hmmm?" mumbled Jack, gripping at the back of Gray's neck, his voice betraying his need to be kept under Gray as the hand on his hip pulled him up. Bodies were already way past any spoken heat as they sought out each other, now grinding, rubbing—playing. If the "Sir" hadn't shown Gray that Jack was getting close to being back in full sub mode and needing a full Mastering, then his voice and body betrayed him now. I heard it, and from the look of Gray, how he held his arms and body around Jack, all to let anyone else know he'd slaughter anyone who contemplated disturbing what lay inside, he saw it. "Better Dom up a little, then, Gray," whispered Jack, giving a nip at Gray's lip, once—twice. "Make it fucking good."

Gray leaned down for a rough kiss, then breached him hard and fast.

Jack cried out, and it was caught against Gray's lips, need now pure fight and heat as the grip into Jack's hair ensured he stayed still for the rough kiss and touch Gray wanted. Tongues clashed for a moment, then Jack swore into him with every hard taste that Gray forced between his thighs. They'd had eleven years together, and it showed; how Gray took such effortless control with a hard pace that Jack rode so bloody well. Each time Jack looked close to losing it, he'd break breathlessly from the kiss, twist his head away, control his breathing, then attack Gray with nip and lip, calling Gray out on each drive into him. In return, Gray stopped each initial cry of heat off Jack, covering his mouth, stifling the cries in his hand, then leaning down and whispering *hush, hush-hush* against Jack's throat—biting viciously to make him cry out again just before taking him harder between his thighs. Tender and brutal, fight and heat all executed in such a basic position. But give Jack his professional dues, he knew exactly how to fire and match that control, twisting away from the hand on his mouth, crying out, body raising up into Gray's, pushing him further to fire the need to control. Neither looked ready or willing to break first, and I was left nearly climbing up the walls to get in on the action, just break all the cries, hard slap of flesh against flesh, and bites of defiance.

Giving a smile, Gray tugged me close and demanded access to my mouth. I let him in, chasing his tongue, and didn't catch on to why until Jack cried out.

"Uh-uh. *Fucking cheat.*" Jack curled up into me, biting at my hip. Seeing us kiss, there was that switch, and Jack seemed to lose all control. He came, and his cry made me lose mine, our come now mingling on his stomach.

"Seriously, Jack?" said Gray, sounding really pleased; breathless, but pleased. "Just a few weeks of edging? You're too fucking easy lately." Giving a smile as I sat back on my heels out of the way, Gray came down onto Jack, his pace not slowing. Jack eased back onto the bed as Gray bit at his throat, as he marked and claimed the spoils with his rough fucking.

"Christ," cried Jack, stretching beneath Gray as though he'd come again when Gray cried his release, fingers digging hard into Gray's ass, encouraging every last inch up him. And knowing Jack, maybe he had come again.

Heavy breathing hit the air, all of ours, then Jack rolled to his side and pulled a pillow over his head. "I'm fucked as a Master sub." He groaned. "The Circle's gonna kick my sorry ass out for this shit. Mike will be sticking photos of Jan up all over the MC base and will be pissing himself behind the cameras watching the *too-fucking-quick* fallout." He waved a defeated hand. "Carry on. I'm fucked. Useless and peachy fucking fucked," he said, sounding half asleep already.

Both Gray and I shared a look, a few deep breaths, then chuckled. "Well," said Gray. "At least we shut him up."

"Cured his headache too."

Gray patted Jack's thigh. "Bless the delicate petal."

"I can still fucking *hear* you," mumbled Jack. "You tag me as any part of a flower again, you can both fuck off and find a new place to live."

"This *is* my place, Jack."

"Yeah. My place," mumbled Jack, and something softened in Gray's eyes.

"You'd live here?"

Jack chuckled. "So long as I can bring my things." I yelped as Jack smacked my thigh. "Right, things? Just need to buy him the collar to prove it."

"Hey," I mumbled, rubbing at my ass, although the thought of being Jack's *thing* had me grinning. Moving in was something else entirely, though, and so too was the collaring. That wasn't my thing. I clamped my lips shut maybe a little too quickly. Even Gray had lost his smile.

Jack had gone so still too, all tensed, his grip on the pillow a little tight. At first I thought he'd caught on to my lack of committal, lay there a little stung at the rejection, but his body was too rigid, that slow inhale... exhale... or more how that cover was pulled a little too tightly against his stomach, fingers rigid and pale at the knuckles.

I frowned just as Gray got off the bed, ditched his condom in the basket next to the bin, and headed in the direction of the en suite. He came back a moment later carrying a damp cloth and towel.

"Here." He tugged at Jack's hip to get him to turn around slightly, get his head from underneath the pillow. Looking down, Jack took the cloth, and with a concentration that defied logic, he started wiping his abs clean with long, slow strokes.

Christ… come. Back in the dojo when me and Gray had fucked him, he'd wiped the come off his stomach with such a look of disgust. His head eventually saw even that as nothing but dirt to scrub off his skin? How cruel was that?

Gray knew the signs to Jack's OCD a lot better than I did. And despite Jack being back on his meds, and Gray, in Jack's words, "Dragging his ass to bastard, psycho nut-case sessions," for his *Don't… torture me* conduct disorder, there were these more obvious signs of how much Jack wouldn't ever really escape both conditions. At best he had coping strategies, at worst… Gray and I were there to catch the fallout. I could understand Gray's agreement to Jack's time off from Dom training, even though Gray seriously ribbed him for it. Despite how Jack's voice and look said he needed that intensity, his head needed time to adjust, to pace, to settle back into routine. As Gray had said, slow and easy. In every way possible.

After a moment I took the cloth off Jack and made sure he was clean. He offered this shy smile, and I leaned down and kissed where I'd spilled my come on him. He loved sex to the extreme and beyond; he just seemed to have difficulty in the comedown from sex. It had eased over the last month, but there were still moments like this that threw him back a touch. Glancing at Gray, he just offered me a frown.

Giving a sigh, I kissed Jack again, loving his murmur as I feathered more nips just below his navel, gently nibbling at the toned skin above his pubic hairline. Jack stroked through my hair, back arching slightly, and gave such a soft murmur of my name. Christ, he reacted so effortlessly to every touch, and it made talking nigh on impossible. I worshipped every inch of him and his goddamn complications for it.

"Jan," said Gray.

"Hmmm?" I gave him a look, not happy that my hard and fast run of vampire bites along Jack's navel had been interrupted, also not liking how Jack's soft chuckles had stopped as well.

"Mobile." Gray shifted his head, indicating to the bedside unit. I hadn't even heard it go off, and with a grumble, I reached over and grabbed the phone. Thumbing the messages, I glanced down at Jack after seeing the text.

Work...

... Mr Hammond's report due by Friday.

"Anything important?" mumbled Jack, arm over his face as he tried to hide his smile.

"The office."

"You're on holiday. Tell them to fuck off." Jack peeked up at me, and I was going to toss the phone aside and steal a kiss when a missed message from earlier popped up.

"Jan?" All frown and worry, Jack raised up onto his elbows. "You okay?"

Flicking a look at him, then more so at Gray, I put the phone back and eased down, making sure Jack got the message to move with me so I could cuddle.

"Just work," I mumbled, hiding in Jack's throat. A stroke came at my back, and as Jack never let me out of the cuddle when I tried to start some more sex, he maybe knew there was a lie in there somewhere.

"You okay?" he whispered.

It was still close, the concentration on his face as he'd wiped at his abs. "Yeah." I held him a little tighter. Seemed communication was still a little hard, and Jack and Gray's quiet saw it too.

CHAPTER 3
WORKING ORDER

Jack Harrison

WITH THE BATHROOM tiles cool under foot, I jerked as arms snaked around my waist, making me nearly cut myself shaving. Bare chest and PJ's shaped me from behind and—fuck me, the bloody bastards 'round here knew how to sneak up on a guy. I huffed but did a lousy job of sounding pissed as I wiped off the excess shaving foam with a towel. "Not forgiven you for ganging up on me last night, Richards."

Jan laughed softly and feathered kisses along the back of my neck. I glanced at him in the mirror, loving seeing him there. "Yeah, laugh it up. But just remember what fucks around…." I tried to think of some grouchy comment to add to that, but it was touching five in the morning, and my nuts were too busy playing Hide and go Shrink. Jan brushed a touch along some bite marks on my throat, and Christ: I'd been marked? Gray usually kept his touch professional and discreet, yet I couldn't remember Jan going dark and vampire on my throat last night. Down by my dick, yeah… but not my throat!

"Hmmm," said Jan as the towel went in the wash basket. "Remember what fucks around… what?"

"Just doesn't get fucked by me, okay," I snapped, but fuck knows how I got there—I twisted slightly and managed to tongue him deeply and get high on his sleepy taste. "That was a real cheap shot, kissing Gray to make me come."

"Yeah?" said Jan, and he rutted against me from behind. "You lost me at 'Jack's just had a shower and he's all naked and drip drying in the bathroom.'"

"Y'know I never said that, right?" I shivered as he drew his hand across the wetness on my abs, all to run down the outside of my thigh. I was still naked; he wasn't.

"Said what?"

"You even in the same universe as me this morning, Breakdown? You still can't seem to get over this BDSM nakedness thing." I chuckled, but Jan only sighed.

"How about you skip work today, pull a sickie, and we get all X-rated in the bed again?"

I leaned back, my head now on his shoulder. "And have Gray take the piss over me pulling a sickie outside of the Masters' Circle too?" I grumbled. "Sure, like I'm gonna hand him that piss-take on a platter." Giving a sigh, I looked down at the bathroom unit. The photo of Gray sat at perfect angles to the sink, and I controlled my breathing. Jan seemed to stop his kisses and looked over my shoulder. Reaching past me, he went to pick the photo up, but I jerked into life, stopping his hand, hating how hard my heart pounded with having him nearly disturb it. Giving a kiss to my shoulder, instead he took my hand and eased it down so I could pick it up.

"Gonna have to get one of you and Gray together," I mumbled, bringing it closer and seeing Gray, dark sunglasses and suit, getting out of his MC's signature car, a black Merc. "Well, if I could fucking tie his ass down long enough to keep him from dodging camera shots." Bloody MI5 ops.

Jan kissed my neck and then gave a gentle lick with his tongue, almost soaking up the moisture there. "How long did it stay all casual before you had to straighten it?" he whispered in my ear, and I offered a smile.

"Six days. Longest yet."

He sighed and ran a touch up my arm, angling the photo so it hovered above the unit. "Seven this time," he said, and I let the photo fall, go all casual next to the sink, with lines out of angle. Scary. I couldn't remember when I'd straightened it, before, maybe after I'd gotten out of the shower. Coping strategies: leave something for as long as possible, leave it out of sync with life while ignoring the need to put it right... but that come on my abs last night...? I let out a snort and felt Jan tighten his hold briefly. OCD bullshit in front of the boyfriend, real fucking peachy.

"Seven days this time," murmured Jan, and the weight on my shoulders seemed to ease. Yeah, more than.

"Anyway." I turned and pulled him into a cuddle. "Morning, gorgeous."

"Mmmmm." His hands wandered down to my ass. "Morning, things." He gave a yawn, then stretched all of his body to the full, still making no apology for the state of his pyjama-covered hard-on. Lips briefly met mine. "Everything okay?" he said, sounding so fucking tired.

"Hmmm?" I licked my lips, not wanting him to move too far from them. "What?"

Jan was quiet, and it forced me to focus on him a little more.

"Nothing you need to talk about?" He peered around me to the photo, and his stroke at my abs was as distracted as his look. He remembered the come there too. I pulled him back, fully intending to tongue our way through this discussion, but ended up looking at him, his sleepy, messed-up hair, soft eyes…

My heart slipped, and I pulled him into a hard hold and closed my eyes. Life was good, damn good, nothing out of place, all lines, moods, and bodies in perfect sync. Perfect. An OCDers dream, or nightmare, one of the two. My head just couldn't quite decide which one. Fuck. I pushed it away. Giving Jan a kiss, I breathed him in deep: a mixture of cologne, deodorant, pillow and duvet; a gorgeous scent. "The talking I need to do will make me late for work." I made a point of rubbing my semi against his thigh, and the slap to my ass made me wince.

"In that case, don't work too hard, Jack."

I gave him a frown; he sounded distant again with that. "That other text last night? What pissed you off? They riding your ass in the world of finance? Because I know people who know people that maybe know a few more people who can make them *all* go away."

Jan was lost for a moment, his gaze back towards the bedroom. "Yeah, scary world at times, Harrison."

Bad time to make a joke. "Not always," I mumbled, seeing that same look he'd had back at the dojo a few months back after Gray had killed Mark Shaw and his prats. He shook ghosts off after a minute, mostly because he came in for another kiss.

"Work," he mumbled, giving a smile.

"Bollocks," I said, scowling. Jan gave a chuckle, then went back to the bedroom. A shave, cologne, fresh jeans, T-shirt, and pull on of coveralls later, I was back in there with them. Halfway between zipping my coveralls up and seeing Jan had drifted off next to Gray, the look of them together kept me still. I'd caught the alarm before Gray had gone Katana on the thing and diced it to toast-sized offerings for waking him. It was rare he did time off from work "officially," although considering he kept his mobile close wherever he went, sat on the bedside unit now, I guessed his ass was still on-call. And, note to dick, what a fine fucking ass that was. He (Gray, not his ass) had a long trip coming up in America in a week or so that was tied to MC business. I'd had to cry out of it due to sorting my garages, which had pissed Gray off as we were meant to be spot-checking some rogue Dom club in the States, and it had earned more piss-taking off Gray. Maybe this was Gray relaxing before that. He guarded one side of the bed, sheet pulled down to his waist, revealing more than his kick-ass body, with its hard lines and tanned suppleness against a pure white backdrop. He was ten years older, but you wouldn't have called that unless you had his birth certificate in hand. Then you'd have to learn to run very quickly if he knew you'd touched his goods.

Jan was the other side, his body not as hard and defined as Gray's, just this soft tone that matched everything else about Jan so fucking gorgeously with his tousled brown hair, light brown eyes....

"Work," I mumbled down to my dick. "And not the sort you're all fired up for again." Grumbling under my breath and flicking an envious glare at the space between them both, I headed on downstairs.

In the main reception area, Ed had already ordered the mail, and I pinched mine from off the letter table. Letters were divided between two addresses, here and home, and the usual shit cluttered my hands. Gray's looked a hell of a lot more interesting, all stacked and ordered and looking twice as big as mine—with a couple of packages thrown in to boot too.

Sweet. One flat brown package looked very teasingly suspicious.

Giving a grin, I picked it up, felt along the edges, then gave it a rattle close to my ear hearing the distinct sound of a disc hitting a DVD case.

"Mail-order porn." I tutted a few times in disgust. "At your time of life? With your connections? Oh the fucking shame of it, my old mukka."

"That's not yours, Master Harrison."

Giving a grumble, I didn't even bother looking behind me. How the other half fucking lived. "Morning, Ed. Off to burn the Master's breakfast?" I got a grunt in return off the butler.

"Off to swindle a few customers out of cash at that so-called garage?"

"Play nice, Ed. What happens if your car breaks down in the most inconvenient of places and I get the callout?"

"I'd check your pockets for my wallet and then expect you to stand aside and watch a real mechanic fix it." He was heading off in the direction of the kitchen, grinning.

"You have a nice *fuck you* day there, Ed." I even gave him the *fuck you* finger, then dropped it when I caught the act in a mirror. Real mature, Jack.

The package still had my main focus, and I let the

suspect DVD case rest back with the mail, inching it into place so Gray wouldn't notice. Ever. With the Dom training Gray had done, with world-wide clientele and serious bastard attitude to match just who it was we mostly trained, I doubted it was porn. He only had to step into his own library and pick from the amount of scenes he'd supervised to get his kick—or better still, step into Master Dom mode and fuck the hell out of me. Christ knows my body was missing it far more than my work head wanted to admit.

The smell of coffee was an instant draw into the reception area as I pushed through the garage workshop doors, then ran my hands under the antibacterial hand wash, stopping as I reached for it a second time. *Fuck.*

"Coffee, boss?" said Sam in between offering one to Aid, and I nearly kissed him as he came over with said steaming mug in hand.

"Lifesaver." I took a long sip, slipping a gaze over to Aid. "Morning."

"Morning, Mr Harrison." Aid looked up from the client book, his mug of tea close by. At least Sam was taking care of the managers. Aid had been promoted since Steve had shifted over to the Strachan garage. To be honest, I'd have thought Aid would have gone with him, but it seemed the bid to keep him here by waving a manager's position under his nose, much to Steve's crossed arms and scowling, had won him over. Fucking strange, that. Aid had fallen into the role well: opening up, running through the client list, assigning the mechs to different jobs.

"What's in the book for me today?" I helped Sam finish up rolling the blinds in reception while still sucking the life out of my coffee.

The ruffle of pages came from behind us. "Two Nissan jobs and an Escort."

"What's up with the Nissans?"

"Clutch and gears are lagging on the one, and—" The sound of more pages being fingered. "—according to the owner, 'the brakes are squishy' on the other."

Sam chuckled as he warmed up the customers' drinks machine. "Gotta be a woman, that last one."

I frowned at him over my mug. Half of the coffee was already gone as I double-checked that the roller doors were up in the main workshop. "I know enough guys who can't fix a car." An image of Jan wearing coveralls and trying to figure out boot from bonnet without the aid of his mobile phone, laptop, and a whole weekend conference thing going on not really helping things there.

"Yeah, I know, but—" Sam shrugged one of those damn *couldn't give a shit* shrugs. "—squishy. It's gotta be a woman."

"Bet you it's not."

"Bet you it is."

"Bet you it's not."

"You're on."

"What?" The coffee took on a stale taste as I looked at him. "I'm not betting on customers."

"Ooooh. Coward."

Like fuck. Giving a scowl, I pulled out my wallet. "Twenty." I held up the offending money. "Where's yours? And Monopoly don't count."

"Aid?"

"Fuck off." Aid closed the client book. "*Aid* by name but not by nature, especially on the finance side. No scabbing off upcoming wages either."

I laughed. Christ, had I made the right choice there. "So. Sam?"

"Hmmm." Sam dug deep into a few pockets and came out with a packet of mints, a condom, and a ten. "How's that?"

"Better than nothing." The ten was taken and handed over to Aid. At least the johnny wasn't used, and Sam had that back, very fucking carefully. "What the hell are you doing bringing condoms to work, Sam?" I mumbled as Aid moved off into the workshop.

"We got talking. Me and Liam." Sam leaned against the reception desk, messing with his coverall zip as I thumbed through the appointment book. The book was really only there for me. All appointments were logged on the computer, but as I hated the sodding things, the book was kept close at hand. Aid was doing a good job of keeping the routine up, and routine—"Liam?" I gave him a sideways glance. The bruises Liam had given Sam for sleeping with his girlfriend had long since faded, but the hurt was there in Sam's eyes over the past few months from missing whatever else they'd both shared. Considering Liam was one of my top Shotokan students, Sam had taken one hell of a beating, but were they sorting things out now?

The door behind clicked open and mechanics started filing in. The merry among them said morning, and I didn't begrudge the odd few with attitudes. Hell, it was Monday, and I was the first to push a few guys out of the way and nut the bastard, especially when Gray and Jan were at home all tucked up in bed, nice and fucking naked like.

"Yeah," said Sam, not looking so sure now. "We, y'know, tried sorting some things out. Although it almost went a little beyond, y'know—"

"Sorting things out?" I finished my coffee, although a little taken by Sam's humility. He could be a sweet shit when he wasn't ringing the git bell, and he had all those first-time blushes going on now. But it seemed he was making a little headway with dealing with his sexuality issues. "Be careful," I added, trying to stop him looking so uncomfortable with being able to talk about it. I'd hate to be twenty again.

Sam tried to inject a little of the old Sam as he held the condom up and made a point of staring at my throat. "I am. How's things coming along on the condom front for you, boss?"

"Work," I snapped, inching up my collar and seeing this was leaning towards some shit comment over Essex, and not liking it.

Sam managed a grin, went to push away, then rested back against the counter when a customer came over, big and biker-looking—definitely male too. Didn't mean it was the owner of the Nissan with the "squishy" brakes, and it didn't mean I would win the battle of the sexes bet. Yet. But—

"Hi, I'm here about the brakes on my Nissan."

I resisted smirking at Sam as he sulked a gaze to his feet.

"Yeah, my missus called it in. Seems they're... squishy?"

Fuck. Sam licked a finger and did the typical *one to me* salute as he turned away. Sod. Twenty pound down, I got to work on the Nissan. By twelve, I was finished with the second one and in desperate need of a little privacy for lunch; that, and the burning need to piss on Steve's Strachan parade kicked in too. The second garage had broken even in the first few months and was doing really well for a start-up. Just hated having someone else control things without me around. I wonder if Steve had noticed.

Up in the office, I hovered over the phone, fingers brushing over the handle. It would be good to hear Jan's voice now, but that would come over as desperate, sad, and bloody OCD-stalker nuts. Christ, would Gray love that handed to him. Asking Jan to move into Gray's with me was a heat of the moment thing, and I knew it had made him uncomfortable. Getting to know him, hell, even just some of his friends from work, was the priority. Well, when I actually managed to pin his ass still, actually talk, and get over the need to fuck him senseless. All that bollocks could be blamed on the honeymoon-period, but I'd been with Gray for eleven years now, and I hadn't gotten fucking him out of my system.

Jan really didn't know what he'd gotten himself into.

So terrorising Steve it was, and I hit his number instead and settled back into the chair.

"Jack—five minutes; five minutes to opening after dinner and you couldn't bloody leave it for one day, you—"

No chance there to even say "afternoon". I grinned, maybe liking Mondays a little better today. "Afternoon to you too, Ste. How much money have you made me today?"

CHAPTER 4
ENSURING RANK

Jan Richards

I'D TAKEN A big chance booking time off work and hoping Gray would be okay with it, letting me just hang around his. When he'd announced he'd booked time off too, I'd eyed him up, and he'd returned it. That had been us, more or less, for the past few months: just watching each other, seeing what we each brought to Jack's table. Jack couldn't take time out this week from setting up the Strachan deal, so that meant what? That Gray had booked the days off to spend time with me? Things weren't exactly tense between us. When Jack was around, Christ, we all just seemed to burn and gravitate into one heated mass, usually with Jack as the white-dwarf core. When he wasn't here, everything was quiet, watchful.

Having spent some time at my home today just sorting out bills, I was up for some relaxing around teatime, which, to me, meant looking around Gray's art collections, well out of sight from prying eyes, in the north side of his manor. It didn't really surprise me when Gray found me in there.

"You love your Welsh art," I said, trying to pay attention to the latest oil on canvas near me. Thomas Jones's *The Bard* took prime position in the exhibit. With the invasion of the English in full swing on Welsh land, the man in the painting was caught threatening a suicidal jump off a clifftop as "the last Welsh bard". But it also proved men *could* multitask as the artist had captured him glancing back over his shoulder, placing a curse on the English. I'm surprised Jack didn't like this one. Although I guessed he'd be tempted to draw in the usual one-finger salute, stating "Now that's cursing someone".

"One of Jones's best," said Gray, leaning against a glass case housing some fancy Japanese sword not too far from me.

Feeling a little nervous, I managed a chuckle. "You're just borrowing Jones's own words and too scared to come up with a better interpretation."

"Oh, you think?" Now he looked interested, ready for a fight.

"You work for MI5, so please note I'll record any slating of the English and post it to the director-general, allowing for a formal dressing down." I took a breath. "Possibly followed by showing Jack any disciplinary action you receive from the director so he can chuckle and throw popcorn at it."

Gray raised his hands, gracefully backing down with a chuckle, then started to head for the exit. "The Spanish element to your surname," I said to him, making him look back.

"Hmmmm?"

"Was that down to the Grand Tour or is your father or mother Spanish?" It had been a rite of passage for many upper-class noblemen to tour Europe in a bid to expose them to classical art and culture, so the Spanish line must have come from somewhere. "Your ancestors, they must have gone through the same thing if your Spanish line goes further back. Hence your Spanish heritage." I looked at the painting, then around me. "And your love of art would come from that too, no doubt." I was with Gray again. "Maybe your British army and MI5 bloodline as well? Raoul tradition?"

"I never served in the army."

"Of course you didn't. Like you were found under a thistle bush, with no paperwork leading back to who your parents are either."

Gray just smiled, and I shook my head at him. "You're done for, Gray. You play me up any more with Jack, I'm letting your boss know about your Spanish ties, but more how you keep a firm tie to your Welsh rebellious roots with that copy of *The Bard* on display back there. Not to mention the painting of Owen Glendower in the main reception hall."

Gray lost his smile a little, a flicker of… what there? Grief? Anger? "You brought in the Welsh rebellion connection, I never did," he said, turning away. "And on a linguistic front, when talking to a Welshman, it's Owain Glyndwr. Owen Glendower is the English proper noun variant. Not wise to call a Welshman by an English name, not unless you want a war." He paused. "That also isn't a copy of *The Bard*, Jan."

Shit. I should have known that.

After following him through to the hall, I picked up the book I'd left on the sofa's arm from yesterday and settled down. Gray had a set time for martial arts practice around seven, and it looked like he was settling to do that just now. "You want a drink, Abstract?" said Gray as he went over to the bar. His abstract comment got him an unhappy glance over the top of my book.

"Problem?" said Gray, his lip curled in a slight smile as he glanced over from pouring the drinks.

I had a love for abstract painting, fine dabs off the tip of a paintbrush, feeling, expressionism, but the pet name was due more to my outlook on life, or more to my being on the outside of the BDSM world, terrified of dipping my toes, and running away screaming when I did. Abstract: minus any discernible balls, in Gray's book. Great. He'd taken to calling me that name a lot lately.

"It's an improvement on what Jack calls you."

I sat up on the sofa. "Yeah, I got the Breakdown digs from when my car broke down a few months back when we first met. That's fine coming from him." Gray came and handed me a whiskey. He was sipping water from the look of it, and I smiled my thanks. "Has he got any pet names for you?" I said, looking up at him.

"Bastard, mainly." Gray struggled to hide that smile behind his glass, and he gave a slight shift of his head. "Amongst anything else I can make him cry out."

"You don't tell him anything about your Welsh history? Your roots?" I raised a brow. "Your Spanish heritage?"

"You know quite a lot about art history, Jan. What university did you attend?"

"You know what university I attended, Gray."

"Hmmm. A strange mix that; accounting and art history."

I shrugged. "Not when you think about it; art is just

mathematical angles and points in full-blown colour and depth."

He shrugged, seemingly satisfied. Maybe. "Jack comes around to things in his own time. I don't push."

"Over your history? He's had eleven years," I said, maybe a little sad with how Jack's way of thinking was ruled by his disorders despite his obvious coping strategies. "It really takes him that long?"

Gray gave another little shrug. "He gets there eventually."

That moving-in comment last night was out of character, then, maybe showing more how he was slipping slightly, supported by how he'd struggled just a few moments later with the come on his stomach. Yeah, I could understand why Gray wouldn't want to push Jack's boundaries without considering a full risk assessment first. He'd agreed to overseeing my training as a Dom so quickly just a few days after I'd met Jack, and gone against the other four Masters doing it, but in many ways now, it was probably Gray's way of monitoring Jack's reactions in a controlled environment. If Gray had said no, knowing how stressed Jack had been back when I met him, Jack's conduct disorder could have no doubt kicked back in. Jack would've disobeyed Gray more through a need to disobey than choice and sense. And I'd learned the hard way why saying *Don't* around Jack was always dangerous business.

Ice and whiskey clinked against the sides of my glass as I eased back into the sofa.

"How do you think you're going to get on with Jack training other Doms, Jan?" said Gray eventually.

The question made me a little uneasy. "Why?"

Gray gave that *answer the question and don't mess about* smile.

I shrugged. "Jack's in his element. It doesn't take anything away from how he feels for me, or me for him. Well, that's the theoretical answer. I haven't seen that tested yet." And that was as honest as I could get. I didn't know how I'd react when whip came to… Jack getting laid.

Gray nodded, then drank. "Jack chooses his contracts here, after the Masters have vetted the potential Doms and sent them through to me for final appraisal. He's usually handed six files, of which he'll choose up to four, depending on intensity of the scenes. I can't allow you to observe those scenes for privacy issues, unless of course there's a reason I deem fit to overrule that and include you, but I can have a word with Jack and see how he'd feel about you sitting in with him when he chooses his contracts." Gray finished his drink as what he'd said made me sit forward slightly. "I don't want you feeling isolated," he added. "No secrets on exactly what goes on and whom Jack will be with." He tilted the glass at me. "If you'd prefer not to know, nobody will think any less of you."

"You sure?" I cocked a smile. "No abstract digs on lacking any balls?"

"Maybe one or two."

Great. Just the ones that matter. "Can I have time to think about it?" I asked quietly. Part of me wanted to know who Jack would be with, what he'd be put through, how things could go wrong, and how they would be handled. Part of me didn't. But I wasn't soft over why Gray was offering this. If I disrupted Jack and threw his head out a little with my feeling uneasy, then it ran into potential dangers for Jack during a scene. Would that be the overruling point he mentioned? That he'd allow me into a scene—desensitise me so that I wouldn't worry and pull Jack out of his game in the process? And where exactly did that leave Gray and Jack now that their relationship had changed slightly? "How are you going to be seeing Jack touched by trainee Doms?"

Gray fell quiet. A little too quiet. "I've been there for every Dom he's trained, bar you. Nobody touches him without me around and without my knowing how he will be touched. And then there's the MC security, and then Jack himself."

"Yeah, I know security is tight." I narrowed my eyes. "I'm talking about you personally. How he is with us, I don't know if I could watch him be like that with someone else. Can you now?"

"It's work with trainees, to the point Jack never quite moves away from the trainer's mindset. You can see it in his body, the way he tilts his head, how he listens to make sure he constantly knows the Dom's position, his intent; there's a constant between subbing and the instinct to Dom the scene if the trainee steps out of line. To most he's not a true sub; it's just another role he slips into." He pointed over. "It's what riled you: his taste of the trainer over a lover."

"But to you?"

Gray shrugged, but it wasn't as dismissive as the act steered towards. "There's something about him if you can reach past the bastard. Move him away from the training, give him the right stimulation, he's a stunning collared sub."

I glanced down at my drink. That was said from a lover talking about his sub. "And yet you hold back on collaring him yourself," I mumbled.

"Hmmm?"

It had been too quiet for Gray to catch. "Jack," I said

quietly, "you've never collared him."

"It's written into his contract that he's not to be collared away from a Dom training scene—"

"You wrote that clause yourself."

"Yes. Those few days with you were the longest he's worn one."

"But you're not me and you're not just any Dom; you're his—a Master," I mumbled quietly.

Gray's look was a little distant, but like with every other question that touched down too personal with him, he didn't answer. Putting his glass on the table next to me, he winked and walked back over to the floor. He seemed a little on edge, maybe because of me, maybe because of the personal discussion, or maybe with not being able to take Jack in full Master Dom mode, I couldn't really tell.

I eased the pull of trouser on my semi-interested hard-on as Gray warmed up. I'd love to see it. For all of my sins, I'd love to see that chemistry in a full scene, all of the whips and chains on Jack, how Gray managed to turn Jack on so much by being behind all of those toys. But also how Jack stirred Gray, kept him so on edge.

Gray warmed up, then calmed his body for a minute before running through a few supple flips, turns, and kicks. We didn't sleep together without Jack, so there really wasn't much time to investigate each other without Jack thrown into the equation. I wasn't quite sure what Gray thought of me, or if I even registered in his world without Jack here. But watch? It didn't hurt to watch. I liked how he kept watching me too, sometimes changing the look in his eyes from distant to something entirely darker. That look... Jack was right: Gray made life damn dark and sexy—

Vibrations from my pocket threw me a little, then I

realised a message had come through and I pulled my mobile free.

Call me, Jan.

Rob.

I choked back a sob, not really realising a shadow now blocked out the message. Gray held his hand out. "Give it."

"It's nothing. It's..." I couldn't finish, not without letting out a deep groan. "It's personal."

"You're touching my fucking sub, in my fucking home. It doesn't get more personal than that." Gray held his hand out farther. "You have the decency to show me anything that could disrupt it."

Hand shaking a little, I slapped the phone in his palm, and he made sure I didn't drop my gaze before he read it. "When did this start?"

"Last night."

"In bed?" He flicked a look at me. "You sure?"

"Yeah, of course I'm fucking sure, I—" But Gray was already moving over to his drinks table, and he picked up the phone, dismissing me.

"It's from Rob's number," I called over, and Gray nodded as he glanced back. "Mike, personal favour. Can you run a reverse text search for me?" He read out my phone number, then waited a moment. "The owner is supposed to be deceased. What I need now is a trace on where that phone was last used, as close as you can get." He paused, then a moment later said his thanks and dialled another number. As the receiver went back in its cradle, I frowned and went over, hearing a ringtone. He'd put it on loud speaker.

Gray leaned against the wall and put a finger to his lips as the ringing stopped.

"Hello." Life seemed to stall at hearing the familiar voice.

"Lisa Kershaw," stated Gray.

"Yes."

"Deepest sympathy on the death of your husband, Robert, and, of course, your youngest daughter."

"Hmmm, thank you. Who is this?"

"You're welcome." He unfolded his arms. "You have been texting Mr Jan Richards on behalf of your deceased husband. Please stop, Mrs Kershaw."

Quiet. "I have, have no idea what you're talk—"

"I do," he said simply. "Don't do it again."

"I... I—"

"Lisa?" I shuffled a little closer to the phone.

"Jan?"

"What the hell are you doing, honey?"

Gentle sobs drifted over the phone, and I frowned at Gray.

"You, you stayed away from the funeral, Jan. I was, was so grateful."

Jack had been with me that day. I hadn't felt right going to Rob's funeral, not as Rob's hidden lover.

"But the flower." She choked back a sob. "That goddamn flower. You left a blue moon rose at his graveside."

Gray was looking at me. That detail didn't need clarifying, though. I had, but I still nodded at Gray. "Lisa, look—"

"Do you know he started growing them in the garden just after we met?" she said, her voice cracking over the phone. "I thought they were for me. He'd give them so much care, so much bloody attention, Jan. And every time you two split up, he'd take one for you with him. At the grave... Ryan, he thought his dad had left it. He thought Rob was sending my boy a message." Her voice went calm. "I wanted you to know how he felt, how shit you'd made us both feel."

I hadn't known. "The roses... I didn't know, Lisa. He never told me." I thought he'd bought them, just a peace-making gesture every time he wanted to break the relationship off, that he'd... Ryan. Rob's seven-year-old. He shouldn't have been put through that. "I'm so sorry."

There was gentle crying. "Just wanted to let you know how it felt, being reminded. I'm... I'm—"

"It's all right," I said quietly. "I know what grief does to you." More than. "Just, no more. Enough now."

"Mrs Kershaw," said Gray, not giving her time to answer. "That's Mr Richards being polite over the issue. But understand, if this continues and he receives any more texts that disrupt, I don't share Mr Richards' politeness. Are we clear?"

"Who—who the hell are you?"

"Good evening to you too." Gray cut the connection, then handed me the phone.

As I tucked it back in my pocket, I glanced at him. "You can't control who talks to me, Gray."

"You hide shit like this again whilst you're around Jack, you won't be talking to *him*, forget who's talking to you. You listen when we say communicate."

I looked away, trying hard not to bite back at everything that comment suggested or how that trainer tone was now there in Gray's voice. "All due respect here, Gray." I kept

43

my voice flat. "You're not the only one here who cares about him. Your house, your sub, but my boyfriend, okay?"

"It's nothing to do with who cares for what, Jan." Gray's voice was just as controlled as I turned away and went and sat down. "It's to do with not repeating past screw-ups on your part."

"Who cares for *whom,* not *what.*" Now I looked at him as he came over. "He's not a piece of BDSM equipment to be stored away in a black zone until you want to use him."

That hit a bad note with Gray, but he was far from perfect too. I knew that, and maybe Gray didn't like just how much I did know. "*Jack's* tough enough to deal with whatever 'boyfriend' issues you have," said Gray. "When you find yourself struggling to tell him what's hurting, which you are, you tell me."

"You saw his reaction to having come on his abs. I was worried about him. He needed his routine back, not tugging from under his feet with this shit again."

"When it comes to Jack, your one worry is me. He's been hurt enough over you and this Rob. That doesn't happen again. Not to the point he's whipped for it."

"I—" My screw-ups had never been mentioned until now, and that bite back at him stopped there. Jack had been whipped for what had happened when both Rob and Mark Shaw had come on the scene. Then when Rob and his toddler had died? What followed? I never wanted it repeated.

"Good," said Gray, satisfied. "You make sure you—"

"Oh for godssake, take your bloody boots off," shouted Ed, and Gray moved back over to the hall floor as noise suddenly came from behind, the hall door now opening. There were a few curses, and I managed a smile.

"Hi, Jack," I said, not even having to look, but as calm as Gray with dropping our... disagreement now Jack was home.

"Right," said Jack, not sounding happy as boots hit the floor. "A guy works his bollocks off all day and comes home to find that neither one of his blokes could get him some decent grub on the table." With oily coveralls and steel toe cap boots, Jack came and crashed on the settee next to me. His black hair was damp, and a slight flush touched his cheeks now that he was in the warm air. Mid-November, no doubt the weather outside was sticking to its usual manic-depressive state and throwing a good bout of cold-shoulder into the mix too. Jack was shivering slightly, but he still managed a gorgeous smile.

"Looks cold out," I said.

"Freezing." Jack eyed me up. "Not that you office guys would know cold if it bit your bollocks off and ran down the street doing hamster cheeks with them."

I gave him the finger as Gray glanced over, first at me, then barely seeming to bite back the need to add to Ed's disgust and tell Jack to take his boots off. Jack kept his body clean to his OCD extremes, but that didn't mean he didn't leave his butt prints about with his coveralls.

Jack stretched, then giving a wink, he lay down, his legs coming up on mine. "All right, things?"

I chuckled. "Peachy." He gave my leg a kick that said *stop pinching my words.* "Rough day?" I asked, passing him my drink.

He palmed at his eyes. "Expensive." He sounded tired, then took the drink and downed it in one, which surprised me: he did alcohol about as often as he did social. No amount of pleading from me had managed to pull Jack into a nightclub over the past few months.

"My fault for terrorising Steve. He threw in a few moans, added how he needed a new compressor, two pit jacks, and fuel retriever. I'm gonna have to think about selling my ass to keep him in garage equipment, not to mention the cost of office supplies."

"That would mean you actually getting your ass back into BDSM gear to sell it," said Gray to us as he continued with his kicks.

"Awww." Jack grinned at me. "Lock him out of his dungeon for a few weeks—"

"*Months*," shouted Gray.

"And he's as grouchy as fuck."

"Yeah," said Gray. "You had a shower yet? You're getting grease on my sofa."

Jack shifted his ass, obviously getting more deliberately comfortable. "Don't hear Jan complain about my ass like that."

"He's a gentleman, I'm not," said Gray. "Get the fuck off my chairs."

"Hear the class go out of the window with that. It was a sofa a moment ago."

"*Now*."

A groan, a kick off of his boots, Jack pulled off his socks, then headed over to the music system that sat behind the drinks tray. After flicking it on to play, he went to where Gray worked his art on the hardwood floor and stood watching him.

"Problem?" said Gray, stopping his run of kata to face him.

"Nope." Jack looked Gray up and down. "Just thought

I'd come train with you for a while."

Gray folded his arms, a very suspicious look darkening his blue eyes. "Why?"

Jack was up to something, and hell did this look interesting.

CHAPTER 5
TEMPTING THE DEVIL

JACK STOOD THERE in the hall, just inches from Gray, and he was doing a really lousy job of looking innocent. "Well, thing is," he said quietly, "you know if there's any chance of you playing torturer on me, I need as much exercise as possible to keep supple, toned...." He pressed his body in close, drifting a touch over Gray's trousers. "All hard. Inviting." A sigh was given as he slipped a look down to where his hand played. "Hmmmm." He frowned, that head of his already with Gray in some deep, dark dungeon. "Invite me to play," he whispered. "Please."

Gray went to say something, either that or drag Jack down into the cellar by the scruff of his neck and screw the hell out of him, but music kicked into life, some eighties rave track that Gray only shook his head at.

He pushed Jack away, and, giving a huge grin, Jack fell in at Gray's side, facing me as he calmed his body. After a little warm up, Jack followed Gray's moves with the same skilled attention, his kicks and flips all in perfect sync with Gray. Yet when Gray turned his back on him—Jack suddenly moved in close, doing this little dance in time

49

with the heavy beat, hips adding an extra kick to moves that I swore should be X-rated and on some shelf somewhere. Air-spanking Gray's ass came into play, then he moved in with every obscene indication of air-humping him. There were no mirrors in here, no arrogance with either of them watching themselves work out, so Gray was none the wiser.

As Gray turned around, Jack fell back into the perfect martial arts partner, all decency and full control. Yet when Gray turned his back… Jack settled back into another bout of *I wanna fuck you* dancing, and I choked laughter as Gray looked in my direction for the second time. He glanced at Jack, but Jack only shrugged and mouthed *what the hell* back at him.

It was inevitable that Jack would get caught out; you could even see it written in his chaos chart that something would go wrong somewhere. A faster song came on, and Jack got a little too cocky, singing along and turning his back on Gray as he danced his latest obscenity.

I stopped the music mid-track, and it forced Jack to look over at me as I put the remote on the table.

"Saw that one, didn't he?" said Jack, and I nodded, unable to talk as I snorted laughter, pointing at Gray as he stood behind Jack, arms folded, no doubt plotting which area of the Thames Jack's body would float best in.

"Uh-huh," said Jack more to himself. A sniff, a glance over his shoulder—he was suddenly bolting over the sofa, missing me by inches, Gray going psycho on his heels. The sofa got a jolt, then I was tipped onto the floor, forcing Gray into a skid by me.

"Go get him, kid," said Jack, already halfway out the door. Gray steadied me as I got to my feet, then he was off after Jack. I raced after the cries as they tore through the mansion, out to the pool, all in time to see Gray grab Jack by the waist and unceremoniously dump him hard onto the wet concrete. Jack was laughing hard, now struggling to breathe as he fought underneath Gray.

"Stop…" cried Jack as Gray tried to catch hold of Jack's wrists. "Now you…" He was struggling to take a breath. "You know you'll only get your hands dirty. Can't… can't have that now, can we, my old mukka?"

I made it over, and Jack took full advantage of Gray's distraction, pushing him off and shouting "yes" before he scrambled to his feet. Gray followed after him, but Jack, looking like he was about to slip over on the wet concrete, forced Gray to reach out.

With a wicked grin and a shove at Gray's shoulders, Jack sent him into a very cold November pool for his considerations.

"Fuck—oh yes." He started fist-pumping the air and giving "Rocky, Rocky!" shouts as Gray surfaced, leaving Jack doubled and laughing. "Had to cool you down and, well… who's the daddy now, eh? Who's the fucking duh-had-dy?"

Jack landed heavily in the pool close to Gray and quickly surfaced, spitting out water as he looked up at me. "*Richards*, you're fucking well meant to be on my side!"

I gave a light flick of my head back into the pool to prove it. "Twelve o'clock," I said, folding my arms.

Jack glanced back, saw Gray coming at him, then giving an "oh fuck," he swam as fast as he could for the steps. Gray caught him just as he reached for the first rung, then dunked him under the water. Four more times with Gray doing that, Jack was left crying no more, and I went over and helped pull him out of the water, followed by Gray.

"Shit." Ed made me jump as he was suddenly there, handing Gray a huge heated towel and an umbrella against the pouring rain. Jack looked at him hopefully, but Ed just snorted and walked off.

"Well fuck you very much, you old fuh—"

"*Jack.*" Gray looked him up and down. I followed a moment later seeing what held his distraction. Jack's drenched coveralls hugged every shape and contour of his body, the rain seeming to fall a little harder, chuckling a dark *Missed a bit, love, let me just wet it here for you.* Gray's eyes smiled, liking the offer, but there was something else in there that seemed to quiet Jack.

"You're in serious shit, Jack."

"Really?" he said back to Gray. "You mean the whole *piss you off, you fuck harder* thing?" That grin of his was torture on the balls. "Hadn't worked that out yet. Thanks for the heads-up, mukka."

Gray went in close. "Yeah," he said quietly. "You keep that heads-up real close, Jack."

Grinning, Jack looked at me.

"What?"

"You." He added a scowl. "One thing, you couldn't just give me this one fucking thing."

"Your annual bath? You're halfway there, Jacky boy."

"Oh. Take the piss out of the OCD working class, is it, today?" he said, looking between me and Gray. "It's all right for you city boys. All suits and ties, but the rest of us who actually move ass for a living, we get the piss taken out of us because we know how to play dirty—"

"*Get.* You get dirty, Jack."

"Yeah? Whatever," he said, flashing his eyes. A sneeze,

he looked at me thoughtfully, then Gray. "You notice he's the only one that's sorta dry?"

I gave him the finger. "That's all you'll be riding if you try it. I've got my mobile on me."

"Oh, hear the sexual non-in-your-end-o on that," said Jack, inching his way over. I let him get a little closer, then bolted back for the house. A clip at my heel sent me down onto the sodden grass, and I had enough time to turn over before Jack, wet clothes and dripping hair, dropped on me. Shaking his head, making sure I took a shower, he waggled his eyebrows. "Just finger-play?"

He was getting hard.

"Telling me you'd moan at just finger-play?" I said back at him.

"That a threat there, boy?" He gave a smile, a grind of hips. "I'll make you cry first."

Fuck.

"Hmmm." I fought a deep blush. "What's with the 'mukka' thing?" I breathed, looking up.

He bit back a chuckle. "And you're the one with the council upbringing, hmmm?" He sneezed, just managing to turn his head away. "Old mukka," he said, wrinkling his nose and giving a sniff. "My old friend?"

"Oh," I mouthed, then let a slow smile creep in. "Don't... kiss me."

Jack narrowed his eyes. "Pull that shit, hmmm? You know it doesn't work with soft lads like you?" But the fight was there in his eyes, the itching to disobey a command, but give me exactly what I wanted in the process. And it was a fight he'd wrestled since he was a teen. "Nope, not gonna work. Ever," he added.

"Yeah? Don't... *kiss* me, Jack."

He pulled a face, groaned, his conduct disorder scratching, needing to get to the surface. We'd looked at doing this over the past few months, as cruel as it seemed, but it was part of the aftercare, that gentle repetition that would get him used to it, and the need to disobey "don't" commands would ease.

"Don't… fuck me, Jack."

He failed to stop his grin. "Oh, well, if you put it like that, Richards."

Before he could touch down with a rough kiss, a towel dropped on his head, making us both wince.

"Hey." Jack pulled it off, and Gray smiled down at us. "What?" he said. "You can come and fuck about too, mukka. Talk dirty to me, I might let you fuck him. Like how you keep eyeing up my things lately."

Something played in Gray's eyes. "Real good to see you back in full swing, Jack. Real good."

He disappeared and Jack's smile dropped. "I shouldn't be worried, right?" He looked down at me. "I mean, I really shouldn't be fucking worried about that tone, should I?"

Oh, he looked good worried.

A sniff, he got up, pulling me with him, and shook himself like a soaked rat again. I winced, pulling back slightly as he soaked me. "Look." He was roughing up his hair. "About you moving in with me here. I—"

"Jack, can I go first?" He looked at me a little worried. "Just hear me out before you get mad, please."

"Mah—" Something in Jack's eyes slipped, a pull back to old *Don't… screw with me* times, to where it had taken Jack getting whipped before I'd managed to talk to him. I quickly went in close, and in between gentle kisses, I told him about the two texts from Lisa. He slowly pushed me to arm's length.

"Gray?" That look in his eyes was dark. "He's sorted it, yeah?" I nodded and let him know about Gray's call as he looked back towards the manor. "You get any more," he said eventually, now back with me, "you tell whoever is closest, yeah?"

Despite him being wet, I snaked my arms around his neck.

"You okay?" he whispered, cuddling back with this grip that threatened to break bone.

"Am now," I said quietly, nuzzling into his neck. "Didn't mean to keep it from you."

"Good." A kiss to my head. "Because she does it again, I'll trace the fucker, then I'll—"

"Phone call, Master Harrison."

We both looked back to the manor hearing Ed call down. "Oh for fuck's sake," Jack grumbled under his breath. "*I'm full into a Mr now, Ed,*" he shouted. "*Fucking call me it in front of the boyfriend at least.* Please."

Ed just snorted, and as we started towards the manor, I winked at Jack. "He likes manners, or at least you trying to manage a few without swearing."

"Old fucker makes me swear."

"Suuure, it's all *him.*"

Jack glanced at me, then pulled me in for a cuddle. As we made it into the conservatory, Jack paused to take off his coveralls and boxers, leaving him naked to the elements.

He gave a huge kick-ass grin, and I closed my eyes knowing what was coming as he headed on in.

"Jack—get some clothes on for—"

"Phone call, Ed," said Jack, innocently. "This way, right?

But thanks for calling me Jack." I could even picture the naked, two-thumbs-up look that Jack would be handing out in there.

Gray was hiding a grin as I went in. Jack had disappeared, but Ed was sat there on the arm of a chair, looking very pale.

"Everything okay?" said Gray. I nodded, going over and giving him Jack's wet clothes.

"Yeah," I said quietly, "it is now."

"Good," said Gray as I followed Jack's wet footprints into the training hall to get my book. Jack gave me a wink as I mouthed an apology. He shook it off and told me to hang on. He'd grabbed a towel from those on offer in the adjoining steam room and wrapped it snugly around his hips, giving him some decency, yet still all so indecent with how his damp hair dripped water onto his shoulders, all to run teasingly down his abs. "Yeah, okay. Thanks, Michelle. I'll be there."

Picking up my book, I cocked a brow hearing the woman's name. "Michelle?"

Jack was scratching his head as he put the phone down. He frowned at Gray when he wandered through. "Suppose that's down to you?"

"What's down to him?"

Gray just smiled, ignoring me.

"Jack?" I was back with him now. "Who's Michelle? What's he done?"

Gray came over, clothes now changed, hair still damp, but looking very at ease as he poured himself a drink.

"Seems I'm wanted at the MC base," said Jack, folding his arms.

The base? Oh. I buried my grin. "Feeling better are we, Jack?"

Jack came over and forced Gray to turn around, drink in hand. "Appears so," he said. "Wonder where they got that idea?"

Gray shrugged. "With all the CCTV the Masters have at their disposal, Jack, they no doubt saw it. That and heard you screaming like a pansy when Jan pushed you in the pool."

Jack pinched Gray's drink and downed it in one. "Yeah. Real strange that."

I chuckled. "When?"

"Thursday after work," said Jack as Gray picked up the whiskey decanter and offered it back to Jack.

"Another one, Jack? You starting back with the MC after such a long, long—long absence, lubrication is best started early."

I couldn't get it together enough to stop chuckling.

"Oh, laugh it up, Richards."

I was.

"Let's see what you're like after no sex for three days."

That sobered me up. "No sex? Three days? What the hell?"

Jack offered me the whiskey. "I can't be touched or touch anyone else for three days prior to inauguration." He looked at Gray. "Only saving grace is that you're on no-touch street too, boss."

"Both of you?" Gray and Jack looked at me. "But that doesn't go for me, right? I mean… I'm nothing to do with the MC. Whatever rules you two live by… they're yours, not mine?"

Jack came over, backing me up to the settee. "Been here before, Richards." A strong grip went to my hair, enough to force my head up, and a kiss ghosted my jaw. "Those hands of yours wander over any part that my hands have already claimed, I'll fuck up parts you don't even know can be fucked up."

Christ. This switch… "How, Jack?" I breathed, kissing at his jaw. "You can't touch me, remember?" Jack answered that with a bite to my throat, one hard enough to mark, to claim, to completely mess with my head and groin. Yeah, if he said wait, I'd sit in the corner next to Ed's dog waiting happily for the call to heel.

"Includes playing around, Jack," said Gray, sounding all formal, but I caught the merriment in his eyes. "Back off."

Jack didn't look too pleased at the interruption, even let his look challenge Gray for long enough. But with a cock of a head from Gray, he backed off, actually took a step away, hands behind his back, head down. Christ, I loved how Gray stilled his every kickback against control.

"Mr Raoul," said Ed. He was back by the door, stood there with a hand covering his eyes. "Shall I set up the bedroom in the west wing for Master Harrison?" For a butler, every comment he made regarding doing errands seemed so… sarcastic in general.

Jack groaned a few expletives as I stared at Gray. "He doesn't even sleep with us?"

"No shit, Sherlock," said Jack, but he instantly curbed his annoyance and winked at me. Giving a hard sigh, he went and stood nose to nose with Gray. There was a brush of his nose along Gray's jaw for the second time now, and the need to find out the *what* and *why* behind it nearly killed me. Jack kissed Gray so gently, that switch flicking to sub. Then shifting down to Gray's neck, feathering more gentle kisses, Jack discreetly rubbed the back of his hand against Gray's cock.

"Better make Thursday good, Gray," he murmured, giving a slow smile against his throat. "And I mean *fuck me like the devil* good."

Gray's eyes were purely all for Jack now. "Got something special planned for you, stunner." That slight smile was all for Jack too. "Something really... fucking... peachy."

CHAPTER 6
THURSDAY

Jack Harrison

NO SEX, NO touching, not even a cuddle up on the sofa—come Thursday, even a smirk off Jan had me in the mood for stripping him naked and fucking his clothes, even if it meant I rolled around the floor wrapping his scent on me. The alternative to no sex had been too ball-busting. Gray and Jan had spent some of the daytimes at the art galleries in London, followed by evening meals with all three of us. Ed introduced the basic bangers and mash to the menu, and Jan had sat there like a kid, munching through the sausages, not really catching on why, but by the time the meal had finished, I'd sat there banging my head on the table, calling Ed all the fucks under the sun. Yeah, I'd heard Ed chuckling from the kitchen, or maybe that had just been Gray.

But Thursday… Today. I made it back to Gray's for six and ensured the mail table was my first stop. With my head buried in places that would make even the devil chuckle, I'd not had time to grab it that morning. Sure enough, my letters were stacked in the pile marked *boring*. Some flyers, paperwork from the MC base, disclaimers, yep, all the usual crap there. Gray had obviously taken his, leaving *almost* nothing to mess through. Almost....

I grinned at the smartly dressed package on the table, even though it did look big enough to house a few books.

Shifting slightly, all accidental like, just to get a better look (hell, it was coming up to December, Christmas prezzies, and all), I ran my eyes over the address printed on it.

Jan.

He'd had mail redirected here?

A little uneasy, I left the package there and headed for the shower in Gray's bedroom. "Anyone here?" I called out only to have things remain pretty quiet. Even Ed had disappeared.

Jan had called at dinnertime to let me know he was out with Gray for the day. Maybe he'd said why they'd be late back; I just hadn't caught it with the amount of background noise from the garage. Strange Ed wasn't around, though. He always polluted some space around here, all green gasses and evil laughter as he slaughtered a few council kids in the kitchen, snob that he was.

Water hit my shoulders, and the assault felt good, maybe a little too good. It was just a formality going over to the MC's; I'd spend about fifteen minutes on my knees, saying a load of *yes/no and thank you* bollocks to the other four Masters. But afterwards? I sighed and closed my eyes, letting my head fall back so water ran over my face. A stroke at my abs, a few shivers chased the wake of my fingers.

Tonight meant serious, *serious* subbing. And Gray in full Master mode? After he hadn't fucked as a Master for nearly five months?

My cock sobbed happily, all *Go on, Jack, just the one, baby. He won't know.* But the no-touch rule was there for a reason, and it stole a breath. Giving a moan, denying every natural instinct to give my cock what it danced in the rain for, I stepped out and switched the shower off.

"Hey, things."

"Fuck me." I jerked around hearing Jan. "You trying to bury me, Breakdown?"

"Go you with all that tough-guy karate training there, you big girl."

Jan grinned and grabbed a towel. Shirt sleeves rolled up, he moved in to dry me. Shoulders took his attention first, then he worked gently down to my pecs. He had that slight curl to his lips as his gaze followed his hands, and I narrowed my eyes. "Okay, what you up to?"

"Hmmm?"

"That grin. Gray's whispered something in your ear. Don't make me hurt your ass finding out just what it is."

Jan knelt, and breathing became suddenly hard when he ran his tongue along my cock. "Focus," he said quietly. "That was Gray's first word for tonight."

Damp lips slipped over my head, and Jan's warm mouth, moist, yet smooth like the finest wet silk took me nearly to the root an—"Fuck, oh-kay." I ran a touch through his hair. He used throat muscles to suck me in deep, and I groaned. He was learning to play dirty pretty quick. "Jan, too, fuck—too much focusing. Stop."

My cock slipped out of his mouth, thudding back against my abs, and Jan smiled up at me, hand now massaging my balls. He was dressed in white shirt and trousers, looking so smart, so sexy, and there at my feet. Fuck.

"Hmmm." Jan tapped my cock. "Gray said control might be a problem with this."

"Yeah?" *Spark plugs, think sparkling slugs.* "Gray, he, he

63

whispered *what* then?"

Jan grinned up at me. "That he'd fuck you into the land of dry heaving cocks if you come."

I weighed the options up, the mass of bodies, threat of a sore cock. Jan. Gray. So I grinned. "That's meant to put me off *how?*"

Jan kissed his way up my abs, my chest, then stood, grabbing my cock and coming in close, kissing my neck, nipping—licking. "You'll leave me frustrated." A gentle bite. "And I might just have to strip naked and play at your feet again."

I groaned and looked down at his hand, how it played along my shaft, his thumb occasionally running over the slit. A grip in his hair forced his lips still and close to mine. "Way too much focusing. You need to fucking stop." Jan groaned as I bit at his throat, bruising the skin.

"Sorry," he mumbled, sounding drowsy, yet feeling nice and hard against my thigh. A kiss brushed at my jaw, then my lips before he pulled away a touch. "You're gonna be late, gorgeous."

I waggled my eyebrows. "You think?"

Jan chuckled. "You're dead, my friend. Carry on winding Gray up, he'll turn on you."

"Yeah? Seriously?" I stroked his ass. "Listen." I gave a deep sigh. "About what I said the other night." I knew this came out of the blue. "About us moving into Gray's."

"Jack—"

"I know. Just hear me out, okay?" I rested my head against his, putting sex and playfulness to one side. "It scares the life out of me," I said quietly, and he tried to pull away. "Everything that we are, it's going so good, so bloody good, Jan. Yet there's that part of me who's terrified to move in case I knock what we have off balance." I glanced down at my hands as I took his in mine.

"I know that's really fucked up and selfish. Life is about working together, yet...." I shrugged. "Routine... I like you, this, us, as it is, and...." I was struggling to explain. "There's been a lot of change in the last five months and—"

Jan managed to pull away. "Jack, is this what's been bothering you lately?"

I shrugged, and arms snaked around my neck as Jan hugged me close. "Not everyone hides something beneath the surface," he whispered, giving a gentle kiss to my cheek. "And if going casual with us is how you manage...."

I pulled back, screwing up my face. This was no casual shit.

Brushing hair out of my eyes, Jan gave such a soft smile, then went on, "Meaning, if you need to keep turning us a certain way until you're okay with moving on to the next stage, I'm good with that." I got a deep kiss and a taste of a mint-chocolate Jan. "You, you're enough for me. More than enough. You.... Just keep talking to me and let me know what's going through your head, okay?" Jan rested his forehead against mine. "And for what it's worth, I'm not ready to move in yet either." He gave a shaky sigh, and I chuckled.

"This talking thing," I said quietly, my nose brushing his cheek, "best if it works both ways, Richards?"

Jan nodded, and he seemed to breathe a little easier with it.

"Good," I said quietly, "'cause I was getting a bit worried when I saw your mail on the table just now."

"I have mail here?" Jan pulled away, looked at me, and frowned. "Maybe Gray's bought me something... good."

"Good?" I bit back a grin. "You going kink on me, Richards?"

He let his hand wander down to my ass. "Talking about

kink," he said, pulling back, "who's going to tell Gray about us not moving in?"

I made a point of looking at a watch I didn't have on. "Oops. Gotta go see a man about a fucking."

"Hah. Coward, I knew it," he chuckled, and I stepped back to pick up the towel.

"Listen, we're not going to be long," I added. "How 'bout you—"

Jan sniffed. "The Mercedes is already warming up. I'm driving you in. Gray's gained clearance with security at the Masters' Circle."

I frowned. "You okay with waiting? We can leave my Merc there, get one of the guys to drive it back, then mess around in the back of Gray's Rolls, with him driving, wind him up some more. A few hours of serious BDSM with Gray, then one hell of a fucking afterwards with you. That gonna make up for having time with Gray?" My frown deepened. "With MC business, he usually keeps things pretty private with me."

Jan gave a slow smile. "I don't mind waiting, Jack. Seriously. Don't… enjoy the next few hours."

That last comment earned the finger off me, followed by a long kiss.

~

Me and Jan pushed through into Regent Manor, southside of the Thames, knowing that the conference hall we needed was a few floors up in the Gothic architecture. We took the elevator, waiting just long enough for the doors to close before I backed Jan up against the wall and tongued him deep, my thigh splitting his legs and rubbing hard into his crotch. We both wore suits, my black on Jan's finely tailored charcoaled grey, both with shirts tugged free and going for full disorderly conduct in a few short seconds.

"They…" Jan searched every inch of my ass, pulling me in, pushing away, then pulling me back in again. "They have cameras in here?" He groaned against my kiss.

I was busy digging a hand down into his suit trousers, rubbing my palm into his cock, all to hear him groan again. "Yeah." I breathed heavily against his lips. "Wanna give security something to talk about and—"

Jan surprised the hell out of me by switching position and forcing me up against the wall.

"Fuck talking," he hissed. "Security will be tossing themselves raw by the time I'm finished."

Something had got him going despite having the cameras here. He'd hated the idea of them back when I'd been Dom-training him at his home. I wish I knew what the fuck it was that had changed that tonight. The doors opened, and Jan was suddenly away from me, tucking his shirt in and straightening his suit as though nothing had happened. Mine was dishevelled and I was left half manhandled up against the wall, watching him.

By the time we reached the waiting room outside the main hall, Jan had this *butter wouldn't melt over my need-to-be-fucked body* look about him, and I knew I was still staring, still trying to tame the roughing up his touch had left.

"Well go on, then, Jack," said Jan, taking a seat and picking up a magazine, all nonchalant like. "Best not to keep the Masters waiting." He even waved me on, casually.

Fifteen minutes. I made sure my shirt was tucked in. Yeah, fifteen minutes—ten if I could hurry it along and miss out a few *hail Masters, I promise to be a good bloke.*

Hand shaking a little, I pushed on through to the main conference hall.

All five Masters and Mistresses were seated at the head of the conference table, and I stopped just short of the hardwood floor, removed my shoes and socks, then took my place on my knees in front of them. The pull on my trousers as I eased down did more to ease the Jan-ache in my cock.

Ten minutes in here. Five, if possible.

"Was there a problem with the lifts, Mr Harrison?"

I let out a cough after Brennan spoke. "No. Hmm. Apologies." I forgot the "Sir" on that and added it quickly.

"Hmm," said Brennan. "Perhaps we need to have maintenance look at them as you're nearly fifteen minutes late."

Brennan, as usual, sat at the head of the conference table. Gray was to his left, Mistress Carr next to him. To Brennan's right were the remaining two Masters. One of these days I swore I'd find out their names, but Mistress Ball Breaker and Master Gruff would have to do for now. And as I was required to keep my head down and only look up when told, asking for names wasn't something I wanted to be bringing up right now, not with knowing just who these Masters were beyond the MC and who selected them.

"Traffic, Sir," I said quietly. "Apologies."

"In the lifts? How odd. Yes, well." Sounded like the bastard was smiling. "Your punctuality is an issue for your Master to resolve, Mr Harrison. For now, good evening."

CHAPTER 7
MASTERS' CIRCLE

"EVENIN', SIR." I nodded at Brennan as he sat at the conference table, then just gave a slight indication either side of him to the others seated with him, including Gray. "Masters, Mistresses."

Replies were given back, papers shuffled about. "I have the doctor's report here," said Brennan. "It declares you fit and well to return to the full Master sub role of training Doms." Again more shuffling of paper. "No scarring from your stitches... excellent. Our psychology department and Master Raoul have also given clearance for you to return to normal training duties due to there being no shows of physical and emotional stress."

I hid a smile and hoped to fuck Gray never saw it. Throwing him in a November pool wasn't probably one of my best ideas for skiving work.

"How do *you* feel, though, Mr Harrison?"

"Erm." That caught me off guard. "Fine, Sir."

"You have been prescribed medication and cognitive therapy again for your disorders. How are you coping with them?"

They'd heard all the gruesome details over Mark Shaw's *Don't… let me fuck with you* head games. Of course they would have. "Hard at times, Sir, I won't lie." I smiled softly, loving the thought of Jan and Gray together. "But I have first-class support."

Quiet. "Thank you for your honesty, Jack. It's good to see." And with that, he sighed. "Neither I nor my peers have any reason to withhold reinstatement of your position. You will be allocated clients on our next training rota, just after Christmas. Are there any particular preferences over your choice of client?"

"Which departments are on the rota, Sir?"

More shuffling of paper, but the answer came from Mistress Carr. "We have eight from the Ministry of Defence, two from the Criminal Investigations Department, also eight civilians ranging from public to the private sector."

"With the Ministry of Defence, are the personnel serving?" The raise of my eyebrow was hopeful. Serving MOD soldiers meant specialist training provided by Gray, which meant nothing to do with sex; Gray was training real bastards with an aptitude for upping the creativeness of interrogation scenes. With a deep masochistic side, I sometimes got to sneak into some and let them… play.

"Ex-servicemen for this rota," said Carr. "Four looking to Dom, two to sub, the remaining two wishing training on the technical side."

"All looking for employment or just personal experience?"

"Employment."

I nodded. Maybe more satisfied. The Masters' Circle was

government funded and tax deductible for a reason: one of their core focuses was providing job opportunities for ex-servicemen, whether it was behind the scenes in security, and at worldwide locations, or just a release for all of their stresses with Dom training or sub training. But they also provided training for those who served in most government departments, and for different reasons. Gray focused more on the Doms or training interrogation officers. To be honest, I didn't mind. Any man that showed enough balls to serve always put him at the top of my *To Do* list. "MOD, please, Mistress Carr." That was her area, and with how she and Gray always had their heads together, it wasn't just an area she stood pretty in.

"Excellent. Thank you, Jack. Your preferences match your Master's, so we have no conflict of interests."

Yes. Less than five minutes. Three to be precise. I said my thanks, nodded, and moved to stand.

"Not yet, Mr Harrison."

Fuck. Head still down, I eased back to my knees, needing to look up at Brennan. "Apologies, I thought we were done."

"I can see that." Again, it sounded like he was grinning. "It's been brought to the Masters' attention that, for your last contract, you refused to use your safe word."

I resisted looking at Gray.

"Is this the case?"

Considering it surrounded using a safe word around Jan? Fuck, yes, it had been the case. "Yes, Sir. Master Raoul was made aware of the issue."

"By Mr Richards, not you?" added Brennan.

A rhetorical statement, but I answered anyway. "Yes, Sir."

A heavy sigh. "You've been with us long enough to know that our Master subs are given those safe words so that security who are observing a training scene will know when their assistance is required. If they know a Master sub is deliberately withholding their safe words, or has a history of it, trust becomes damaged. In an environment where training is mostly focused on non-civilian personnel, you can understand the potential concerns that will raise for our security teams."

"Yes, Sir. Circumstances surrounding my last contract were…" I frowned remembering Jan's hurt after I'd hit him. "Emotional. The fault was entirely my own."

"In certain ways," said Brennan, "it removed you from the Circle and out of harm's way. Nobody would have felt the loss of a Master sub more than those sitting here."

I frowned. That had been meant sincerely. "Thank you, Sir."

"However, understand that the price for breaking trust between a Master and his sub, and ultimately the people who are employed to keep a Master sub safe, is a serious violation, one that no Master here will tolerate under any circumstance, Mr Harrison."

I closed my eyes. Just great that I'd start back with another flogging on my record. Or worse. "The fault is mine," I said, keeping my voice as calm as possible. "Master Raoul—"

"Called enough."

I looked up, just briefly.

"There were faults all around, Jack," Gray said quietly. "You've already taken punishment for events you had little to no control over. Enough. More than."

"The Masters are in agreement," said Brennan.

"However, you've been a Dom trainer for nine years now, Mr Harrison. Trust and respect, you have ours; do not force us into a position where we have to question whether we have yours. Ever."

Life calmed just for those few seconds. "Understood, Sir." And my thanks after that was aimed solely at Gray.

Brennan nodded. "But as a first-time trainee sub would be required to do, I will ask you to now state clearly to the Masters your personal safe word. What is your personal safe word to let a Dom know you wish for him to stop the scene?"

I blushed, somehow finding this more uncomfortable than a flogging. "Hmmm. Mercedes, Sir."

"And what is the Masters' Circle's security safe word, the one that you would use if a trainee Dom fails to listen to your call of Mercedes, and thus poses a dangerous threat that has moved beyond your control?"

"Mercedes-Benz, Sir."

"What does that second safe word initiate?"

"External safety protocol," I said. "It alerts security observing the scene to how they are needed to end proceedings with the safety of the sub solely in mind. Mostly where the Dom has failed to stop the scene and moved beyond a Master sub's consensual zone."

"State an incident where you would use Mercedes-Benz, Jack."

"Now," I mumbled, and it won a few chuckles from those at the conference table.

"Apart from now," said Brennan.

I buried my blush. "One clause in my standard contract clearly states that I will not entertain incest themes in any way, shape, or form with a trainee Dom. If a Dom were to challenge that midway through a scene and threaten physical violence to force an incest scenario, Mercedes-Benz would be used if I couldn't—" Beat the shit out of the Dom. "—stop the scene myself."

"Will you fail to use either of your safe words again, Jack?"

"No, Sir," I mumbled quietly, and it earned a few more chuckles.

"Good. Enjoy your evening, Mr Harrison." I caught his smile then. "A Master has the right to re-test the mental aptitude and fitness of his Master sub. No cameras, no CCTV equipment, just you, him, and whatever tools of the trade he wishes to test your mind and body to the full with." Quiet. "Will you allow Gray to re-Master you, Jack?"

Name the time, date, place, and I'd be there, saddle thrown over shoulder, cowboy hat on, naked, willing to ride the rough until he stopped bucking through exhaustion, but for all of the smart-ass answers I could have used, "Please," was the only breathed reply I managed. It won a soft chuckle off Gray, and I quickly added a "Yes, Sir," hating the sub mode already slipping into gear there.

~

The doors to the main hall closed behind me, and Jan had enough time to stand before I was over, pulling him up, backing him against the wall, then kissing the fuck out of his mouth. "Merc. Now."

"What?"

"Move." I gave him little choice, making Jan nearly fall as I forced him into a stumble down the stairs. I wasn't waiting for the lifts.

"Jack?"

"Shush." We passed the security guards, Jan doing this whole salute thing as the two guards shared a *what the hell* moment. As we made it to Jan's Merc, Jan's back hit the passenger side door as I pushed him up against it. Hands sorted blindly through his pockets as my mouth caught his, hips grinding into hips.

"A little desperate to get laid there, Jack?" breathed Jan.

Still hunting for Jan's car keys in his trouser pocket, the hardness he had going on distracted me for a second. "Just, just get in the fucking car." We crushed in close, breathing heavy, heated, touches all out of rhythm. "I want to play the fuck out of your body, I—"

The keys were pulled from my hand, and Gray threw them to Jan.

"You touching my sub when he's been marked off-limits to everyone but me, Jan?" There was no anger there in Gray's voice, just that flick of a half-smile, but the bastard part to the Master Dom was there, and it had Jan fumbling to push me to arm's length.

"I, hmmm." The keys jangled in Jan's hands. "No. Just—I'm just warming his-the, warming *the* engine up for you." He was suddenly gone, heading for the driver's side, and leaving me dropping my head against the black Mercedes-Benz.

"You'll make a proper Master when you grow up, Jack." Gray sounded like he was smirking. Then he came in so close behind, his light breath, then a gentle nip on my neck had me forgetting all about Jan for a few cock-teasing seconds. The feel of him behind me had my legs inching wider apart, hands slipping behind my head, and body and mind going for full and silent submission right here in the darkness of the car park.

"In the Mercedes," whispered Gray, "you touch no one. You *do,* however, touch yourself without coming. Clear?"

"Mmhm." A release of a lock went somewhere, and I twisted my head. Gray held the passenger door open. Oh, right, in *that* Merc. Managing to drag myself away, I ducked into the back, Jan not helping the issue when he looked in the mirror and caught my eye.

As the door was shut, the draught disturbed my hair, helping to cool things down. Then with the car barely shifting as Gray eased in, everything heated up having him so close.

One hand gripping onto the headrest behind, I inched down, already easing my trouser belt open, then ghosting a touch into my suit trousers. Fuck me. I'd been touching myself for years, knowing the twists and turns that got me going, but Gray brought this to a new level playing this shit out in the open.

Strokes were kept long, slow, and even on my dick, the play hidden beneath the protective cover of white shirt and black tie. Feet were flat on the floor, hips occasionally shifting up as teasing became too much. I kept my gaze twisted away from Gray, almost into my arm as I gripped onto the headrest behind, eyes screwed shut. Tonight was all about Gray, about what got him going, what he wanted—needed…. And Gray was a watcher from any distance, all that covert stance. To start with at least….

Jan was quiet, unnaturally so. The Merc kept a constant pace, yet when I looked, Jan's knuckles were white, his eyes completely fixed on the road ahead.

This was the niggling concern in amongst lust-land,

always had been: that he'd get pissed off with me and Gray training Doms together for a living; that he'd have to stay on the sidelines as a vanilla doing nothing but licking at the edges of our world. Gray was a player of the highest order, and if he'd taken to playing Jan off against me now, not allowing him to touch when it came to a re-Mastering scene just between me and Gray, I'd do more than just have a few words on forcing him to the sidelines.

Strange how I settled for playing my own body, tracing a touch through the perspiration slicking my stomach, mixing it with the pre-come. Gray was a bastard, but he was also a Master. Mine. He wouldn't fuck life up in such a way. I trusted him, body and soul.

"Stop." Gray's soft voice stilled intent, and I managed to gather enough sense. We'd pulled up onto his drive. Jan's quiet niggled at me a little more, and I wanted him out and inside so I could see if he was okay. He'd been under a lot of stress lately. Maybe all of this was getting to his vanilla side more than he admitted.

"Jan," I started to say, now decent as I went around and pulled open his door. He graced me with a glance, nothing more. After shutting the door behind him, I let my head fall a touch as I made my way into Gray's hall, making sure I went first.

Moody. Yeah, I could still do fucked-up and moody.

My jacket found a home in the cupboard as Jan and Gray followed in. Giving a deep sigh, I waited for them to close the main door behind us before I could find the balls to face them.

"Look, Jan—"

Grabbed by the shirt, pushed back against the door, Jan came in hard and heavy with a kiss that nearly cut my lip.

"Fuck." It was all I could manage as Jan tongued me deep, his hands—everywhere. Tugging my shirt free as he backed away, Jan then pulled me through the lounge, past Gray's study, down a few stairs, through a long hall, and finally into a studio Gray kept solely for me and him. All of the usual BDSM toys blurred at the edges seeing Jan in front of me. I wanted to warn him he wasn't supposed to be in here, private sessions between me and Gray were kept just that: private. But he slid down on his knees and nuzzled against my cock so fast I lost breath. "What, what the fuck's gotten into you?"

Gray slipped in behind, and a nibble at my ear sent shivers down my sides. "Something special tonight," he said quietly. Was he smiling? "Hard and soft torture. And Jan and all his soft-lad approach has… voyeuristic tendencies, but only when it comes to us. It's what got him going with the cock cage you wore a few months back. Those needs just need… encouraging. *Encourage* him, Jack."

Jan eased to his feet, wiping at his mouth. "Strip," he said, backing away from me and pulling off his own shirt so he was reduced to nothing but grey suit trousers. "Please. Just for me, martial arts guy."

And there it was: that move away from BDSM. Just Jan's soft nature in such stark contrast to Gray's bastard side. Damn his soul, he'd sharpened that damn sweet talent too.

As I slipped off my tie, then shirt, he moved over to a white leather Tantra chair and straddled it before easing on down, face on to us, and flicking at the clasp to his trousers so his hard cock was on full display. He waited until I was naked, then—"Kneel."

After giving a quick glance over my shoulder, still feeling Gray's teasing bite at my ear, I knelt with my head down. This shared hard-soft command was something fucking new.

"You have your Master here, Jack." Jan was so quiet, so calm, now gently massaging his cock. "Teach me. How do you ask for his touch?"

I glanced down, knowing what Jan was asking for. Every sub had their way of asking; mine went back eleven years, something very personal to me and Gray after... Martin had fucked things up for me, and it was something that Jan had every right to ask to share as a lover. Gray stood just behind me, and without looking, unable to look, I blindly traced a touch up the fine cut of his trousers, coming to rest at his pocket. Gripping there tightly, I turned into him and reared up, upper chest now crushing against his hip, cock riding his leg as his stance spread mine. He smelled so fucking good, and I ran my nose along his belt, hands gently gripping at his ass, before I eased to my feet. Letting my hand rest gently on Gray's neck, I gently nudged my nose at his jaw. The fact that he reacted, shifted to allow me access to his throat and brush a kiss there was his approval to continue.

Fuck. The toned muscles of his abs played under my fingers before I shifted down to the clasp of his trousers and unzipped him. With one side of his trousers inched open, I pulled out a small portion of his shirt to expose a fine line of tanned hip.

Giving a frown, I rested my head on his shoulder and found my cock.

"Christ. Gray," I mumbled, moving in so close my shaft brushed his exposed hip every time I stroked. I fucking loved him just being by me, with whatever it was that he wrapped around my body. He could be half a world away, and I'd still feel his shift of gaze in my direction. I sighed, content just to stay there, mark his tanned hip with light tastes of pre-come, letting anyone know who came within half a fucking continent that I'd floor the fuck for getting close. "Shit," I mumbled.

Gray gripped my wrists, breaking concentration, and I looked at him just before his step forward insisted I take a few steps back. The curve of my ass hit one of the bondage tables, and Gray eased me down, forcing me to arch onto tiptoes until I lay flat.

He came down with me, lips to neck, and then ran kisses along the length as his body blanketed mine. A nudge at my jaw to lift my head and expose my throat was his demand as my Dom; my shift of head to allow him access was my submission. All quiet, unspoken, but then words sometimes got too hard between us to speak. So this... this was us. He bit, sending shivers through me that fucked with every vein in my groin. And from here, I watched Jan, the look in his eyes as he sat there stroking himself, his gaze not straying from us.

"Fuck." I hid in Gray's shoulder. Too much. Together they were too fucking much.

Gray eased back, making sure I stood, the bondage table again digging into my ass. "Hands up. Above your head," he said. A moment later, a metal cuff circled one wrist, then the other. Gray liked his shackles, numerous ones tethered at various heights to the ceiling.

Hands never lost contact with my body, feather-playing down my arms, my sides, coming to rest on my hips, and then encouraging me to turn around and face that table. A leg eased mine open, then Gray's touch ran down my thighs as he knelt and chained my feet apart with the bondage straps tethered to the base of the table legs.

It forced the lower part of my cock against the wood, and I gripped onto the chain, biting back a groan as my shaft rode the ridge.

A stroke came at my cheek, and then the room went dark as a blindfold was eased into place. Soft groans hit the air—Jan's.

"Sex slave," whispered Gray in my ear, stirring more shivers. "Always did like this look on you, stunner." A collar slipped around my throat, and a heavy leash was left to rest between my pecs, the leather end hitting my cock before resting on the table. Breathing became my only focus; collars were bad history for me. Gray knew that but stopped any kickback from my mouth with a cat o' nine tails. I cried out, my cock instantly fucking the table as the cat struck my back. Six more came, two at my thighs, but hit with such precision and quickness the arch of my body was already lost to more strokes on my back.

A slight draught, a sudden change of direction, I cried out as the whip hit my abs.

"*Fuck, you bastard.*" I meant it, and in reply the cat hit the tip of my cock, the part that the table couldn't hide, and with such fine precision. Then an even more bastard strike hit my back, and I bit back more abuse, body arching away from the whip.

Drawing a finger trail through the perspiration coating my abs, a touch traced down to my cock, brushing my tip, slicking me up, then wrapping the end of the leash around my shaft.

"Like that, Jack?" Jan whispered so fucking softly, and I groaned, at first thinking it had been Gray's touch. But Gray made his presence known from behind, a cane cutting across my ass, and Jan took advantage of the push forward into his touch, circling my cock and angling it down beneath the table.

"Come on, Jack, ride it," said Jan, that ballsy bite to his tone. Breathing his name as I gripped harder on the shackles, now forced up onto the balls of my feet, I fucked Jan's hand with the leash circling my shaft, the ride somehow kinkier under Jan's innocent touch. Another strike of the cane had me crying out, the intensity racing around my hips, into my groin, making my shaft nothing but heat encased in a vice. Gray met each pull back with a slice of cane across my ass, and it only forced me back into Jan, this time with a twist of head into my arm that yelled I was getting close to coming.

"Enough," said Gray, reading the signs. "Long night ahead, Jack." His hand traced the small of my back, a gentle mapping of marks that only stung more under his tenderness. "Control the fall for me, stunner." Giving a teasing bite at my shoulder, the bastard *was* smiling. It was in his voice as he whispered, "Re-Mastering is now in full session."

CHAPTER 8
RE-MASTERED

GRAY RELEASED MY hands, and the instinct was there to rub at them, to relax, to find control and let Gray play.

"Down." The grip on my collar ensured I did just that, taking me face-first over the bondage table. "Arms above your head." Shackles were pulled down over the main body of the table, and I rested my head down, forehead to hard surface, feet still spread wide and hands receiving the same lack of freedom as they were bound close to my head.

A gentle brush of hand against my balls, the undeniable touch of a patch on skin came next, one on my inner thigh, then another to the right. Two more were taped just slightly down from that, one left, one right. Wiring traced up over my ass, touching the burn on my cheeks, and then two more patches were placed on the small of my back. I knew what they signified: enough kick, enough voltage to—

"*Fuck.*" The first jolt was just enough to accompany the humming already running from fingertips to toes, and I closed my eyes, squirming into the shock. The second jolted me slightly, tightening the muscles across my lower back, between my thighs, and I shifted under the onslaught, the shock travelling my length and making it kick back into gear after the flogging. One more, two, three times—then I lost sight of my whereabouts as the high voltage had me up on my tiptoes, body and mind humming to bastard-filled currents that had me crying out hurt.

Maybe. Fuck. Maybe.

A pause came, long enough to leave Gray running his hand over my shoulders, and I swore if I could see it, there'd be that blue spark between his fingers and my skin, that electrical charge he always seemed to send through my body, voltage kit in hand or not. And then muscles were tightening again under the onslaught of electrical current. I was crying out, the fuck was I crying out. Hurt, agony, but more, just… *"Fucking… more."*

~

It took me a while to realise my hands were free, feet having already found a more natural position, and I stumbled from the table, a little puzzled as to when exactly Gray had stopped, or how long I'd lain there.

"Down."

"Fuck." No hand on my collar this time, I instantly followed Gray's command more on instinct than sense. The blindfold was still in place, either that or Gray had really sent me blind, and my hands found the floor in an attempt to ground me.

A touch ran under my jaw, shifting my blinded gaze up.

"Calm it," whispered Gray, and the scent of his cologne, so close, it was enough to let me know he was crouched in front of me. "Breathe," he said. "It's been a while, and I'm losing you. I need to see you pull back. Control the fall, stunner. Your blackouts with your disorders are always a concern."

After taking off my blindfold, he walked away, and I heard him open something, a box? It had that *clip* sound as a lid was shut; then he came back over. "Full submission."

No questioning, no fight, no mouth, just natural submission. Inching my knees wider, linking my hands behind my back, I eased down and rested my forehead to floor. These were the times when life had no complications, just sensation, just sense. Just Gray's sense and my quiet sensibility around him.

A gentle tug came at my collar, and it was removed a moment later.

"Holding the same position, lift your head."

I did, and Gray crouched by me. In his hand slept a new collar, and I frowned. I'd not seen this one before. It was the traditional leather that Gray liked, but this one was a strange metallic silver with two matching D rings. An inscription lay on the inside, something I couldn't read from this distance. A smile touched Gray's lips.

"Would you wear this collar, Jack, and not remove it until I have spoken to you in the morning? I want to discuss how good it would look to see it on you permanently."

"Sir," I mumbled.

"Repeat what I've said."

"Not to remove the collar until morning, not until you've spoken to me."

"Good." Brushing a touch against my cheek, he shifted slightly and slipped the collar into place. Then he picked something else up. In his palm sat a smooth, round stone;

no bigger in diameter than a flattened tennis ball but looking heavy as it sat there in his hand. "One kilogram," he said quietly, "about the weight of a bag of sugar." He reached over, and the weight of the stone pressed down close to the base of my neck, dead centre to my shoulder blades. It was left there as Gray stood. "Control. Under no circumstances is the stone allowed to fall for the next half-an-hour, is that clear?"

"Sir." The weight of the stone felt a little heavier, my shoulders aching just a touch more as Gray came back over and knelt just a few feet from me. "Hands out in front, fingers linked."

Unlocking my fingers from my back, I stretched my arms out in front of me, now seeing the long lengths of rope in Gray's hands. The style was undeniable: Asanawa white jute rope, and I think I groaned. Gray was Kinbakushi. Rope bondage was more than just an act, it was a sexual expression, and fuck, I'd grown up loving the ropes as a kid. It took time, patience, and I closed my eyes to the feel of the rope constantly binding my wrists partway down to the elbow, then knotting together. The silk feel to the rope crisscrossed over my back, then was made to create diamond shapes over my ass, down one leg, then the other. All the time, the jerks from the pull on rope were met with a will to keep my body as still as possible so the stone didn't fall. Rope slipped down my crack, circling one hip, then the other, and I was left to control my breathing with deep intakes in, long breaths out, loving how the rope brushed against my cock as I shifted slightly.

He finished by pulling my linked hands back over my head. Elbows still touched the floor, fingers now able to brush the rock on the back of my neck as he tied my hands in place. I was bound in almost a defensive position, on all fours, protectively covering my head with my arms as white diamond-shaped rope bindings coated my body. Each time I breathed, the rope around my chest strained, the fine strands creaking and groaning, almost acting with my body to breathe out my pleasure.

A hand brushed gently at my right hip.

"Still with me, stunner?"

I couldn't speak; breathing was now so deep it felt like I was a few breaths from sleep. "Sir," I mumbled quietly, content to be bound, collared, and naked at Gray's feet.

The gentle sound of a camera shutter opening, then closing disturbed the quiet, and I kept my head down, hidden. I didn't mind photography; Gray knew that, just so long as my identity was kept private. Lighting must have been prearranged, just a soft mosaic surface on my body and the floor surrounding me. Christ. I'd have loved it if Gray himself had been caught in the background, just half-hidden in the shadows. Part of me wanted to stretch comfortably into the soft light, just revel in Gray's threat.

That gentle click of the camera shutter came from every available angle, as much care and attention to detail shown with his photography as he did with his rope binding, close one moment, then distancing himself the next.

"Fucking stunning, Jack." A pause, another camera shot, then things fell quiet, and I twisted into the rope on my own, happy to get some relief with the rope riding my cock, flattening it tight against my lower abs. I could stay like this for hours; I'd been left like this for hours by Gray many a time, and I groaned into the free play time on the ropes now.

The strike of a match made me still, and the scent that hit the air as a long block candle was placed just in front of me, teasing every part of my body with what was to come next, it made me choke a laugh. "Fucking *vanilla?*"

"Control, Jack," said Gray, but he laughed that softly.

"Fucking vanilla-scented? A few months off from training Doms, and I get a fucking vanilla candle?"

Gray tipped the candle, enough to reveal the build-up of white-hot wax, and I writhed, *th'fuck* did I writhe. He tipped it a little more, and a single drop of wax teetered on the edge of the candle, gathering like a full pearl tear, then spilling, hitting the floor, heating, then cooling into a small white pool. So close that the scent of vanilla mixed with polished mahogany of the studio flooring.

Fuck. The thought of fire-play infected my body, and I twisted, writhed, half wanting to run, half wanting to fall and just fucking *feel* the burn.

Gray eased to his feet, and I caught my breath, trying to gauge where he was, listen for his footsteps—just anticipate where the burn would come. My shoulders? Ass?

I arched like a cat, the stress on the rope crying out the thrilled hurt as hot wax dripped onto the small of my back. Usually it would run off the skin, but the diamond shape of the rope caught it, held it still, giving everything that extra few seconds of burn, and I hissed out as Gray made sure each drop filled the shape of the diamond. I wasn't exactly crying stop now—more… just—"Fucking *more.*"

"You spoke?"

The taste of salt was on my lips as I screwed my eyes shut. "Suh—" My voice cracked, broke. "Sir, yes, Sir, please."

The rope keeping my hands behind my head was loosened, and I let my hands find a natural place on the floor as a stroke went to the back of my neck.

Gray's hand encouraged me up so I was kneeling, hands in front of me, almost hiding my body's love of his touch. He was knelt there in front of me with something held in his hand. He offered the rock forward. "You kept it in place at all times."

I found Gray's shirt, pulling him in, kissing his jaw, throat, lips. A kiss brushed my cheek before he stood, then a soft chuckle came from the corner. "Remember that cold November pool, Jack?" Gray whispered in my ear.

That made me pause. *Th'fuck* did it throw a little cold water on things, how I was collared and all naked like at Gray's feet.

"Did you keep that heads-up real close?"

A touch ran under my jaw, then a grab at the leash tethered to my collar pulled me up. Jan stood smirking by the bondage table, his cock topping his trousers, and it took me a few steps to realise I was being led back to *the* corner.

"Fuck." *Denial corner.* I'd spent many a night there with my balls being stretched for one violation or another.

Tethered halfway up the wall was a thick, heavy chain. The sort used to restrain security dogs. It lay in a pile on the floor, a huge, sleeping snake waiting to crush a few bones. Told to stand just a few feet away, I waited as Gray went over and grabbed the end. He hooked one end into the back of my collar the next moment, and the weight of the ball-freezing chain was dropped down my back.

"Mmmm," said Gray, brushing kisses along my throat as his hand feather-played my back. "Tempting, Jack," he said quietly.

"Yeah?" Pulling him in close, I roughed his lips up, growling against them, "*Fucking come on, then.*" A grip went to my hair, making me wince as my gaze was forced to the ceiling, instantly culling any heat.

"Do you know why you're here?" said Gray, calmly.

"Sir."

"Why, Jack?"

"Fucking you off, Sir."

"How did you fuck me off, Jack?"

"Slipped and, all innocent like, accidentally pushed you in the pool, Sir."

The grip tightened in my hair, this time forcing me to shift my stance slightly under the pressure. "'All innocent like,' is it?" His breath brushed my jaw, and damn, I failed so pathetically to stop my groan.

"No," I murmured, Gray taking any twist of devilment away with how he held me. "No accidents," I said quietly. "Us. 'S all that matters, Sir."

"Good answer," he whispered quietly, lips brushing my jaw. "Down."

And he made sure I did just that before shifting over to the wall. A few moments later, he came back with some handcuffs, fine silk, and a heavy tripod, the latter he screwed into the floor.

"Shit." I groaned. The adjustable arm on the tripod stood level to my cock, and on the end of it a rubber cock sleeve tempted even the most worn out of cocks into life. Tight, gorgeous on the cock usually, but studs lined this one. I hated fucking studs. Ribbed was better, but Gray knew I liked ribbed, hence the studs. Bastard.

"Hands," said Gray.

Still bound by the rope, I offered them up, and he cuffed one, then the other, before slipping the small chain to the handcuffs over a special rung on the cock sleeve of the tripod, which he then screwed shut. It didn't give my hands much room to move, maybe play with my tip if I was allowed to, nothing more.

Jan had inched closer. "Shit," he mumbled, and I had to look away as he played with his own cock. Gray lubed the inside of the sleeve, then paid wicked attention to my cock, slicking me up, forcing me to look down and grip the sleeve to stop myself fucking his hand. He dipped my cock towards the rubber mouth, then a grip at my ass made sure I pushed in.

"Mmmm." The studs ground into my cock, sending white stars playing a tune in my eyes.

"Don't move," he said as I moaned, instantly threatening to fuck the sleeve there and then. But seeing Gray pick up the long silk strand, I did as I was told, nearly crying *bastard* as he started to wrap it around the base of my balls. He circled them four times, tied an intricate knot, and then tied the end of the strand to the bottom of the adjustable arm on the tripod, giving a pull to make sure my balls were stretched with my cock already deep into the sleeve.

The hurt was there, but so too was the instinct to fuck out of the sleeve. I did just that, and it came at the price of pulling viciously on my balls. *"Bastard."* I groaned and quickly fucked back in, which didn't help one bit, because now I just wanted to fuck back out again and enjoy myself.

"Looking good there, Jack," said Gray, hiding a smile and rubbing his palm against my tip.

I groaned; like hell did I groan.

"You try and play nice for a few minutes," said Gray, and I watched him stand, watched him look back at Jan, watched Jan stare at Gray, then I cried all the *fuck God, yes pleases* as Gray backed Jan up against a wall. In one smooth move, Gray took hold of Jan's wrists and stretched his hands high above his head, all for Gray to pin both there with one hand, Jan's now crossed under his. Jan instantly pushed his body into Gray's, and Gray let his free hand trace down Jan's arm, over his chest, down to his cock as it topped his trousers. Last time, these two together like this as I'd been forced to watch had all been about punishment—mine. Now this was just about them, about Gray ensuring rank, about Jan learning how to follow. Because Gray was pure top at heart, and he was topping Jan now.

"Jesus," breathed Jan, and I was right there with him. Every muscle was alive and moving under Gray's touch, Jan writhing and trying to bite back his need to stay calm, cool. But as Gray stroked his cock, the kiss Jan gave to Gray was full of everything he needed to get out. Bodies were suddenly moving against each other, pulling, pushing, grinding—Jan trying to pull his hands free and touch in all his gentle ways; Gray keeping control and looking in every need to tie Jan up and fuck him senseless. They were contradictory, both so fucking far apart in mind, body, soul—work, and they clashed in ways that probably weren't supposed to go together: Jan trying to calm things, Gray to rough it up, and all it left was one ball-busting heated mass of touching, want, and downright cock-teasing cries.

As Gray released Jan, now gripping the back of Jan's trousers, then tugging them off his ass and letting them fall, I kept quiet, feeling the pull on my scrotum, but not wanting to spoil their moment together with my frustration. Jan distractedly kicked his trousers away, showing how they needed to focus on each other, to know I was okay with that. Th'fuck I was okay with it. I just needed my hands free to film it, or find a way to get over there and join in.

Gray slipped a touch down Jan's outer thigh, and in one frustrated move, he lifted Jan onto his hips, Jan now forced to rest his shoulders and head back on the wall. After slipping on a condom, Gray took him hard. Jan's sweet cry into taking Gray nearly pushed me over the edge, forcing me to grip my tip to stop the fallout.

Using the wall as leverage, Jan rode Gray just as hard, both of their bodies crying out the tensions playing through them. Jan came hard, quick; then Gray seemed to force control with a cry and pull free. He hadn't come, but he seemed a little startled, a little out of breath with nearly losing it.

I managed a grin. Jan got you like that, and I fucking loved how even Gray was nearly caught in his gentle trap. He eased Jan to the floor but pressed his body in, both breathing hard, smiling, watching. They always seemed to watch each other, and I loved seeing that intensity, how lost they were in each other's look and touch. Then Gray seemed to shake it off and glance over.

"How you doing, petal?"

"You fucking, fucked up—" My abuse got heavier, but I shut up as it made Gray come over. A gentle shove, he knelt behind me and a hand gripped at my throat, forcing my head up.

"Missed me?" breathed Gray into my ear, and the threat of his freshly coated cock against my ass was there.

"*Christ, yes.*" I'd missed the bastard.

"Said I'd fuck you into the land of dry heaving cocks," breathed Gray. Jan was now in front of me, kneeling, grabbing around the sleeve to make the ride tighter. I groaned; it was all I *could* do before time started to disappear from memory. Gray let his arm snake around my waist and pulled me back into him, adding extra pull on my balls as I was forced to take his cock.

"Welcome back, Jack," he whispered heatedly as I cried out, taking him full force. "Missed fucking you like this, kid, so fucking much…."

CHAPTER 9
SLEEPING WITH THE PACK

Jan Richards

I WASN'T GOING to be the one who woke Jack this morning; he looked so tired lying there, facing me as he slept. The alarm had gone off ten minutes ago, stirring them both and forcing Gray to smack it into snooze. He'd let his arm automatically find Jack's waist, and he'd pulled Jack back in close, forcing a smile from me. Gray had removed all of Jack's BDSM gear, with the exception of one item. The stunning silver-grey two-inch leather collar, one ring on the front, one on the back, slept on Jack's exposed throat. No doubt something more conservative would be chosen if Jack was out in public, a discreet chain maybe? Only not now. Now he looked every part the sub: visibly claimed, sexed-out, and exhausted in sleep. With how the colour matched Jack's eyes perfectly, it had been chosen specifically, maybe echoed by how Gray had whispered something against the back of Jack's neck, gently kissing the exposed skin above the collar before settling back down again. Jack had been lost, too far gone in exhaustion to offer up anything other than a whispered breath of names: Gray's, mine. They'd both fallen back into a deep sleep neither wanted to be dragged from, not without killing somebody in the process.

Trust me to be the one to step into sleeping pack territory. I stirred, just slightly, wincing in the process. I didn't know you could screw a guy dry, make him come so much that his dick would give up eventually and dry-heave nothing. With Jack being chained in that corner, I'd worked him hard, but Gray? I'd cried out towards the end, reduced to watching as Gray had taken play to the bedroom. Jack had been in such a strange bloody state. I'd seen it kick in when Gray had been shocking him, then again after Gray had taken him for the first time in "the corner". Part of me had been damn well impressed with how much Jack's body could take to reach that level. Hell, even Gray had broken a sweat eventually, but he'd damn well made sure he'd taken everything from Jack in the process.

One hand tucked under his pillow, the other across the top, almost hugging it and managing to half-cover his face and collar in the process, Jack slept on. There'd been no going casual with his photo afterwards, no worry over OCD, being touched, or having come on him. I couldn't imagine Jack relaxing enough to reach this state with a trainee Dom. From what Gray had told me, Jack took time out alone after a scene. It allowed him the time to deal with how the comedown after sex played havoc with his mind: BDSM cares and needs always balanced with Jack's care plan for his disorders. But now, half cuddled up to me after play had finished, Jack had seemed as though he was dozing under the touch of Gray's gentle stroke of cloth to his abs, thighs, and ass. He'd been utterly relaxed, just soft malleable clay that Gray could manipulate into anything he wanted. Yet Gray had simply made sure that the whip marks were taken care of, painkillers taken, fluids kept up, then settled in behind Jack, whispering in his ear. I'd crashed soon after, loving the gentle tones Gray used, even though at times I swore they weren't just for Jack but directed my way too. I was just glad Gray was there for everything, because there were times, yeah, I could have really lost myself, or ran screaming from the studio with what I was doing.

I brushed gently at the soft hair on Jack's arm. If this was how he was every time Gray Mastered him, I understood why Gray kept it private, why he'd never let it be filmed. It wasn't how Jack performed mid-heat, how his cries could make you drunk as the need to satisfy them played havoc with the unskilled handler, but in the right hands afterwards, Jack became so quiet, every ounce of disorder, chaos, mouth, and attitude dropped. And there was nothing more calming on the soul to lie next to. Part of me swore that the search for that quiet was what drove Gray, because the moment Jack quietened, so did he.

But it would be a long time before my body was ready to do anything like that again. And if I'd been given the voyeur tag by Gray, maybe I could hide in it for a while. "Jack." I gave him a tentative shake. "Hey."

"Hmmm?"

"Jack, you're going to be late for work."

Giving a grumble, he grabbed the duvet and disappeared beneath it. "Fuck work."

I chuckled and tugged it off him.

One grey eye came open. "Just a few more minutes, Mom, yeah?"

"Yeah, you lie there, cuddle up," I said quietly, inching

closer and drawing his leg between mine. "I'll just go phone your garage and tell Sam you said he's in charge for the day."

"Huh?" His head came off the pillow, the links on the collar giving soft, subdued clinks. "You up for bankrupting me, Richards?"

I chuckled, then moved in for a kiss. "Just *focusing* you."

He scowled, kissed me back, then hid back in the duvet. "But my ass hurts, my arms hurt, my hips hurt, my—"

"Petal got a headache too?"

I flashed my eyes at Jack as he came out from under cover and tried to look back at Gray. "Boss is up, baby."

Up on his elbow, Gray looked down at Jack. "You getting your ass into gear? Because—"

Jack instantly eased his nakedness on top of Gray's, quieting even Gray as he took him down to the bed. "Hmmmm, morning." He gave Gray such a long and deep kiss. "Last night," he breathed against Gray's lips, then Jack looked at me, reached over, and pulled me in for a kiss, "fucking good." He turned back to Gray and sighed. "Fucking love-the-bones-off-you-both fucking good."

Gray smirked. "For us working you?"

Jack nudged Gray's cheek with his nose, asking Gray's permission to lift his lips up for a kiss. I understood it now, the private signs behind asking and gaining permission to touch, and kept quiet while the tender protocol played out as Gray allowed him to kiss.

Jack finished tasting Gray, then murmured, "No. For being the bastard I'd always do."

"Yeah? Love the bastard, huh?" Gray was trying hard not to look bothered. "Then get fucking dressed."

Jack gave the biggest puppy-dog eyes. "Use me, lose me, huh?"

Gray reached up to stroke Jack's jaw, then let the tips of his fingers slip down to the silver collar. Just between skin and silver-grey leather, he played his touch along it, his look a little lost, then he finished by hooking a finger in the D ring. Cocking his head to the side and frowning slightly, Jack let himself be drawn down into a gentle brush of lips against lips.

No. Everything Gray needed to say was there, in that look, that kiss. He wouldn't lose him; maybe use him in so many wicked ways, but never lose him.

Then he tipped Jack off onto the floor.

"Ah. *Fuck*. Right," said Jack, a mass of legs and arms. I saved the cover but missed saving him as I cried laughter. Grey eyes came up, peering over the bed like a war machine coming in for a sneak peek before an attack. "Like that, is it?" A Dracula hand came into play, stretching long shadows over the duvet as it reached to pull it off.

"Touch that and you're fucked MI5 style, Jack," said Gray, not even looking.

The hand drew back, withered away into its own shadows, and I chuckled, watching as Jack grumbled his way to his feet. He reached up and tugged the silver collar off, mimicking Gray's comment, then sliding the leather into the bedside table drawer. Gray went quiet, seeming to listen as the drawer slid shut, then as Jack headed over to the bathroom, his goddamn sexy ass and everything on glorious display, Gray turned his back on me and pulled the covers over him.

Frowning for a minute, I threw back my side of the covers, sat up, stretched, and then glared back at Gray's clock. Six. Jack had had about two hours sleep. I felt rough, so Christ knows what he was going through. After wincing as I pushed to my feet, I headed on through to the bathroom and relieved myself as Jack grouched like hell in the shower. Flicks of water came over, hitting my shoulder, my ass, and I shouted over my shoulder, "You know it's me here, not Gray, right?"

Jack stepped out a few moments later and did his shaggy-dog thing, shaking himself, wet hair soaking me.

"Yeah," said Jack, coming over and turning me around for a cuddle. "Kind of figured that out when I didn't get a cheese grater along my cock."

Shuddering, I pushed his wet body away, and he huffed. "You too?" Those grey puppy-dog eyes came into play again. "Love me, leave me?" Then he winked and tugged a towel off the rail and wrapped it around his waist.

I started brushing my teeth at the same time as Jack, although he kept glancing my way, and I caught his smile.

"What?" I said with a mouthful of toothpaste.

"You were a ballsy bastard last night."

I blushed, looked at the sink for salvation, then spat and rinsed. Jack followed, giving a final wipe to his mouth.

"Sorry," I said, conscious of just how I'd spoken to him.

"Don't be. It's good to hear what you like, how you like it, that you're ballsy enough to voice it. Turns me on like fuck."

I gave him a half-smile. There was no trainer voice there. Just Jack. And good to know I was still ballsy in his eyes. I had a lot to live up to lying next to Gray.

"You were pretty out of it at times," I said, and Jack gave this *uh-huh* sound. "Worried me a touch." Jack looked at me.

"Worried? Why?"

I shrugged. "Just your blackouts and things."

Jack stopped what he was doing for a moment. When he looked at me, he looked a little sad. "I trust Gray." He smiled as he brushed the back of his hand against my cheek. "I trust you. It was a good environment last night, everything just right: people, lovers, and a bastard thrown in to lead the mix too."

I laughed as Jack folded the towel up so carefully before putting it back.

"Jack, didn't Gray ask you to keep the collar on?"

"Hmm?" He glanced back.

I pointed to his throat. "Last night. I remember—"

"Jan, it's okay. Jack's late for work."

I frowned, trying to see around Jack, back into Gray.

"Shit." Jack caught his arm on the door handle and stood there rubbing at it. "Collar always comes off after a scene," he mumbled before heading back into the bedroom and starting to sort out his work clothes. Scratching at my head, I followed soon after, going over to the wardrobe and pulling out my jeans and shirt.

"Hey, what are you doing?"

I glanced at Jack as I fastened my jeans. "Driving you to work. You didn't get much sleep and you were pretty out of it by the time we finished."

Jack straightened, looking more than a little stiff even after Gray's aftercare. "That's…." He frowned, but it came with a soft smile. "Jan, you hardly got any sleep too, you soft sod."

"I know," I said, tugging my T-shirt over my head. "But it wasn't my ass that got double-ended last night."

Jack chuckled. "Good point—good times—but good point."

We made it downstairs, and Jack went over to the door and started thumbing through his mail. "Ah." He pulled out a brown package and rattled it against his ear.

"Is that even your mail?" I went over and grabbed my coat. Gray had moaned the past few mornings how his mail had been tampered with, and we kind of figured who was responsible. Jack stood there confirming it all as he rattled the package close to his ear again and grinned. "Yours."

"From yesterday?" I pulled it from him with a scowl and opened the brown package. "Looks like Gray's getting in the Christmas spirit." Two books were inside, and I flicked through the first and nodded, already lost. I recognised Gray's handwriting attached to the note inside.

Try something a little more hardcore than abstract, Abstract.

I chuckled, only to have Jack frown. I showed him the note, then held up the books. If he could have vampire-hissed, he would have. "Since when did he start buying you stuff?"

"We were out yesterday discussing doing an art collection here, which I'm looking into this afternoon, and I'd seen this one." I waggled *Imitations of Original Drawings* by Hans Holbein, also wanting to run upstairs with it and lock it in a safe somewhere. "It's a collectable."

"Cars are collectable," said Jack. "That—" He even pointed. "—is a book."

"About fifteen grand's worth of book."

Jack gave a whistle. "And that one?" he asked, looking like he wanted to prod it from fifty paces to see if it bit him.

I looked at the collection of abstract art. "'A piss-take,'

as you'd put it," I grumbled, and Jack laughed.

"Fucking peachy. He's good at those too," he said.

"What the hell do I get him in return, though, Jack?" I put the books very carefully onto the table and sighed. "I mean, with Christmas a few weeks away—"

"Well, you could promise to see if Santa's sacs really are never-ending when it comes to delivering the goods."

I leaned in close. "You're on about Santa's nuts, aren't you? That's…." I weighed the options up here. "Gray, wearing nothing but a Santa's hat, a black one, with *BDSM badass* printed on it? You holding a *Santa, please stop here* sign next to your ass, all wide-eyed, expectant, and on your knees?"

Jack choked a laugh. "That's definitely one for the MC suggestion scene box. And are you a fucking mind-reader? I've been threatening to get Gray a bloody badass hat for years. Always said I never had the bollocks. Speaking of which… you've just perverted everything pure and innocent about Christmas. You bhaaaad man, you."

"Me? You were the one on about Santa's sacs."

"You up for it?"

"Fuck yes," I breathed.

Jack grinned at me as we reached my Mercedes, then scowled as his phone went off. He fumbled for it as I pulled out my keys and unlocked the Merc.

"Hey, Dad." Jack winked at me. "What's up?"

I smiled at the mention of Gregory, especially with all the politeness that Jack fell into around him. We hadn't met yet, but we'd spoken on the phone a few times. Things took time with Jack, I was slowly getting used to that, but he was more than worth the wait.

"Ah, sorry," he was saying, and my ears pricked up as he winced. "Mom? Complicate the issue by using Dad's phone, why don't you," he said, rolling his eyes at me before we got in. I hadn't spoken to his mother, not yet. She'd been away for a few months after the divorce.

"Sure," said Jack, getting in the Merc as I unlocked it. "I'll make some room in the books for today. *Ci sentiamo.*"

I waited before he slipped his phone into his long jacket before saying, "Something you want to tell me?"

Jack started fiddling with the radio. "My old lady's garage is overbooked. She wants to know if she can bring a client over today to ease her workload." Jack relaxed with a wince, his movements still stiff and awkward. "Always throws me when she uses my old man's phone like that."

"Jack, you've just gone a little Italian."

He looked over, frowned.

"Something you *need* to tell me?"

He blushed, so badly it forced him to look away. "I'm mostly English, Jan. Bacon butties 'n' all. My mother, she's something else, coming from sunny *not-fucking-freeze-your-knackers-off* Cinque Terre. She met my old man when she ran into the back of his Land Rover with her Jag. He was on a business trip there. Sorry. Details...." He frowned. "I get there eventually, y'know. *Ci sentiamo* just means 'talk to you later.'"

Forget that. I was trying to stop the whole *come to Daddy, baby* reaction hearing him speak just two words. "You and Gray, I swear, you need—"

"Fucking? Because you know I can speak a little Italian, mostly swearing, but I can do this deep, sexy Banderas voice—"

"He's Spanish."

"I can do this deep, sexy De Niro voice."

"American."

"Seriously? With the whole De Niro thing? 'Cause it sounds like it's got an Italian suffix twang to me."

By the time I pulled up to Jack's garage, I was still trying to stop the tears, the chuckling was that bad. Jack. He really was bloody hopeless with nationalities. No wonder he hadn't caught on to Gray and his Welsh connection.

CHAPTER 10
DON'T…

Jack Harrison

"JACK."

That came from Sue, and I tugged my head out from under the car. A few hours after Jan had dropped me off, I was elbow-deep in an oil filter, although the swearing flying through the air suggested it felt more like I'd been at it for five hours. Sue was grinning over from reception. "Your mother's here. I've taken her up to your office."

Easing up, I winced at the aches, knowing I really should have booked today off. My old lady adding to an already packed workload wasn't gonna help either. If she was shifting work over, you could guarantee it was going to be a big job. Muscles feeling the strain a little more, I washed up before heading on up to the office.

"Hey, Mom," I mumbled as the door pushed open.

She glanced over from by the main desk and it wasn't hard to see why my old man had fallen for her. She was business through and through, with her tailored suit—

always trousers and matching jacket—thick, long black hair that was tied back to reveal the full blackness of her eyes. Even at sixty, she was something to look at: slim, tall, with time just seeming to stand back and appreciate her beauty as she matured next to it. "This job you're on about? What are we doing and how long are you giving us?"

There was barely any other reaction from her, even after I'd pulled her into a brief hug. She offered me a weak smile, nothing more.

"Where's the owner?" I tried to peer down to the car park. "He meeting you here? Can I get you a coffee or something?" I really needed to get on with work and get back to Gray's, see if we could all lick our exhaustion together.

My old lady glanced around. "No. No, *grazie*." She clutched her black business carry case, looking from me, to the door, to the door, back to me.

"Mom?"

"I, I've just got back from Italy."

I offered a small chuckle. "Oh-kay. I kind of know. Dad told me. Good trip?"

"I was at your father's and was supposed to go to the garage. Just go and meet my client and arrange for his car to be towed here. I was tired. Your dad asked me over for a coffee, and I thought—"

"Mom." She was rambling, sentences unfocused; not herself by a long shot.

"He got something for me in the post."

I frowned. "Something to do with the divorce?" That would explain it.

"No." Nothing else was given, and I rubbed at her shoulders, hating how she seemed to pull back a touch.

"Are you happy, Jack? With this Jan?" Black eyes rested on mine. "Your dad told me about him, and, well, are you happy?"

I gave her a smile. "Yeah. More than, Mom."

"Then you—" This time she definitely pulled away. "You don't need this now."

I caught her arm. "What the fuck's wrong, Mom?"

She was startled with that, and I already regretted letting my mouth slip. Her lips had thinned, not quite angered, more fearing letting any words pass them. And she kept fidgeting with the damn carry case, running her fingers over the leather clasp, feeling the button. "I..." She finally pulled her bag open and reached inside. "He'd ordered me this CD for Christmas. Said he'd wanted to replace the one I'd lost." She pulled out a brown wrapped package, certainly looking like a CD with the size and shape. Taking it from her, I saw that the end had been neatly sliced open. My old lady had a thing for letter openers. Not that I could blame her, so did I, only not in any sense she'd ever understand.

"*War of the Worlds*," she said with a shrug. "I lost the Jeff Wayne version when I left, so he said he'd order me a new one." There was a ghost of a smile. "Always trying to build bridges. This came today."

Giving her a brief look, I reached inside the package and, yep, there it was: tripod aliens with big eyes on the cover. "I remember listening to this in the car on the way to school." I snorted a smile. It had scared the hell out of me.

"Yes. There's a key ring in there too. It has a light on it. And, Jack, there's a message."

After a slight frown, I opened up the DVD case and quickly caught the small purple keyring that fell out. I'd seen enough over the years; having certain car parts marked for theft prevention, you'd need one of these UV security lights to read the markings. And the message…

Don't…

… look at the CD, J.A.C.K.

For a moment I didn't move, every letter of each little clause, all formatted in true Mark Shaw head-fuck style, it stalled everything bar the fall of the low afternoon sun catching the lettering.

"Jack."

I looked over the disc itself, flicking the LED light over the alien landscape. On a slower sweep, a message came up under the gaze of the purple light. A website address, then:

Don't…

… panic when watching the porn sites, Jack. Music… book… DVD.

I went over to my computer and started to type in the web address.

"Jack…"

"Shush." I shouldn't have looked, it wasn't even down to any conduct disorder that I did, more a need to see. This was the internet. Public *fucking* domain.

Tacky and crude images showed a porn site banner, then:

Don't…

… watch the pup bound and fucked by Bear in woods.

Life slipped off the clutch for a moment as images started playing on screen, then—"*Fuck you!*" All wires snapping, the monitor ended up on the floor when it refused to stop choking out the sick line on screen. "*Fuck… You!*"

"*Jack!*" My old lady was over by me, trying to grab at my arm. "Please, not the computers! Your records."

Stop. It had to fucking stop. Mark. The *fucking cunt.* He'd filmed Cutter's first fuck with me. And there it was—my grass-stained ass on display on the smashed-up screen, taking over five hundred likes already. I kicked the shit out of it.

"*Jack....*" My old lady was tugging at my arm as Sam slammed the door open.

"What the—"

"*Jack,*" my old lady shouted through Sam's words. "Stop. That man... He-he tied you up. Did he... hurt? You cried hurt. Did he—"

"You *saw?*" I groaned, hands going to my head. "You—" Life became very fucking small. CD? Book? DVD?

My old lady's CD... A book, DVD. *Jan's—Gray's?*

"*No.* For fuckssake, *no.*" I took the stairs, my old lady's calls following me, but losing them to my own as I shouted for Sam to move out of my fucking way.

~

It didn't take me long to get to Gray's, mostly because the journey was a blur, and I pushed on through to the manor. A yelp came from behind the door. "Fucking move," I snarled as Ed jumped back. UV security light in my hand, I started pulling at the mail on the table, tugging out drawers and looking for Jan's books from this morning. "Where are they?"

Giving a disgruntled grunt, Ed started to pick up the rubbish I'd scattered on the floor. "What?"

"*Jan's fucking books.*" The drawer shattered at Ed's feet, and he yelped as it caught his knuckle on the way down. "The DVD, the one Gray ordered. Monday, the DVD, the—"

"Jan has just taken his books through to the Marquis Gallery, east side, to start an art collection in there; the DVD—"

Gallery.

I bolted past the lounge plus four more rooms, through a long corridor, then came to a stop outside of another of Gray's studios, one I usually avoided at all costs due to the amount of torture that went on in there.

"Jack?" A little startled, Jan looked up from the art he was unwrapping. His grin widened, then he was suddenly over, tugging at my arm. "A new art collection's going in here." He pulled me over to the huge brown painting he'd been unwrapping. "Gray and I didn't have time to go to the museum this morning. Gray worked on this, giving us the first print, and, Jack...." He looked back at me. "You should see it."

He pulled off the cover, and the frame that came into view was stunning, all white and no doubt some expensive shit of Gray's taste, and the black and white canvas....

Hands went to my head. Oh fuck, oh fuck. Not the collar.

I was used to Gray taking prints from different scenes I'd worked; pictures never really did anything for me. This one was from last night, all hands, knees, and paying homage on the floor, grey collar to boot.

"Fuck."

"Stunning, isn't it?" said Jan. "It's you, and I mean you. See, the rope?" He outlined it from where we stood. "Arms are made to bend back, almost protectively over your head; everything that binds you internally, your disorders, it's brought to the surface by the rope. And yet at the very point vulnerability seems to want to consume, you offer your body and mind with no complications, no judgments, just you: sensuous submission to life and disorder in soft light and shadows. Your history caught in erotica."

Caught. "Where's your books, Jan?"

"Hmmm?"

"*Your fucking books?*" He jerked at the cry as I started searching the gallery, pulling at the brown paper littering the floor. I found one sitting on a display case, the abstract book, and grabbed at it.

"Jack. What the hell?"

Using the UV light, I scanned the back page, the front, inside, then out. Nothing. I tossed it back at him. "The other one."

"What?"

"*The fucking other book, Jan.* Where is it?"

"In the lounge, on the coffee table—"

I was gone before he could finish and made it into the lounge. The second book sat in isolation on the table in a protective cover. Giving a snarl, I pulled it free and checked the front cover with the UV light, then the back, the outside, then inside where—

The purple of the light caught something on the first page, another website address, this one a little different and—

Don't...

... make me laugh anymore, Jack. You're killing me. Seriously. Take a breather before you do yourself some damage.

Love always, Mark.

Giving a cry, I tore the page in two, reducing it to shreds as Jan cried out, trying to tear it out of my hands.

"*For godssake, Jack. Stop. Please. That's—*"

"What the *fuck's* going on?"

I glanced back and refused to groan. Gray was back by the lounge door, his attention half distracted and on Ed's hand.

"*Bastard.*" I threw the book up the wall with such force it hit the fireplace, dislodging some fancy candles and sending them to the floor.

Gray was suddenly in my face, pushing me against the settee, and I nearly stumbled onto it as he came in nose to nose. "What the fuck's your problem, Jack?"

"Nothing."

"Nothing?"

"*Nothing*" was growled through my teeth. I pushed him aside and shifted for his study. Ed brought his mail here, but it had been nearly a week ago. Gray would've opened it. Drawers were pulled out of the mahogany desk, then I started on his DVDs.

"*Jack!*"

Gray's shout didn't stop me, just heated life, and added to me tearing up his study. "*Where the fuck did you put it?*"

"What?" said Gray, now standing back, arms folded, a dangerous sign within itself.

"The DVD." I slammed a drawer shut but didn't even glare back. "Where did Ed put that fucking DVD you ordered?"

"This one?" Ed stood by the door, holding a DVD case, and I stopped. "Gray ordered me a copy of *Downton Abbey.*

114

I'm useless with technology, and—"

Giving a snarl, I started to shift for him, but Gray, grabbing my coverall collar as I passed, shoved me up against the wall with a thud. His gaze fell on my hand, on the UV security light, and—"Gray," I said quietly. "Don't, please. You can't… don't see that."

A look at me, Jan, he took the UV light and headed for Ed.

"Ah. Don't—" Hands went through my hair. "Please…." Gray flicked a look at me as he reached Ed. "Don't watch that, Gray, please…."

Holding the DVD in one hand, Gray opened it up and ran the light over the inside. A glance up at me, he headed out of his study.

I waited, listened, not daring to move, to breathe—not even when Jan turned away and headed out after Gray too.

CHAPTER 11
JAN, MEET CUTTER

Jan Richards

SOMETHING WAS SERIOUSLY wrong. Something out of that book had Jack climbing up the walls, enough to tear up over fifteen grand's worth of art history. Part of me didn't want to know; another part of me *had* to know.

Noise came from the lounge, the kind of grunts and groans off a TV you'd turn down at night time so no one else would hear you, and I slowed my pace.

Side-on to me, Gray was standing by his laptop with his arms folded, his face giving nothing away. I frowned but couldn't quite bring myself to go over. "DVD?" I said quietly, resting against the doorframe, but Gray shook his head.

"Porn site."

My heart fell. Amongst the recently posted, there was a screenshot of a painfully young-looking Jack. Gray homed in on the title for a moment, enough for me to read it from here. It was the same intro found on most sites, yet somehow very much in a class of its own.

Don't…

… love the Cub in slap-kink with Bear.

I rested my head against the frame, just hugging my stomach, and watched as Gray clicked on the play button.

A simple master bedroom came on screen. It allowed room for a bed with a brass frame and headboard, made up with crisp white duvet covers and soft pillows. Each side had a bedside unit, and a lamp was on one, but barely added much light to the cream-coloured room.

Three men heated life up in there. Well, two men and a young boy just touching eighteen. One man sat in the corner, watching what was going on in the bed, a smile plastering his face as he stroked his hard-on. He was naked, but then so were the two people writhing on the bed.

Cutter was an easy spot. Mark Shaw had him bang to rights as a thug who loved to cut up young men: a skinhead, three times bigger than Jack, and most of the muscle looking as hard and as up for it as what went on between his thighs. He had a tattooed scalp, some political racist slur that ran down his neck, and Jack, he was the naked teen struggling underneath him.

Jack's hair was longer, wilder, his body youthfully thinner, still deeply tanned and coated in a thin sheen of sweat. Cutter had just flipped him onto all fours, his arm snaking roughly around Jack's neck, his free hand pulling at Jack's hair to twist his head and get access to his mouth. He kissed hard, rutting just as rough, pausing from his kiss only to grin at the youth he held.

"Want it, boy?"

"Not tonight, luv," said Jack, smiling, "got a headache." A growl, Cutter shifted, tossing Jack onto his back, and

Jack's dick came into full view. My heart sank, because for all of the fight Jack offered, he wanted it. He wore nothing but this black rope necklace with a black cross sleeping on a bigger silver one. Tiny sterling-silver balls, three one side of the rope necklace, three on the other, gave it that youthful look, a little expensive too. I didn't look below that necklace again. Jack looked young, way too fucking young for me to focus on anything lower than that necklace.

"Smart-mouth fuck." Cutter slapped at Jack's cheek, but Jack only grinned a little more. It won him a harder slap. "What you got for me now, boy?"

Jack nipped at Cutter's jaw, feeding it.

Another slap, this last one was hard enough to snap Jack's head to the side and leave a stinging redness to his cheek. "Oooh," groaned Cutter, "like it, don't you, boy?" His hand crushed between Jack's thighs, making him groan. "Yeah, like it rough, all right, don't you, Jack?"

Even his name hadn't been cut from public viewing.

After shifting back, Cutter grabbed Jack's ankles, then pressed them together before forcing him to bend at the knees. Feet now flat against Cutter's chest as though he wanted Jack to push him away, he grabbed Jack's wrists and locked them behind Jack's knees with a huge hand. "Got something to fuck that mouth out of you, boy."

Cutter leaned all of his weight over Jack, trapping Jack's hands with the pressure he put on Jack's legs, a reverse of the position that Gray had used when he'd bound him on the floor, only with Cutter using his whole body to swamp Jack and keep him still. Two more slaps cut his lip, to which Cutter wiped at Jack's mouth, then forced his thumb into Jack's mouth to take the taste of blood. Then Cutter rubbed his dick against Jack's ass and the cameraman made damn sure he focused in on exactly where Cutter was going to claim, pre-come crying a line of desperation over the tanned smoothness of Jack's cheek. "C'mon, tough kid. *Cry for me*. Fucking c'mon."

A wide-angle view saw one hard fuck into Jack that only had Jack arching his back, crying out, then… then he was writhing beneath Cutter, calling him out with each hard fuck up him, biting at Cutter's lip, his jaw, his—

Every ounce of fire there, only now with Cutter.

Unable to watch anymore, I turned away and headed back to Jack. He wasn't in Gray's study, and Ed looked up from tidying up the mess and shifted his head out towards the conservatory. "There," he said quietly. By now, Gray was with me, and I followed him towards the patio doors. Jack sat with his back to us, on top of the white stairs outside, staring past the pool, the summerhouses, off into the trees opposite.

Gray had held the door for me, and I went and stood a few stairs down from Jack. I was taken back to the day when Gray had whipped him in front of the Masters, to when he'd taken a beating for me. Afterwards, he'd looked so ghost-like, his face ashen, hurt, and he'd had this damn silence that had driven me to dark acts. I went to call his name, break the silence, but someone beat me to it.

"Jack."

A woman stood over by Ed, and the likeness to Jack was striking; there was no mistaking who this woman was. Dark hair, tanned, tall, yet slim, the suit she wore tailored to her body well. Strikingly handsome came to mind with both of them but for different reasons. "Elena Fortello," said Ed, as Gray straightened. Elena must have taken her maiden name after the divorce. "She followed Jack in. I thought—"

Gray nodded, and something seemed to stir Jack as he looked back and groaned. "Mom, has Dad seen that too? Does he know?"

Elena took a few steps forward, stopped, and looked torn with not knowing what to do. "No. I thought…." She looked at Gray, me. "I thought—"

"Don't tell him." Jack frowned. "Please, Mom. Don't tell him, 'kay?"

Christ. I went and knelt by him. "Jack." He needed to hear it was okay, only I fell quiet. How he felt about the internet, about being naked and there for thousands to see, this was one of his worst fears. I'd heard his comments over the webcam when the cameras had been installed at mine. It had messed with his head back then, now this just finished the job.

"You received a website address too?" Gray was talking to Elena.

"On a music CD this afternoon that Gregory ordered for me. It came in the second post, but Jack—" She stopped herself, her gaze flitting to Jack.

"But Jack, what?" said Gray.

"He wrecked the computer in the office. I—"

Gray's jaw tensed. "Do you have the CD?"

"Of course."

"Why?"

We all looked at Jack when he spoke.

"Why do you need to see any more of that?" he said as anger crept into his eyes.

I stroked at his cheek, but he wasn't quite with me when he looked back. "Jack, he needs to trace the source, to try and find out who sent it. He needs to see how many—"

"There's more footage? Not just the one in the woods?"

"You saw one of you in the woods?" said Gray.

"You didn't?" A glance back, Jack then buried his head in the arms across his knees. "Fuck. Oh fuck—"

"Jack." Elena took a few tentative steps closer but seemed to fall to the wayside.

"I'm going to need the packaging, if you please," Gray said to her. "All of these have come inside ordered packages; they've been intercepted at some stage. I'll need to run checks on postal areas and prints." A look down at Jack, he came over and crouched by us. "Have you received anything, Jack?" he said quietly.

Jack shook his head, face still buried, hidden. Gray stroked at his head, and the contact made Jack look up, but it was directly into the trees, away from everyone.

"I told you Mark's footage had been destroyed, and I'm sorry. In all honesty, we simply hadn't been able to trace it," said Gray, which wasn't entirely accurate. It wasn't just Gray who had lied to Jack: I had too. "I—" started Gray, but Jack shook his head.

"It's all right." He gave a sniff, then wiped at his nose. "I'm not seventeen, Gray. I knew there was a possibility something would turn up." He gave a cold snort. "I knew you both were talking bullshit back then. I just didn't...." He shrugged. "I've just had enough of this bollocks and...." He looked at Elena. "Not her, not them, not home for godssake."

Gray leaned forward and kissed Jack on the head. "I'll sort it." As he pulled back, I glanced at Elena. Maybe Gray had forgotten himself for a moment, maybe he was past caring, but that was a pure and open display of feeling on his part. Jack hadn't told his parents about Gray yet; Gray preferred his privacy. And Jack? For all the chaos he seemed to bring to the table, he tried to keep waters as calm as possible for those he kept close.

Jack offered a short, sharp laugh. "Don't you ever get sick of sorting my shit?"

Gray pulled him in close. "No." He let go, his gaze a little too deep into Jack's, like he knew what he was going to say now would tear him up. "Jack. I've got to get in touch with a friend, and then a colleague who deals with child protection over the internet—"

"What?" said Jack, sharply. "Why the hell would—?"

"That link I've just seen, there's two videos of you on there. In the second one," Gray looked at me, "you were barely seventeen."

"So? Sixteen's this country's green-light fucking limit," he snarled. "And I fucking loved that shit, right?"

"But it's been posted on the internet with an international market whose minimum age limit for this material is eighteen years."

Jack groaned heavily.

"That makes it an illegal upload," Gray said quietly. "I can get the sites shut down almost immediately via Child Protection and CEOP, the Child Exploitation and Online Protection Centre, but I also need to talk to a friend about finding the location of the uploader, first."

"Mark did it," snapped Jack, forcing Gray to ease back.

"The date of the upload was after Mark had died, and mail has been intercepted since then," said Gray.

That earned a second glance from me. I hadn't even paid attention to those details. Even if Mark had uploaded them himself, it still meant someone else was playing head games now. Mark was dead. Like Jack needed that shit; like we all needed this shit now.

Gray let his hand find Jack's neck. "I need to know you're okay with me doing this. You'll have to talk to no one but me, if that makes it easier, but I need to trace that link and the people in it."

Jack looked away, his lips thinning.

"There are few people I trust when it comes to these issues, Jack; barely any when it comes to you," said Gray. "We'll ensure no one else sees this footage that doesn't need to, but that means finding out how many sites these videos have been uploaded to, and how many videos there are."

Jack stiffened slightly. "Can they trace where the upload came from?"

Gray sighed. "Most of these kinds of uploads are done from a public source, like library computers. But sometimes a basic location is all we need to trigger other leads."

"The site wasn't British," I said quietly, and Gray nodded at me.

"American."

"But the upload could come from anywhere?" I added.

Gray confirmed that with a nod as he stood. "I need to get Child Protection and CEOP in on this and make a few calls, track the IP address of the uploader." He mouthed a *look after him* towards me. I gave Gray a nod and watched him head back up the steps, phone in hand. He went over to Elena, and they seemed to watch each other for a moment before Gray gently took her arm and led her back into the mansion, no doubt needing information on the how, why, and where behind her CD.

Looking down at Jack, I sat next to him on the step, eventually following his gaze into the trees. After a moment, I nudged his shoulder with mine. "Love the bones off you, martial arts guy." Jack looked at me. His hands were crossed over his knees, close enough for me to reach up and brush his fingers with mine. "We both do," I said quietly.

Jack glanced down, avoiding my gaze, but his fingers caught mine on a second swipe, and he held on to them. "Don't know the fuck why, at times."

I pulled free of his hand, gripped under his jaw, and pulled him in for a hard kiss, startling him a touch. "Then you're a fucking idiot, Harrison."

He sighed and rested his head against mine. "Didn't want you to see that," he said quietly, and then he brushed his lips against mine. The kiss heated up, Jack giving everything—maybe needing everything back in return, needing to know everything was okay.

I let him know it was, biting at his lip, diving back in with clashes of tongue. Just a kid. He'd just been one fucked-up and complicated kid back then, and I growled against his need to feel that everything was okay.

He pushed me down, my back now against the steps, and brought his body on top of mine. "Love the bones off you, Richards," he breathed in between tonguing me deep. "Don't ever forget that, okay? Please. No matter what you might see." Jack let out a sigh, but it sounded unsteady as he nuzzled into the curve of my neck, now letting his hands trace my arms, then sneak around to cuddle me tightly. "Can't have my old man seeing that, Jan..." he whispered. "It's bad enough with you, Gray... my mother. But my old man?"

He seemed to grip on a little tighter, and I returned it, adding a gentle kiss to the side of his head. "He won't, Jack. Gray will make sure he won't."

I felt him nod, and then he pulled away, gripping my arms and pulling me up with him, only to pull me close again. After a moment of just holding on, he went to start towards the manor but paused, looking a little unsure, looking as though he was trying to listen out for voices and hear what was being said. How much of his youth had been spent like that? Listening to whispered voices? Taking his wrist, I tugged him forward, and we headed on into the house to see Gray come off the phone. He looked at me as Jack went over to Elena.

He spoke something, some whispered Italian that, from the drop of shoulders and inability to look at her, spoke a thousand apologies. Fantasies were now given a firm reality check seeing it. Elena pulled him into a cuddle. "Don't be stupid, luv. You've got nothing to apologise for." She pulled away to hold Jack at arm's length. Giving him a kiss, she pushed away and went over to Gray. "I don't know how or why Jack came to you, I don't really care. But you look after him now. You know where I am if you need me." She held out a hand, which Gray looked down at. "Take care of him, Mr Raoul," she said as he shook it. "You find who's sent these and you make them stop." Elena glanced back at Jack, at me. "I'll make sure Greg hasn't received anything like this. I'll check the post again and our computer system."

Jack seemed to tense.

"Discreetly," she said back to him with a smile. "You...." She frowned. "You just keep safe, honey. This..." Elena swept a hand towards what Gray held. "It means nothing. It changes nothing."

Jack looked away. He seemed unable to speak, and I went over to him, then thought *fuck it* and pulled him in for a cuddle.

Elena nodded, perhaps content in the knowledge Jack would be all right. We'd all be all right. As she left, Gray's phone interrupted us, and I glanced over. He frowned as he listened, not even acknowledging the caller by name. After only a few moments, he put down the phone and came over.

"Pack enough for a week, Jack, you're having a break."

"What?" Jack was already shaking his head, looking at me.

"Don't piss me about. Jan's coming too."

"I am?"

"You are," said Gray, and I scratched at my head.

"Gray, I'm in the middle of a week's holiday from work, and I was hoping to book Christmas off too. They won't allow—"

"It's already sorted. Get your passport."

I stared at him. "What do you mean sorted? You've been in here for twenty minutes."

"It's sorted," said Gray, a little harder.

"Gray, I have the garage to look after too," said Jack, adding his own protests. "I can't drop everything."

"I've arranged for one of the MC's top mechanics to take over with the aid of Steve. And Jan—" I didn't like being Gray's focus, or the half-smile he offered. "You're under investigation by MI5."

"I'm *what?*"

"Helping." He was actually smiling. "I meant you're helping MI5 with their enquiries."

"Tell me—" Life just drained through my feet into a puddle on the floor. "—please tell me you didn't say anything like that to my boss? That's my accounting career up the chute."

Gray's smile was a little wicked, but damn Jack, it infected him too, and that was damn good to see.

"Consulting," Gray added finally. "You're consulting on an overseas account that you've highlighted as a concern to G-Branch counterterrorism due to the substantial amounts of money you've witnessed changing hands on paper. You will be unavailable for a week starting tomorrow, and, of course, the trip is fully funded by MI5."

I sighed relief. "Could work," I said to Jack's laugh. Then I tried to bury a *hell, yes* smile. "Give my reputation a serious boost, if nothing else."

"Which is the cover story your boss will give to your colleagues. I told him you were really having colon suction to clear out your tubes."

I choked at Gray's words, and I wasn't even drinking anything. "*What?*"

"Just kidding," said Gray, and he even threw in a wink. "Although a week away with Jack, you're guaranteed to get sucked senseless in some form or another."

Oh, well. I tried to suppress the need to rush over and stuff Jack in a suitcase, let alone any clothes. That was the decider there; even Jack had let his eyes darken into the land of *let me at him.*

"Oh, hang on a minute," said Jack, shaking it off. "You're due in America for MC business tomorrow."

Gray grinned.

"And I didn't want to go to America on damn MC business when I have my own to finalise."

Gray just smiled some more.

"We're going to America, aren't we?" said Jack, his

shoulders deflating. "That rogue club you were on about?"

"Yes," said Gray. "And you're working."

"Fuck," said Jack. "I can't stand fucking flying, not to mention people—not to mention bastard, ponced-up people who fly."

"I fly," I said. "Regularly. Is this another dig against vanillas, Harrison?"

"Yeah, but—"

"I'm an international traveller too," said Gray. "That a personal dig at me?"

"Fuck. No. But—" Jack tried again, only to have Gray hit Jack's shoulder.

"Digging your grave with two shovels again, Jack. Shut the fuck up and get ready." Gray glanced at me then and narrowed his eyes. "Jack will be working over there too, Jan. He'll be assessing Doms and their psychological status to see if the Dom club they work is a good source to incorporate into the MC. Or whether they need shutting down because it isn't."

I fell quiet now. "Assessing? Including sleeping with them?"

"If the need be," said Gray, and his attention went to Jack. "Jan isn't MC, Jack," he said quietly. "He's struggling to reach a decision over just being with you when choosing a contract. Keep MC business away from him at all times."

"I know MC rules," said Jack.

"Your head's not in the right place and you fucked up over not reading a contract last time. You may know the rules, but don't ever forget them. I see you struggling or forcing Jan into a position that compromises his peace of mind, I will pull you up."

"I'll take care of Jan. You just make it clear to your Doms over there to keep their distance from him and don't piss me off."

Gray went over to his desk and brought some files back over. "Read the contracts, learn the Doms. Don't fuck up, just take this time to get away and ease your head, let alone your fists."

And that seemed the decider there. After tucking the files under his arms, Jack pulled out his mobile and started making a few calls.

CHAPTER 12
FAR FROM OKAY

Jack Harrison

I'D FUCKING HATED the idea of America and had remained stubborn and quiet all the way there. Yet a week later, after getting no news of any more links, or Gray not telling me there'd been any more links, we touched back on home soil, and I couldn't help but chuckle at Jan as we stepped through customs.

"Say anything, Harrison, and you're dead," he said, staring at me as I did a double-take of what he wore.

"Not saying anything, honest." Yeah, like *fuck* I wasn't gonna say anything. Give it five minutes, just five fucking minutes—just enough time to see him squirm and blush his way through customs, and I'd start. Despite hating the idea of MC work, we'd met some pretty special people at Diadem, the Dom club over in America. And two particular wind-up merchants over there, Gabe and Darrek, had topped off things nicely by giving me and Jan lovely parting gifts.

Ed was waiting for us outside of the airport with the Rolls. He stared at Jan, then me. "Gray, get them to take those off, or they walk." I chuckled as Jan coloured again. "Brits Suck" was printed on the front of our caps, the reason why now forever locked firmly in America with Gabe, Darrek, and that bastard of a lead Dom, "*I know Gray better than you*" Trace. Well, okay, and it was also locked in the recesses of my perverted mind, ready to press play again when I needed it. Jan had come alive over there, instantly connecting with Darrek, and more than getting a kick out of watching Gray test out Gabe's Dom skills. After pissing Gray off, the bastard had left me with Trace, and yeah, I'd found out he knew Gray, all right. For now, poor old Ed was true Brits all the way through, so "Brits Suck" wouldn't go down well with him at fucking all. Shame.

"Semantics, Ed," I said, patting his stomach as I passed him.

"That's what's bothering me," said Ed, with a scowl.

"'S not so bad," I said, winking at Jan. "You should see what the American lads got in return."

Ed groaned. "I don't want to know—ever."

"I don't know." Jan finally managed a smile as he looked at Gray. "Wouldn't mind going back, myself."

Although Gray smiled, he was the only one still looking a little distant. Something had gone down over in America; well, apart from me seriously pissing him off over not reading the contracts and really screwing up. Again. There had been a personal issue with Trace and the link surrounding the porn sites. I didn't quite know what happened with the link, just that Gabe had disappeared with Gray a few times, and Gray had come back not looking happy. As for Trace?

The porn sites had been taken down via Gray's Child Protection and CEOP sources, that I did know. In all honesty, America had been a good place to forget, just live for a few days, *enjoy*, even though I'd gone there with one hell of a chip on my shoulder and caught the backlash off Gabe for it. I'd worked for the MC for so long, any club outside of that seemed lowdown and more than dirty, especially when it came to a pussy of a Dom who had never fucked his clients. But Gabe had been anything but a pussy, in fact I could compare the amount of days I could last in a cock cage to just how rare it was to find a Dom who got me going sub so effortlessly. I'd made some good friends, the exceptional few I'd kill to have working over here with me at the Masters' Circle.

But now we were home, and despite the crisp, clear skies, that dirty feeling returned. All nice and heavy like, pressing on my chest, making it hard to breathe. I got in the Rolls with Jan and watched Gray have a quiet word with Ed, their glances in the Rolls' direction making the topic more than just a painful kick in the bollocks.

"You okay?"

I gave Jan a weak smile.

"Missing America?"

That spark was still there in his eyes, although there was a tinge of sadness now. "A little," I said quietly.

"You think Gabe and Darrek will take us up on our offer? Maybe come over?"

I snorted. "Not without Trace."

Jan laughed softly. "Aw, Jack. Those baby greys have taken on a very dark shade of jealous-green lately. It's not Trace's fault he's biker-fit, tanned, chiselled jaw: completely Gray's wild taste. I could see why he and Gray—"

"Tracey," I snapped. "His name's fucking Tracey, all right."

"Oh, yeah," said Jan, and I groaned at the devilment there. "Should go down really well, the guys at the garage learning you were wrestled down and tied to a bondage table by a guy with a girl's name. Street cred' will really take a dive."

I gave him the finger, and that just made him laugh more. "You find out anything about Trace and Gray's history together?" Jan waggled his eyebrows. "Y'know, who managed the fight for top all those years back? Two top Doms like that…"

I groaned, *th'fuck* did I groan with that image. Trace had as much bastard in him as Gray, and, give the bastard his due, he had that same kick-ass physique too, only Gray wore a suit to temper his, while Trace was all jeans, long legs, T-shirt, and biker-fit look. Add Gabe into the mix, it had been Dom heaven for one glorious, fucked-up week. But no, neither Gray nor Trace had given any details on who had topped who. Bastards.

The Rolls shifted slightly as Gray got in. Ed was acting chauffeur, and life became dull in the blur of traffic as we pulled away. "You going to tell me what Gabe found out in America?"

Jan passed Gray a glance. Yeah, he'd been watching him too.

That ability of Gray's to weigh up every thought before he spoke was really starting to piss me off now. "Are you—?"

"At first the link was thought to have just been uploaded to an American site, but sources also confirmed that it might have come from America's shores too," he said through my agitation, and I snorted, maybe realising for the first time the coincidence of where exactly we'd been in America.

"By any chance the state where Gabe and Darrek lived, right?"

"Yes." Gray rested an elbow on the window, fingers brushing his bottom lip. Was his head still back in America? Gray was unusually quiet, and I didn't think it surrounded just me. "Gabe actually picked up that the signal had been bounced from another country, with a time delay on uploading," said Gray.

Now I frowned. "The signal was delayed? What do you mean?"

"Just that the links had an upload delay of about four months from when they were first posted, and from a different country than first thought."

"Not America?" Jan was frowning. "Four months… that's still after Mark's death five months ago. So, what? Someone he knew is getting Jack back?"

"Maybe not one of Mark's men, no," said Gray. "Jack? What are your thoughts?"

I shrugged. "Those packages were tampered with by someone who knew both of you two, my mother. Mark didn't know who Gray was, that was the whole point behind his mind fuck: he wanted you," I said to Gray. "He just didn't have the intel to do it. Maybe Keal's involved in some way? Bastard has the intel, especially since—"

"Yeah." Jan stiffened slightly. "Since I messed up over talking to one of Keal's men in a club a few months back and planted Jess smack bang in the middle of the MC, where Mark Shaw needed her to be."

"Bollocks, Jan," I said quietly. "That shit over Darren

and Jess happened when you were in a bad place. Forget it." Jan's drop of gaze to my thigh, to the long-since-healed scald that made me want to visit Darren again and say hi MC style. Only nobody had seen good old Darren since Gray had got his hands on him. Strange that. Jess had been moved on too, but given protection with the MC over in the States. Last we heard, she'd just settled down. "I was going to say especially since Keal was nearly sent down a few years back for smuggling drugs in via his sex trade. He knows Gray via MI5's part in that. And from Darren, he'd know where you live now, Jan. And yet the packages were only sent to Gray's and my mother's, not you."

"Maybe." Gray narrowed his eyes. "The distributer of those films certainly has access to more intelligence than Shaw did. The original upload came from Corsica. Added to how mail was intercepted here, that's a lot of personnel. Surveillance has been tracking Keal's movements," said Gray. "His whereabouts are accounted for during the times the link was uploaded from Corsica."

I sniffed. "He's sex trade; Keal has more than enough contacts abroad."

"There's nothing on his hardware that I've been able to trace."

"You've had access to this Keal's computers?" said Jan, eyes a little wide. "Don't you need a court order for that?"

"Sometimes," said Gray, and he left it at that.

"What about his son, Logan?" I asked. "I never usually hear much about him, other than how he's always around to offer a *get-out-of-jail* card for his old man." I half-smiled. "Pity, he's the looker in the family."

Gray levelled his gaze and Jan didn't look too happy either.

"Professional observation, nothing more," I said gently.

"Logan has no history of working with his father." Gray still sounded... off. "But there's always that possibility. Keal also knows where I live from all the times he's placed surveillance on me."

"You don't mind?" asked Jan, looking confused. "That he's watching?"

"It's usually the first sign he's doing something he shouldn't be."

"Ah," said Jan.

"And if it is Keal," I said just as evenly, "he knows my folks now."

"Ed informed me that nothing new has come through here, and surveillance was put on your parents, Jack," said Gray. "They can stay there for as long as you like."

I nodded as Jan said, "There was nothing at mine." He took some water from a bottle he'd kept in his pocket. We'd checked his Villa out Saturday morning before we'd left, then asked Ed to do regular checks throughout the week too, same with my place.

"Doesn't it cancel Keal out, though?" asked Jan. "If Keal knows, through Darren, where I live, the packages to me would have been sent to my home, not to yours, Gray."

"Just means someone was watching where we were spending time together, Jan," I said quietly.

"And someone who knew how to stay hidden," added Gray.

"What about the deliveries themselves?" Jan messed with his shirt sleeve, a sure sign he was uneasy. "Anything off them? I mean, you've checked prints and things?" Jan's question was aimed at Gray, yet he interlocked two fingers with mine as I started tapping on my knee. All the right touches, at all the right times with this soft lad. He offered the water, then only smiled as I shook my head, my gaze fixed on the offer of shared germs.

"Both wrapping and packages have seen too many handlers," said Gray. "Those that could be pulled drew a blank." He gave a thin smile. "But that's just the basic with checks, Jan. CCTV of the van's delivery plus times of deliveries are being checked to see where and when there was opportunity for the packages to be tampered with, as well as checks on personnel history of the delivery depot itself."

"And?"

"Jan, it's not TV," Gray said, giving a wipe at his eyes. "Intel takes time and people." He looked at Jan and gave a thin smile. "But they will be found. The best thing for you—" He looked at me. "—for both of you is to get back to normal."

With little choice *but* to get back to normal, that's pretty much how the next few weeks in December flew by. Jan was the saving grace, using his dinnertime to come over to the garage now that he was back at work. Eventually things started to settle, to find some normalcy. Enough, at least, for me to fail to resist dragging Jan over to the nearest Christmas Forest store and choose a Christmas tree—a big motherfucking one with huge pine needles Ed would be cleaning up for the next twelve months. I'd grinned to myself seeing the look of disgust on his face as me and Jan had dragged it into Gray's manor. Gray hadn't been too impressed, just standing there, arms folded, watching me and Jan wrestle it into place with a few expletives off me; then we'd decorated it. Or tried to, at least. Even Jan had stood back at one point, screwing up his face in distaste when I'd pulled out a spanner to dangle from a branch.

Hey, it was tradition, in our house at least; welcome the New Year in with no car troubles. Gray didn't know this shit; it was the first Christmas we'd spent together away from all the formality of the MC contracts. It was going to be a damn good Christmas.

The sex afterwards had been a great way to get into the holiday spirit. Gray had fucked hard, sweat lining his body, maybe needing to burn off work stress. Maybe. He'd been quiet, and I didn't mind being his stress-release point when it came to work; the harder, the better, and all that shit. If it helped organise his head with a rough session with me, Jan sometimes taking to just watching, I didn't mind. Christ knows I understood that more than most.

"Come on, Jack."

I glanced back at Jan. He sat at the kitchen table, demanding breakfast, every relaxed smile going now Christmas was just under a week away and today was his last day at work for two weeks. It's why I made damn sure I was up to get him and Gray coffees and some poached eggs on toast before they went off to work. Jan had done all of his Christmas shopping, keeping all of his goods locked up in his home, away from prying hands. I still hadn't done too much, and that included the guys at work. Gray was pretty easy to buy for: I knew he had a love of Japanese swords, and my wage from the MC would cover what I had planned for him. Jan was something else. I knew he liked his art, but unless it had a picture of a car in it, I was useless at that sort of thing. I was hoping Gray would be able to help, at least enough to get Jan something he'd really go nuts over, well that he'd go nuts over my nuts for at least.

"You know I'm starving over here," said Jan, and I grinned before taking his breakfast over to the table. Ed sat reading his paper, and he eyed the toast and eggs I slipped in front of him.

"No coffee?" he asked, glancing at Jan's as I brought that over next.

"You've got no manners," I said, hiding a grin as I took my seat.

Ed flicked his paper at me, and Jan got up with a sigh and poured Ed a coffee.

"One thing," I grouched to Jan as he sat back down. "You couldn't give me this one small thing." Jan only rolled his gaze.

"Thank you, Mr Richards," said Ed, finally folding his paper onto the table. I grumbled, seeing him put it casual compared to all the breakfast plates I'd arranged. I pushed it into place only to have Ed narrow his eyes at me.

"I'm baking today, Mr Richards," said Ed. "Would you like me to add Danish pastries to the list?"

Now I scowled. "Danish pastries? You never cook me any Danish pastries."

"You're not Mr Richards."

"Bastard," I mumbled, then, "That egg of yours is two days out of date." I snorted satisfaction seeing Jan choke a little. "Teach you to butter up the butler and get my share of the DPs."

Jan growled at me, then carried on eating as Ed poked at his eggs with his knife. Hell, that made my Monday morning. "You booked Christmas day off?" I said to Ed, really hoping to fuck he had.

"Nope."

Fuck. He hadn't.

"Why?" he asked.

I shrugged. "Just wondering who was going to be around."

Jan's ears pricked up at that, and he cocked his head like a puppy hearing food dished up. "Got some plans, have you, Jack?"

"Maybe."

Gray padded through in a suit, looking shower fresh as he arranged his cufflinks. He took his seat, and I went over and served breakfast. Fresh coffee was put on too as Ed disappeared out into the corridor, no doubt to go and get Gray's mail, either that or run screaming from the eggs.

"Hmph." I snorted as I put Gray's food on the table. "That old bastard does know I wouldn't poison him, right?" Ed's breakfast hadn't been touched. "Fuck me. Try to do a good thing."

Ed came back in as I said that, carrying the mail. As usual, Gray's pile looked far bigger and far more interesting than mine and—

"Not yours, Jack," said Gray, taking his. Ed threw mine on the table, then sat back down, occasionally throwing me a glare, chewing his food extra slow as if to pick up on any traces of arsenic. Prat. I knew Gray had access to shit that didn't have any taste and that wasn't traceable under autopsy. I'd opt for that.

Ed was sniffing at his plate now.

"Oh for... look." I pinched a slice of toast off Ed's plate. "See?" I said through a mouthful. "No laxative."

"Now your germs are all over it."

I choked, having to cover my mouth before I did myself some damage. "Are you taking the fucking piss, you old bas—"

"*Don't.*" The sharpness in Gray's voice silenced the

breakfast table. "Show some fucking respect when you talk to him, Jack."

I frowned down at Gray, Ed, then at the table, until Jan finally filled the silence around the table with a cough. "Jack," he said softly, "those plans you were on about for Christmas day?" He had this gorgeous look about his face.

"Dunno. Breakfast with my old man and lady. Dinner here?" I shook myself out of my mood. "Night time's pretty free. You?"

"Same. Well, breakfast with my mother, not your folks."

I grinned, then eyed Gray. "You?"

He was reading through his mail. "Don't know yet." He glanced at me. "Dinner. Here."

At least that confirmed we'd be eating here, together, although the semi-monosyllabic exchange was starting to piss me off. I smiled over at Jan. "What time are you finishing tonight?"

Jan shrugged. "I'm in a meeting until seven, but after that…." His gaze said *I'm all yours, baby.*

"You?" I said carefully to Gray.

"MC's Christmas dinner."

"Tonight?" I frowned. "Since when?"

"Since the MC has been in business, Jack."

"No, I meant I hadn't heard anything."

"You don't do social."

"Yeah, all the same. I usually get an invite I can go native with and burn outside as I dance around the campfire."

Gray glanced over before taking a sip of coffee. "And that's my problem, because?"

Christ, was he in bastard mode today.

"Why? What have you got planned?" chuckled Jan, still munching through his breakfast.

I kept my face as innocent as possible. *"Un po' di istruzione orale, con enfasi sull'orale, lascia perdere l'italiano."*

Ed choked on his toast as Jan's food failed to find his mouth. "M—mmm?" Jan stuttered. "What?"

"Italian language tuition, well… learning."

"That is *not* what you said, Jack," choked Ed, and I was tempted to pat his back, but I'd have probably broken a few thin bones in the process. And—

"Fuck," I muttered, forgetting just how much Ed had travelled. "Well, there was *some* mention of Italian oral lessons—"

"Oral, you mentioned *oral* tuition, with less emphasis on the Italian, more on the oral. Period."

"Ah?" Jan turned a deeper shade of red as I chuckled. Ed was as sharp as Gray sometimes. "Well, hmmmm." Jan found his watch, even made a point of staring at the time. "Look at that, I'm, well, gonna be late for work."

I bit back a smile. "Come on, soft lad, I'll see you out," I said, getting to my feet and heading out. I saw Jan to the front door, and with a kiss, he was gone. Scratching at my head, I padded back through to the kitchen. The clock touched seven, letting me know that I was running a little late too, but I needed food. Gray sipped at his coffee, sliding some mail under his pile as I took my seat. "Anything interesting?" I asked.

"Do you live here?"

"No, but—"

"But what?" Gray focused on me.

"Nothing." I flicked a look at Ed. "Can you give us a

minute alone, please?"

After a moment, Ed nodded, then pushed back and left without a word as I went over to Gray. Pushing the table back enough to hear it scrape protest on the tile, I heard Gray's hard sigh. A gentle touch at his shoulder kept him there, and I went in close, straddling his legs, and gently asking him to look up with a light brush along his jaw. He did, eventually, and I kissed his lips.

Something settled into his return kiss, and it was enough to ease any gripes and groans that I was feeling.

"You okay?" I said quietly. Gray let his hands dust my hips, gripping gently, then pulling me into his lap.

"Just tired," he mumbled.

I briefly caught his bottom lip between my teeth. "Tired? You sure... Sir?"

Blue eyes held mine, hands now running down my outer thighs, then back up to my hips. I shifted into Gray's touch, loving the feel of my body up against his. "Define respect for me, Jack," he said quietly.

Giving a frown, I kissed at his jaw. "What I'm holding. You."

His touch traced up my sides, coming to rest at the zip to my coveralls. As he leaned forward, kissing at my neck, he pulled the zip down and let his touch trace under my T-shirt, now digging fingers into my sides.

Something was mumbled so quietly against my neck, then, "Do I scare you that much, Jack?"

The light breeze of his lips against my neck stopped, and I lifted Gray's gaze to mine. The look there gave nothing away, and I traced the soft curve of his bottom lip with my thumb. Something played in his eyes, I couldn't tell what; he looked away from me far too quickly. "What the hell's going on?" I said quietly, kissing at his cheek. "What th'fuck have I got to be scared of around you?"

He mumbled something else I couldn't catch, and I eased off him, kissing my way down until I knelt between his legs. Through the material of his suit trousers, he was already hard. I traced over it, breath and light play of teeth over his shaft earning me a soft sigh. After unbuckling his belt, I teased him free, closing my eyes and letting my hands run up the inside of his thighs, knowing the image well: white shirt, tie, clasp on his trousers undone. "Fear I've known," I mumbled, kissing his cock gently. "I've forced enough into people in the past. But you? Me?"

A hand ran through my hair, slow strokes as I took him in my mouth. As much as I knew my own body, I knew Gray's better, how he liked to be touched, to be tasted. The grip in my hair tightened, and I allowed Gray to pull me away slightly, then rest my head on his thigh. Again that stroke came through my hair, enough for me to relax and push Gray's shirt up a touch to expose his hip. As I nipped and licked at the toned skin there, the tip of Gray's cock played down my neck with each gentle stroke he gave to his shaft.

"Like seeing you calmed, Jack."

He kept my head turned slightly to the side, not allowing or wanting me to move and take control or to touch, just stay. And I was content not to take control, just to stay, bites and kisses now getting a little rougher on his hip knowing he was getting close, his brush of tip against my neck matching my need to see him come. The grip moved from my hair, now resting on my jaw and forcing me to expose every inch of my neck. His slight change of breath was the only indicator that he had come hard as I bruised a bite at his side, staking my claim at his hip, albeit a very discreet one.

Fingers stroked alongside the line of come on my neck, and I closed my eyes, loving the touch. "Forget the party tonight," I mumbled quietly, denying my need to wipe the come off for a few seconds more. I needed just a few seconds more of this, maybe needed a lifetime of this. "Stay with me tonight, with Jan. If you're tired, we'll get some kip, nothing more."

He said nothing, and I looked up, flashing my eyes. "Or I have ways of keeping you up all… night… long."

A thumb traced my jawline. "I'm peachy, stunner." He looked so sad. "Real fucking peachy." Then he smiled a little. "You want to do something for me?" He gave a slight smile again. "Fuck Jan hard tonight. I like fucking you when you're exhausted from touching him." There was a hard sigh. "It'll help me get through the formal bollocks of the MC Christmas dinner, if nothing else."

He sounded so dejected with that, and that was a first. BDSM was his lifestyle; he protected the MC aggressively, so this… this was something new.

CHAPTER 13
COLLARED

Jan Richards

I FOUGHT A yawn as I pulled up to Gray's manor and let a security guy check over the inside of my car. As he waved me on, Gray's Merc wasn't in the driveway, no doubt signalling he'd left for the MC's party. Jack's black Merc wasn't curled up on the court either. He'd had to work late, or it seemed he'd decided to go to the ball after all. Damn, please let it be the former. Alone time with Jack was rare now.

Keys in hand, I pushed on through to the reception hall after kicking off the snow, half expecting Ed to be there. He wasn't, and unable to bury the grumble in my stomach, I headed on through to the lounge, intent on finding the dining room. Sometimes Ed left something on the table: a sandwich, something light. Mainly for me and mostly done to annoy Jack. But the only thing keeping the mahogany dining table company today was a bucket full of ice. Peering inside, I didn't even see any wine.

Spoilt, Jan. You're getting too bloody spoilt.

Arms snaked my waist from behind and a kiss feathered my neck.

"So, Mr Richards." Jack murmured. "You promised your soul to me for a few hours."

Christ. He'd said that the first day we'd slept together, and I loved how he remembered these things when others seemed to pass him by so easily. I turned around, slipping my arms around his neck as he traced my waist. He smelled good, he *felt* even better. He wore a white shirt, black tie loosened at the throat, hair tousled, wild, and black suit trousers shaped his ass so perfectly. All of him just looked as though he'd been caught mid-heat, and he'd given the V to finalizing his look, knowing his clothes wouldn't stay on that long anyway.

I grunted as he shifted, backing me up against the wall, forcing me into it. Hands were all over me: hair, chest, sides—one forcing my neck up so he could bite at it, the other digging down into my trousers and rubbing hard over my shaft. Giving a groan, arching into his touch, away from the wall, I let the heat play out for a moment, then managed to breathe, "What's got into you tonight? Gray play you up before he left for the Christmas party or something?"

"Mmmmmm, said he likes knowing I'm fucking you," mumbled Jack, then something slipped around my throat and was tugged into place before being fastened.

"Collar?" Christ…. "Jack, you know I'm no sub, right?"

"Humour me," he said gently. "Run with one of my fantasies, then we'll get to yours. Promise."

"Hmm." I was lost to how Jack kissed along the collar, body grinding in hard as he pinned my hands to the wall.

"Fucking love Gray, how he marks," he murmured, and—oh. Did he taste me wearing this or himself? His... compromise for Gray. There seemed so much sadness there too. He bit a little harder and—

"Jack... Fuck me..."

"Don't," snarled Jack against my lips, and a thumb brushed my jaw. "You keep that sweet mouth shut."

I smiled, then gave a lick at his thumb. "Screw you, Sir."

Jack chuckled, and that touch to my jaw traced around into my hair, where he rubbed strands together almost distractedly. "Taking the piss, huh, things?"

"Just a little... teach."

He forced my head back hard, straining the muscles. Now he reared up against me, his one hand crushed almost painfully into my balls, the threat clear enough against the backdrop of my grunt.

Christ, take away his tone, I'd forgotten he did this for a living, making play so fucking professional.

"A little?" said Jack against my neck, squeezing harder and nearly forcing out a cry.

"A lot." A smile. "Don't... kiss me, Jack, please." I liked to play too.

A brush of lips came at my jaw, the threat there still against my balls. "Say please again."

"Please." And it came, no begging, no role-playing, only that need to be us. A brief touch of his lips played mine. Soft, so tender, betraying every hard grip in my hair, every cruel threat against my groin. This Dom in his natural environment, he wasn't so tough, just wanted loving, and he purred and calmed so goddamn contentedly when he found it. But something had set him off; I didn't know what, just wanted to fall at the feet of whoever or whatever it was that was pushing this side of his need and—

"Jack's car's around the back. Jan's is in the courtyard. They're here somewhere," called someone from the hall, and Jack was suddenly alert, head out of my neck and looking back towards the dining hall door. "I'll check in here, then get some supper ready," said Ed.

"Fuck no," breathed Jack, and I dropped my head against his shoulder, chuckling.

"Aw come the fuck on," he murmured as the door to the dining room eased open; then he was suddenly away from me a touch, hurriedly tucking in my shirt with heat filling his cheeks, a quiet chuckle bit back as he caught his bottom lip between teeth.

"There you are—oh—" Ed stilled in the doorway, and Jack shuffled away, suddenly whistling, scratching at his head, and gazing very innocently around the dining room.

"So, Jan." Jack managed to find some art on the wall. "This is a really interesting picture—"

"Painting," I mumbled under my hand.

"And obviously by some bloke—"

"—Woman—"

"—Bird. Who likes…" He seemed to really struggle as he looked at it, shrugging. "Grass?"

"Landscapes," I added quickly as I went over.

"Landscaping."

Oh for… I looked away, trying not to chuckle.

"Hm. You two hungry?" said Ed, coming in and narrowing his eyes, then grabbing at the ice bucket on the table.

"*No.*" The shout from Jack startled me a touch, let alone Ed. Jack reached over, trying to pull the bucket back, but only sending a few ice cubes onto the table from the tug of war that went on now. "Let me get that, Ed. I'll—"

Ed tried to wrestle it off Jack, and I couldn't understand the fascination on Jack's part as he wrestled the old man, looking ready to throw him to the floor and go down on him with an elbow if Ed didn't let the bucket go.

"*Jack.*" Christ. I had to stop myself from joining in and trying to get it off them. What was his problem?

"It's okay, Jan. I'll take it," said Ed, face a little red but definitely full of hard determination over not letting Jack win. "It's been in the family for genera—"

"Yeah, yeah, it's old like you," said Jack, and he seemed to curse and spin away when Ed managed to pull it from him. "Fuck…. It's why I chose it."

"Please, don't choose it again. Ever," said Ed, frowning distastefully, then heading for the door. "I'll arrange something proper for you gentlemen to eat. You know, so you don't have to resort to cannibalism and carry on eating each other."

"Fuck," mumbled Jack. He shifted just a second afterwards and slipped in front of him. "At least let me carry the bucket for you. It looks heavy." He even tried to grab it again.

Ed came to an abrupt halt and glanced warily at Jack as he slowly pulled it away. "What's in the bucket, Jack?"

"Nothing."

"Nothing?"

Jack gave his best smile. "Nothing, I swear." He lost it as Ed reached in the bucket and pulled something out from amongst the ice cubes.

"*Jack.*" I doubled, choking laughter, now fighting a deep blush for both of us.

Ed held up a very homemade-looking ice dildo, one covered in a red and ribbed condom and giving a huge, thick cucumber a run for its money.

"Oooh, suits you, sir," said Jack, snorting a chuckle, and I groaned.

Ed raised a brow, looking so much like Gray now, and Jack shuffled his feet a little, his smile faltering.

"I…." Jack scratched at his head. "I can explain that."

"I'd rather you didn't."

"Really?" He actually looked a little perplexed that he didn't have to offer at least something. "Because, well, you really only need a bit of ten-inch ribbed tubing, lube the inside, line it with a ribbed condom, then fill it with water and—"

"I really insist you don't finish that," said Ed, dropping the dildo back in the bucket and turning away.

"At least let me empty the bucket for you," said Jack, glancing back, giving a helpless shrug before going after Ed. "My mess. I clean up my own messes."

"Then start by dressing yourself."

I couldn't stop hiding my chuckle anymore and finished tidying myself up. Jack still looked ruffled: shirt pulled out on one side, buttons undone—everything about him caught mid-heat and up for it.

"Kinky. Would you like me to dress for any particular occasion?" said Jack as they started to disappear down the hall.

"Decency?"

"Ouch." He sounded genuinely hurt and cupped his ears. "You talk to your mother with that mouth? Decency… what a wicked word. Keep it away from my debauched hearing, okay, you old fucker?"

"I will so long as you never use my walk-in freezer for fashioning sex toys again."

"You know people get paid millions for ice sculpting."

"Not when it's cock-shaped, Jack. They just get arrested."

Whatever else was said was lost to the length of the corridor, and I closed my eyes to my own chuckling and tried to ignore the growling in my stomach. Food. I needed food.

Giving a last glance around to check everything was back in its less-heated place, I took a left out of the dining hall and headed into the kitchen. The ice bucket was on the side with a plastic bag around it, evidence bagged and tagged, and I bit back another chuckle wondering if there was a note attached to it somewhere telling Gray exactly why, where, and, well—*it was Jack*. Again.

I managed to pull a salad sandwich together as noise drifted through from the bottom of the stairway. Making sure everywhere was again tidy, sandwich in hand, I munched my way through one half as I followed the noise.

True to form, and obviously having gotten away with poisoning the Doms and subs at the Christmas party so he didn't have to don paper party hat and hit the Wii dance party, Gray was back and obviously letting off a little seasonal steam with Jack. From the sounds of the kicks and grunts, they were sparring.

Sparring?

My cock found sudden life.

Both were shirtless, Jack in just his black suit trousers, Gray in lighter charcoal, and both barefooted. Gray had tempted me with a few lessons, but this sport was something worth sitting back and watching when it came to Jack and Gray. With Jack, it was a way to keep his body toned, a way to give back to the kids he taught, but with Gray, there was something about his stance that told me he humoured Jack, held back—because the kind of fights Gray got involved in only upped the missing person statistics. I'd seen that first-hand.

Jack could hold his own. More than, though. He swept Gray's feet from underneath him, sending him to the floor, all to shout, "Fuck yeah." Jack then did this victory flip, landing lightly on his feet, adding a little dance to finish, and shouting, "Oh, yeah. Who's the daddy. Who's—"

He caught sight of me, and he was already trying to hide his grin, his eyes also dancing with plenty of pleading on not saying anything over the ice dildo, the bucket, or maybe more how it all involved Ed. "I thought you were tired?" he called over.

I was? Finishing chewing some of my sandwich, I padded over to the row of tables. "Don't mind me." I rested back against one, enjoying the show, and waved them both on. "Continue. Please."

Gray had gotten back to his feet and was looking over as he dusted himself down. After a moment, his smile fell.

"What?" I stiffened slightly. His stare was long, hard…. Then he looked away, and I frowned. The weight of the collar around my neck kicked in, and my heart slipped to my stomach. Something was wrong with the collar. After resting my plate on the table, I reached up to slip the collar off. I hadn't known, or more noticed in the heat. The silver collar Gray had used on Jack now slept in my hands. The one Gray had asked Jack not to remove….

"Hey." Jack didn't look too happy, and he started to come over. "Did I say you could take that off an—"

Gray caught his foot as he passed and sent Jack tumbling to the floor with a *hmph*.

"You have a problem, you pick on me. Not him." Gray reached down and pulled Jack to his feet. Pushing him away, Gray then sent a kick to the back of Jack's legs that would have taken him down again, but Jack jumped out of its path with a chuckle.

"Ooh." Jack waggled his eyebrows. "Gray… he wants to puh-lay." Only it didn't look like it to me, not even as Jack took up a stance, body side-on to Gray, legs wide apart, and wiped a thumb over his nose. He did this *come on, then* with his hand, still missing the change of current in the air, and—"Better Dom up, Raoul. Make it real fucking peach—"

He caught a kick to his ribs that instantly sent him down, doubling over on the floor with a grunt, followed by a quick glance up that said that had more than hurt. "Fuck—"

I eased off the table as Jack staggered to his feet, looking pretty badly winded, one arm now across his ribs.

He ducked another kick, then—"Fucking peachy, Jack? That shit too?" Gray caught him in the ribs, and Jack looked a little confused, and doubled, wincing, at a kick that was about as friendly as the last one.

"What?" Jack caught Gray by the ankle as he finally managed to defend against another kick, then pushed him away, taking a few paces back. "Fucking *time out*," he snapped angrily, and that meant he was one step away from calling his safe word. I'd learned that over the past few months with his contracts. "You're being a dick, Gray." Only that sounded more concerned than when he'd called me a dick a while back.

Gray was already coming at him with a roundhouse kick. Jack ducked, but at the last moment, Gray quickly changed direction to anticipate Jack's move—and caught Jack a vicious blow on the jaw with the back of his heel, followed by a vicious backhanded blow across the face.

"*Gray.*" I was off the table, going over as blood spilled from Jack's split lip and a bloody nose. "*Jesus fucking Christ. Stop.*"

Jack stumbled back a touch, his back hitting a table, forcing out a grunt, and Gray was suddenly on him, grabbing his wrists—forcing him down over it.

"*Life still fucking peachy for you now, is it, Jack?*" shouted Gray in his face.

"Off," snarled Jack. I was there, trying to get Gray to do just that as he grabbed Jack by the jaw. He brought Jack up close, close enough I swore he wanted to lick the spilled blood, taste it.

"Fucking push it. Go on, you cunt. I'll show you how *fucking peachy* a real bastard gets. One who never did need a collar to ensure the pup knelt at his fucking feet."

Jack went to say something, but Gray never even gave him chance, just pushed him away, leaving Jack there frowning. He went to push up too, looking seriously confused, then something washed through Jack's eyes and such a heavy hurt hit his look.

What the fuh? Stepping heatedly up to him, wiping the blood from his lip, I gave Jack a hard kiss, then pushed away with a snarl and went after Gray.

He was in the darkness of his lounge, pouring himself a drink as I went over and pulled him around to face me. "What the fuck was that in there? You hit him, you bastard."

CHAPTER 14
TRUST, RESPECT

GRAY PULLED AWAY from my grip on his arm, then took a long drink of his bourbon, ignoring me by doing that whole denying a sub acknowledgement by not looking.

I put my face in his, forced him to look. "Trust? Respect?" I snarled. "Where the hell did all that go, huh? *You drew fucking blood.*"

Gray let his hand fall to his side, his drink spilling over his fingers as he gently tapped his thigh. "You want to see trust and respect? You want to see that fuck of a sub's trust and respect?"

Gray went over to his computer, touched a few icons, and the flat screen came online. A few more taps, a room came into view, voices, laughter, singing—a house party from the sound of it.

I moved a little closer.

Bodies packed the lounge, music blared in the distance, and paper peeled like a scab from the walls, pulling dry plaster away with it. No lightshade kept the ceiling light company, taking with it every ounce of taste as every now and again, whoever was holding the camera would get jostled.

"Smile for the camera, Jack," said a voice from behind the lens.

All his youth came into view. Caught taking a swig of beer away from all the other partygoers but one, Jack stood next to Steve. Steve. They'd both been under Cutter's knife, but the home movie made their history more real, more vivid. Although he was a good five years older than Jack, Steve looked so much younger than him, paler, thinner. Jack's smile was shy but with an edge that told the camera user he'd get hit if he didn't get lost. And he proved it a moment later, smothering the lens and pushing the camera up. The image on screen blurred for a moment as Jack was heard saying, "Get the fuck out of my face."

The camera focused on Jack again, but now from a safe distance away. Jack's black hair was shorter this time, shaved at the sides with tram lines giving him a hard-edged fashion look, yet certainly carrying that un-tempered look that he still hadn't managed to shake in maturity.

Jack looked irritated that the camera was back on him again, and it took Steve's tug at his arm to stop him coming over.

"Don't shoot the messenger" came a voice from behind the lens. "Cutter's got a few friends out back, Jack." A pause. "Wants you, baby."

Mark Shaw. How could you not recognise Mark Shaw's voice? And yet Jack had forgotten all about him growing up. Not surprising, really. His head wasn't in a good place back then. Yet Mark had still taken exception to Jack forgetting, then of course even more exception to when Jack had gone under Gray's protection to get Cutter sent down. Mark had attachments to Cutter that were even unhealthier than Jack's.

"Get the fuck out of my face, then." Jack gave Mark the finger and took a fresh beer from those on offer on a very ill-looking paste board spread with a cheap plastic tablecloth. His empty beer went in a black bag underneath it. Everything going on there looked wrong on so many levels all ready. Mark kept back, casting the camera at Steve, who only shook his head. Then Mark followed Jack through the crowds of teenagers. Jack seemed to snake through them, politely so, until someone stepped back and knocked into him, spilling Jack's beer and crowding into his personal space.

"*Th'fuck off.*" He shoulder-shoved the older kid out of the way, making him fall. A cheer went up through the lounge, beers held high. Then the other boy was up, inciting more cheers now he was back in Jack's face again.

"You—"

The youth staggered back, then fell to the floor, cupping his nose as blood poured from where Jack had headbutted him. Not even drawing breath, Jack went in, kicking the hell out of him until Steve rushed and pulled him off. Things had fallen pretty quiet as Jack squirmed out of Steve's hold, then turned and shoved him back.

"*C'mon then, Jack,*" said Steve, squaring his stance to fight. Jack moved in, pushing him up against a few guys. They pushed Steve back into Jack, and the jolt snapped Jack out of whatever bloodbath was going through his mind. He suddenly threw his arm around Steve's neck and pulled him in for a hard kiss on the forehead. Cheers went up and Steve fought to pull free.

"Hey, Jack, get a room."

Jack let Steve go after a moment, only to keep him close

with that arm around his throat, his free hand roughing up his hair. Whatever was said between them, and something was said, it was lost to the crowd, then—"Steve's pure straight," he snapped at whoever had shouted the *room* comment. "Kind of like him that way too." Jack went to push away, but Steve caught his sleeve. Whatever pleading went on in Steve's eyes as he looked towards where Jack was heading, it was ignored as Jack pulled angrily away.

He pushed through into the back, the men only chuckling and shouting at the beaten boy to get back on his feet and stop being "such a pussy". Steve was caught helping him to his feet as Mark followed Jack. Pushing through the door, Mark panned his camera around a backroom where three men stood talking. Cutter was back on screen, full-frontal this time, and what little hair he had on his head, his beard made up for. It was long, just biker-style. Unkempt. Eyes were the only remarkable thing Cutter had going for him: startling forest green, like nature at its fullest just before drought weather set in. Seemed Jack had a thing for eyes, only Gray's... well. Gray's were better. But the draw was there with Cutter's. His muscled body wasn't tempered with a touch of fat, but he was big—huge, stocky. Jack had summed him up as a bear. I agreed, but one that was prepared to stand back, let others attack, then go in for the meat once the prey was dead. Christ, was Jack naturally drawn to the bastard type too? Was that part of his disorder? Seeking out males more dynamic than himself to lose himself in? Had he done the same with Gray?

The other two men looked just as hard. In fact, it looked like Convicts Unite in that back bedroom.

Saying nothing, Jack knelt by the door. Damn strange. He had every polite manner there of a kid waiting for an adult to finish talking, or a—

I shifted uneasily, casting a quick look at Gray.

Eventually Cutter glanced over as Jack began to fidget, occasionally glaring up at the newcomers. Giving a small smile, he came over and stroked at Jack's jaw. Jack instantly shifted into the touch, lifting his head, just lightly. The black rope necklace had gone, replaced now with a small silver chain housing a small padlock. Cutter rubbed it between his fingers, then rubbed distractedly at the necklace he himself wore. A silver key sat quietly on a thicker chain, and Cutter winked down at Jack before heading back towards the men.

I waited, half praying for Jack to reach up and take it off, show some sign of discomfort, of how it tore at his head to wear a collar, but….

But?

Unease ate more at my insides.

"C'mere, boy."

Mark followed Jack as he padded over and caught Cutter pulling Jack in close by the back of the neck. Jack barely reached chin level and seemed content at the kiss that went to the back of his head. Pinching Jack's beer, taking a swig, Cutter swung an arm around Jack's neck, leaving him face-on to the other guys and the camera as he drank.

"Causing trouble out there, our kid?" Cutter grinned over at the two men, his eyes flashing.

"Fucker spilled my beer," mumbled Jack, looking down and wiping his T-shirt.

"Where?" After putting the beer down, Cutter dug his bloody huge hand into the front of Jack's jeans. "Here?"

Jack chuckled. "Oh yeah, right fucking there." He seemed to watch Cutter rub hard into his dick. "Idiot there said you wanted a word," said Jack, glancing briefly at the cameraman, then back over his shoulder, having to twist and look up slightly to look at Cutter.

"Yeah." A bite went to Jack's ear. "Meet Smithy and Rus here. These two guys are old friends of mine, and I promised them a team-building session before that job in a few days." Jack gave a slight smile, and no shyness was there, more an echo of Jack in his older years, come all the experience and kink in young eyes. "And," added Cutter, "I need all the crew on that job, but it sounds like you've just floored one for no reason. Seems you need a team-building session too, huh?"

"Hmmm? What'cha got in mind, Sir?"

Cutter rubbed Jack's dick. "Let's just feel our way through it, hey?" A grin. "See what crops up?"

It was hard, watching what happened next. Cutter took a fresh razorblade from off the bedside table and lifted Jack's shirt. Seeing Jack's reaction—that lowering in his eyes: heated anticipation—I wanted to groan.

But seeing him as the blade cut a small path on his abs…?

Jack said the touch of a blade on his skin made colours explode in his mind, wiping away the need for any of his meds, any therapy. And it was there: pupils dilated like with any drug, body relaxing into the harm. Instant sensation overriding thought, taking any sense. After slipping off his shirt, his jeans, boxers, leaving nothing but the silver chain to show off his tanned youth, Jack shivered, only he looked far from cold. Both men in front of him paid little attention to the chain, one only signalling that the door should be shut.

Given all the privacy they needed, Cutter ran the flat side of the razorblade over Jack's hip, not cutting, but leaving

Jack looking down at it, this bite to his lips, a frown that begged—pleaded for the blade to go just a little deeper, or simply tease him more, not cut, just keep him high.

"Oh, yeah, kid. Feels good, huh?"

"Hmm," murmured Jack.

Making Jack face the bedside unit, Cutter bent him over it, now running the blade over Jack's ass, sweeping it down between Jack's legs as he kicked them apart. The blade disappeared, touching Jack's scrotum, then a sharp pull back was given, a cry off Jack—then the blade surfaced with a slight touch of blood staining the silver.

One man on screen gave an awe-filled "Fuck".

I looked away. "Gray. Enough, yeah? You know this. Don't do it to yourself." Because I knew where his head had gone with this. But Gray didn't move; he looked *imm*oveable.

Cutter kept Jack there for a moment, hand on the small of his back, watching with a tilt of head as Jack rode whatever high he got from the cut between his legs, hands gripping and tightening on the unit.

"Fuck me." One of the men came over, laid a hand on Jack's left ass cheek, his right. "Yeah." A lick of his finger, the man pushed it into Jack, fuelling Jack's ride from the cut with a deep fingering.

"Tight?" said Cutter.

The man grinned up. "Fuck, yeah."

Finger pulled free, he pressed his hand flat on Jack's right ass cheek and opened him fully again, his look on Cutter. Cutter unzipped himself, and Jack grunted as a thick dick started to feed into him, the man holding him open now rubbing Jack's cheeks around Cutter's dick and giving encouraging coos to fuck him harder.

"Tight." Cutter rode Jack long and slow, knowing just that, with each prolonged push finished by a hard snap of hips. Every stroke forced a rough breath of air from Jack, and it pushed Cutter over the edge as he grunted, pulling out and wiping come on Jack's ass. Jack stilled, hands seeming to grip the unit for a different reason, his knuckles white.

"Stay," said Cutter as Jack went to move, and he encouraged him to do just that by holding him down by the back of the neck. The man who had enjoyed himself by spreading Jack's cheeks took his place, slicking his fingers with the come that ran free and taking time to lube Jack to make the ride easy. At least Cutter looked after Jack by making sure both dicks were suited up, although he ignored every other sign going wrong with Jack, how tense his body was. The man took more time taking Jack, savouring the ride with a sickening look about him that said he loved youth a little too much. The third, he just pounded in, smacking into Jack's ass hard enough to knock the bedside unit into the wall each time. Cheers went up outside, banging coming on the wall that matched the pace of the knocking going on in the bedroom, and laughter chased each one.

Fired up with watching, Cutter worked his dick hard for a second time as he took his place behind Jack. It would have been easier on the soul to see Jack fight against it, show some sign that he didn't want to be there, but as he glanced back over his shoulder, saw Cutter, there was a grin, a shine to his eyes that said he enjoyed the change in handler, and it held me still. Mark had been right: Cutter took Jack like Jack was a man used to being rough-fucked by a nutcase, not an eighteen-year-old kid screwed up with his conflicts over ODD and OCD and hiding it in the kick of being cut.

Cutter wrapped an arm around Jack's throat, pulling him up, back into him, and then a hand went over his mouth and nose. My frown deepened. Take it back a few months to when Gray taught Jack a lesson on orgasm denial, that was Gray controlling Jack's breathing, that was… I fought down sickness. Yeah, I knew where Gray's head was now.

The two men each took one of Jack's hands, stopping him from tearing Cutter's grip off, and Cutter took him hard as one man counted to thirty before Cutter would let Jack take a quick breath again.

"Yes, boy," he growled, another man covering Jack's nose as well now. And Jack fought, trying to twist out of it, or force Cutter to play harder. Cutter certainly came harder, forcing the last few ounces into Jack. From the camera angle, how Jack's dick was trapped between his abs and the unit, Jack came hard too, his cry not allowed to fill the room as Cutter kept it forced back in his throat. "Fucking yes."

He let Jack go, only to have Jack collapse, fighting for breath, onto the unit; then Cutter's hands were all over Jack's damp back, touching, mauling—feeling. "Get dressed. We've got work to do on that wholesale job over the next few days. And if that was Jeff that you smacked about out there, you make damn sure you two kiss and make up before the job."

As Jack stumbled back and started tugging his jeans on, Cutter and his brood headed for the door. It came open and Cutter barely glanced at Steve as he came in.

"Everything okay?" Steve watched every move of Jack's, yet still seemed to be conscious of exactly where Cutter was as he gave him a wide berth.

Jack didn't look up as he fastened his jeans. Cutter glanced distractedly over his shoulder at Steve. "Kid's fine. Real fucking peachy fine, ain't you, kid?"

Christ. I groaned. No. Now I knew where Gray's head was. Times…. Just how many times had Jack used that phrase? How many times had I *heard* Jack use that since I'd known him? Only it wasn't his—it was Cutter's. He *still* kept Cutter close in his own, unique way.

I felt like throwing up. I was going to throw up.

And Gray, it looked like he'd been constantly battling it since he'd first seen this video: one Dom losing to another even after all these years.

CHAPTER 15
FEELING THE CHILL

"OH YEAH, REAL fucking peachy that, ain't it?"

Both Gray and I looked back to the door.

Head resting against the frame, arms folded, Jack was framed in the shadow of the doorway as he watched us. "Said that every time we fucked, did Cutter. Barely even heard it half the time."

"Jack," I said. Gray had stiffened, dangerously so. "Just… just give us some space for a few minutes, yeah?"

Only Jack's focus was purely on Gray as he came over.

"Kind of his catchphrase back then," he said softly. "Loved saying it when I'd fucked a few mates off and had to kiss and team build there too. But that, that was purely just the bonus when it came to Cutter getting some." He smiled, but there was a dangerous deadness to his eyes as he stood nose to nose with Gray.

After taking Gray's drink off him, Jack weighed it up in his hand, watching it play around the edges as he tilted it slightly. "This from the porn site in Jan's book, hmmmm?" he said quietly. "You found it and couldn't resist watching it over and over again, when I'd specifically asked you not to?"

Gray never replied.

Giving a nod, a snarl—Jack threw the drink at the monitor. "*Well ain't that just* fucking peachy, *you dick?*"

Glass from the tumbler mixed with the shattered monitor, sprinkling shrapnel inches from all of us.

Gray shifted, backing Jack up against his study desk, pushing him down again before the glass had even settled.

"After all these years—*you bring a cunt like that with you into* my *home?* My *fucking home?*"

"What?" snarled Jack in his face. "Got a fucking problem with me all of a sudden?" Jack pushed his forehead against Gray's, pushing him up, away from the desk. "Only it's confusing me a touch. See, I'm your biggest reminder of shits like that—with the shit I've pulled—and you've got footage spanning nine years of people fucking me in all sorts of roughed-up positions—*you've* fucked me in all sorts of roughed-up positions, even whipped the skin off my back when I've fucked up—and yet you—" A shove at Gray's shoulder, Jack pushed him away a touch. "—you turn that fucking upper-class nose of yours up at me for my fucking mouth?"

"*Because your mouth's still stuck around his cock and you don't hear me.*"

Jack stalled. "What?"

Every ounce of calm was back in Gray. "During the re-Mastering scene, what did I ask you to do for me?"

There was a frown, then Jack fell quiet, wiping at his mouth, shrugging.

"The collar," Gray said quietly. "I asked you to keep it on until I'd had a chance to talk to you. I said I'd like to discuss how good it would look on you permanently."

Jack's face screwed up, looking more lost as he tried to think back.

"To discuss collaring you, Jack." I groaned, almost shouting it at him before Gray had to go through each word letter by letter. Jack wasn't stupid. "You took it off, then tonight, you put it on me. His offer as a Dom, his gift, and you—"

"You...." Jack stumbled for the words. "I.... You, you didn't say that, you—" Distance was in his eyes. "You asked to collar me? I.... Everything was just so fucking good that nigh—I just—"

"Didn't hear me. You—"

"*Was lost in a fucking scene*," shouted Jack, then his eyes widened a touch. "So you hitting me, it's, what? You being fucking jealous over someone I fucked when I was a teenager? Years—no, *decades* ago?"

Anger ran in Gray's eyes again.

"No." Jack nodded. "Not that simple with you, is it? Always head fucks with you bastards. So, what?" His look searched Gray's eyes, but it seemed to try and get in at his soul more. "You.... Back to teacher, is it? Was—was that some kind of fucking test on your part?" Now the fire was there. "You wanted to see if I'd remember mid-scene—or if I'd screw up, huh? *And I went and fucked up?*" He laughed a little. "You really are a fucking prick who doesn't give a shit about anyone beyond teaching them fucking lessons. You get a kick out of watching *me* fall as you play your head-fuck games, huh? *Ones I've tried to avoid since Cutter, and you, you fucking hit me for it, you—*"

"—Fuck," snarled Gray, and—

"Hey—no-no-no." I caught hold of Gray's fist, coming

between him and Jack, and nearly spinning Gray a 180 before his fist even hit its target. We'd been here before, last time with me on the receiving end. "Back off," I said as calmly as possible, but Gray was looking past me to Jack.

"No head games, no tests," he said coldly. "Just us, Jack; just an offer to step forward into definite Dom/sub territory beyond MC formality. It turned out to be the wrong time to ask, nothing more. It always turns out to be the wrong time to—" He bit that last clause back, tensing his jaw.

"The wrong time to ask me anything?" Jack finished for him, but paperwork had been knocked off the desk in the scuffle. After picking one up, he stood looking down at a letter, this deep frown to his face as he read. "Oh right," he mumbled quietly. "You wanted to step forward into normal Dom/sub territory away from MC formality, hmmm?" He half offered the letter over, but Gray didn't take it. "Because you look and smell like Cutter wanting to fuck someone over when he didn't get his way to me." Letting the letter land back on the desk, he looked at Gray, me, then left.

Gray gave this snarl, pulled out of my grip, and went after Jack like a bulldog having already tasted blood. It was a twisted replay of a month or so ago, when Jack had wound Gray up over his karate moves, dancing behind him, then getting caught out. Only now there was no trace of laughter as I went over to the desk.

Turning the letter around to face me, Jack's invite for the Christmas party was there and open on full display. Gray had opened it but not given it to Jack? Why?

Giving a frown, I left it there.

Again I caught up with them out by the pool, only rain had been exchanged for a heavy fall of snow that should have given Gray's pool area such a gorgeous night setting. Gray cut over the loungers and took Jack down, sending them both into the snow without an ounce of friendliness as he pinned Jack down.

"*You put me on his fucking level again—you little fucking cunt?*"

Giving a cry, Jack pushed him off, got up, looking just as pissed as Gray eased back to his feet.

"*My mail?*" said Jack as I caught up to them. "Why hide the MC's fucking invite? What right have you got to open it in the first place—*it's against the fucking law.*" Gray caught hold of his arm, but Jack pulled away, making Gray nearly stumble. "What is it? You and your mates from work got together over the last few weeks for a little Saturday-night movie session, all to watch that shit, and you got some ribbing? Some flak for homing Cutter's cutting slag—so you get a sudden case of embarrassments and feel the need to put me in a box and hide me under your bed? *Because you know how fucked up that is, right?*"

"Easy." I tried to back Jack off, hands on his chest. "For God's sake, please. Ease down."

Jack didn't seem to hear and pushed my hands off. "Fuck me." He laughed. "I mean, as far as art goes, I know I don't exactly communicate on the same level as you and Jan, right, mukka? Which fucking pisses me off because I've never rammed my MA down your throat, how I can run circles around you both where mechanics is concerned."

"*What?*" I said.

"But I know I'm the best at what I do, both with the MC and my garage," said Jack, again purely focused on Gray. "I train people so they don't fuck up and hurt someone."

"*You role-play,*" snarled Gray. "This… nothing is serious

to you. Mechanic one minute, pretend sub the next, boyfriend another. *This isn't a role-play scenario to me, Jack, this is my fucking life as best as I can live it.* And I... I need you to explain why you keep failing to hear that from me."

"*Hear you?*" cried Jack. "Jesus *Christ*, Gray—I live my whole fucking life *by* you. But I fuck up. My head, it completely bypasses sense, and who I want to spend the rest of my life with gets fucked up in the process. You've *seen* it, you fuck." Jack pushed him back. "It took meeting you to stop me blacking out and waking up in someone else's bed—to stop me walking into Martin—fuck beating the shit out of guys and wrecking a few hotels, and you stand there shouting deaf role-player? No matter how much I'd give my fucking life to be collared by you full-time, it won't stop the fact I'll always be more screw-up than man when it comes to being anyone's anything. So, yeah, I shift and switch roles, I turn this way and that, because it fucking scares the life out of me when it comes to standing still and risking screwing up how much I fucking love you. That's what I'm scared of: *fucking losing holding onto you!*"

"*Jack.*" I had to stop this some way, but again Jack pushed me aside.

"And if it comes down to it—" He nodded angrily at Gray. "Yeah. I think that's been your problem all along too—you're scared of where my head goes. That's why you never let me go top, why you let me switch with everybody else but not do the basics of just topping you, why you let me role-play. It's fucking safer for you to let me hide in roles." Jack threw his hands out, laughed, then sobered pretty quickly. "You know what—fuck you very much, Gray. You don't particularly like me or my disorders after watching that shit in there, after what we've been through all these years—you could have just told me to fuck off and not come back." He lost so much of his fire now. "I'm long past needing you to kick the shit out of me to get your point across."

Gray had stopped talking, but fists clenched at his side. Jack nodded down at them, then seemed to lose all fight as he looked up at Gray. "Out of everything else, I didn't want you to see the collaring, Gray. And... and...." He frowned. "I'm sorry, all right? For what I said in there, here. You're nothing like Cutter." He paled, looking a little sick. "When you're watching that, trying to find out who sent that shit... just please remember I'm sorry, that I love the fucking bones off you." His face screwed. "I wasn't his collared sub, not by any standard that the Masters' Circle recognises." He stared at his own hands. "He wasn't a Dom, not by any standard I recognise when I see you." His face creased slightly. "And I'm sorry. I missed it; it felt so fucking wrong wearing his collar, but yours... I just forgot to say how fucking good it felt...."

Jack looked away, back to the line of trees, and seemed to shiver. "We're all right, aren't we?" He was back with Gray. "You and me. Us?" He shrugged, maybe defeat, maybe just an unwillingness to push Gray to a distance even though he was hurting. "We can deal with all this shit?"

Gray glanced at Jack's throat, and for the first time, he let all of his defences down, that look seeming to evaluate how many more years it would take, or even if he had any right asking, seeing how it tore Jack apart. Then he looked away. "Maybe we both just need some head space. A time out. You should go home for a while, allow me time to find the uploader to these links. I'm not a good person to be around at the moment. I should have seen that. It's my fault, Jack, not yours."

Jack tilted his head slightly, giving a frown. "Yeah, right. Sure." His eyes had such a strange look to them. "Back to the formal MC shit, are we, now? All head space and time out? Back in the black?" He nodded, then glanced down. "Okay," he said quietly, wiping a hand over his face before finding me. "Jan, call me tomorrow, yeah? I'm gonna go clear my mess up in there, then I'm heading home for good. Fuck all this emotional shit."

"Jack. *What?*"

He came over and I got a kiss to my cheek before he paused briefly, resting his head against mine. "'S all right," he said quietly. "I didn't, I really didn't want you to see that shit in there—he had no right *showing* you that shit in there—and I'm sorry, so fucking sorry." Then he was gone, heading for the house.

Gray took my attention. I was shivering against the snow, but if Gray was cold, he hid it bloody well. "Answer me something," I said to him quietly, now going over, our shoulders almost touching. "What happens to you when it comes to him, hmmm? Those links have been sent to people whom Jack cares the world for. You more than hold the intelligence to know why, and yet you still fall for it and take it out on him, not them."

Gray looked at me. "Who the fuck are you to tell me anything about Dom/sub relations, Jan?"

"He loves you," I said quietly. "If someone outside of your world has to tell you that, Gray, then screw your formal Dom/sub relations: you're still missing what it is just to be in a normal Dom/sub relationship. When he's stripped bare, when you've taken everything he has to give, when he has no mouth, no complications over his disorders, just quiet—he's been under your touch, he's lying next to you. And that's Jack when there's no roles, no playing, just him, just you—just us. If you see that bare honesty as pretence where you're concerned, Gray, then you're right to call for a time out, but not for Jack's sake here."

I left him there and headed back into the lounge. Jack crouched next to Ed, picking up the broken monitor as I went and knelt by him. "Jack."

He pulled his arm out of my reach and snarled, "Need to clean. My mess."

"I'll do this, you go take a bath, relax, just—"

"Fucking fine. You two do it." He threw some bits back on the floor, pushed to his feet, and headed for the lounge door, yet was forced to stop when he bumped into Gray. For a moment I thought Gray would snap out of it, say something to Jack, but he didn't, forcing Jack to nod, confirm whatever was running through his mind; then he turned away, heading for the reception hall. The way out. Home.

"Jack, for God's sake." I pushed up and went after him, glaring at Gray. "It's gone ten at night; the snow's too thick out there," I said, following Jack through to the main reception hall.

No shirt, just half-soaked suit trousers, Jack rested against the door and slipped some trainers on. A long coat came on next as he took it from the cupboard.

"Don't drive in this," I said, going to him. Not with how you're feeling, baby.

"He stays until morning, Jan," said Gray, coming into the hall and leaning against a showcase. "He's not wrapping his Merc around a tree and having it look like MC Doms are stupid enough to drive in this, and he's certainly not dragging Ed out at this hour. He takes head space tomorrow."

I stared, completely dumbstruck by Gray. "What did you just say?"

Rooting for car keys, Jack found them in his pocket, showed them to Gray, then hurled them down into the hall. "Lest I bring the MC down with my shit anymore, eh, Gray?" He smiled thinly at me, but there was a lot of hurt on display in his eyes. "I'll walk and get Sam to pick the car up in the morning. Can you see he gets the keys and my things?"

"I said head space period, nothing more, Jack," Gray called over.

Jack laughed. "Yeah, you're still being a dick, Gray. Your way or throwaway, right? Well you, you go right ahead and sort your business shit out all calm and collected like there. In the meantime, for showing Jan that shit in there—" He flipped the finger. "Fuck you, you cunt."

"Jack, plea—" I tried to get his attention, but he was already back with Gray now.

"For what it's worth, I learned 'fucking peachy' off my old man as I sat watching him work on engine parts in our kitchen. I was five years old the first time I heard him say it. My old lady went apeshit. But then—" He gave a shrug. "—it's also a phrase that's pretty common. Cutter just liked to copy style, take what was yours, and keep it for himself. I wasn't going to let him keep anything of my old man's." He looked at his hands. "Christ knows he had enough chunks out of me." He was back with Gray, barely. "Things slip by me at the best of times, but some things don't go away, not how I feel about you, about Jan. If you'd have asked, told me it was screwing with your head, I'd have told you and stopped Cutter's head fuck. But all that bullshit over trust and respect just gets locked behind MC doors when I clock out of a night. Party tricks, right?"

And with that, he pulled the door open and walked out.

"You…." I looked from the door, to Gray, to the door, back to Gray. "That's an hour and a half's walk," I said, unable to understand just what the hell had happened here tonight.

Gray walked past me, going for the door. After picking Jack's keys up and putting them on the mail table, he shut the manor down.

"No way." I went for the door, but Gray's hand on my arm stopped me.

"I told him to wait until morning; he didn't listen," he said flatly. "It's his decision to leave, not yours."

I pulled away, my laugh sounding a little hysterical. "Fuck you, Gray. He wanted to know you were all right with him, that it was okay for him to be here—basic fucking BDSM communication when a sub knows he's hurt his Dom and just wants to know they can move forward once it's sorted." I ran a hand through my hair. "Why the hell didn't you say it was okay for him to stay? Is all that emotion so fucking hard to let go in your world? Do you even have any or is it all just really party tricks like Jack says?"

Gray came in close. "Don't ever fucking push it enough to find out, Jan." I eased off with that, just a little. "Jack can't be here. He, more than anyone, should fucking know why."

Movement back in the hall saw us both look back. Ed pulled on his coat.

"Where do you think you're going?" snapped Gray.

"Jack is inappropriately dressed, as usual. I—"

"You care? When you won't even tell him who you are?" Gray snorted. "Just clean his shit up, that's all we ever do around here. I'll talk to him in a few days when we're both ready for it. This is no place for him to be," said Gray, heading over for the stairs. "And he's a Mr now. More than capable of finding his own way home in the dark and moving on from a Master."

Yeah, right. I undid the locks and ignored the anger that came off Gray as he added, "You don't fucking follow him."

"Screw you, Gray. You've seriously fucked-up, and you know it," I said back to him, seeing that he'd paused on the stairs. "I'm not your staff, and I'm certainly not here as a BDSM tool for you to withdraw and punish Jack with. You want to force him into self-black, that's your problem. Me… I'm going to find my boyfriend and let him know that shit belongs in his past, where he wanted it kept."

I grabbed my coat and didn't bother shutting the door as I turned my collar up and ducked into the falling snow, heading for my Merc.

CHAPTER 16
HIDING

OUTSIDE IN THE snow, it took two attempts to press the button on the key ring for the Mercedes to unlock, then I was in, slipping behind the wheel and shivering away the night as I shut the door and started the engine. After a look back at the manor and slam of the front door, I reversed down the long drive and pulled out onto the main road. Left would take me farther into the countryside, and I doubted even Jack and whatever it was surrounding his ability to "walk" for miles would choose that tonight. So instead I opted for right, helped by the night guards pointing the way. Jack had been gone about ten minutes, and hopefully he would have kept to the main road. Snow fell thick and heavy, forcing me to a crawl and to switch wipers and lights to full beam.

Just five minutes into the drive, I wondered how far Jack could have gotten—certainly a hell of a lot farther and, from how I hadn't seen him yet, a hell of a lot quicker than me. I came to a crossroad, a little fingerpost helping to show the way, just. Snow covered a bench, at least a foot now, leaving the trees and branches close by heaving and glistening in the frost-bitten air. Picture-card gorgeous in the moonlight, but bloody bitter on the balls when all you had on were thin trousers and a jacket. Even the heating didn't seem to take off the bite.

As I rounded a corner, lights flashed over a figure, head down and buried in a turned-up collar. Slowing the car, I set the windows down. "Jack."

He glanced over, and from how he tried to blow warm air into his hands without shaking, he was freezing.

"Christ, baby." I reached over and opened the door. "Get in the bloody car."

He didn't seem to need much prompting, slumping in the passenger seat and closing the door. Hands struggled with the door, and I quickly set the window up and switched on the heated seats.

Jack curled up to the door, trying to find some warmth, and we didn't speak: Jack concentrating on the basics of getting heat back into his body, me so tempted to stop the car and cuddle up with him in the back.

We pulled up outside of Jack's half-an-hour later, and for a moment Jack panicked as he tried to search for his house keys. I think he'd just realised they were on his car key ring, and that it was back at Gray's, keeping warm in Gray's manor. Why the hell hadn't Gray warned Jack about that? Bastard.

"Fuck," he mumbled, and I left him searching as I opened the door with my set. Jack had given me a spare set about a month ago, but I hadn't used them much with how we mainly stopped at Gray's. I'd given him a key to mine too. A frown from Jack, I let him go through, then shut the door behind us. Jack was already dropping his coat on the stairs and heading up for his bedroom. After making sure the alarm was taken care of, I slipped my coat off, picked Jack's up, and a curse from upstairs had me frowning as I made my way up. Heading into Jack's bedroom, I saw him shivering like hell as he started pulling drawers open.

I knew what was wrong, what he was after, but the photo was at Gray's too. Christ... he needed to straighten his world... to try and control the chaos.

Catching a glimpse of the magazine on the bedside unit, I took it to Jack.

"Here." I wrapped my hand around his waist and rested my cheek on his shoulder as I offered him the magazine. He looked at it and physically relaxed, breathed out a shaky sigh, then took it. His body trembling, hand very unsteady as he held the magazine out, my hand helping his keep it steady, he let it drop casually on his set of drawers—then straightened it. "Okay?" I said quietly. After a moment he shrugged, and I tugged at his arm, pulling him towards the bed.

My clothes came off, Jack not the only one shivering now in the coldness of his bedroom, and I threw the big duvet back. Jack stripped, then he was in bed next to me as I pulled the covers over us. Jack seemed to instantly seek me out, pulling his nakedness onto mine, bodies cool but warming to the contact as we lay facing each other. The quilt seemed to have buried Jack, leaving just strands of his black hair on the whiteness of the pillow. He rested his head just below my chin, cuddling in so close, and his breath brushed my shoulder as he shivered.

He was hiding, and not just from the cold. Giving a frown, I kissed the top of his head. "You okay?"

He shook his head, just slightly, a no, and dampness kissed my neck as he shifted, seeming to want to get closer.

"Easy." Running a hand through his hair under the cover, I pulled him out from hiding. "Jack...." I let my hand fall to his cheek and brushed at the track of a runaway tear.

Jack closed his eyes and let his forehead rest on my jaw. "Thank you for coming after me," he said quietly, and his leg slipped between mine, his body still needing more contact, warmth, but not just from the winter cold. "So fucking bitter tonight."

I didn't know whether he was talking about the fresh-fallen winter land out there or Gray. Most likely the latter, but his breathing had deepened, and he was nearly half into the land of exhaustion already. I made sure the duvet was pulled as tight as possible around us, even though my shivering had stopped with having Jack and his warming body next to me.

Gray hated Cutter, with good reason too, but this was Jack here.

Our Jack. Not Cutter's.

"Shouldn't have missed the collar..." he mumbled, and I pulled him in closer.

"Can I ask you something?" I said quietly before he slipped under. "About something you said?"

He mumbled sleepily against me, then, "About the art comment, didn't mean it. Just... just pissed off, just—"

"No," I said, kissing his head. "Not that. You, you said that you'd woken up in someone else's bed, with the blackouts."

Quiet, a harder grip came around my body.

"What did you mean, Jack? You said you walked into Martin."

There was the briefest of shivers. "Don't...."

"Hmm? What? Who's Martin?"

"Likes the ladies. Nurses. Doesn't like... me. Hates Gray. Likes to... walk."

"Walk?" I stroked at his back. "This Martin likes to walk? Where to, baby?"

"Bed," he mumbled.

"To sleep with women?"

"Walked to Gray when it mattered...." A tear fell against my cheek as he rested back down. Christ, tonight had really played with his head. "Love Gray so much, Jan. Can't let Cutter fuck this up for me, not with him. He's struggling seeing Cutter's collar. Should have stopped, thought. Should have taken my head out of my ass, kissed the fuck out of him, just told him how much I loved him.... So many should haves, too much fucking past."

"Easy. Easy."

"I'll call him in the morning. Sort this shit out right, yeah?"

"Yeah, in the morning, baby. Get some sleep. Rest." But he was already there, and I let my breathing match his, needing the calm.

~

The sound of the shower woke me first, and I eased an eye open expecting daylight to filter through the arm across my face. Instead the darkness still made itself comfortable as a sleeping partner around me, and the cold outside sapped all of the warmth out of Jack's side of the bed. Giving a frown, a blind fumble under the covers found that Jack wasn't there. Then the run of the shower came back into focus. No light came from under the rim of the en suite door, just a constant patter of water and an occasional sweep of steam as it played with the chill of the room. The heating had been cut back on with spending so much time at Gray's, and I pushed the covers back, knowing Jack would need some warmth after he got out. I'd never known him to take a shower during the night before, not without being worn out through sex. After managing to slip on some of Jack's pyjama bottoms, I headed into the hall and sorted through the cupboard, finding the heating switch with the aid of a light. Somewhere off in the distance, a door opened, and glancing back, I yawned and switched off the light.

"Just seeing to the heating, Jack. Be through in a minute."

Rubbing at my shoulders as the soft thump of the combi heater mimicked a deep heartbeat, I padded through to the bedroom and glanced at the bathroom door. "Jack?" The sound of running water still echoed softly in the bedroom, and wiping at my face, I headed over to my mobile phone and picked it up off the unit.

Jack's magazine was out of place, dropped casually and on the verge of falling off the edge, onto the floor. That hadn't been where he'd last dropped it, and I glanced back to the bathroom as my fingers hovered over the touchscreen phone. That was twice now in the space of only a few short hours that he'd gone casual. Cleaning now, was that through necessity, compulsion—or just needing to wash off past memories? My heart sank a little. Giving a hard sigh, my attention was back with the phone.

"I told him to wait until morning; he didn't listen."

Gray's words drifted on back through the cold of the night. Gray had asked Jack to stay, maybe not the right way—but he had tried to get him to stay in his own way, give it time to cool down overnight. He'd tried to step back from his anger but failed as miserably as Jack. But then they were both still struggling as lovers, to move beyond their usual D/s roles that usually gave them their safety zones, their *distance* when feelings got too complicated.

So yeah. I sniffed. Gray was struggling too. And despite anything thrown about a few hours ago, he'd want to know Jack was home safe. He was in a bad place and needed his mind easing as much as Jack's. Would he even be asleep now? I doubted it.

Jack's home. Safe.

I frowned, knowing more needed to be said in the text but lost with how to fix this.

… gone casual twice and in the shower now; I somehow doubt you're doing too good either. We'll sort this.

Abstract.

A hand slipped over mine and the mobile was taken from my hands. I jerked, giving a smile, expecting to see Jack. But a wide and unfamiliar smile was offered, sex indiscernible until the feel of a huge body pressed into me from behind, making the mass of shadow more than male and heated as a hand swamped my mouth, culling my cry.

"Shush, shush. You'll have plenty of time to cry for me, sweetheart."

Giving a look towards the bathroom, I tried to yell, this strangled whimper that sounded more hiss than anything; then I was hurled face-first onto the bed, half on it, half off as shadows and heated breaths suddenly bled into the bedroom. I tried to count how many, three, four… then a metal bar pressed into my mouth, and a grip to my nose forced me to take a breath and welcome it. Hands were grabbed, a knee digging into my ass to keep me still, and cold cuffs slipped over my wrists. Someone else held onto my hair, forcing my face into the covers to demand cooperation or risk suffocation.

"Easy, pet." This voice wasn't the house of muscle who'd taken my phone. This one came effeminately sweet as a hand gripped my jaw, forcing my head up and back while some sort of watch dug into my cheek. A squeeze came roughly at my ass. "Play nice, I'll feed you real well." The hand slipped inside and rubbed between my cheeks. "Yeah, feed this pet real sweet, I will."

"Not yet," whispered the house of muscle. His mass of shadow dwarfed all the others that were shifting quietly around the bedroom. Occasionally he'd point at certain things, and they were picked up by other moving shadows. With a look at me, he came over, climbed on the bed, and then sat crossed-legged by me. "Mind if I borrow a few things of yours, kid?" He slipped the phone back in his pocket, then breathed close to my ear, "Of course, starting with that slag of a boyfriend of yours?"

I started to struggle, then cried out when my arms were grabbed and jerked up, that knee digging in my ass to stop me easing the near-suffocation of my face in the covers.

Giving a tut, Muscle Man shook his head at me. "Nice to meet you, by the way." He winked over. "You can call me Vince. The nice man who wants to pet your ass, that's Henry."

Names. I went still. Names were a bad thing. Faces.... Christ. I could see their faces even in the dark, and Vince, his eyes were so bloody alive.

Vince looked over to the en suite and gave a heavy sigh. "Any idea what we can do to fill the time while princess in there preps his asshole for me?"

"Oh yeah," whispered Henry, and I choked back a sob as the jingle of a bracelet or watch came with the sound of my pyjama bottoms being pulled down off my ass. "Got plenty of ideas, me." I bit back a cry, my shame, as he bit my ass cheek, then pushed a finger in. Now the jingle of a watch matched hard fingering and, grunting into the bit gag, I closed my eyes as ragged nails grated me from the inside. "Fucking nice and tight, boy."

"Pull your finger out of his ass, Henry, save it for later." Vince sounded annoyed. "I was thinking more along the lines of a DVD, anyway."

Henry left me alone, and I stilled on the bed with a touch of my ass on display to the dark shapes that moved quietly in the room. As I breathed heavily into the metal gag, people were pulling things out from drawers, packing them in a case, but being so careful and quiet with it in the process. Vince brushed my face, wiping the hair from my eyes. "You and that boyfriend of yours, you been watching a few porn sites lately, hmm?" said Vince. "You like that slut of yours as a kid? Him getting hammered by Cutter?" Vince grinned, showing perfectly white teeth against the black backdrop. "Little fucker's got a mouth on him, ain't he?"

Pulled off the bed, I landed on the floor between the bedstead and bedside unit. Henry slipped behind me, then pulled me back, almost hugging me from behind as Vince moved over to Jack's DVD/flat screen combi on the far wall. After inserting a disk, silent images of Jack flashed across the screen. He was back at the party, being told silently that Cutter wanted to see him in the back. "Hmmm, nice tight package, that." Vince was back sitting on the bed, cross-legged, watching. Another man stood by the bathroom door, a fourth shadow stood quiet over by the window. A kiss graced my head from behind. "Smell good, pet." Henry licked at his own finger, his gold watch making that cheap jangling sound with it fitting loosely on such a thin wrist. "Taste even better. See?" He stuffed it close to the mouth bit, and I shook it away, nearly gagging. My ass still hurt from his fingering. I wanted him nowhere near my mouth with it.

"Pack it in," hissed the third man over by the bathroom door. "There's a time and place for that. Keep him fuck-free until then."

"Fuck-free, Doc." Henry hugged me. "They didn't say nothin' about finger-free. And I've got ten of them." I tried to get free as he waggled them for everyone to see. "Heel, pet." A thin arm around my throat pulled me back.

"Shush." That came from Vince. He barely turned around, his head tilted slightly as he watched the DVD play out. "Favourite scene's coming up. And... here." Jack's ass was held open by one of the thugs on screen, and Cutter took him raw. "Yes, get in there, my son." Vince fist-pumped the air, mocked doing a silent wolf-whistle, his smile all the innocence of a devoted football fan seeing his favourite team score a goal.

He stopped as the shower was cut off in the en suite. "Oh." He winked down at me. "Play time."

Tears misted my eyes, and I started kicking the hell out of the unit as Henry let me go and scrambled up to his feet. Like Vince and the others, he disappeared out of sight. One hid behind the door, one went flat on his stomach on the floor by the other side of the bed, Vince out in the hall, and I tried to cry out as the light came on in the bathroom and the door eased open.

"Jan?" Towel wrapped around his waist, Jack was there, roughing up his hair with another. "What—" My heart beat hard. Silent images played out quietly on the flat screen. Jack saw them—then found me.

"*Jan.*" Towel dropped, Jack crashed down by me. "*What th'fuck?*" I started to shake my head as Jack cupped my face. "Fuck." He wiped away tears, then tried to pull the gag free. "Who—"

Vince came from behind, and Jack must have seen something, maybe the startle in my eyes. He started to turn, to stand. But for all of his huge size, Vince moved surprisingly fast, grabbing Jack around the neck, pulling him back, up, as someone came out of nowhere and jabbed something into Jack's arm.

Jack fought so hard for a few more seconds, his terror on me, for me, then whatever hope of him getting away was lost to the close of his eyes, to the complete relaxation of his body into Vince.

"Yeah." Vince smiled as he thumbed along Jack's throat, hugging him close. "There you go, princess, you catch a few winks before we start." He eased Jack to the floor, left him there on his side as he came over.

"You too, sweetheart." I got a pat to my cheek, then a needle punctured my arm. "Your slut over there." He looked back at Jack as heaviness hit my senses. "Gonna teach him to be a good boy and stop fucking things up for people. And you, Jan." He looked at me. "You get to come along too, you lucky boy, you."

CHAPTER 17
STRAIGHTENING OUT THE KINKS

I WOKE TO a strange taste in my mouth. Polished wood numbed my ass, and a familiar scent made me screw my face. To match the polished wood, Jack's CK One cologne lightly dusted the softly lit room. Then came a draught of his shower gel, as if his en suite was just a few steps away. The pain in my wrists was something new, so too was being on the floor, and I eased my eyes open. Darkness still hugged me close, and the crisp whiteness of Jack's duvet, his bed—

I stiffened. The towel he'd dropped wasn't there anymore, but Jack's bedroom—we were still in Jack's bedroom!

How could we still be in Jack's bedroom? It didn't feel like it, but….

Above my head, a metal ring was attached to the wall, and a thick chain rattled as I tried to ease the hurt in my wrists. Lights were still off, but no shadows moved in the bedroom now. I blinked a few times, needing to focus, to get a sense of why, of where—

"Jack?" The bit gag was gone from my mouth, but it didn't stop how sore and broken my voice was as I tried to find Jack.

Movement came from the bed, and someone climbed out. A moment later Vince padded his nakedness over.

Naked.

His dick was thick, hard, just stopping short of his navel with a red, bulging tip that left smears of pre-come on his skin. He was big, painfully so, and as he crouched down, he scratched at his balls and gave a yawn. "Keep it down for a moment, yeah? Princess is still trying to sleep over there."

That stole every part of me.

Shown by a mirror on the ceiling, which Jack would never do, he lay his stomach on the bed, head buried in the pillows, arms tucked underneath them, all half-hidden by the covers, He slept there, or looked every part fast asleep at least. The gratuitous shaping of a silk sheet hugged his body, showing the fine contours, but he was also naked. It confused the hell out of me: I was his polar opposite, chained, but dressed in suit trousers, shirt, tie, and tailored jacket. And it wasn't just any suit, but one from my wardrobe at home.

But Jack, Jack was naked, and Vince had been next to him. Naked.

"You never fucking touch him," I said in a flat, calm voice. "I mean—ever. You'll end up dead."

"Yeah?" Giving a sniff, Vince patted my cheek, then stood and padded back over to the bed. "Kind of envy you, Jan," he mumbled. He drifted a touch over the silk shaping the curve of Jack's ass. "You get to lie next to this every single night."

"Keal." My breathing went so fucking deep, heart

pounding hard. "You're with Keal. And you're fucking dead for this, I swear to you." The bedroom window wasn't too far from me, slightly ajar, shifting the blinds just a touch. Ken, Jack's next-door neighbour, he was always at home. He'd hear if I—

"Fucker, you touch him, I swear to God you'll end up dead and lost to any public fucking records. You—" Crying out, I kicked the hell out of Jack's bedroom unit, thudding against the wooden floor, anything that would make a row. *"He'll find you. Christ, will he find you and tear your fucking fingers off for even breathing by him."*

Vince glanced up into the corner of the bedroom, to where a red light blinked. "Yeah, *he'll* tear my fingers off, hmmmm?" He shifted the silk sheet off Jack, giving a distant smile at the full offer of tanned nakedness, then he laid his body down, his whole frame completely swamping Jack's and pressing him into the mattress.

"Off." I stilled.

Hands traced up Jack's arms, showing that he wasn't tied down.

"Heard he likes playing rape." Vince kissed lightly at Jack's right shoulder. "Gonna be good to see how loud he can cry when it comes to the real deal."

"Get the fuck off him."

Vince glanced back, just briefly. "This bit, it's just for you, Jan, to show you he's mine from now on in. Then you count the days waiting for that someone to come and tear my fingers off for touching him." He ran a hand down Jack's side, petting, digging into the toned skin on his side, his hip. "Personally, I've got a feeling nobody's gonna miss you pair. Fucking shame that," he mumbled. "I know I'd miss this."

Vince reached to Jack's thigh, gently pulled his leg up until it was bent at the knee, then he eased his hips down, one hand on his dick and seeking out everything in this world he had no fucking right to claim.

Christ… no. "The man who owns Jack," I said it so quietly as Vince groaned and pushed in, "he'll find you. He'll find you, and there'll be nothing left of what's between your thighs for touching him."

"Owns?" Vince set a gentle pace inside Jack. Jack… still lost heavily to a sedative from how even rape didn't pull him into the nightmare. "You don't own something like this," he said, brushing his lips over Jack's neck. "You fuck it." He held himself deep in Jack. "Yeah," he breathed quietly, "thought he'd be tight. All the workout his ass gets."

"He's not fucking conscious."

"Oh, point taken. Not okay to rape when he's unconscious, but okay by you to rape him when he's awake." Chuckling, his rape came slow, not hurried in any sense. Just taking, knowing there was all the time in the world to take with an unconscious mind and body.

"Sick—you sick fucking—" I tried to shut it out; the soft slaps of hips against ass, the rhythm the mattress was made to take, the sighs, the slicked-up sounds, the kissing and gentle bites at Jack's shoulder—the absurdity of how easily it was all allowed to happen.

Vince picked up his pace, now enjoying himself a little more, making sure Jack jerked underneath him with each harder pound. He looked close to grunting out his come, even groaned it, then suddenly pulled back, his dick still hard, not spent, but slick from loving where it had been.

No condom—the bastard hadn't used a condom.

Giving a satisfied bite to Jack's shoulder, then a slap of his ass, Vince climbed off and came over. Hand on slick dick, he crouched and tutted at me. "Nice vocals there, Jan."

Slick. I looked away from how slick his dick was, how tight his balls were, more than up for finishing the ride.

"Gonna have some right fun, us." A hand brushed my lips. "Don't go quiet on me, kid. Stay focused." Giving a glance back over his shoulder, Vince gave a whistle. A moment later, the bedroom door eased open, casting a little light over the floor from somewhere downstairs. The shape and shadow looked thin enough for Henry, but there was also that clink from his wrist, the sound of a cheap watch knocking against the handle of the door that told me it was him. He threw something over, and Vince caught it—then a sniff at his fingers, Henry climbed onto the bed.

"Oh, sweet fucking ride." Henry straddled Jack's hips, pulling out a hunting knife. Watching the play of light off the blade, he ran it over Jack's shoulder blade, his glance back at me a sly one now as he was caught like Gollum and his precious in the light of the door.

"Don't." I shifted, and Vince grabbed my hair, forcing me to stay focused as scratch marks on Jack's shoulder blade were left visible in the wake of Henry's knife.

"He won't," said Vince, "so long as you do exactly what you're told, and I mean *exactly* what you're told now." He held up a mobile, Jack's. Had Jack's been in his jacket? He never really was up to date with how mobile phones were meant to be… mobile. "When you speak," Vince said flatly, "you keep a nice, calm voice, Jan. If you don't?"

The knife sliced over Jack's left shoulder, not deep enough to scar, but enough to leave a trickle of blood weeping and running away in terror from the blade. Jack stirred, just slightly, with a drugged-up mumble that had him gripping at the bedsheets.

"*Stop. For God's sake, stop.*" Henry did, but the tip of his blade drew distracted patterns in the trails of blood that tried to escape.

"Then be a good lad, Jan," said Vince. "Now, repeat what I say. When the speaker answers—"

He forced my head up, making me struggle to breathe as I watched Henry play in Jack's blood. "When the speaker answers," I mumbled.

"You tell him you're taking Jack away for a break."

Slow circles were drawn on Jack's toned skin, some toddler's attempt at twisted blood art. Him? "I'm taking Jack away for a break," I said coldly.

"You'll be back after Christmas."

"Christmas—"

Henry leaned down and licked at one of the scratches.

"—back after Christmas."

"Good boy," said Vince, tapping my cheek. "Keep it short, keep it sweet. He starts asking any questions, you say bye." A rougher grip in my hair. "What do you say?"

The bottom of Henry's lips was red as he pulled away and licked across them.

"Bye."

"There we go." Vince thumbed through Jack's phone and pressed it to my ear.

"Mr Raoul's?" said the voice over the phone. Rachel.

Life came sharply into focus as I twisted to look at the phone. A finger pressed just as sharply against my lip.

On the bed, Henry dragged the knife down over the tanned curve of Jack's left ass cheek, slowly dragging it this way, that.

"Can… may I speak to Gray, please, Rachel? Jan Richards." I hadn't spoken to her before, but remembered Jack using the name a few months back when he'd had to call Gray outside of the MC.

Vince had called Gray. Yeah. Who else would he be calling?

Quiet, then a voice came through. "Jan?" He sounded tired, like he hadn't slept in a few days. He hadn't slept. Had it been a few days? "Where have you been?"

A tear slipped free. Henry was running the fine point of the blade towards the crease of Jack's ass. After only a moment, it paused against his most vulnerable access point.

In that one instant, that hunting knife was closer to Jack than Gray would ever be. "Gray… I'm taking Jack away for a while."

Quiet. "Let me talk to him, Jan. Now."

Henry used the flat of his hand to open Jack's cheek, just to show where the point of the knife played, what would fuck him this time. Another tear fell. "Head space. Please. He needs—" Christ. Fingerprints already marked Jack's hips. Had Vince…? "Hurt." Vince stroked at my cheek. "I'll make sure he talks to you when we get back. We'll talk. Just… hurt. He's hurting too much." Christ, he's hurting far too much now, Gray.

Nothing was said, then the line went dead from Gray's end. Life cut off completely.

"Oh well played." Vince got to his feet and threw Jack's phone over to Henry. "You can get some sleep now." I got a kick at my feet. "Don't need you for this next bit."

Henry came over as Vince went back over to the bed. I never took my gaze off how easily he slipped in next to

Jack and pulled him close.

"Come on, you, up you get," said Henry.

I did, and every ounce of fight I had came with it. Other men came into the room, and all Vince did was fluff his pillow as I was dragged out fighting and screaming for both of us.

~

"Here we go," said Henry, and my back hit the bed hard in Jack's spare room as Henry and his men dumped me down, leaving me needing to throw up as the world carried on spinning. Before I could get up, a mass of hands dragged me farther up the bed, and mine were chained above my head. Rope around my ankles made sure I was spread wide just before my shoes and socks were tugged off. "Comfortable?" mumbled Henry.

There was no option of a reply as a gag bit into my mouth before being tied.

"Awww, pet. It's been a rough day for you." A needle was passed over, and I started to struggle. "Let's make you happy for a while, let you sleep. You look like you'll have such a sweet sleeping face."

Jack. I tried to cry out at that.

"Hey, hey," soothed Henry, giving a smile. "Vince is gonna teach him to be a sweet pussycat." The needle dug into my arm. "Nothing for you to worry about just yet."

Life started to get dark very fast.

"Nothing to worry about but... me."

CHAPTER 18
DEATH-PLAY

SHOUTING WOKE ME first. Then the sound of hell breaking loose seemed to slip away just as quickly as mugginess tried to pull me back under. Feet taking steps two at a time added a pulse to all of the cries that seemed to go up all over the place. A door came open in the distance, and Jack seemed to cry a thousand and one obscenities.

Jack.

Fucking Jack.

The spare room door came open as I writhed on the bed, making sure the metal bedstead knocked and banged against the wall, answering his fight. It seemed to go quiet for a moment in another room, then Jack was shouting my name, calling life out as more thuds came from his room.

"Shut him the fuck up." That came from Vince as Henry was pushed into my room. Then, staring at me angrily for a moment, Vince was gone, disappearing into the hall. A hand jammed hard against my mouth, then Henry threw his body down, pinning me still and nearly choking me with how he pressed the gag deeper into my mouth.

"Shush-shush, pet," he whispered heatedly against my cheek, his dick hard and jamming into my thigh. "Jack's just woke a little early, is all. Grouchy shit, isn't he? Vince'll get his men to sort him out, you'll see."

I tried to cry out, to pull away from the hand on my mouth and how my own body hurt when I moved, but Henry followed every move I made, covering my nose and holding on when I refused to stop. The cries and shouts were more sleep-filled from the other room, the thumps and shouts from other men less hurried, more bruised-sounding, exhausted.

"See?" whispered Henry. "Jack's getting some happy juice. He'll learn eventually."

A shadow cast over us, and with sweat dripping from his forehead as he wiped across it, Vince looked down at me, then Henry. "He's needed again."

"Did your pet see your face?"

"No," snapped Vince. "And shut the fuck up with the questions. C'mon, I'm gonna wash that fucker's mouth out and teach him some real manners." Vince ran his eye over me. "Make him a little happier, Henry. It's show time."

Something was pulled from underneath the bed, and after a moment, a case flicked open. Henry flashed a smile over, a needle ready in his hand. "Just a small prick now, love. Christ knows lover boy's used to something bigger by now. You too. It coming back yet?"

Life started to blur at the edges, and for a moment I just wanted to stare up at the ceiling, watch the play of light over in the corner, how a red light blinked on. Then I was moving, a tug at my arm pulling me up, off the bed. Feet dragged along the floor, making scraping noises on Jack's carpeted floor, which was weird because I swore he had wood flooring throughout. Easier to wipe clean, keep the dust off.

As I was pulled into Jack's bedroom, I cried out, finding some life seeing Jack naked and on the floor with his hands cuffed behind his back. Henry pulled me to my feet, hissing quietly at the two men who stood around Jack. One nursed a bloody nose whilst a third man sat on the bed, gripping around his own ribs. Just off to his side lay an empty syringe.

"Jack," I mumbled as Henry tugged off the gag. Jack stirred, just a slight shift of body, a soft groan from over on the floor. *Fucking get up. Come on, baby. Move. Fight.* You can fight. You can more than fucking fight this, baby—please.

Another groan from Jack. Blood stained the floor as he lifted his head a touch. No…. Where Gray had cut his lip, Jack had a few more twins that almost kissed it. Knuckles were stained red, some bruised, and… fight… someone had already tried to make sure he didn't, but—

"Jan?" Not even looking over, he seemed to have difficulty lifting his head any more as heavy tiredness laced his voice.

"Stay with me, Jack. Please. Stay with me, baby."

Running water from Jack's en suite caught my ear, and I frowned, wondering why it was making a noise with Jack out here. Then Vince, all naked, came out, brushing past me and Henry, wiping his hands on a towel before going over to the bed. Reaching down, he grabbed something from underneath, strange in itself as Jack never kept anything under the bed, nor on the floor. Vince straightened and was fastening something in place on his face. When he looked over, two huge, round, slick black eyes stared over. It would have been laughable, but the black leather gas mask looked welded onto Vince's face, stretching the leather to obscene degrees to fit his huge skull. Shaped to frown at the brow, a permanent disapproving look darkened it, a grid for a mouthpiece giving Vince a metallic rasp when he breathed.

"What the?" I mumbled. "Just… what the—"

Arms out wide, Vince did a slow circle, showing off his full naked glory. None of it seemed for my benefit, or Jack's as he kicked at Jack's shoulder, stirring him slightly and forcing a murmur.

"As your Dom," said Vince, his voice distorted as he came down and pulled Jack onto his back, "I have preferences." A stroke went to Jack's jaw as Jack's eyes widened, startled by the strange face, the stranger voice. "One of them is rape."

"*No.*" That was me.

Vince eased to his feet and another kick went to Jack's ribs. "Don't… safe word me, Jack. Don't… beg me to stop."

Jack went to say something, but a fist stopped him, snapping his head to the side and making him choke blood onto the floor.

My cry strangled, I tried to get to him. Henry tightened his grip around my throat, keeping me up even though the world was spinning enough to take life from underneath me.

"Didn't hear you, boy," snarled Vince. "What did you say?"

Jack was left groaning on the floor. "Merce—" Vince kicked him in the back.

"What was that? Can't hear you, boy."

"Leave him the fuck alone."

Vince looked over at me, then nodded at the two men left standing.

Grabbing at his arms, Jack was dragged into the en suite. Then we were moving too, Henry dragging me backwards towards the en suite, my feet going from underneath me as my shoes left scuff marks on the polished floor. When the fuck had I put on black shoes?

~

I hit the tiled floor hard in Jack's en suite, crying out as bones jolted in my wrists before I stopped my head from splitting on the floor. The world didn't stop turning even though I curled up there crying for it to.

Jack was on his knees in the bath, body soaked, gasping for air with hands still cuffed behind his back. The two other men had disappeared, leaving Vince standing in the bath behind Jack. Vince said something to him as he pulled Jack by the hair. I couldn't focus long enough to hear it. Then—

"Don't... cry out your safe word," said Vince in Jack's ear, and again, as soon as Jack started to open his mouth to answer, to rebel, yet give Vince everything he wanted all the same, Vince pushed him back under the water, silencing him.

"Fucking stop," I mumbled, trying to force my body to move. "Kill him. You'll—"

Vince pulled Jack back out of the water. "Safe word. What is it?"

Chest rising and falling heavily, looking as though Vince needed to keep him up so he didn't fall, Jack again went to cry it out, but Vince pushed him under the water as he did.

"*Mercedes,*" I cried out for him. "It's fucking Mercedes, and he's trying to say it." Henry skirted in behind me, pulling me back so my head almost rested in his lap. "Let him say it, please."

"Easy, pet, easy." A stroke came to my hair. "Let Vince work his magic."

With the splashing of water came hard and hurried gasps for air as Jack was pulled free again. Hair covered his face in thick, wet curls, almost hiding him from view, and he was shivering as if Vince had only run water through the cold tap.

"If you don't tell me your safe word," said Vince, his breathing just as hard now with the effort to keep Jack under the water each time, "I won't know when I'm breaching your comfort zones, boy."

Again Jack went to cry it out, to get this all to stop, and again Vince took him underwater. It seemed to last longer with each one, leaving Jack more and more exhausted as he was pulled up.

"No safe word?" snarled Vince. "You want no fucking mercy under me, boy? Fair enough." He stepped out of the bath and grabbed Jack by the waist. After lifting him out, Vince dumped him hard on the floor, then reached for something in the bath. The cat o' nine tail's leather strands were soaked and dripping, and without drawing breath, Vince laid into Jack.

There was a lot of power behind him, each pelt on thigh, on Jack's stomach, his groin, and then his legs as he tried to curl up, away from the beating instantly causing red welts that crisscrossed like crazy, paving over Jack's body.

I tried to crawl over, take some of the blows, let him

hide. But Henry was there, hooking my hands over a curved piece of metal close to the toilet, and a pat went to my head. "Just keep talking to him, pet. Let him know you're here."

Vince had straightened, the end of the thick cat still held in his hand. Jack shivered on the floor, trying to shift up, to sit, but the movement was almost impossible with how the cuffs still bound his hands behind his back. Giving a shake of head, Vince gave him one last whip across his back that made sure he stayed down.

"Don't... tell me your safe word," said Vince, water running from off his leather mask. "Don't... stop the rape." Jack mumbled something, then as he tried to focus and answer, Henry moved in with some black duct tape and wrapped it tight around Jack's mouth.

"Bastards," I mumbled, trying to slide down, to get my body to move, if only to lay down next to Jack and cover him up. Nightmare... Jack's wide eyes cried one huge nightmare, how he needed this to stop, but wasn't being allowed to call it. "You sick fucking—"

Then Jack went still and quiet, forcing me still as something dropped close to his head.

Henry had pulled a photo of Gray out of the bathroom cupboard, and having dropped it there casual on the floor, Jack was left staring at it. How had they known?

Black marker now in hand, Henry wrote a single message on the bath panel, close enough for Jack to see.

Don't...

... straighten me, Jack.

I groaned, but as Jack eased onto his stomach, tried to shift, to get close and just find some comfort in normality, in ordering all chaos, Henry slipped something around

Jack's neck. The dog choker was pulled tight, then Henry crushed his foot onto the loose end that clinked on the tiles. Jack was choked to a stop, barely able to breathe let alone move with having Henry's foot tread on his collar. As Henry held him still, Vince kicked Jack's legs open now he was flat on his stomach. He knelt between them, running his hand over the damp curve of Jack's ass, seeming to fall so quiet as he watched his own hand play.

"Don't… straighten the photo," breathed Vince, quietly, head tilted as if to watch the play of light on the small of Jack's back.

Henry inched the photo closer, almost touching Jack's cheek.

"Don't…" said Vince, "straighten the photo, Jack."

Looking down at Gray as Gray got out of the Merc in the photo, a tear slipped over Jack's cheek. The fight was there, not to listen, not to disobey, then the battle was won and lost within just a few short seconds as he eased down and brushed his nose over the photo. Maybe not even to straighten, maybe just to feel, just to get close to—

Gripping Jack's hair, making him cry out, Vince pulled him back so he was now on his knees, looking down at the photo. As he did, Vince took the thick end of the cat to Jack's ass and rubbed it up against him.

"You touching something you shouldn't, boy?" said Vince quietly. "That's a serious fuck-up. But I promise I won't fuck you with this. All you have to do is use your safe word. What's your safe word?"

"*Mercedes*," I mumbled. Blunted studs lined the leather, the handle itself as thick as Vince's dick, but studded—this one was fucking studded and threatening rape. It would tear Jack's insides up.

"Last chance," said Vince as Jack struggled to cry out. "Don't... tell me your safe word?"

He couldn't, not with the tape on his mouth. *"Fucking Mercedes, Mercedes-fucking-Benz,"* I cried, throat tearing as the cat pressed against Jack. "Mercedes—Mercedes-fucking-Benz, please. It's Mercedes-Benz, let him say it..."

"No? Nothing?" Vince tutted, then Jack cried agony as he took the handle of the whip down to the root. With everything else that came, I shut it out, curling up in the corner, covering eyes—ears, repeatedly whispering, *"Mercedes... Mercedes-fucking-Benz...."*

"You can rest now," said Henry. The offer of a cover left me wanting to throw up. Jack had been left bruised and bloodied on the bathroom floor. Still naked. No comfort. No cover. Yet me...? A bed. Jack's spare bedroom all warm, softer lights....

"Tired, pet?" Henry pulled something out from underneath the bed, and a red light in the corner of the room blinked to try and take a look.

"Don't... worry about Jack," purred Henry. "His ass'll be sore, but Vince'll take real good care of him when he lets him wake up in a few days. You just wait and see." A stroke came at my hip, then gently slid over to my dick. "You just sleep now, pet." His voice was so quiet, breath light against my cheek as he lay down on the bed with me. "I'll look after you, promise. Just get some sleep. Please..." Another injection stung my arm. "Yeah..." Fingers traced down to the clasp on my trousers. "You just... just sleep... I like you... sleeping, pet...."

CHAPTER 19
PLAY IN SESSION

Jack Harrison

MOVING STIRRED ONE fucked-up waltz inside my head, and the stab of hurt in my ass and back encouraged me to stay lost in the feel of cool silk sheets. The pillow made a soft ledge to grip onto, and I groaned, barely shifting my hips and stirring anything else. Voices swam in and out of focus, making it hard to think beyond the softness of the bed, and I pulled the covers up over my head, wincing against the fucked-up mixture of sound and sense.

"Jack?"

The cover was tugged off my head, and I twisted into the pillow, not wanting the onslaught of light or the confusing sound of voices to get any closer.

"Come on, honey, up you get."

Whether it was day, morning, I couldn't tell. Didn't really want to, just needed to lie down for five more minutes, shut out the cries. Life swam in a shit-load of hurt, my ass, my shoulders, and it didn't help when the bed depressed next to me and a hand rubbed at my side. "Fuck."

"'Nother bad night, luv?"

"Hmmm." I coughed, voice sore, broken, not really understanding the sweetness of the voice in the backdrop of cries and struggles. "Mom?"

"You okay, honey?" Black eyes frowned down at me, my old lady's face taking on a highway of lines as her Italian came through now. Her hair was loose, which she never usually did, black curls surrounding her face, nearly hiding it. She'd eaten something hot and spicy. Maybe a curry? But curry... she fucking hated spicy food. "You were crying out," she said, giving a frown.

"Jan." I twisted around, grunting out hurt. I'd been wiping tears off his face by the bed. He'd been bound... gagged, then.... "Ah." I tried to move, to sit up, but there was a stab of pain in my ass, and the feel of sheet scraping along my body forced a sharp hiss.

"Oh, honey." Hands pushed down at my chest. "You've got this illness bad. Take this."

A glass of cool orange juice touched my lips. "Mom," I mumbled, the world and all its soft covers swimming for a while. "Jan. Hurt—"

"Shush." A hand under my arm helped me sit up, then encouraged me to lift my head. "Your throat sounds sore."

The glass touched my lips again and panic hit for a moment. Lips... water... fighting for breath. I downed it in one, taking a deep breath afterwards to chase away the rush of fear that crushed my insides. Hurt seemed to instantly ebb away and numbing took over. It felt so damn good, because I chased whatever threatened to rise in my head back down.

"Maybe…." My old lady rubbed at my cheek. "Maybe I should go call Vince?" She offered a smile.

Vince? I looked at her, tried to focus, but the lines on her face were blurred at the edges, giving her this warp-drive effect every time she moved. "Gray. Need Gray. Argument an—" The world tipped upside down and I dropped my head between my knees. "Whoa, fuck…."

"Easy, honey. You're really sick. Get some more sleep."

I lay back down, my arm dropping over my face.

"That's it, baby," whispered my old lady. "You stay here. I'm gonna go and give Vince a call."

"Vince?" I mumbled something, shaking my head. "Just Jan, just need…." Jan. There was something wrong with Jan.

Pissed.

Jan had been so pissed, and scared. He'd been crying and scared as he lay on the en suite floor, shouting, curling into himself. *Mercedes… Mercedes-fucking-Ben….*

The comfort of pillows and soft sheet surrounded me again as the sound of voices forced my hand off my face. I'd fallen back to sleep, only this time making the mistake of trying to get up too quickly. The light through the windows swam in and out of focus, blurring life beyond the blinds, and I dropped my arm back over my face to block out the dizzy assault and the sting that came with moving. No good, life still did one fucked-up waltz in the backdrop, and I groaned, wiping a hand over my face, hating how much my hand shook. A glass of water sat on the bedside unit, and I held back throwing up as I reached over and grabbed it. The ice-coolness was everything I needed, soothing the burn in my throat, the hurt in my body and ass.

Giving a wipe at my mouth, I blindly gave the glass a home back on my bedside unit. "Shit." Closing my eyes, I tried to stop the swaying going on with my bedroom as I stood. Satisfied I wasn't about to end up arse over tit on the floor, I made it over to the wardrobe. Jogging bottoms came out, and I slid the door shut as voices came from outside, not panicked, just calm, and the world became calmer hearing it.

Calm. Fuck. I needed Gray's calmness now.

Wincing, I pulled one leg through my jogging pants, then the other, then made it over to the door. Red flashing irritated the fuck out of me, and the camera above the door had me staring. Mike. There were no details there of sorting through schematics with either him or Gray. Nothing that said MC cameras should be here. In fact, Gray, he'd been pissed and angry, I—

"Jack." My old lady's eyes widened a touch seeing me open the door and step into the hall. She came over and a hand was suddenly pressed against my chest as the floor nearly crept up on me. "Jack, love, you shouldn't be up." I palmed my eyes, then realised she wasn't alone as I looked from her to the big wall of muscle standing at the top of my stairs.

"Fuck..." I frowned up at him. "You...? Gray. Where the hell's Gray, M-mom?"

My old lady frowned. "Oh, honey." She was talking to House of Muscle. "Vince, I'm really sorry. I don't know what's wrong with him—"

"*Who th'fuck's Vince?*" I shouted at her. "Gray. Where is

he, Mom? Jan. Where's Jan?" I gripped onto the doorframe as sickness turned my stomach, then pushed at Vince as he came closer. "Get th'fuck out of my face."

"*Jack.*" The sharpness to my old lady's voice jerked me slightly as it grated through nerves. "What the hell is wrong with you—"

"It's okay, Mrs Fortello," said Vince, and I found myself looking up a whole fucking lot as he came over, the expression in his brown eyes a little sad. "Jack's just tired, is all." I grunted as he tugged my grip off the doorframe and shouldered my arm over his, his arm slipping around my waist and forcing a hiss as he caught soreness there. "Let's get you downstairs, see if we can clear your head a bit, okay, baby. You—"

"*Th'fuck off.*" I slammed a hand against his chest and tried to break a few chest bones. "Get... get the fuck off me, you asshole. Gray—"

"Easy." Vince tugged me along the hall, taking my weight a little when the world went black for a moment.

"*Fucking shit,*" I bit out as pain travelled up into my spine.

"Oh-kay." Vince rested his hand on my stomach to stop me from falling. "Not good, you—"

"You touch me again, and I'll fucking floor you. *Jan—*"

Shuffling came from my spare room. There'd been shuffling in there before, a day, maybe two days ago, I swore there had, slight thuds of metal bedstead knocking against wall, and I tried to crane my neck, echoes of thuds and answered cries tearing me up. "Jan?" He'd been so fucking pale, so fucking terrified there on the floor.

Snarls hit the hall—mine—and I was trying to get past Vince, push him out of the way.

"Fucking Jan." The world started to spin as I looked back, my old lady crying out at the struggles, and it seemed to make matters worse as the world carried on spinning as I lost my footing and started to fall....

~

"Jack, c'mon, our kid. You with me? I need to know you're okay."

"Hmph?" I jolted awake. I lay on my settee, legs drawn up, feet flat on the arm with someone behind me. A kiss went to my head as I struggled with the time slip. "It's all right, our kid. Take it easy. You've had it really rough lately with this sickness. You need to calm down."

"Jan?"

Another kiss came to my head as I struggled to keep my eyes open. "No. Doesn't matter, though, kid. You just get better."

Not fucking ill. I wanted to tear the huge arm off my chest, especially when he (Vince?) laced it around me and pulled me in close. But tired... I was so fucking tired. Sound and images from my TV kicked into gear, but they were one continuous blur, making it too hard to try and keep up with them. The ceiling looked much better: no movement, no colour. I knew I was staring but couldn't really help it.

"Okay, now we know you can wake up with no problems, you get some sleep, our kid." Another kiss, another slight flare of wanting to nut the bastard, then it was gone. Tired. I was just too fucking tired.

~

Somebody shook me, and I mumbled that they really needed to fuck off now. I liked my settee: I'd chosen it specifically for this, when life became too fucking muggy to drag my lazy ass upstairs. But that shaking came again, this time with a bout of chuckling.

"Come on, Jack. Get your ass into gear. Want to show you something."

Whoever had been my pillow was now gone, a cushion now in his place, and I groaned, liking it that way. Hands grabbed under my arms, tugging me up into a sitting position. I followed the movement through, leaning forward with arms resting across my knees, then dropped my head, half rubbing at my eyes, half just wanting to lie down and sleep again.

"Still feeling rough, hmm?" There was a stroke to the back of my head, and I looked up, narrowing my eyes. Square jaw, head tilted slightly, he looked alien in familiar surroundings, but that sadness was there to dark brown eyes, and soft brown hair was shower fresh....

"Jan?"

Hurt flickered in brown eyes, and it put such a weight on my chest. I hated those eyes looking so fucking torn. "Name's Vince, Jack." Sadness seemed to deepen. "Don't you remember, baby?"

"Sleep… here." I frowned a gaze around me. I'd gone to sleep on him here.

"Yeah." Brown eyes seemed to lift a touch. "That's right, you fell down a few stairs and went to sleep here on me yesterday."

"Yesterday?"

"Hmmm. I left you here; you looked like you'd hit someone if they moved you."

The pull in my body didn't hurt so much today as I rubbed a hand into my forehead. Vince's touch replaced mine, feeling for something.

"Christ, Jack. This carries on, I'm getting the doctor in." His hand dropped to my neck, stroking gently and—

"Sick." I gripped my stomach, cramps nearly creasing me in two as a bitter taste came to my throat. "Need to throw u—"

"Hang on." Vince was gone, then a bottle of fresh water was pushed into my hand. "You've barely taken any fluids over the past few days. You need to drink."

I took the water, needing to ease the soreness in my bones, and nearly drank half before it was pulled out of my grip. "Slowly." Vince sat back and gave a worried smile. Perfect teeth. His teeth were so fucking white and straight. "Look at this." He was grinning. "Got something that might clear that head of yours a touch."

He was gone, and the flick of a switch assaulted my head. "Okay." He winked as he came back over. "Tell me what you think."

The usual two-tone pastels to my lounge were complemented with a real Christmas fir tree, soft blue bulbs, and silver streamers that were tacked to the ceiling shifted in the breeze. Huge white Santa faces with white beards had attached themselves along the main feature wall, all with rosy cheeks and big smiling faces.

What the—

"Your old man came over while you were out of it and helped," said Vince. I looked at him.

"My old man?" There was a tug, desperation to see him.

"Your old man," said Vince, moving over to the tree. "I think your mom called him this morning. As things have been—" He looked back at me and offered a soft smile. "Well, a little odd lately. I think they wanted to help. Your old man wanted to wake you, but I kind of advised against it."

"My old man, he…." Ignoring the heavy weight at the mention of my old man, I looked at the base of the tree now. It took its usual spot, my white corner unit shifted out into the hall and the tree placed neatly in its place. A few needles had fallen onto the cream carpet, just a few, three to be precise.

"Jack?" Vince joined me as I made it over, and he pulled at my arm to stop me from grabbing at them. "What's up, kid?"

I pointed at the base of the tree. "Needles."

"Well…." Vince looked down. "Yep."

"Floor," I mumbled quietly, itching inside at how out of place they made everything. "I've got to—"

"Leave them." Vince tugged at my arm. "There'll be a lot more by the end of the day, no doubt by the time Christmas is over. Evergreen my fucking arse. There's a few days left before the big day, and the tree's already crying rape in the corner." I was taken into the kitchen and sat down at the breakfast bar. Vince disappeared, and the silence of the kitchen left me wondering if he was real.

"I was going to save this until Christmas."

He was suddenly in front of me, a long rectangular box in his hand. "But you've been feeling so sick since we got back from Turkey, I thought I'd give it to you now." The box was put in my hands. "Go on," said Vince. "Open it."

We'd been to Turkey? Images were there of a plane,

feeling pissed off, not sitting by the window, hating sharing germs in the cabin with a bunch of air riders. Vince looked so expectant, brown eyes so wide, waiting, needing. Giving a tug at the black ribbon, I eased the lid off and sat staring down at the contents.

The necklace looked familiar, couldn't really think why, though. It was this black rope, interspersed with small silver balls at regular breaks. Hanging from it was a sterling silver cross with a smaller black one in the middle.

"Lost this," I heard myself mumble.

Easing back with a sigh, Vince nodded. "Yeah, I remember you saying." I frowned at him, but Vince was focused on the necklace. "A robbery or something."

"Fight."

"Hmm," Vince nodded at me. "Some twat up an alley by your house."

My turn to frown. "Gray."

Vince scowled. "I don't think so, baby. The guy beat you pretty bad to get at your wallet." He seemed to lose all of that Christmas cheer, seemed so sad. "Don't give that bastard a name and let him own you."

I rubbed at my head, hating how thick it felt. "Here," said Vince, and I was jostled slightly as he took the necklace, moved my hand from my eyes, and slipped the fine quality of the necklace to rest cool against my throat. "There you go." It fastened into place. "Looks good." A kiss brushed the back of my neck and every muscle tensed in my body.

"Hey, easy." Vince seemed to put some distance between us as I glanced up to the corner, at the safety of the camera winking there. "How about I get us something to eat? Maybe some coffee? Maybe that will pull you back into the real world?"

"Coffee." I nodded, needing... something. "Coffee's good." Vince was up, heading on into the kitchen before I could put the movement in order.

"I've got to go to work in about an hour. You going to be okay, Jack?"

"Nights?"

"Hmmm?"

Darkness was creeping up to the windows now, or they were black at least. Which was fucking weird considering it had been morning a while back. "You work nights?"

"I know it's a bastard. But I promised Karl that I'd work the next two nights up until Christmas Eve. That gives us Christmas Day and New Year's Eve together."

I rubbed at my head. No one should be alone for Christmas....

"You okay with that? Your old man said he'd get a manager in to cover your garage while you're off your feet."

"Hmmm?"

A mug of coffee was set on the table by me. "We'll get you better, kid. You'll see. For now you drink your coffee, try and eat. We'll sort you out. Just don't..." He smiled across at me as he sat down. "Worry."

CHAPTER 20
THE TASTE OF THINGS TO COME

Jan Richards

A TAP AT my legs forced my eyes open, and I lay there staring up at the ceiling, shivering against the cold. Clothes were long gone, only a soft pad under my ass offering comfort. Everything below the waist was sore, legs all stiff and refusing to move. Sleep had come and gone, the only constant being someone snuggled up to me—climbing on top of me. There was little fight except against the tiredness, against the creeping feel of what would happen if I closed my eyes, what would happen if I kept them open. Voices had filtered through from the hall at one point, arguing, shuffles—more heavy thuds like Humpty Dumpty had been given a hand off the wall. Then Henry had slipped a hand over my mouth despite the gag still biting into it. I fought through the fog bank, tried to cry out Jack's name, but after that, sound had been subdued, and I'd been forced into sleep again.

"Come on," said Henry, tapping at my leg again. "Bet

you're hungry?"

I flinched away as he brushed a touch down my side, the *clink, clink-click* of his cheap gold watch serenading his path.

A soft whistle was given, and in the evening light, two men pushed through into the bedroom. Tubing was brought in, one end having a funnel attached. Another man also carried a strange-looking gag, and I started to shake my head seeing the round wire shape, the kind used to keep a sub's mouth open wide, ready and waiting.

"You keep quiet, now, pet," whispered Henry, and I grunted as my gag was pulled free. The need to cry out was instinctive, and a hand clamped over my mouth and nose. I tore my head from side to side, at first to get free, then just to try and breathe. Henry jammed his thumb in at the corner of my mouth, giving himself enough room to get the bottom of the bit gag fixed over my bottom teeth. A grip of my balls plus my cry out allowed him to force the rest into my mouth.

"Sweet," said Henry, tying it in place, then running his thumb over my bottom lip. "Can think of a few things to put in there." Giving a grin, he leaned over and spat, wiping at his own jaw as spit and slime hit the back of my throat, making me gag. "Can't do this without lube," he said, chuckling at his own joke.

A grab at my hair, my head was kept still as Henry took the long tube and slid it back and forth over my tongue. "Relax those muscles, pet. Let me in." Plastic tubing touched the back of my throat, causing me to gag again, then Henry took every care with forcing it down my throat. I writhed as a mixture of wanting to throw up and choke hit me. I settled for choking as tears forced free.

"Doc," Henry shouted back over his shoulder. "Don't make me come out there and force my cock up your ass to get you in here."

There was shuffling back by the door, and a short, stocky man came and knelt on the bed by Henry. A packet of liquid and the stink of bourbon came with him. The packet he seemed content enough to sit there shaking; the bourbon he'd already drank from the smell of it. The doc made sure the funnel was fixed in place on the other end of the tube, but his hands shook so badly that the tube shifted deep in my throat, forcing me to choke and arch my body into each one.

"Christ, give that the fuck here," snapped Henry, and he grabbed at the tubing. "You feed him."

"Okay, okay," said the doc, now looking down at me. "Just fluids, enough to keep your stats up and—"

"Don't fucking talk to the bitch, just get it down his fucking throat."

After he gave a tear at the corner of the pouch, I choked as liquid slid through the tube, leaving an ice-cold feeling in my stomach.

"Almost done," said the doc, looking a little more cheerful. He left the bedroom, then someone else pushed on through.

"You're awake. Good. How you doing today, kid?" said Vince, removing my gag. Henry shifted off the bed so he could sit down. I gave up looking any lower than his waist; I didn't want to see any lower than his waist. Images swam in and out of focus, but his voice? With or without a black gas mask as he'd stood behind Jack in the bath, no amount of drugs could drown out echoes of his voice, no matter how much he whispered and tried to disguise it. He gave a heavy sigh, and a hand grabbed my jaw, forcing a look at his face.

The bedroom was lighter, maybe late afternoon, and the soft shades helped highlight how he could have been the happy council refuse guy that sorted your bins. He wasn't the sort to avoid. Quite good-looking, with dark brown eyes, soft brown hair. No… Not brown. The roots were darker. Black. Christ—had he dyed his hair?

"Get the doc to keep an eye on him for infection. Fluids need to be kept up too." Vince sniffed at me now. "And wash him, for fuckssake, Henry. He stinks of your come."

"I flushed his ass out," Henry whined in a high voice.

The padded mat beneath my ass? Heat… disgust filled my cheeks.

"The catheter took care of the rest."

I strangled a groan.

"Yeah? Not good enough." Vince sighed. "Go get the shower ready. Princess is still asleep, idle fucking arsehole that he is. For now." He patted my thigh. "Let's get this one cleaned up in the meantime."

I found some life, kicking and crying to go anywhere but the bathroom.

A hand crushed into my balls, shutting me up.

"Jack…" I said, suddenly calm. "Where is he?"

"Don't worry your pretty little head about him. Not until I need you to," said Vince, and a rattling came as he messed with the chains above my head. "But we need to keep you looking and smelling your best for him."

A blindfold slipped into place just before I was forced to my feet. Things were unsteady for a moment, life teetering close to the edge and threatening to fall without any protest as I stood there. Then Vince fire-lifted me onto his shoulder, slapping at my ass. I winced but stayed quiet. "Not sore here, lad?" Vince chuckled. "Your cock's too soft, Henry. If you can't make him cry, I'll have to take him off your hands and give his ass a real workout."

Henry mumbled something as Vince carried me out. Footsteps sounded a little odd once we were out of the bedroom. More like polished shoes on concrete. It also took us over fifty footsteps to reach Jack's shower. Jack's spare room was next to his main bathroom, so it should have taken maybe eight at the most. A chill came across my bare ass, dusting over the small of my back, almost as though we'd stepped outside, or maybe into somewhere spacious like a long corridor. Wrong. Everything just felt wrong. Yet as Vince dumped me on rough tile and pulled off my blindfold, Jack's bathroom came into view, right down to his laundry basket and antibacterial hand wash. The "no touch" hand wash that he always insisted on.

"First things first," said Vince. I managed to roll to my side, resisting throwing up as he lifted the toilet lid, then regretted it as he pulled his zip down and tugged out his dick. I turned away as urine splashed onto my face.

"Better." There was a thick sloppy sound, then he tucked himself away. "Your turn, sweetheart."

Pulled up by my arm, the world turned as I was dragged to the toilet and forced to stand there. Vince came in hard behind, digging a clammy hand around my shaft, and I groaned.

"Mmmm." Resting his chin on my shoulder, Vince looked down. "Okay, so maybe I know now why a guy in Jack's fuckable league would go with a guy like you." His breath stained my cheek. "That's a damn good cock you've got there, Jan." He angled my tip towards the basin. "Meaty. Bet you've loved forcing that up him, hmmm?"

"Don't *force* Jack to do anything," I mumbled, looking away, any need to relieve myself disappearing with how he held on between my thighs.

"Yeah? Might have to look at that." He started massaging my dick. "Let's see some action from this, y'know, being as you've just curled up for the past few days and let me fuck your boyfriend."

"Fuck you."

"Nah." He bit at my shoulder. "I like tops. A bit like Henry when he sees the right kind of pet." Fingers rubbed at my ass, and I winced from how sore I still was. "Your ass knows what he feels like, right?"

Life numbed, or maybe fell a few shades greyer, because all life and colour no longer existed.

We stood there for ages, and I started to wish it on, nearly calling my body out, anything to get his hands off me. I waited a long time. Then as Vince cupped my root with finger and thumb, my balls with the remainder, digging and massaging, heat flushed my body as nature kicked in.

"There we go. Good boy." It seemed to last forever, then seeing it trickle to nothing, Vince gave a few good shakes. "You need anything else?"

I quickly shook my head.

"Prefer Henry cleaning it out for you, hmmm? Kinky fuck, ain't you?"

I stiffened, and Vince chuckled. Getting a tug at my arm, I was pushed under the shower. Vince's grab at my cuffs took my hands up, over the showerhead, leaving me nearly tiptoeing.

Water came on almost instantly, forcing me to drop my head and splutter against the assault. It was ice-cold, causing me to writhe, but then heat came through, enough to make sure the dirt was cleaned away. Vince disappeared, and I was left hanging there with water splattering the tiles as I closed my eyes and let it wash away everything.

Someone touched my shoulder with a sponge, and I bit back a cry, jerking against the spider contact.

"Christ, you're a bloody soft sod," said Vince, and he gave a snort as his nakedness brushed against mine. "Fuck knows what Jack sees in you." He washed himself first, occasionally nudging me as he moved. Then the rub of sponge came over my shoulders, slow circles that seemed in no way hurried, sweeping the small of my back, then around to my abs. The familiar scent of coconut hit the air, one of my favourites from back home.

Vince dragged his nose over my shoulder. "Smell fucking good, though." He pulled back and a kick forced my legs apart. Feeling the sponge slip between my cheeks, I gripped onto the cuffs. My groin was cleaned, the sponge then slipping down my legs, seeming to spend longer on my feet as he bit gently at my left ass cheek.

Hands pulled my ass open, and Vince sucked in a pained breath. "Yeah, you're sore down here. Henry been riding you hard after all?" He fingered around my hole and I jerked at the contact, trying to move away. "Hey." A slap came at my hip. "Jack doesn't bitch-wince like this. Fucking man up, you pussy, otherwise I'll pass you around to every man here who can manage to get even half a semi on." He pushed his finger in, and I bit back a cry at a slow fingering. "See, you're learning. No damage up here yet, though. Have to keep checking these things, right? Poor Jack and his ass needed licking better after taking the thick end of that whip. Had a few tears going on. Gonna love splitting him some more," breathed Vince, again giving a rough bite at my ass cheek. Then he was back to his feet, cleaning my arms, then hair as I screwed my eyes shut. Jack....

"Better," he mumbled, taking the showerhead down, careful to push the cuffs farther back so I couldn't easily slip free. I tried to force my hips into the wall when he crouched and spread my cheeks with one hand, then washed my hole.

He was back to his feet and the showerhead was fastened back in place. "All done." The water stopped running and I was left shivering into the cold, or maybe from whatever was in my system. Part of me was missing the numbness that came with a full dose. Hands drifted down to my hips. "You look good wet, Jan. Hmmm." A full hard-on pressed into the small of my back, pinning me against the wall. "All fresh and clean."

Bites went to the back of my neck, fingers now digging hard into hips as he took hold and started rubbing his dick between us.

"Gray will cut your fucking balls off," I said flatly. He knew about Gray; how he knew didn't interest me anymore, but if he'd done his homework that well, he'd know what Gray was capable of.

Vince grunted, maybe losing pace, then giving a sigh, he patted my hip. "Still counting on him to come charging in on a white BDSM bondage horse, hmmm?"

I kept my breathing even.

Another sigh. "Well let's put you out of your misery, eh?"

He was gone. After a moment he came back in close again, reaching around me. It took a moment to recognise both mine and Jack's mobiles in his hand. One went on the shower stand, my phone, and Vince came back to me, thumbing through Jack's.

"Right, so after your call allowed me and Henry to rape

the fuck out of you two—" I got a nudge. "—thank you for that, by the way." Vince snorted a chuckle. "We found our Jack rambles a bit when he's on the drugs. Seems you all had a falling out recently, hmmm?" He sniffed and flicked on a message. Today's date was Saturday, December 23rd. Six days? We'd been here six days? Then the date of the text message came into view. Two days after the argument.

Maths and numbers; I was okay so long as I had maths and numbers.

Call.

Just a simple order, but one that had Gray written all over it.

"Left that there for a day," said Vince, "then sure enough, Jack got another."

Jack. Now.

"Well, thought we'd better reply." He thumbed the sent box.

Fuck you, Gray.

"Got to keep up with that fucker's more colourful way of expression, right?"

My stomach turned. Vince was back thumbing through the inbox. "Ah, here we go."

Jack. Fucking call me. Now. Don't use Jan to call again.

"This Gray dude," said Vince, "such a nasty fuck to Jack, ain't he?" He was back thumbing the sent box. "Kind of took a wild guess that those porn sites had finally got to you all, and no doubt poor old Jack was the target of his shit, so I thought I'd help them both along."

I need a break from this shit. We'll talk when my head's in a better place, not when you damn well demand it.

Time out… There was no time out attached to that message. Gray will know, Gray will…

"We had no more calls after that to Jack. But…." Vince picked up my phone and put down Jack's. "You got a call a day ago. Which you missed, then promptly apologised for."

And there it was, in black-and-text white.

Gray, apologies. Jack's going through a rough time at the moment; he's barely talking to me and is using my phone to "go casual". He's promised he'll talk to you when he's in a better frame of mind. I'll give you a call in a few days to let you know how he's doing.

"Decent guy that you are. To which Gray replied."

Fucking call me on Jack's phone, Jan. It's not rocket science.

"Now, you being mister soft lover and nothing to do with Gray's Master Circle," said Vince, "I thought you'd take exception to being spoken to like that. So."

Another message flicked up in the sent box.

For god's sake, Gray. Not the heavy tactics now, please. Just let me have these two weeks to calm him down. You don't sound in any state to talk properly to him either, not yet. I'm not going to call you, not until I know you're both calm.

A strangled groan hit the air. I knew it was mine, and a sympathetic pat tapped my hip. "Come on, Jan, I understand, like, totally how you feel. The guy sounds a right twat, right? I'd have said exactly the same thing."

"*You did, you fuck,*" I shouted, only to hear Vince chuckle.

"Well, yeah." And he thumbed the last message that came in.

Two weeks. No longer. When you get back, Jack sees me, and me alone.

Look after him, Jan.

Please.

I choked back another sob.

"And just in case you're thinking 'but he's MI5, he'll do his check on the mobile signal and see we're not, well, away, he'll know something's wrong,' our tech guy could convince Gray he's getting message updates from NASA if he bloody well chose to do so."

"He'll know. He'll fucking know. There's Jack's dad, his work, his—"

Vince showed me a few other texts, those to Jack's dad asking for cover, apologising, saying he needed time away, a cover-manager for the garage until after Christmas. Texts to Steve to see if he was okay, that he'd be away for a few weeks and to get in touch with Greg if there were any problems.

"Let him check away, Jan," said Vince quietly. "Everyone has the same old story. You and Jack, well—" He gave a chuckle. "—you're having a real good time out together over Christmas without good ol' Gray."

Jack didn't do social, but he did do family. He was big on family. Gray would know this wasn't normal. He'd fucking know.

"So, Jan." The mobiles were now back on the shower unit, well away from the water, Vince pressing his body back into mine with his dick never thicker. "Just you, me, Jack, and whatever I can think up to do to you."

"Don't," I said quietly.

"Oh." He nuzzled into my neck, smiling. "Say that again. *Please.*"

"Mr Vince." A voice drifted through into the bathroom, followed by harsh radio feedback. "You're needed elsewhere. Leave Mr Richards alone."

I hadn't noticed it when I was dumped down by the

toilet, but back above the door, and keeping a full watch on the bathroom, sat a camera with a single red light.

"Eyes forward." A grip to my hair forced my head into the wall. "Henry, get your fucking arse in here and take care of this shit."

"Coming, love."

"Hmmm." A kiss graced my shoulder. "Looks like princess is starting to stir. Let's go see if he's starting to play ball." A needle punctured my arm, making me cry out. "You can come play too."

CHAPTER 21
WHITE CHRISTMAS

WOOD FLOOR STAYED cool under my body as I curled onto my side, naturally finding a safe foetal position and hugging my knees to my body now that I could move. Jack's cologne was all around me, mixing with my own, and part of me wanted to question why my neck was damp with traces of my favourite when I was otherwise naked to the elements. I'd loved it when Jack had added mine to his collection, that sweet intensity on his face as he'd taken it off me and inched it into position in amongst his. Everything found a place in his life eventually, even if he did need to go casual sometimes and throw everything out of order.

Easing a hand under my head, I groaned as I tried to push up. Life waltzed around me, turning my stomach with it, and I choked bile onto the floor.

Not clean…. I looked around, under Jack's bed, over to his computer desk, anywhere just to try and spot a towel. Mess like this would drive Jack to casual, and casual wasn't good, it meant he was struggling, and struggling… Jack had been struggling so much in the bath.

"Fuck." Palms flat on the floor, I kept my head down as life continued to spin. I licked across my lips, tasting salt, tasting tears. Out. I needed to get up, to get out and find Gray, find a—

Mobile.

There on Jack's desk, not far from the monitor, sat his mobile. Staring. I knew I was staring, taken with the light on the screen, almost as if someone had just finished using it and had tried to put it back to sleep in the darkness. Light looked so good in the pitch black around me.

"Move." It took me a moment to realise that had fallen from my lips. "Fucking move, Jan."

Noise came from the bed, stealing my attention, but only for a while before I was back with the light on the phone, now getting to my knees and trying to blindly find my way over. Gray needed to know Jack. He needed to know that wasn't Jack in those videos. Just a kid, Jack had just been one screwed-up kid, a kid that was struggling and fighting for breath as he was being raped in the bath, just a kid. Just ours, just—

Another shuffle on the bed, this time followed by a soft groan filtered over.

"Jack?"

He mumbled sleepily, and I was suddenly crawling over to the bed, dragging myself up, pulling Jack onto my lap and kissing repeatedly at his head. "'S okay, baby. 'S okay." On his back, an arm over his face, Jack blindly found my arm, mumbling something, then tugging me down. "C'mon, baby," I said, choking back tears. "Need to go. Need to… to move."

"Wrong…" Jack murmured, then he twisted onto his side, pulling me down with his hand finding the back of my neck. "Something's wrong." Jack added more pressure to my neck, forcing me to lie next to him. As I sank into the warmth of the covers, he was instantly coming in close, leg going over mine, arm snaking around my chest as he hid in my shoulder. "So wrong."

Life spinning as I grabbed his shoulder, I tried shaking some life into him. "Gray. Need... need to go get Gray. Find... just get Gray."

"Jan?" Jack gripped harder, almost trying to climb inside me. "Stay. Christ. Don't go again. Don't hide from me... please."

I choked a sob, wanting, needing to hide too, somehow registering the black necklace around his throat as it dug into my arm while I held onto him. "Don't want to hide, baby." I kissed his cheek. "Stay with you. Stay."

The bed shifted as someone lay down behind Jack, and I stiffened as slick, black eyes peered over Jack's shoulder, huge round holes that reflected my blank stare in alien orbs. Breathing was strange, filtered through a black gas mask that almost seemed welded to the thick skull it shaped.

Not real. That wasn't fucking real. Just some dream. Part of one huge messed-up dream.

"Yeah, Jan's here," a voice whispered in Jack's ear. "He's always right fucking here for you, kid." Jack fell deathly still as I cried out.

Someone came at me from behind, slipping in close, tearing my grip off Jack and pinning my arms behind my back. Hands were cuffed in the struggle, Jack lost to his own as a grip to his hair pulled him back, away from me, then forced him face-first into the pillow.

"No." An arm went around my throat as a thick, naked

body pressed Jack's into the mattress. *"Fucking no."*

"You touching Jan without my permission?" Hands pinned level to his head, Jack cried out as thick legs forced his open. "That's one huge fuck-up, Jack. And you know what happens with fuck-ups, don't you?" Jack grunted as a dick pushed into him. "I make you cry, boy." Each pound of Jack into the mattress travelled up my body and matched my cries as I tried to get closer, to get the bastard off Jack. Then I cried more when a grip to my hair forced me closer to Jack. My chest brushed against Jack's side, my groin against his hip as I was forced to feel every struggle he made to try and get free, every hard pound of groin into his ass as he was forced to take the man above him.

Giving a cry, the man in the mask grunted, holding himself deep in Jack for one second, then fucking in a few last lengths to make sure he took everything his balls had to offer. Finished, he pulled his hips back slightly, then stroked along his dick, the last few traces of come were strangled from him and oozed out onto his fingers, then he wiped it on Jack's back. Breathing hard, heavy, Jack went very still.

"Off him," I mumbled. "You—" I fought against the choking grip on my throat, trying to kick, trying to snap the masked man out of his trance, how he stared at Jack. *"Get that fucking come off him,"* I cried.

The black gas mask shifted in my direction, then he eased down by Jack, never letting his gaze shift from mine. Pushing at Jack's shoulder, forcing him onto his side, facing me, the man took a hold in Jack's hair, then made sure Jack looked at me. Pupils were dilated, greyness focused somewhere else, on something else, on the crawling inside his body. "'S okay, baby," I whispered, trying to shuffle closer, rest my head against his, just try and give him something else to ground him away from the come on his body. Nobody had heard our cries yet, that was nothing new for a street like this; always looking the other way. But Gray... "They fucked up, baby," I whispered. "He knows, he'll come, he'll find you. Time out. You never said time out," I mumbled. "He'll fucking know it wasn't you. You wait and see. He'll be here."

Something was whispered in Jack's ear, and the briefest flicker of a frown crept to his face. The whisper came again, this time accompanied with a thump to the ribs that had Jack doubling into my shoulder and crying out.

"Don't... kiss Jan, Jack."

I stared at the man in the mask. Pulling Jack's head back, he whispered again in Jack's ear.

"Don't... kiss him, you fuck."

The confusion was there, that need to fight the whispering in his head, but also something else, the need to hide, to find comfort, to take comfort...

Jack came in, shivering, holding so tightly he hurt my neck and stopped breath. There was a gentle nudge at my jaw to get my attention, Jack asking me to respond, needing a response, needing comfort, needing security, and tears ran down my cheek. He wasn't asking for me, he wasn't after my attention, my comfort or strength. He asked for Gray; he needed Gray now.

"Christ, baby. Stay with me," I mumbled, kissing at his head, allowed to kiss at his head, his cheek, not caring where so long as I felt him against me, so long as he felt me. "Don't listen to what they say. Stay with me. Stay with—"

Jack was pulled onto his back and a fist split his already cracked lip. *"Told you not to fucking touch, whore,"* snarled the man in the black mask, then Jack instinctively covered his head from the beating he took from huge fists.

Quiet.

I'd struggled, fought, and shouted out for so long watching the assault, that when everything fell so quiet so quickly, it held me still. Huge grey pools were watching me. Blood ran from Jack's nose, his mouth, and when he blinked, a runaway tear mixed with a line of blood spilling from a cut just above his eyebrow.

And again the black mask moved in close behind him, coming close to Jack's ear. "Don't... fuck Jan, Jack."

Grey eyes blinked at me.

"Shut it out," I whispered quietly, shaking my head. "Don't listen, baby. Shut it out."

He frowned, just slightly, stirring more blood down his cheek.

"Don't... get your dick and fuck it in his ass," said the voice again.

Another tear falling, Jack shook his head, just slightly.

"No?"

"No," he said quietly, and as he shook his head slightly again, it matched the slight trembling going on with his body.

"Good boy." A touch ran down Jack's arm. "We reward good boys here," he said quietly. "We let them cuddle. Would you like to cuddle Jan, Jack?"

Giving a frown, eyes not leaving mine, Jack nodded.

"'Course you would."

A huge hand gripped my leg, pulling it onto Jack's upper thigh. Feeling a slight jostle from behind, a dick was tugged free, pre-come smudged on my ass before sliding down and nudging against me. "Cuddle, you fucks," breathed a voice in my ear.

The head punched through, making me grunt at the same time the man behind Jack slipped a hand between Jack's thighs.

"Think he can take my whole fist?"

Jack cried out.

"He's got to have had two cocks up here." A rooting deep in Jack pushed his hips into mine as Jack tried to escape the assault. "Yeah, start small, just three, then—"

Jack cried out again as hips and groins were forced to clash against each other. His arm was tugged around me, his hand taken up to my hair and forced to grip in a lover's embrace.

"Yeah," breathed the masked man, "looking fucking good together there, boys."

Something slipped in Jack's eyes as our bodies were pushed and knocked against each other, a look of humiliation, shame, hurt, but none of it for himself—for me. His look was for me. Then it was lost as a grip to his hair forced him into my throat, forced him into hiding. And then life lost all colour, all taste, all focus but for slick black eyes, for the constant rhythm of our bodies being forced together. Hurt. It didn't even hurt after a while, not even as the man behind got onto his knees and started pushing harder into me. Amongst all the grunts and groans, the slap of bodies, feeling Jack's hips clash with mine, hurt was pushed into the darkness, and it was surprising how fast that numbness came, how even needing it to stop was lost to how many times I counted how the red light blinked down at us from the corner of the bedroom.

A hand stroked between my thighs. "Christmas Day

tomorrow, pet." Breathing was heavy, heated, tired. "Might be a bit rough for you." A chuckle. "Gonna need something for the sting, I think, some loving to carry you through." Henry grunted his orgasm, pulling out his dick, then pushing it back in. "Fuck, loving…"

"Yeah," groaned Vince. "Looks like it's gonna be a white one this year." Vince wiped some of Henry's come on to Jack's cheek. "Merry Christmas, boys."

CHAPTER 22
CRACKER, JACK?

Jack Harrison

"… THIS SNOWY CHRISTMAS afternoon from Five Live."

From the kitchen, the sound of the radio kicked in, or it had been playing for a while, and I just hadn't known. Heat from my head burned into the arm over my face, and it seemed to match the burning going on in my body.

"Fuck." I licked across dry lips, groaned. It felt like I'd slipped up over siphoning petrol out of a tank and rammed the tube down my own throat. It brought with it a heat and gut ache that had me coughing and nearly throwing up.

"Hey, easy. C'mon." A hand gripped under my arm. "Let's get you up and off the settee." Feet eased onto the floor, I rubbed at my head as Vince's face came into view. "You've been in and out of it for a while," he said, moving my touch and feeling my head. "This carries on, I'm really getting the doctor in." That sounded familiar, like he'd said it before, only I couldn't remember when.

Then shuffling came from over by the bay window. I glanced over, just quickly, then looked back at Vince.

"Jack?" Vince followed my look back to the bay window. "Something spooking you, kid?"

Hands bound out of sight, tears streaking down his face, running over the gag in his mouth and falling onto a fine black suit, Jan sat there, propped up against the wall underneath the bay window. Face looked clean, pale, hair looking so soft.

"Jack?"

Vince stole my attention. He frowned at me, but my gaze skirted to Jan, just briefly, before I quickly found my feet.

"Jack—"

Don't...

... look.

Don't...

"Fine. I'm fine."

A rough groan came from the corner as, giving a sigh, Vince rubbed roughly at my hair. "Yeah? Then merry fucking Christmas, you ass," he said, giving a chuckle. From the kitchen, some BBC station was wishing people Merry Christmas again, then music drifted in on the back of turkey and stuffing.

Shifting my feet and catching my toes on the edge of the coffee table, I ignored the shuffling noises in the corner and looked up to find a few unwrapped gifts on the table. Little bits of Christmas paper littered the floor in places, and a few more gifts were under the tree, stacked Jenga style. The muggy feeling in my head wasn't here so much, and I missed the numbing escape it gave as I picked up one of the boxes back on the coffee table, trying my best to ignore the bits of paper on the floor. The latest CK One cologne printed neatly across the box. Somebody here had done the Christmas shit with getting up and opening presents, but like fuck could I find the memory that said it was me.

"One of your favourites," said Vince, and I glanced up as he came in carrying two glasses of some sparkling shit in two long stem glasses. I couldn't remember him getting up and leaving. He stepped between me and the table and sat down next to me.

I turned the cologne over. Yeah, I liked this one. Maybe. Again shuffling and mumbled noises came from over by the window, again I ignored it; damn my soul. I ignored him and his hurt-filled need that cried for everything to stop. Just stop. Real... nothing was fucking real. Or what was real, it hurt to think about... hurt everyone more.

Vince held out one of the drinks and I let the cologne rest back on the table before taking it. The long stem glass was cool, like it had been chilled, and I nearly took the contents in one, loving the coolness on my throat, the ease it brought to the agony going on in my body.

"Just some sparkling water," said Vince before taking a sip of his. I took the rest of mine. "Dinner's all on. Should be about forty minutes. You're looking damn good."

I was in black suit trousers and white shirt, the collar loosened with an even looser black tie around it. No shoes, no socks, no will to look at the man hiding under the window. Fucking hurt. Dreams... fucking hurt.

"Thanks," I mumbled, finding interest in my hands.

"Good." Vince pulled me back into the settee, and an arm went around my shoulders. "You're looking a little better too. Not so pale and all virginal." Vince was chuckling, and I smiled. That's what people did at Christmas, right?

"How'd that call go with your dad this morning?"

I frowned. Something came through, talking, wishes of Merry Christmas, asking how the garage was doing again. My old man hadn't sounded happy, neither had my old lady. "Fine." I think.

"Your mom called afterward," said Vince. "Said we should get together for New Year's Eve." He was finished with his drink. Strange enough, I looked down and mine was full again. I took another long sip, welcoming the relief, trying not to focus on the coughing that was coming from beneath the window. "She wants to know if all of us should go to the Thames," said Vince. "Maybe bring the New Year in with the London fireworks display."

"Don't…" I rubbed at my head again, shivered. "Don't do social."

"Bullshit." Vince even choked. "We met at a nightclub with you going all slutty over my ass. You remember?"

Not knowing how to respond, seeing the light and life in his smile, I searched for the memory.

"Hmmm?"

"Yeah. S'pose," I mumbled.

Vince's smile widened, and he pulled me closer and kissed my head. His hand pushed at my jaw, making our lips meet. The feel was strange, his lips out of place against mine as struggles came from over by the window. I pulled away before he could explore my tongue with his.

"Burning," I mumbled.

"Huh?" Vince was up and pushing past me. He called out a second later. "Good nose on you, Jack. The potatoes were nearly dry." A curse. "You're gonna have to get your ass back into gear and take over this shit. I'm useless at cooking."

Glass still in hand, I let my head fall back against the sofa and closed my eyes, shaking like hell now. The shuffles and muffled cries from by the window demanded all of my attention, but I didn't give in, refused to fucking give in. It would only hurt us more if I did. Growling hit the air, and the emptiness hitting my stomach made itself known, aggressively so. To the point it nearly had me doubled and willingly blocked out the noises coming from my window. I was so fucking hungry.

"I'd let you cut the turkey," called Vince, and it was followed by a chuckle, "but I guess it needs a real bloke, not a delicate princess like you." The grip on the stem glass threatened to break it, then, "Get your pretty ass to the dining room, Jack. It's already set up."

Leaving the stem glass to roll on the settee, I pushed up and started to head for the kitchen. On the unit sat a paper, *The Sunday Times*. The date said December 24th. Yesterday's? Didn't matter. The world was doing a fucked-up waltz again, and I reached down to pick the paper up, let it go casual, let life find order, chase away the man behind me an—

Don't...

... straighten me, Jack.

I pulled my hand away.

Fire. Everything was on fire, including the need to keep the fuck away from touching casual things and risk burning my fingers again. Frowning down at the paper for a moment, I forced my way through the dizziness and made it into the kitchen. "Take this," said Vince as I passed. He held out a cheap silver bucket with a few opened beers in it.

Classy.

Tugging the bucket close to my chest, I hobbled on through to my dining room, using the wall as a guide. Vince had already set everything in place. This red plastic Christmas mat was spread over the long table—hell, he'd even put the table back in—and it had a matching red table runner, candles, some strange red plant in the middle, with two places set opposite each other with bright red mats. Colour. A whole shit-load of colour and chaos.

I eased down into a chair closest to the door, breathing easier as the bucket was set on the table. Life went black for a moment, and I rested my head down on the arm across my placemat. It would be so easy just to sleep, forget, not dream, not about—

"Hey, up."

I jerked up at Vince's voice, sitting straight. He was standing next to me with plates stuffed full of food, but I couldn't shift my attention from the corner.

"Jack, you okay?"

Jan was back, chained up by the patio doors, hands now above his head, shirt pulled out, jacket all ruffled. I flicked a look up at Vince.

"Don't… see him," I whispered.

"Who kid?"

"Jah—" I stopped myself, and a moment later, Vince put the plates on the placemats and crouched next to me.

"Jan's here?" said Vince.

Giving a glance to the corner, I nodded.

"The corner?"

Not looking, I nodded again.

"Take no notice, kid. It's hard, I know, but don't let him

spoil Christmas day for you. He'll go away eventually. I promise. Nightmares always do."

Jan struggled in the corner, tears streaking down his cheeks.

"Focus on me, kid."

I looked at Vince. He'd sat opposite, and for a moment the food stole every manner I had.

"Hungry, hmmm?" Vince chuckled, picking up his knife and fork. "Before you start, hand me a beer, beautiful."

I'd already taken my knife and fork and was ready to start. Annoyed, I quickly reached over and passed him a beer. Mine came next, then I went back to tackling dinner. Things had fallen quiet in the corner anyway.

"Oh, hang on," said Vince, and I frowned as he got up and disappeared back into the kitchen. Two crackers held in one hand, he came and sat back down. "Here." He held one out to me. "Tradition, Jack."

Cologne, such a strong scent of cologne hit the air. Not mine, someone else's—Jan's, and enough to make my stomach turn. All I could do was stare for a moment, fighting back the vomit, not wanting to look into the corner.

"Jack. C'mon." Vince waggled the cracker, shaking the contents from side to side.

Taking a swig of beer first, needing that swig of beer, I gripped the cracker. Vince pulled hard, snapping my arm forward, and he added a shout when he saw he'd won the prize. It went the same way for the second one.

"You've yet to beat me at this, Jack." Vince tossed a hat and some plastic thing I couldn't focus on at me. "Go on, put it on." The hat got another finger push in my direction.

Something about a hat. Not a thin yellow one like this,

but black—thick fur, a white trim. *BDSM badass* printed on it, or Jan had wanted Gra—"Hmmm," I mumbled.

"Jack, come on," said Vince.

I looked up to find he was already wearing his, a purple thing that sat lopsided on his head. One edge had crumpled like a reluctant halo that had been dumped on the wrong head and was crumbling under the shame.

"Don't." My yellow paper hat sat there like a used condom: deflated. "I don't do—"

"For me?"

Vince took my attention. There was a sadness drooping his eyes, and he seemed to wash it down with another swig of his beer. "Listen, you don't have to—"

I glanced at the corner, but Jan wasn't there anymore. But Christ, those brown eyes. I picked up the hat and put it on. Vince nodded, softened his gaze, then pointed at my plate. "'S all gettin' cold, kid. Tuck in. Oh, and Merry Christmas."

"Uh-hm. Merry Christmas." Another growl of my stomach agreed with the "tuck in" part, and I took a mouthful of mash and two veg in one. Two more forkfuls took its place, but I'd barely swallowed before I choked, my hand stopping me throwing up all over my dinner.

"Jack?"

Chair pushed back, I stumbled into the downstairs bathroom, and the porcelain goddess took my homage, the taste that hit my throat a mixture of liquid acid mixed with that gritty painkiller feel. Looking didn't help. It had that dog-food appearance, brown mush, with a smell that was just as bad. "Fuck."

"Easy, easy." Vince rubbed at my back. I was well into the land of dry heaving coughs, and it threatened to tear my ribs and lungs apart. "Soup," Vince murmured angrily. "I should have just given you soup. Fuck. I'm sorry, Jack." A strong grip under my arm pulled me to my feet and my weight was taken. "C'mon, back to bed."

"Clean up," I mumbled, looking back towards the dining room.

"It can wait, kid. I'll do it later." Vince huffed, shifting my weight slightly as he tugged me back through the kitchen. "Let's get you settled down."

I hit the softness of the mattress upstairs and let my arm fall over my face as Vince pulled the covers over us both. "It's been a long morning, Jack. We'll just rest up for a few hours, yeah?"

"Hmmmm," I mumbled, then—

"Fuck," said Vince, and he was suddenly gone, out of the bed. The TV flicked on. The bed took his shape again, then he was back in, snuggling up to me, the covers pulled over us. "It's getting on for three." Vince sniffed and rested a hand on my stomach. "Queen's Speech is on."

Sure enough, a run of music declared just that, and I groaned. Giving a pat at my stomach, Vince chuckled. "I know you hate this shit, but I like to see how the other half live. I grew up moving from home to home, living the council life." Another pat. "Unlike some spoilt princess here, eh?"

A sob escaped, one small enough to jerk my body, but not really knowing why or where it came from. Something about council-bred, about running away from any fights, too soft to stand and fight.

Vince didn't look too soft to stand and fight. It fucking hurt too much knowing that.

"Hey." Vince tugged my arm away and brought his body

on top of mine, nearly pushing me deep into the mattress with the weight and making me try to jerk free. "It'll be all right, kid." A wipe came at my cheek, at the tear that had fallen. "You're doing good. Real good."

A feather of thick lips went to my throat, the odd nip of teeth. "Let me make it good for you, Jack, if only for just a few moments. Please." Vince's hands interlocked mine, drawing them up the bed. "Hmmmmm. You look fucking gorgeous in this suit."

Another run of kisses came, this time at my jaw. It didn't make me shift my throat; he didn't have permission to touch—

"Will you let me make it good for you, Jack?" He sounded so quiet. "I need you to say you're okay with this." His leg parted mine, and he swelled against my hip. Fuck, was he big. "Please," whispered Vince. More kisses moved down to my collarbone, kissing, nipping. "Tell me you want me."

Hands traced down my arms, then my sides as he worked his kisses onto my stomach, just ruffling up the shirt to start with, moving gentle strokes up, down with his touch. Then he started to unbutton my shirt, a kiss following each undone button as he eased the soft material open.

"Mmmmm." A tongue licked at one nipple, leaving it wet against the cold air before teeth nipped. "You want me, don't you, Jack?" Letting his free hand sneak inside my trousers, he brushed against my boxers, then bit at my other nipple, making me cry out. I blushed, the fuck did I blush. "Oh yeah." Heat filled his voice now. "Look at this. You want me, all right."

Giving a tug just behind my ass, Vince inched my trousers over my hips, taking my boxers with it, and then his mouth was on my cock as it hit my abs.

"Christ." I groaned, my arm going over my face, hiding from how he made me feel: a basic kid's reaction of see no evil, hear no evil; everything pushed away, especially how uneasy I felt with having Vince sucking on my cock. All his noises, flick of tongue against my slit, so right in many ways, but wrong in so many others.

A kiss went to my shaft. "Beautiful, kid. Thank you." Vince slid his huge body up mine, hard friction against my groin, hips, then lips tasted mine, and I tasted myself.

"Let me fuck you, Jack."

I frowned, my arm still hiding it.

"Tell me you're not interested in taking me," he dipped his hips, "I'll leave you alone."

I needed ties to council-bred skills, to soft brown eyes, to a tender soul, to calm, to control, to a darker soul that contrasted so fucking perfectly with council-bred skills—

I hid in Vince's shoulder and pulled him down before slipping my arms around his neck. "Better Dom up, make it fucking good," I mumbled.

"Jack, yeah. That's it." There was a rush to get my trousers pushed down and off, a rush for him to get his cock against my skin. I didn't look; fuck knows feeling its threat was enough to have me tensing. Vince slicked up his fingers, then rubbed them up and down my ass, my legs now parted by one of his. "I've missed this," breathed Vince.

Grabbing his cock, he guided it to my slicked-up ass, and I instantly put a hand on his hip, stopping him. "Johnny." Panic was there, one that had life fading into grey around me.

Vince just laughed. "We've been doing bareback for

years." And his first push in with his tip made me cry out, that feel of thick head stretching muscle, filling and pushing through the sting, pushing past my body's own instinctive reaction to push him out. "Don't need no johnny." The length fucking killed my stomach let alone my ass as it slid in root-deep. Sex came hard; quick rabbit strokes that had me grunting more pain than pleasure.

"Feel my arms, Jack."

"Huh?" I breathed. Raised up, Vince kept looking at one arm, the other, muscles all tensing with every move his hips made. "Fucking feel that muscle there, our kid." The next hard fuck pushed through the pain, forcing me to groan confusion.

"Yeah. Open them baby greys, Jack."

Like fuck.

"Look at me."

Heat reddened Vince's face, down to his collarbone, sweat dampened his brow, and the fact a brown stain leaked down at his temple from his hairline didn't stop what was going through my body.

"Yeah, that's it. You remember me in here." He fucked in my ass once, twice, now pinning my hands down just above my head. "Like that, Jack?"

Someone else was above me, smiling, so close to orgasm as I'd hid in the covers; someone else holding my cock, encouragement, slow—gentle. "Fuck, Vince. C'mon, baby." He did and I arched underneath him, meeting his body with mine as I came, riding the heat of Vince's cock as he increased his speed, grunting out his come just after I'd called his name. Vince's weight crashed down a minute later and kisses and bites showed appreciation. Hands squeezed my ass cheeks, my hips, making me wince.

"You keep that in your head, Jack," he breathed heavily. "You remember how good my cock can make you feel. How quick it can make you come."

The comedown drained me of everything pretty quickly, pulling me under fast. I barely felt Vince slip to my side, hand pulling me close and onto my side as I started to fall asleep.

"No more dreams, Jack. Not about Jan. That'll keep him at bay." A kiss went to my head. "I hope to God he lets you find some fucking peace for tonight…."

But soft brown eyes blinked back at me from over by the wall, and I blinked in return. Jan was back, bound with his hands above his head, tears streaking his face as he continuously shook his head at me, always shaking his head. Or maybe he was just shaking, period.

Don't…

… touch him.

Head twisting away, I closed my eyes.

"You okay?"

I looked down at Vince, his come sliding down my ass.

"Christ, Jack. You feel like you have a baseball bat up your ass." He eased up off me. "What's wrong?"

"Clean," I mumbled. "Off."

"Clean?" Vince gripped at my arm and sat me up. "You're saying this—" He ran a finger in the line of come, then wiped it on my cheek. "—is dirty? *My* come is dirty? 'Cause it just looks damn sexy to me. I like seeing my come between your thighs after I've fucked you."

"Dreams." My fingers, digging so hard into the mattress, were hurting now. "Clean. Need to—"

Vince reached over and picked up the juice. Where the

hell had the juice come from? "Okay, now I know you're nuts. Take this instead. This needing to be clean shit, it's pissing me off now."

I looked towards the en suite, towards the towels I knew that hid in there. "I need...."

"Drink," said Vince. "I bet I can get you back to sleep without cleaning your abs down. Then maybe you'll see how this fever is just playing shit with your head." He put the drink in my hand, even lifted it to my mouth. I took a sip, then downed it in one just to distract myself from looking at the en suite. A ruffle went to my hair, and the motion caused my head to spin. The glass went on the bedside unit for fear of it breaking on the floor.

"Jan still here?" he said, and I risked a quick glance over my shoulder. Only shadows hugged the creeping darkness and I sighed relief before shaking my head.

"See? You're doing fine, our kid. Just fucking fine." His eyes were a little hard. "Although this cleaning shit is still obviously a concern."

Vince pulled back the covers, got in, and then tugged me down. "We'll sort it, though, kid. Don't—"

Quiet.

"—worry."

CHAPTER 23
CHRISTMAS BLUES

Jan Richards

"C'MON, PET. YOU'VE been looking down for days."
Henry sat stroking at my stomach, but I didn't register it
too much. The spare room was pretty quiet; it had been
quiet since Boxing Day. Laughter had come from
downstairs, the front door opening to the sound of clinking
bottles, shouted hellos. The party had gone on for a few
hours, Henry keeping me company by cuddling up next to
me in bed. These strange cooing noises had come from
him, followed by constant stroking on my stomach, asking
if I was okay. Then he'd climbed on top of me, took what
he needed, before going back to my side and his petting.
There'd been no fight, the blinds enough to hold my
attention. I hadn't felt it when he climbed on top of me; I
hadn't felt anything since Christmas night, since after I'd
seen Jack let Vince fuck him, since everything that had
come after Jack had complained about come between his
legs.

Scared, Jack had been so fucking scared to look over, yet most of that terror had been directed at me, every time his eyes had settled on mine. Like I was nothing but a bad dream he wanted to hide from.

But the worst had come after Jack had shivered and asked to clean the come off him. After Christmas night, lessons had come on how only real men got dirty, how—

I bit back a cry as a knock came on the door. Henry pushed back the covers and got out of the bed as someone came over. Vince sat down, taking over stroking at my stomach, but it didn't matter. Nothing mattered. Not even how real men got dirty now and allowed someone to fuck them and leave come on their abs for just a little longer…

"Henry tells me you've been feeling a little down," said Vince quietly. "Heard you crying in your sleep a few times after Christmas night." Vince sighed. "And he even fed you some champagne after that to celebrate all the love that's in the air."

"Pet's ungrateful," mumbled Henry.

"Yeah," said Vince. "He is, love. And after all the love and devotion you've shown him." That stroke still came at my stomach. "Final training session." He smiled at me. "That okay with you? We're nearly there, kid, promise. Jack's getting quite the decent chap." Vince leaned down. "Just need to make sure he stays that way when you're around."

Vince started untying my hands. "Get him dressed: make him look pretty," he said over to Henry. "Show time. Let's make it good."

∽

256

Hands cuffed in front of me, collar around my neck with Henry tugging on a leash, I offered no protest as they took me into Jack's bedroom and sat me in the corner. I was back in a suit, black shoes looking so clean, so polished.

The bedroom was softly lit, and opposite, grey eyes stared at me from the other side of the bedroom. The room was bare except the bodies breathing heat into the room: me, Henry, Vince, and Jack.

Vince and Henry wore black gas masks again, but Jack's gaze was solely on my face. My gaze on his.

He remembered Christmas night. It was there in his eyes. How real men got dirty and should never be ashamed of it; how it was nightmares, its lovers, that brought out all of the guilt and need to… not be a man. And I was everything that caused all that guilt… all that… self-loathing and hate.

He was naked, but not chained in any sense, and when I shifted, just easing the aches in my body, he jolted as if a rabid dog had inched a few footfalls closer.

"Not real, Jack," I mumbled. "What they've made you feel, it's not real, baby."

Giving a sniff, Vince went over and crouched by Jack. Pulling his mask up to expose his lips, he said quietly, "Is Jan here, Jack? Is he real to you?"

Jack nodded, just a single shift of head that never allowed his eyes to fall off mine. Because Vince didn't mask his voice now. He stepped into the nightmare, looking to ground Jack, make him… what? Face his fears? Me.

"Real men get dirty. That's the natural order of the world," Vince said gently. "So show him how you handle men who make you inferior, forcing you into needing to wipe gorgeous come off your body." Quiet. "If it helps, baby, hit him. Break him apart for how he holds you down. Nobody holds you down. You like getting dirty. Get fucking dirty."

Vince stroked at Jack's cheek. "Kill him, baby."

Giving a snarl, making me cry out, Jack was over, pulling me from the wall by the hair and forcing me down.

Life drained out of me as his body came down on mine, one hand pinning mine above my head, another gripping hard into my jaw as if he was going to headbutt me. Snarling into my face, forcing my head back stretching muscle, almost waiting to feel muscles snap, for the neck to crush and—

Everything went still, and the grip loosened on my jaw, fingers gently rubbing the fine line. I opened my eyes and Jack looked down at me. He'd twisted my head to the side and cocked his to match the awkward angle. "What... what the fuck am I doing to you, soft lad?"

I nodded, never more scared, but never more calm in that moment. "Stop, please," I said quietly. "I... I just want to go home now. I want you home with me, but I'm... I'm so scared, Jack. So scared. I don't know why this is happening and.... Body and soul. Love you body and soul. Remember... remember that, *please*."

A tear fell from grey eyes, then all of the tension and confusion seemed to drain from his body. He came down, head resting against mine. "Don't..." he mumbled quietly, so bloody quietly, "don't say my name anymore, baby." A sob wracked his body. "Please. Don't look at me. Don't touch me. Hurts, hurts us so fucking badly... Don't...."

The fight was there against his words as he looked down, the need to do what came naturally between lovers despite all the chaos—and his lips touched mine.

As a "fuck" came in the distance, his kiss was hard at first, then gentle, so tender, the salty taste of his tears coating our lips. "Hurts..." he breathed, "hurts more when I don't touch you. And don't.... don't want to see you hurt. Just... don't look for me anymore. Please." His cheek brushed mine. "Leave me alone. I need you to leave me alone, stay out of my head."

I cried softly, cuddling in close, hiding somewhere in the curve of his neck, needing to hide now. "I'm no ghost, Jack. I'm here. Please—"

Jack was dragged off me with a leather strap around his throat. "You touching again? Not getting dirty, boy?"

Vince made sure his mask covered his whole face, hiding his lips, and masking his voice again. Tossing Jack back into the middle of the floor, he started to shake his head. I tried to move, but Henry was already there, chaining me by the throat to the wall. "You touching Jan intimately, boy?" said Vince, all friendliness deliberately buried. Jack snarled, but Vince was there, tying the loose end of the belt that choked Jack to a hook in the floor, forcing Jack onto his hands and knees. "Did I say you could touch anyone intimately, boy?"

Vince eased to his feet and slammed a foot into Jack's ribs. As Jack doubled, Vince headed out of the bedroom, only to come back a moment later carrying a smoking poker, the end shaped into the letter V.

"For pissing your Dom off again, boy. Let's give you a visual reminder of who owns you. Really give you something to clean off."

Jack felt the heat against his cheek first, and it seemed to stir him from whatever he was going through.

"No." That was growled out as he twisted his head into the floor, but Henry was there, pulling Jack onto his side, pinning his arms behind his back and slipping his legs around Jack's to keep him still.

"No?" Vince moved it down over his throat, pausing, watching Jack squirm away from the iron. Then he shifted over to Jack's shoulder, gave another long pause, then moved down over his stomach, just to pause at the fine V of Jack's abs. "But you've fucked me off, boy." He held it close, close enough to make Jack writhe, cry another *no*.

"No?" said Vince. "But you looked at Jan. You *touched* Jan. Don't—"

"Fuck no," cried Jack. "Please."

"—tell me your safe word, and I'll stop."

"Mercedes. *Mercedes.*"

"What's that?" said Vince, tilting his ear to Jack. "Can't hear you, boy."

"*Mercedes, Mercedes-fucking-Benz, Merce—*"

Vince pressed down on Jack's right hip.

Jack's agony and struggles were enough to tear off the necklace he wore as I cried, "*Mercedes—Mercedes-fucking-Benz now. Please….*" This had to stop. It needed to fucking stop.

Vince pulled the poker off, taking skin with it, and tutting in the process. "But you didn't say your safe word, boy." He ignored how I'd cried it for him. "What's your safe word?"

Jack choked on the floor. "Merce—"

"Sorry, can't hear you." The iron pressed into exactly the same patch of blistering skin.

"*Mercedes… Mercedes-fucking-Benz.*" Jack writhed, twisted—tried to double, to hide, to get away from the burn. "*Gray. Gray, for God's sake—please. Mercedes. Mercedes-Benz—Mercedes-fucking-Ben….*"

The hurt that hit the air was unadulterated, and it lasted for only a few seconds before Jack passed out, the smell of burning flesh lasting long after Vince had made sure he'd blacked out.

I sobbed, curling into a protective ball. "Gray, for godssake, please." Same name, but cried out for entirely different reasons, because Gray was being made part of the same nightmare, one where Jack wanted Gray to stop, yet I needed Gray to step in and end it all.

A kick encouraged me to shut up, but it was Jack's groan that had every ounce of my attention as he came to. Henry had gone over to a bag I hadn't even known was there. Reading off a piece of paper for a moment as though he needed to know what to do next, he then pulled out a white cotton shirt. It looked familiar, one of mine? Life blurred too much at the moment to focus. But as Henry pulled out another two items, I went still. He went back over to Jack, first dropping my shirt by him, then dropping the photo of Gray and writing what I could only guess was the same old message next to it:

Don't...

... straighten me, Jack.

Shivering, Jack went quiet, staring at the photo, his nose inches from my shirt.

"Go on, boy," said Henry, smiling. "Touch it. Touch him. Go on. Earn yourself a fucking."

As Jack fought a battle, tears streaking his cheeks, Vince came over to me. A tap came at my face as Jack's struggles played out longer and longer. There was no natural drop to try and touch his Dom... me. "Had enough, Jan?"

I twisted my head away and closed my eyes, shut him out, but a rough grip to my hair forced me to look back.

"Stay focused, kid." Vince sounded almost regretful as a pat came to my cheek. "I'm surprised he has anything left for you. And funny, he must be a damn good actor with me still, because while my friends were downstairs Boxing Day, d'you know he sucked me off in the bedroom? Got such a gorgeous mouth and knows how to fucking use it too, don't he?"

"Fuck you."

Vince snorted and let his thumb brush my lips. "You've got a sweet mouth too, boy. More virginal, more… innocent." He mumbled something else. "Can you still play innocent for the cameras, Jan?" He glanced up into the corner, sweat dripping from underneath the black gas mask.

More noise came from the floor, just a grunt. Jack hadn't moved, his look solely on Gray's photo. Eyes had been wild when I'd first seen him, now something else crept in. Hip blistering, Jack completely stilled, eyes pinpointing that photo, not shifting, head lowering as if counting, calculating, clockwork ticking over in his mind and—

Broke. Something finally broke in his head.

Vince was talking to me, Henry whispering to Jack, neither of them really seeing the tension in Jack's body, what I saw in Jack's body then.

A snarl, Jack jerked back, the first vicious pull back stopped by the collar, then the second snapping the leather free as he writhed and twisted like a dog forced to wear a collar for the first time. Then, suddenly shifting, he was up, grabbing at Henry, headbutting his mask, splitting the eyes, forcing Henry to stagger away, holding his face.

"What the fuh?" snarled Vince, getting up. Other men were suddenly in the room, one pushing Henry out of the way, but then making the mistake of going in first. Jack kneed him in the groin once, twice—pulled him back in for a third, then headbutted him down to the floor. It snapped another man into gear, but Jack caught hold of him, grabbing him by the shirt, and slamming his head into the wall, once, twice—the third with added cries of satisfaction that saw Jack kick the hell out of the man as he slumped to the floor, bloodied and quiet.

"Blackout!" shouted Vince, and he moved fast and hard, rushing Jack from behind and grabbing him by the waist, throwing him to the floor. Jack hit hard, and Vince went down, even his size needing two other men to come rushing in to try and pin Jack still.

Essex. Steve had said Jack blacked out in Essex. Was this it? That utter of blackout of life and sense, just a need to—

"Yes, Jack. Come on, baby," I yelled, life finally kicking into gear. He was pure intent, unfocused, but enough to take down anything that stood in his way, purely because there was no sense of danger, no remorse over action—just pure aggression that even Vince and his drugs couldn't keep out of his system. *"Fucking react, Jack, fucking hurt the bastards, baby, fucking make them bleed."*

CHAPTER 24
VINCE

"GET SOME FUCKING ketamine in here," cried Vince, struggling, holding Jack on the floor and looking worried that he was caught struggling. A moment later, someone scurried through the door. Not the doc. I hadn't seen this guy before. He knelt, the needle he held missing its target twice as he tried to get it into Jack's arm. Jack cried out, seeming to feel it scrape his skin, then it was pushed in, and Vince gripped at Jack's jaw, forcing his head back as the struggles instantly started to ease.

"Fucking calm it, boy," he snarled, as Henry, looking as pissed as hell, pulled a knife out and fell down by Jack.

"I'll cut the fucking cunt's fingers for that." Blood poured from Henry's nose. "I'll peel off his nails one by one and slice through to fucking bone—"

"No," cried Jack as Henry held his wrist down, flattening out his hand. "Christ, Vince! Stop him, for fuckssake."

A finger went to Vince's mouth as he instantly pulled back and gave a gentle "shush" towards Henry and anyone else in the bedroom.

He didn't need to bother. I'd already gone still hearing Jack cry out for Vince and completely bypass Gray.

Vince came back down on Jack, the mask now lifted to reveal Vince's mouth again. "Jack, it's okay, kid. I'm here. Just a dream, just a bad fucking dream."

Jack grabbed at Vince's shirt, pulled Vince in close, all to hide, and I strangled a cry from my throat. "*Not yours. Never fucking yours.*"

"Shush-shush," breathed Vince, his lips so close to Jack's. "Just curl up, sleep." He stroked at Jack's hair, petted him, then planted a kiss on his cheek. "You're safe, our kid. All safe. But you need to stop burning yourself. It's not real. Not real, kid."

"*Why? Why the hell are you doing this? What have we done to you? What—what has Jack ever done to you?*"

Jack relaxed his grip, arms falling to his side, but all heavy, like he'd passed out, and Vince eased off. I saw his smile as he pushed to his feet and came over.

He took his mask off, breathing hard, heavy. "Still think he's yours? Gray's?" he said quietly. "That he gives a fuck about you anymore outside of a dream?"

I started to shake, unable to take my gaze off Jack.

"You're on your own, now, gorgeous," said Vince. Another wipe went to my lips, and I didn't even feel the touch. "Maybe you ought to consider paying real nice attention to Henry with that sweet mouth of yours." He paused. "And I mean real nice attention. Otherwise, what he'll do will fucking hurt you, kid. It doesn't hurt Jack anymore. Well, unless he plays up like that again, then I'll fuck a bat up his ass to keep that aggression tempered. But he's a good lad now. You need to start thinking about being a good pet too, for Henry. You're no use to me any longer now."

I couldn't stop looking at Jack. For the first time, the very first time, I wanted to get at him, shake the fuck out of him, finish everything Vince had started—take the knife, press it against his throat, see the life come into his eyes again just to take it away, just stop. This all needed to fucking stop.

Jack's breathing became a little erratic. Nothing too bad to start off with, just slight pulls in on his lower stomach, then something changed. There was a sudden sharp pull in of breath that showed his ribs, his intake of breath now ragged, strained.

The convulsion seemed inevitable, but the ferocity of the assault startled me as choking came and Jack lost control of his body.

"What..." I groaned. "*What the hell have you done?*"

After giving a glance over his shoulder, Vince hissed and rushed over to Jack. "Leo, get your fucking arse back in here."

The man who had given Jack the injection rushed back in.

"How much?" shouted Vince, hunting around for the bottle Leo had used and finding it rolling a few feet away. "How fucking—"

"Hundred mil, the usual," said Leo, but Vince hissed through his teeth as he found the bottle.

"You fucking idiot. This is concentrate—you gave him ten times the stated dilute dose, you fuck. *Doc.*"

Other men were back in the room, now trying to hold Jack down. "Don't touch him while he's fitting," I shouted. "Are you really that stupid? You'll do him more damage."

"Get the doc," Vince shouted back as the men stepped away from Jack, and a moment later a commotion of voices hit the air as other commands were shouted outside: *get a stretcher, blankets*, all timed with Vince's shouts over the fuck-up of the bottles as the doctor rushed in.

"Jesus, you weren't paid to kill him," the doc snapped as he fell next to Jack. He didn't have that controlled calmness that usually came with someone who'd had years of practice. "Overdoses like this… Fuck. Oxygen. I need some bloody oxygen. *Get me some bloody oxygen—*"

"He's struggling to breathe," snapped Vince.

"*Which is why I need the fucking oxygen,*" said the doctor, his voice heated. "This—" He held up the bottle that they'd used, and the remainder of the contents danced inside. "It handles the respiratory drive well, unlike other anaesthetics. But oxygen—"

"*Then get him fucking oxygen.*"

"He needs a hospital!" shouted the doctor. "This dosage will fucking kill him unless it's properly monitored."

Vince pulled him so close their noses could have shared germs. "Properly monitor it," he snapped. "It's what you're fucking paid for."

The bedroom was suddenly full of bodies, and somewhere it registered just how many people were involved in this, were in Jack's home, but then Jack was piled onto a stretcher, still fitting, an oxygen mask now on his face. Vince looked back over at me, scowled, and then snapped out orders. Life bled from the bedroom, leaving me alone.

I followed the commotion in the hall as far as my ears would strain. Doors opened, closed, shouts came, all forcing my heart so hard against my chest, it hurt.

And then it was quiet.

So fucking quiet.

I forced my breathing to a standstill, hoping to catch something.

Jack.

My head fell against the wall. Christ. "I didn't mean it, baby." I gripped onto the handcuffs, wanting to shout out. I hadn't meant it. "Didn't mean it, Jack. Love the bones off you, martial arts guy, fucking love…."

The shuffling outside Jack's bedroom door had stopped ages ago. Since then, one cough had led to two, then hard barking took over until I threw up. In the darkness of the bedroom, blood intermingled with stomach lining, I tasted more than saw it, and I let my head fall back against the wall, heat racing my body, yet shivering with cold as I tried to ignore the smell. Even the stench faded eventually, just leaving behind the chill, the need to sleep. Henry hadn't been one for sterilising his equipment, the tubing used for force-feeding he'd left on the unit until next time or knocked it on the floor.

"Hey." A tap came at my foot, just gentle at first, not enough to make me want to open my eyes, but then it came again. "Hey, you awake, Richards?"

"Jack?"

Jack crouched in front of me, cocking a smile as huge silver eyes seemed to catch the light and glisten like a pool catching the sunlight waiting to break through the clouds. "You still in the same universe as me tonight?"

"Hmmm." I licked across dry lips, then managed a smile seeing Jack was back on the hardwood floor, running through his kata. "Need a drink," I mumbled, and Jack grinned over. He wore black jogging trousers and a black vest shirt, showing off the toned suppleness to his shoulders, helped by how he'd just half-flipped, landing on his hands and was walking around upside down.

"Just a drink, hmmm?" he said, landing on his feet. A moment later he was over by me, straddling my legs as he shifted my hands above my head. "All the time you've spent with us and that's as wild as your imagination gets? I need... a *drink*?"

I chuckled, hating how it choked into a cough in the end, one that had Jack frowning.

"You okay, baby?" he said quietly. He brushed his cheek against mine, then kissed it gently.

"Just need..." Nuzzling into his neck, I knew tears dampened the soft curve. "Need this. Need—"

"You touching my sub, Jan?"

Both of us looked over as Gray came into his bedroom. It never even clicked where the hell the hall had gone or how the bedroom now blended into view. Jack was pressed up against me, keeping me against the wall, now dressed in white silk pyjamas. My hands had already found a way down to his ass and how the silk smoothed and slipped over the curves of his ass so perfectly.

"Because Jack knows you shouldn't be touching my sub, Jan."

Giving a frustrated groan, Jack eased his body away even though his hands stayed on the wall, keeping his lips so tantalisingly close to mine. "Just saying goodnight," he said moodily.

"So say it and fuck off," said Gray, unbuttoning his shirt, over by the opposite side of the huge bed. "You're still on no-touch street until inauguration."

Jack was doing this scowl as his hand mimicked everything Gray said, then he pushed away, heading over to Gray.

"You don't touch me either."

"No hug before you Master me?" Jack stopped, only having reached the bottom of the bed, doing this whole *c'mere* thing with open arms and waving him over for a hug. "Use me, lose me, hmmm?"

Gray gave a hard sigh. "I haven't used anything properly in months, Jack. Save the puppy-dog eyes for the land of soft and gullible over there."

Jack looked back at me, his eyes hopeful.

"Oh no," I chuckled. "Not my house, baby. Not my rules." Jack was suddenly back by me, and my back hit the bed as he pushed me down onto it. A black silk sheet was tugged over my face, making me lose sight of the world, and Jack eased his body down on mine. A kiss touched my lips, and I stilled as the silk of the sheet was caught between our lips.

"Jack," warned Gray.

I tugged the sheet off my head and looked up. "Technically," said Jack, "I'm not touching him over here."

"Yeah? Suppose you fell, all accidental like?" said Gray. "The sheet just got in the way?"

"Safe sex," said Jack, although we were laughing so hard, it barely came out right. It also wasn't helping having him hiding in my throat, trying to bury it.

"Think you're both funny?"

"Fucking hilarious," choked Jack as I stroked the curve of his neck. He had a damn good curve to his neck, kissable, lickable. I could understand why Gray would want a collar there, staking his claim.

"Jack, out," said Gray, stopping me from doing just that. Jack groaned against the loss, almost as if he'd sensed what I was going to do. After jamming a hand against my mouth and kissing it, he pushed away, leaving me cold as a draught from the open window caused a run of shivers.

"I'll just go back to my cold, lonely—empty room, over on the other side of bollockland, with only the smell of Ed's socks to keep me company." Giving a scowl at Gray, Jack reached the door, then looked back over. "Later, things." He winked, and then he was gone into the darkness of the corridor, leaving nothing but the cold draught from the windows.

I choked a sob, not really understanding why the loneliness hurt so much. Gray seemed just as confused as me as he came over and tapped at my leg.

"Hey. Shut the fuck up."

I blinked, trying to adjust to the light that was coming from the bedroom doorway. The draught was coming from there, not from any open window, and the man crouching in front of me was too stocky to be Gray. He stank of bourbon, even added a run of hiccups to the whole drunk aura he gave off.

Doc. I couldn't see his face, the light of the doorway silhouetted his form, but deep down I knew it was the doc. Fingers prodded at my eyes, opening the lids, forcing me back into cold reality.

"Juh—" I wiped my tongue over my lips, winced. "Where's Jack?" It felt like he'd been here a moment ago, so bloody close. I still tasted him on my lips. I needed to taste him on my lips.

The only answer was the lift up of a syringe in Doc's hand. That was good, right? I mean, Jack had taken loads of these. If the doc held one now, maybe it was time to see Jack. I wouldn't mind this if it meant I would see Jack; I'd see that he was okay.

I was crying again. "He... Jack. Please, tell me he's...."

With the syringe placed to the floor, a tug came at the cuff to my shirt before the sleeve was rolled up.

"Jack?" Life was blurry for a moment.

The syringe was picked up off the floor, and I didn't even flinch as it touched my arm.

"Jack's gone," said the doc.

"Gone? Gone where?" I whispered.

Doc smiled thinly. "I'm sorry, okay. A few days ago...." He looked at the needle. "Too much for his system."

"Jack." I swallowed as a salty tear hit my lips. "'S not gone."

Doc seemed to shake something off. "Yeah. Hurts. This, this will make it so it doesn't hurt anymore. Don't fight it, okay?"

I looked away and didn't fight the push of needle into me. Nothing was worth fighting for anymore.

≈

I woke up crying out, and the grief carried on when I found the world was black and plastic around me. It felt like I was the mouse stupid enough to wander into a snake's stomach. Arms were tight at my side, and this strong smell of leather hit my nose. Fingers took on a life of their own as I scratched, clawed, rooted around, panic giving me something to fight and move for. Just level with my navel, I felt the run of a wide zip and traced it up, inching past my face until the underside of the zip's catch ran under my fingers. Scratching at it with my fingernail, I managed to get it open—then I was tugging it down past my face as far as I could over my body. Somebody had bothered to dress me, suit, tie, the lot.

"Fuck." I sat up, gasping for air, then instantly regretted it as my head smacked into hard metal. The world swam for a minute as I eased back down and risked opening my eyes. Huge hinges were above me, curved like forks ready to lift and hold something, and I struggled to put them and this plastic sleeping bag into context of Jack's bedroom. These hinges seemed to belong to the boot of a car, one that was open, me on the inside, looking up. Car? There hadn't been a car in….

Voices drifted over, and the world moved slightly. Bedrooms didn't shift, or sway and dip as though someone had got in. Cars. Cars shifted with weight.

"I'll get the boot in a sec," called a voice. "Doc's had his fat ass in this. I need to adjust this seat." The car shifted again as the wind picked up, then—"Shut your fucking door. Bloody gust is gonna take it off."

CHAPTER 25
ESCAPE

SOMEONE WAS IN the car, adjusting a seat, and I flinched, wanting to move, but found everything stopped without having Henry there to tell me *to* move, without having the muscle mass and strength to move.

Stupid, so bloody stupid, Jan. Move.

A gust of wind that nearly had me crying out shifted the car, or maybe the seat being adjusted added to it. It pushed me enough to move. After twisting onto my stomach, I eased myself over the rim of the boot. It left me nose to nose with the leather bag I'd been in. A blanket sat next to it and I stuffed it into the bag and zipped it back up just as more wind shifted the car, blinding me with my own fringe. Hearing footsteps, I dropped, more slumped as my legs gave out underneath me, and I shuffled under the car, leaves and dirt hitting my face as another gust of wind moved the car. The big estate allowed ample room to hide underneath, to wait, but the cold, wet concrete underneath me and the smell of oil as sets of feet to my left, then right, all left me shivering. A big building ran alongside of us. Grass was on the other side, a fence just up ahead. It was bright, the sun at its highest, but still so cold.

Where had all the snow gone? Where the hell was Jack's house? His street?

"Come on, fucking hurry up, Leo." The man who had given Jack the overdose? That came from my left as the footsteps to my right came around to the boot. A thump, the force rocking the car, the boot was shut, followed a moment later by someone getting in the passenger side. I made my body as small as possible, kept low to the ground as the exhaust kicked into life inches above my head. It seemed the smartest thing to do a few moments ago, hide here, but if the car reversed, turned left, right, I was in for serious damage.

Covering my head with my hands, I kept as flat as possible to the concrete. Mostly hiding from sight, but also against the wind battering me. After a few seconds, the car pulled off, tyres gently easing forward so as not to cause any damage. I counted to ten, giving the driver enough time to not bother looking back, but also not to draw attention to me staying there if anyone inside the building were to look out.

Once the car was clear, I stumbled back to the building. My back flat against the wall, wasteland was now ahead of me, that big fence to the left, maybe a warehouse to my back, but at least it offered some shelter against the wind. Off to my right, the lack of wind allowed the sound of a main road to filter over.

Running was hard. Concrete and pebbles bit hard into my bare feet as I rounded the corner. It took me past a closed loading bay with huge containers used for transport, an unused forklift, more wasteland, then wood hit my hands as I reached a fence. I scrambled up over it, ignoring the splinters, and dropped to the floor on the other side. I landed awkwardly, my ass hitting a pool of mud, but only inches from a minor "B" road. One car passed me by, horn blaring, surface water spraying up, and I pushed up and ran into the road seeing the next one.

The little Micra missed me by inches, forced to screech to a stop, and I stumbled around to the passenger door and managed to pull it open before the tyres had finished smoking.

Screams from two kids hit the air, and I slumped inside the car, more scared of them than they were of me, hands held up in defence and trying my best to calm down the young mother who was already sorting through her handbag.

"Please, please, just listen." From the look on the woman's face, that wasn't bloody likely. "I'm not here to hurt you, I…" I closed my eyes, gripping onto the passenger door and trying to shut it. "I just need help, please. I need." I wiped at my cheek knowing it wasn't just mud dampening the skin. "I need you to take me home."

The woman opened her mouth to speak, her eyes darting to her kids.

"Please," I said quietly. "I won't hurt you. I just need help. I need anyone's help."

A frown, the woman took her hand out of her bag and offered me her phone. "Call someone," she said through tight lips. "Shut the door."

I whimpered my thanks and took the phone after finally managing to shut the door with the aid of a strong gust of wind.

"Are you hurt?" she said as she slipped into gear and pulled off. I glanced at her, barely, unable for the second time to punch at the numbers. I couldn't focus on any of the digits. Numbers, I couldn't even count on numbers.

"Fuck." I wanted to take that back hearing a kid mumble "Mom," from behind, and quickly looked at them. "A friend…" I closed my eyes, my hand digging into my forehead. "… someone I love is, badly, so very badly…." Say it, Jan, say the word. I let out a groan and dropped my head back. I wasn't going to believe a word those bastards said until I saw Jack's bod—until I saw Jack myself.

"Hey, it's okay," said the woman, and I jerked under the touch that went to my knee. She shifted her hand, now sorting through her bag, and pulled out a bottle of water. "Drink this."

I looked at it, and her frown met mine.

"It's okay; it's safe to drink."

I took it from her and kept to little sips, somewhere remembering that too much too soon could do more damage. Then I was back with the phone. There was only one number that mattered, one person I wanted to damn well see buried next to Jack. Gray's mobile started to ring, but there was no reply. "Jesus…." I bit back a cry. "What day is it?"

"What?" The woman looked a little startled.

"I need to know what… what day is it?"

"Monday, the thirtieth of Dece—"

"The thirtieth—" My stomach sank. How long? Two weeks? Monday? "I know where he'll be."

"Who?"

I gave her the address to Regent Square, and then nothing but getting to Gray and ramming the phone down his throat mattered.

∾

The car hadn't even stopped outside of Regent Manor before I was out and dragging myself across the gravel. Barely reaching halfway, my legs gave way, and I hit the ground with stones digging into my palms and knees. For a moment I stayed down, too numb, just staring at the small bits of grit and stone in my palms. Then someone was pulling me up with a hand under my arm.

"Mr Richards?"

Whoever stood at my side blurred a touch, and my hand instinctively sought something to hold on to as life warped. I caught a security badge.

"Hey, easy," a voice mumbled, then a whistle was given. "Hey, Mike, over here. Can you give me a hand?" A moment later someone else buffeted me as a shoulder slipped under my arm.

"Jan? Hey, you okay?"

Mike. The tech guy who had set all the camera security at my home all those months ago came into focus, as did the security guard to my right. "Mike." My hand went to his chest as I tried to turn around and point at the woman. "Don't let her leave here. You need... need to find out where she picked me up."

"Go," whispered Mike, and the help off the security guard was suddenly gone, nearly making me stumble with the loss. "Easy." Mike pulled me straight. "Where do you need to go, Jan? Who do you need to see?" He sounded calm, so professionally sodding calm.

"Gray."

"Okay. He's on the fifth floor in a conference with the Masters." I was tugged forward. "Can you make it?"

"Fucking move."

We made it through the reception, over to the lifts. I hadn't walked properly for weeks, and it showed. People were either quick enough to get out of my way or were jolted aside as Mike gave a look that made sure they did. Gripping my stomach and hating how much I needed help off Mike to get out of the lift, I saw Simons come at me from some cupboard hole in the waiting room before the hall. He'd been the one to tie Jack to a cross six months ago for my screw-up. I hadn't liked him then, and I certainly hated the fucking sight of him now.

"You can't go—"

"Move." He seemed to scurry back a few feet, his look nervous on me, then Mike. He took the hint to stay out of the way as I pushed away from Mike and shoved through the main doors.

As the doors closed behind me, all talking in the hall fell into silence.

Gray sat next to Mistress Carr. He started to stand, to frown, to fucking say something—Yeah, you come and fucking say something, Gray. I was by him in a few seconds, every intent there of hurling him onto the table, pounding the hell out of his face, already doing that in mind and fucking loving the release, but he beat me to it.

A grab at my jacket, he twisted me around, slammed me down hard onto the table, sending a decanter of water spiralling away as he came in close. "What the fuh—"

"Time out?" I cried in his face, cutting him off. *"He never cried time out in the texts. You... you think he'd stay away from you for this fucking long when he's risked rape just to touch your fucking photo, you cunt?"*

Angered cries were already going up around the hall as

Gray pulled me off the table and sent me stumbling back towards the door a few paces.

"You." Gray pointed at me. "What's gone on, Jan?" he said quietly, looking at me, looking down at my body. "What *the fuck's* gone on?"

"What th—" I laughed, more scared of the sound I made, hands going to my head. "Fuck you, Gray—*fuck you.* You... Firearms. You just take me the fuck to wherever you keep your firearms, and then you... you—"

I couldn't finish that, just crumpled down to the floor at the end of the conference table, head buried in my arms.

"Jan?"

A gentle stroke came to my hair and I looked up to find Gray crouched next to me. I was sobbing, I knew that, but I couldn't find the words to let everything out any other way.

"What the hell's gone on, lad?"

"Gray... they..." I wiped at my nose. "They hurt him so fucking much. They... I think, I think they killed him."

Gray pulled back a touch as I wiped my eyes on my arm, keeping down for a minute as a fresh wave of sobs took over.

"Where's Jack, Jan?" That couldn't have been colder, and the click of a sidearm came, the safety off. Gray was back to his feet, a gun at his side. I pushed up, making sure I stopped inches from him.

"That's mine."

"No," he said quietly.

I held out my hand. "Give it, or I swear to God I'll fucking kill you for it."

"Which is exactly why you don't touch this," said Gray,

turning away. "Brennan," he called back into the room, "make a call to a few of your Met friends. Get them here. Simons, you've seen the state of Jan—why the fuck haven't you got a paramedic up here?"

I barely glanced back at Brennan, at Mistress Carr, but when I did, they had sidearms. The question over why they had been licensed to carry a weapon was there somewhere, but I didn't care.

"I'm going with you," I said back to Gray, bringing him to a halt.

Gray looked me up and down. "You're in no state to walk out of this hall, let alone the building."

"I know names, I know faces," I said to him quietly. "I've been gone half-an-hour. If Jack's still alive, he's my only priority. You." I pointed at the gun. "That's yours."

Gray watched me for a moment, weighing something up, but hiding exactly what that was. A look back at Brennan, Carr, he nodded at me. "You don't move from my fucking side. Clear?"

With the address the woman gave us, we pulled up outside the disused warehouse just one hour after I'd stumbled out of the car boot. Six other cars were with us, two black Mercedes, the rest a bland assortment that looked like they were used to morphing into the background. Three cars stayed at the front of the building, the others pulling around the back. I'd managed to get some shoes on, have some patch-up crap over dehydration from a medic who had come with us, but I was close to blacking out. As I got out of the car, caught another gust of wind, and looked at the warehouse, shivering took over now adrenaline had long since been used, recycled, then tossed withered and useless aside.

"Here." Gray dropped his long black coat on my shoulders as we stood by the car and frowned when I jerked away from his touch. "If you feel you're slipping, starting to black out, you sit down where you are."

"Wasting time," I mumbled, shivering despite the coat, and I started to shift for the warehouse. A hand on my arm stopped me, pulling me back.

"Not yet."

"Gray."

He was looking at Brennan, who held a small device in his hand. "Not yet," he said again, quietly. If it was a thermal camera Brennan was using to see into the building to judge how many people were inside, pointing at the floor wasn't going to get him anywhere. Gray was looking at it too. "How many cars do you remember seeing here, Jan?"

"One, a Ford estate. I wasn't exactly counting."

"Okay," said Gray with a hard sigh as Brennan cast him a look and put the thermal camera away. The dynamics had changed slightly between them, even I could see that, Brennan now waiting for Gray to give the nod.

Whatever arrangements were needed to handle this, they had already been sorted. As Gray shifted, his suit jacket opening a touch and showing his sidearm, I found myself staring, then noticing that Gray saw I was staring. "I've used one of those."

"Yeah?" said Gray, barely looking at me. "You keep thinking that." His voice didn't have that hard edge despite the words, and giving a look to Brennan and Carr, he headed for the entrance.

There wasn't much shouting, maybe the odd hold of hand up to an earpiece, a lot of listening, as I followed Gray in and around the first floor. Old machines rusted here and there, huge transfer presses that looked like they'd seen better days. Plastic wrapping that usually kept pallets and their goods in place drifted over the floor; a glass window showed an office of some sorts off to the left, and beyond that, doors were marked up as toilets. No doubt there'd be a canteen close by.

"Fuck." I doubled, suddenly realising. "Jack's." Gray was there, pulling me up. "We'd been at Jack's—ah, shouldn't be here, could have driven me here an—"

"Jan?" he said quietly, but I pushed him off, trying to back up, get out.

"Jack's," I mumbled. "We were at Jack's."

"Not possible, Jan," said Gray. "I've been ther—" Something was said into his earpiece, making him frown, tilt his head, then he was looking up.

We made it to the second floor, and I slowed my pace seeing men standing outside of a door, one that had them passing strange glances between them, then easing aside to allow Gray in.

CHAPTER 26
HOME AWAY FROM HOME

GRAY PUSHED PAST me, but his touch on my shoulder was gentle as he eased past, his need to see what hid behind that door more of a drive than mine. Or so I thought. For a moment he faltered as he stood there looking in, and his confusion killed everything inside of me. Then he shook it off, and he was in the room, spurring me on as he disappeared.

I didn't understand, or more I couldn't process what hit me. I'd stepped through Jack's front door. To the left stood his coat stand, his stairs just ahead, slightly off to the right. Then a little farther, his lounge came after that. I went on through, and sure enough, the rest was a pure mirror of Jack's lounge leading through to his kitchen and breakfast bar, only this time full of Christmas decorations. His dining room was beyond that, and plates were stacked in the sink. A wok, spaghetti Bolognese sticking to the sides...

I backtracked and eased my way up the stairs. Again to the left was Jack's spare room, and I avoided that at all costs, heading for the shower. Opening the door took me through a long corridor, where his shower room sat at the end. Maybe they hadn't had the room to extend the house properly and add it on, maybe… What the hell did I know?

I went in there first.

Water dripped from the showerhead, threatening to stain the wall, leaking like a lonely tear that didn't know how to stop. I went over, so tempted to stand underneath it, dip my head, and just feel close to Jack again, even if it was only in terror.

"You were cleaned here."

Gray's voice was soft, but it was a statement, not a question. He leaned against the door, in much the same spot Henry had always stood.

"They're gone," I mumbled quietly, leaning back against a wall and screwing my eyes shut to block out Henry's image. The smell of urine, sweat, blood, sex, and my cologne, it stained the air, turning my stomach. "He's gone," I mumbled in an even flatter tone, letting my head fall back as I closed my eyes. "But you knew that," I said quietly, remembering the look Gray and Brennan had passed between each other outside. They'd been checking for heat signatures of tyre tracks; they'd seen more than one set. "You wouldn't have let me up here otherwise, would you?"

A tear fell, then more. "What the hell's been going on here, Gray? What the fuck have they done?"

"You never saw outside of Jack's home?"

"Here, his spare room, his—" The shaking that gripped threatened to tear me apart, and Gray was suddenly there, trying to rub at my shoulders.

"Don't—" I shook him off. "*Just fucking don*—" That one word was strangled into silence and I hit the wall. "*Fucks, fucking sick fucks.*"

A whistle came from behind, up to the right, back in the direction of Jack's master bedroom. Giving a tug at my sleeve to encourage me to move, Gray made sure I followed.

Brennan knelt close to where the hook was still fastened to the floor. They hadn't even pulled that out. I hadn't even noticed. Everything rushed in; the will to get out, forget the screw-ups, and….

Gray eased me to one side and went and crouched by Brennan. After slipping some gloves on, he ran his fingers over the hook, his attention transfixed on the patch of blood just beneath it. Maybe from Jack, maybe from the men he'd beaten.

"A few days old," whispered Brennan, and Gray gave him such a hard glare. Brennan eased to his feet, away, seeing it. Because there it was: that dead look that turned blue eyes almost pitch-black and had men stepping away from him.

Looking at me, Gray came over. "I need you to tell me everything, Jan. And I mean everything, start to finish. No detail left out, as best as you can remember."

I stared at him, that feeling of fresh drugs being pumped into my system making me shiver, because like hell could I do anything but stare at him.

"Everything," he said gently. "Seconds matter."

Shivering came a little harder. I knew how this went. "We… the night you two argued, we got home. We slept eventually, Jack was so cold. People were there as we slept, and when Jack needed a shower in the night, they—" I frowned. "Videos. After I sent you a text to say Jack was okay, Vince, the main bastard in charge, he watched one of those videos of Jack and Cutter while Jack showered. He sat on Jack's bed with me, watching them."

"He had discs with him?"

I was back with Gray, nodded.

"He could have copied them off the porn sites," breathed Brennan in Gray's ear.

Gray barely glanced at him. "Or he's the uploader, or at least knows them." Gray focused back on me. "And?"

I glanced back into the room. People looked around the upstairs now: Carr, other men.

"Jan." Gray stole my attention. "Everything."

"They drugged Jack," I said flatly. "They... when I woke, I was here. I thought, I thought we were at his. Everything, everything looked and smelled..." I glanced around. "Exactly like his. They'd dressed me in a suit, and Jack?" I pointed to where the bed had been, ignored how easily I let it fall back to my side. "Vince raped him while he was unconscious." I frowned. "Then nearly drowned him, raping him with a studded whip. Blood. So much blood. And Henry, right after the branding, he picked up this note that he read. I don't think I was supposed to see it, but... it looked, with the things they did to Jack, maybe like a BDSM list of things to do? And they wrote things on the floor."

"Jan." Mistress Carr was at my side and her hand slipped into mine as Brennan checked the floor over for chalk marks. "Take it slowly. Did they—" She looked at Gray. "—did they touch you?"

I licked at my lips, focused on Gray—needing to focus on Gray. "Vince's rape was systematic: at night, with different mind games, different BDSM equipment and techniques. How he did it... he, he twisted everything Jack knew, taping his mouth shut at first so he couldn't use his safe word, then removing it and not listening when he did cry it. And don't... they used the whole psychological play with saying don't, saying 'Don't... tell me your safe word.'" I fought back that rush building inside of me. "He cried it, Gray. He cried for it to stop and they carried on the rape, raping him and they, they, us...."

"Anything else?" said Mistress Carr quietly, trying to focus my rush away from rambling.

"That phone call to you," I said to Gray, and he narrowed his eyes. "That was just after he'd first raped Jack, when Jack was unconscious. Henry had a knife to Jack's cheek, he cut his shoulder, then threatened to rape him with the knife and—" I shrugged some tears. "I had to make that call, Gray. I needed to make that call an—"

"It's okay," said Mistress Carr, giving a sideways glance to Gray, but like hell was any of this okay.

"They were mostly silent, or whispering," I said, "both wearing black leather gas masks, whenever we were forced together—"

"*Forced* together?"

I held Gray's gaze, denying the memories.

"I need to know, Jan."

"*Fucking mind games*," I snapped. "Always mind games with the masks, twisting everything, raping Jack when we were forced to cuddle up, raping him—" I stopped for a moment. I had to stop. "They made sure that I was the only one that made any noise. And my clothes, they had a selection of my clothes, my cologne, and they put my shirt by Jack when they hurt him. They said they were training him."

Now Gray frowned.

"With your photo too."

"Photo?" said Carr, but I was looking at Gray. "They wouldn't let him go casual with it, and they had the message 'Don't... straighten me, Jack.'"

Brennan was by us, his look as frowned as Gray's. "They knew his disorders and personal coping strategies?"

Gray nodded and looked back around the bedroom. "His home too. And they'd torture him at night with you?"

"At night?" I shrugged a little hopelessly. "I don't know. It would be light in the spare room, dark in here. They..." I wanted to cry at how useless I was and rubbed hard at my arms just to make it hurt somewhere else. "They drugged him constantly, I think. He'd be really disorientated, just trying to hold on, but scared too, and aggressive, so bloody aggressive. Like with everything else, they knew what they were doing until it came to the drugs." I was fighting vomiting. "They gave him a concentrated dose, not a diluted one with the injection, that's what they said. Jack started having convulsions here. They didn't need it." I wiped a hand over my face. "Gray, he struggled, he struggled so fucking badly with his OCD and conduct disorder. The last time after the photo of you was dropped casual out of reach, he blacked out, to the point he nearly killed one of the men. Left him bloodied on the floor. They wouldn't let him free, and you could see the build-up, what they put his body through, it was nothing compared to stopping the need to straighten the photo."

Something flickered through Gray's eyes before it was instantly buried. "Psychological reconditioning," he said flatly, and it was terrifying how calm his voice was. He filled none of his own details in, just focusing on mine.

"Why?" said Brennan.

Gray looked at him. "Remember how authoritarian Jack was when we first met him? Back with Cutter, how he'd exploit Jack's disorders and push for his kickback against the establishment?"

Brennan seemed to search for the memory, then nodded. "Something similar here?"

"Only a reversal, forcing a calming down." Gray glanced at me. "There's a definite link to his OCD and conduct disorder… perhaps to convince Jack he only suffers both under supposed BDSM handling, but that BDSM handling only occurs in a dream-like state?" His eyes narrowed as he looked around the bedroom. Yeah, he'd figured it out like I had. "Maybe followed up by normality during the day, all three: OCD, conduct disorder, and his BDSM liking, they're nothing more than a bad dream to him, perhaps?" He set his jaw tensing. "They knew what they were doing, all right. And to do it, we're maybe looking at a date-rape drug, ketamine, perhaps enhanced with an opiate or the likes."

Gray frowned at me. "What did they give you, Jan?"

I stopped rubbing at my arm. "Couldn't have been the same," I said, shutting out the memory. "It knocked me out and I woke in the boot of a car in a body bag. Maybe the doctor tried to help? Lowered the dosage?"

A look passed between Gray and Brennan. "Jan," said Carr, where Gray stayed silent. "Ketamine is good at maintaining the respiratory system. It's not a drug to use if you have no intention of waking the patient up. And if you woke in a body bag…." Gray gave her a look that quietened her backtrack, and my world became a whole lot smaller. She rubbed at my arm, then squeezed gently. "Not everyone has the same reaction to medication." Her smile was small, thin. "You got away. But we really need to get you to the MC hospital now."

I wasn't meant to get away; I'd seen faces. That was her

whole point. And that left Jack… where? That hit hard and Carr pulled me in close only for me to push her away. "Easy," she said quietly.

Brennan had given a long, angered exhale. "So their MO is if they stop Jack craving BDSM, it cures his disorder…. We're dealing with some sick fucks. Although…" His lips thinned. "If Jack was given ketamine throughout, even here…. It would be pretty useless overall: all of it would just have been one bad dream if Jack ever shook the drug off."

"Towards the end, they didn't drug him so much," I said flatly, remembering how clear his look had been since Christmas day. "So fucking scared…. Him and Vince, they sat eating Christmas dinner as I was forced to watch from the corner, and Christmas nigh—" I stopped that there as Gray levelled his gaze and didn't let it shift.

"Vince…" I mumbled. "He didn't give a fuck about any MO. He just got a real sadistic kick out of his control over us, over raping him." I felt sick. "He told me what he did to Jack on Boxing Day. I heard laughter, beer bottles smacking together, then Jack…." I shut up not wanting to chase the images over Christmas night.

"Don't go there, Jan," said Mistress Carr, brushing her hand at my face, although Gray obviously was going there. "Sounds like they drugged him into thinking that the perpetrator was a safe refuge, that everything else…. It was just a bad dream."

Yeah. That I was a bad dream, that Gray, BDSM…. "Jack…." I wiped a hand over my face. "He was so fucking pale." Fresh tears fell. "Ill and battered. I don't… after the fit, they wouldn't tell me if he was—"

"Did you catch any other names?" said Gray, again focusing thoughts. "Vince would more than likely be a pseudonym, unless he….”

Unless he didn’t expect me to walk away. “Henry,” I said. “Leo, Doc….” I tried to force other memories that should stay buried. “No surnames. I counted about ten different men altogether.” Gray nodded, went to say something else, but a whistle from the stairs had him pushing past me. “And cameras.”

“Cameras?” Gray looked into the corner as I pointed. Wiring was hanging loose, the camera ripped out and nowhere to be seen. I felt like crying that it had been there. I wasn’t lying.

“You need to see this,” a voice called up. A look at Brennan, I eased down the stairs after Gray. We were led back out of “Jack’s,” and twice I stumbled, twice Gray was there to catch me by the arm before Brennan took my weight. Helped up a stairway, I was led into a little room just a few doors down on the third floor.

“Obs room,” said Gray, flicking on a switch and highlighting the run of monitors. Jack’s bedroom came into view on one of them. A few clicks, and other places flashed on screen: Jack’s lounge, his shower, his spare room. Computer hard drives were smashed on the floor, and a phone was pulled off the wall over in the corner. “Get Mike in here,” said Gray, only to have Brennan add, “We can call my CID techs in on this. We’re beyond the MC with all of this, sir.”

I rubbed at my head, everything hurting too much to connect the roles played here.

“Mike’s ex-A Branch, technical support for MI5. He knows the setup for the MC; he’ll be able to tell where all of this—” Gray threw some parts back on a table. “—this shit differs. Also where they would get the equipment and from which supplier.”

Brennan nodded, took out his mobile, and made a call. "On his way," he said as Carr picked up some of the hard drive debris off the floor.

"They chose to break the gear rather than wipe it," she said.

"Hmmm," said Gray. "Any good tech would be able to find a way around wiping files. Hitting the main board shows they at least knew what they were doing tech-wise." He weighed his options up by the look of it. "I definitely think we're dealing with the uploaders to the porn site here. They had the savvy to bounce the signal between countries." Gray glanced at me. "And the phone signals."

He'd checked? Of course he'd checked. "But won't… won't Mike be able to do anything with this?" I said, unable to go into the room as Gray looked over.

"If there's a way, he'll find it." Gray went and picked up the phone—all the wires were exposed. "Harry."

A man brushed past me as he looked into the room.

"Get onto the phone company," said Gray. "Find out the who, where, and when behind the calls made to and from this building; see if there's an internet link and who the provider is. Get a full internet footprint. Also find out who owns this place and who they've leased it to lately. Go back as far as you can. Check street CCTV, see if we can get makes and models of cars that came close to this building. But get forensics into the mock-up of Jack's home first."

"Harry" nodded. Before he left, something passed between Brennan and Gray, a look that had Brennan moving over to Harry and whispering in his ear.

"This is well-funded," said Carr, watching Jack's bedroom scene on the monitor. "And I mean *well*-funded.

Replica of a home setting, premises, equipment. And then there would be wages."

"Wages?" Closing my eyes briefly, I pressed my forehead against the doorframe, then looked at Carr. "People *paid* to watch this?"

"Sometimes just for the thrill of watching it," said Carr.

"But…" I ran my tongue over dry lips. "But this was corrective. You… psychological reconditioning…. A reason, all of this shit, there has to be a reason." The tears I wiped away said there needed to be a reason for all of this shit.

"Other than the porn-site links," said Gray, "did Jack mention anything out of the ordinary happening, about anyone visiting his house before this happened?"

I shook my head. "We've been at yours mostly. And Jack was the one who taught me what to look out for when it came to letting people in."

"But his house has been left open without him being there," said Brennan.

"Jack's next-door neighbour, Ken, he would have mentioned anything unusual like the alarms going off," I said, and Gray nodded.

"I'll pay him a visit and double-check to make sure," said Gray.

"What if it's a past trainee?" I managed to step in the room a little but avoided looking at the screens. "Someone who's been to Jack's? Someone that Mark Shaw got to before he died?"

"If it was a past trainee who Mark had gotten to before he died," said Gray, "Mark would have known who I was, who you were all those months back."

I just about saw the logic behind that.

"And Jack's trained nobody else at his house since, either," said Carr. "I'll still run a check on past trainees to make sure."

"But it is someone who knows Jack, his habits, his lifestyle, his home." I eased against a wall, life spinning again.

"You need to sit down, Jan," said Gray, pulling a chair out. But sitting in a chair that had been occupied by someone who watched every aspect of that nightmare down there, it made me want to throw up.

"No," I forced through my teeth. Showing weakness would get me shunted out of the picture, although as his grip tightened on his sidearm, Gray's look didn't say that.

"Jack's cognitive therapist is new to the MC." Gray was talking to Brennan now, yet still looking over here. "I vetted her before she took him on: married, two kids, settled financially. But she would know his personal and social traits; home would be out of professional scope, but that's not saying she can't be ruled out."

"Got it," said Carr, although I never saw her take out pen and paper.

"A list, you said?" said Gray to me, and I nodded as he narrowed his eyes. "That suggests to me that Vince wasn't in control of this."

"Why?" I said with a frown.

"Doms have their own signatures," he replied, "their own preferences when it comes to dealing with a sub. You said they went by a list. Someone hired him knowing a Dom would be traceable because of his preferences, his style. They needed a non-dom." His breathing seemed to be deliberately controlled.

"A rapist," said Brennan.

"I've already said that," I snarled, but Gray shook his head.

"One with a history, Jan, one who would see the BDSM through because it fed his own desire to control." He looked at Carr. "See who's known. Go with first names, Nina," said Gray, causing her to pause. "He seems arrogant enough to think he wouldn't get caught. Also tie it into the other names: Henry, Leo. Match it up to any DNA forensics pick-up. He'd work with people who shared his MO, people he trusts." As Nina nodded and left, Gray came over to Brennan. "The people who funded this…" he said to him. "They would need someone in the community, someone with connections who's not stupid enough to hand them a Dom, but who would have the right connections that would put them in touch with the likes of Vince."

"Even suggest that a Dom would be traced in the first place?" Brennan narrowed his eyes. "Someone with a knowledge of how the MC base worked, how they'd track things down too? How to hide and pass people on in the sex trade and make connections through it?"

"Keal," confirmed Gray. "That fuck's involved in this all right. Jack called it." He didn't even look at me before he was heading out of the obs room and calling out to no one in particular. "Find out where Mr Ryan Keal is."

"There's no time for a court order," said Brennan. "And Keal will just cry for that greased-up lawyer of his, like he's been doing for the past few years—"

"I can delay any communication from where he is so he can't call anyone," shouted Carr from somewhere.

"Not needed. He's under my culler contract now," shouted Gray. "Keep your teams' hands as clean as fucking possible from here on in. Stay out of any contact with

Keal."

I didn't know what the hell a culler contract meant, but I caught Gray by the arm, and he gave such a hard look. "You can't see this, Jan."

"Jack, he's my priority," I said flatly. "Everything else, that's yours."

That weighing up came in Gray's eyes again, staying there for a little longer this time, but the meaning was buried so quickly before I could read it. "You do nothing but follow my lead." Brennan joined us too now. "We find Jack, you make him your only priority," said Gray. "The rest... it's mine, do you hear?"

"You... you think Jack's okay?"

Gray glanced at Brennan, but no one said anything.

CHAPTER 27
KEAL

GRAY PUT A call in to some friends. MC? MI5? I wasn't really sure, didn't really care. The name Andrews cropped up and he received a message back only ten minutes later giving him Keal's exact location. Considering it was Monday afternoon when most people were just finishing off the work day and getting ready for New Year celebrations, I'd seen Gray only narrow his eyes on being told Keal was at home, apparently having left work only an hour ago *ill*.

"His home," I said, huddled in the car next to Gray. "This Keal, he got any kids? A wife?"

Gray shifted into gear but never replied, not for a good ten minutes until he'd avoided the main streets of London. "A girlfriend who's at work. One son called Logan. Thirty-three and not into Keal's business," he said eventually, his gaze straight ahead.

I nodded, focusing my attention on the car in front and trying to deny the blurring going on with my eyes.

"They touch you, Jan?"

Resting my head on the window, I kept my gaze firmly ahead.

"You told me about Jack." Gray's lips were thin, pale, looking like he was past any kind of discussion. "They… did Vince or any of his men, did they lay a hand on you too?"

"What did you do when you took my call, when you saw those texts?" Bone-tired, I folded my arms, hugging myself. Cold, I felt so cold. "Did you believe them?"

Gray's knuckles whitened on the steering wheel. "Yes," he said flatly.

"Without a time out call? You really think Jack would avoid you for this long?"

"I hurt him again, and—" Gray changed gears. "—Jack…." He ground his teeth, defining the muscles in his jaw. "So fucking unpredictable. Even with his disorders managed, there were never any guarantees. And you? You make this difficult. You—" Whatever else he was going to say, he seemed to stop himself.

"It never crossed your mind to double-check?"

"I fucking double-checked." Yeah. It was there in his eyes. "Steve had messages from Jack checking up on the Strachan side of things. Jack's father had messages to arrange cover for his work. He'd packed his clothes, made purchases on his card over in Essex; you'd also packed and sent regular messages to your mother."

I pushed up. "I *what?*"

Gray's attention was far too focused on the road, the way ahead. "You'd already booked time off work, I checked. I gained access to your mother's house and checked her phone records too."

"You—you broke into my mother's?"

"I checked," said Gray. "Your mother won't find any trace I've been there."

I screwed my face. "What… what did the texts say?"

"That you'd gone away with Jack. You'd be back after the New Year. One on Christmas day wishing her—"

I choked a sob. "Vince, *he knows my fucking mother, where she lives?*" I punched the dashboard a few times, grateful for the pain it brought. Something else to focus on, some other hurt, but barely any strength to do any real damage, barely any strength at all when I'd needed it. "What did you do with Jack's car keys?"

Gray frowned over at me as I looked at him. It scared the fucking life out of me that we had been made to disappear so professionally: no trace, no questions. Or at least questions that wouldn't have been asked for a few weeks, and by then—

"What the hell did you do with Jack's car keys, you fuck? He'll need them when he—"

"Easy," said Gray, quietly, casting a glance at me. "Jan, you're off track a little with your thoughts. I need you calm; I need you to stay focused just for a little longer, okay?"

"You started with the fucking questions." I instantly closed my eyes and bit back the anger.

"It's all right," said Gray, but a gentle touch that brushed my leg made me thump his touch away and sit in silence.

We drove for a while down the A216, then took a right into Rural Way. At the end of the street was a run of land that took us up to a security station. Two security guards sat in the box just before a huge gate, and I didn't question why Gray slowed, already flicking the switch for his window to come down.

"Can I help?" said one beefy-looking man in a black suit

as he stepped over. He leaned down into the window, and barely registering he'd done it, Gray put a Taser to his neck. The guard went down, but not before Gray caught him, then pushed him to the side. Already pushing out, a gun aimed on the second security guard to keep him still in the box, Gray ordered him out.

Urine stains marked the man's trousers as he lay there, rolling on the floor. Gray, his gun and gaze on the second security guard, flicked at something back inside the security box, and the gates rolled open.

"Down," he said to the guard, and the slim man quickly complied. The sound of crunching tyre came, and another two cars pulled up behind Gray's. Brennan and his men filed out, taking charge of the two guards as they were forced into the back of the Mercedes. Gray had a few quiet words with Brennan before coming back. He got in and put his foot on the accelerator.

"Listen carefully," he said quietly. "You don't panic. You can't be harmed in here. You don't get out. When I stop the car, you stay where you are, and you don't move until I tell you. Nobody else from my team will approach you, so if anyone but me even attempts to, they won't be friendly, and you drive away. Keys are in the ignition, I have a spare set. Keep the doors locked at all times."

The curved driveway took us up to a detached three-storey home, and as soon as we drew up to the house, the two security guards who had only curiously watched us drive up suddenly seemed to catch on that something was wrong. Dull thuds hit the Mercedes, and I flinched.

"Ballistic protected." Gray spoke calmly from my side, still driving. Now up by the main doors, Gray was suddenly out, using the Mercedes as protection as he took someone out. I looked straight ahead, gripping onto the seatbelt as shouts, cries, and the dull thud of bullets went up outside and around the car. Brennan and his men pulled up behind us again, and I stared ahead, blanking out the chaos outside. People were getting killed, but it was strange how it didn't matter; nothing mattered. Nothing but getting to Jack, and these bastards were in the way of that.

Everything fell quiet. Two men stood outside of Keal's house: Harry and one other of Gray's men from the warehouse. Blood lined the courtyard, long drag lines where bodies had been pulled across the floor. Part of me wanted to smile, wanted to follow the lines in some morbid game and see what chaos they led to, but I couldn't move.

Time passed, then someone pulled open my door and ordered me out. I sat there until Gray tugged on my arm. He was the only one with a key to the Mercedes, so it had to be Gray.

"Come on."

I got out, and Gray shut the door, his gaze back on the house and mine followed his.

"Jack?" I mumbled, but after watching me for a moment, Gray shook his head.

"Not yet. But you watch some of this from here on in. You need to watch some of this from here on in. Put these on." He passed me some black leather gloves, then indicated to the house. I followed him in a moment later. He wouldn't have let me if it hadn't been secured, and I clung onto that little spark of trust in him, even if it was only a little.

Nothing looked out of place inside, just the odd broken pane in the front door. But with white floor tile and walls, I was led into a lounge that looked pretty enough to welcome prospective buyers with all its white leather. A show home.

Where Keal's men had gone, I had no idea, didn't even ask. In here, it was just me, Gray, and the odd thump from upstairs that made Gray look up every now and again.

Seeming satisfied with something, Gray went and dragged one of the dining room chairs into the middle of the lounge.

"Keal?" I said eventually as movement came from back by the stairs.

"Just joining us," said Gray, pulling up a second chair and twisting it so he could sit and face the second chair in front of him.

"Ah," said Gray as Brennan pushed a struggling man into the lounge. "Nice to see you again, Ryan. How's your boy, Logan?"

"What? What the fuck are you playing at, Raoul?" Keal, hands bound behind his back, tried everything to push back the way he'd come. What the hell you'd expect look-wise from a sex trader, I didn't know, only that Keal wasn't it. He was all grey hair, friendly green eyes, old, about Jack's dad's age and looking Santa-friendly, only without the port belly, and dressed to impress with a very expensive-looking grey suit. He looked at me, and I swore he looked the sort to ask out for a drink. But then his gaze was back to Gray, already dismissing me like any company director bypassing the lowest paid office worker.

"I'll have your MI5 cock on my barbeque for this, you fuck," snarled Keal. "You can't come in here without a search warrant."

"Not here as MI5." Gray patted the empty chair. It was the first time I noticed he wore black leather gloves like mine. Brennan saw it too. "Come chat with me for a while."

"Chat?" Keal snorted. "Fucking cha—"

Brennan pushed him over, nearly making him stumble. "Likes his cupboards," he said, forcing Keal down into the chair by Gray. "Or hiding in them at least." Brennan tied Keal's feet to his chair, legs open, then backed off over to the door. Is that where they'd found Keal? Hiding? I eased down onto the settee, the aches and pains in my body groaning disgust. I was some distance away, but close enough to see the sweat forming on Keal's deeply tanned forehead. Something had him worried.

Gray gave a business sigh. "Three names, one chance to answer a single question," he said, easing back into the chair and crossing his arms. "The funder for the kidnap, Vince, Jack. Where are they?"

All of the fear seemed to drop from Keal and was replaced with a raised brow. "You kill my guards because you've misplaced that fag of yours, Gray?" He snorted. "Really shouldn't leave something of that refined quality lying around—who knows what will trip over and fall on top of it. Still, if you need a new one, I have a few on my list who might interest you, but you really should have come by my office to discuss your..." He smiled. "Weakness."

Gray sighed, eased forward, elbows resting on his knees and still looking so relaxed in unfriendly surroundings. "Nice place, Keal. Lacks a little colour, though."

Something flew past me, making me jerk, and I realised it was rope, very fine rope, maybe specially made. Gray caught it as he stood, nodding a thanks over to Brennan, then wrapped one end of it around Keal's throat, just once, before Brennan was over, holding Keal as Gray set the rope down Keal's back and tossed the rest under the chair. Sitting back down, he unzipped Keal's trousers, reached in, and pulled his cock and balls out. Giving a tut as Keal struggled, he picked up the rope, pulled Keal's balls down, then wrapped the end around them once, twice, three times, making sure the balls bulged into a purple mass as Keal cried out. He kicked the rope under the chair, and Brennan picked it up, stretching Keal's balls as far as they'd go under the chair, then he tightened it all up by throwing another loop around Keal's neck and fastening it.

With a look at me, Gray disappeared into the room behind and the faint sounds of drawers being sorted through filtered over as Brennan stepped back out of the way. Keal looked at me; I held his gaze.

He went to say something, but a clip up the head off Gray made Keal cry out. It had only been a cuff a parent would playfully give a kid up the ear, but the rope around Keal's balls was tied in such a way that even a small slap on the head would give maximum ball torture, stretching the sac so that his scrotum looked like it would crack open and his nuts would fall out.

"Jesus… Jesus," hissed Keal.

"You don't look or talk to him. I'm here," said Gray, and what he held took my attention. One was an extension cable, the other just a pair of standard hair straighteners. Gray hunted for a socket to plug the extension in, then unwound it back over to Keal and dropped it at his feet. After taking a seat, Gray plugged the hair straighteners in and set everything at his feet. "When you do talk to me, it's a simple answer to my question," he said. "And your answer is: where?"

Again Keal went to say something, again Gray tapped him on the cheek, causing the rope to shift and pull on his balls.

"*Fucking cunt,*" cried Keal, which won him another cuff

on the cheek.

"Language. Turns me on like fuck when Jack swears," said Gray, flatly. "But you, you're a worthless piece of shit." He seemed to weigh up Keal's cock. "Not a bad size," he said. "Always helps, that. Believe me. You don't know how awkward this technique can be when you've got a small dick to play with."

"Yeah, you wanna play with a cock? Wait until my solicitor hears what you've done—your bosses will have you bending over, kissing my feet, and taking every cock in my lawyer's whole fucking law department up your ass, you—"

Another slap cut off his words.

"Language," he said calmly. "Three names: the funder for the kidnapping, Vince, Jack; one question—where. Keep focus on that, please." Gray picked up the straighteners and tested out the heat by hovering between the V of the plates. "Expensive make." He eyed up the brand name, then shrugged. "Cheap ones work just as well." He wrapped the long cord around Keal's neck and Keal started to panic as Gray rested Keal's dick between the V of the plates, not quite touching, but close enough to make him squirm under its threat.

"Now." Gray pulled a lighter from his pocket. Damn strange. I'd never seen him smoke. "Can you remember that one question, Keal?"

Keal grunted something, then spat at Gray.

The slap at Keal's face came hard enough to snap Keal's head to the right this time—and force the one edge of the straighteners to scald part of Keal's dick as tension on the rope stretched his scrotum. His scream hit the air, and he instantly squirmed in the chair, forcing the other side of the plate to touch down, burning into the other side of his dick and balls.

"*Oh, fucking—*"

"Language." Gray sat back. "That's three times I've had to remind you now."

"*You bastard.*" Keal snorted through tears, but even keeping still singed pubes from the smell hitting the lounge.

Gray only shrugged. "Not yet, Keal." He leaned forward. "But it's coming." Keal's groin sported red blisters as tears and snot streamed his face. "Now," said Gray. "Where's my sub? It has a really simple answer."

"*I don't know,*" cried Keal, and Gray flicked at his lighter and took it close to Keal's hip.

"Signature marks for a Dom, they're like linguistic fingerprints. All those subtle techniques used to mark the body, they let you know which Dom has handled a sub." The flame of the lighter caught Gray's eyes, stealing all that beautiful blue and taking it into dead blackness. "Really beautiful to read on a body." He offered this smile, just a slight curl of lips as he watched the play of the flame so close to skin. "But do you know, in all the years I've known Jack, he's only ever touched the surface to what I really… like." He focused a little more. "I love him too much to let him know the real bastard." A sly look at Keal. "You know how that feels, right? You like to keep your Logan away from your shit?" He never expected an answer, although Keal looked too tormented to reply as his gaze darted between the lighter and the straighteners shaping his dick. "Yeah, you see it now. Move away from this—" He held up the lighter. "—you'll burn your balls. You don't move, the lighter burns slowly through your hip." Gray flicked it and pressed it into place.

Keal screamed, but tried his hardest to keep still, obviously choosing his hip over burning his balls in the V of the plates.

"Ah… progress," said Gray. "Survival instincts are in force: a will to not get marked too much. Take the lesser burn. Good. You acknowledge choice; that there is a choice here. Interesting how the mind works under threat. Now, let's push that survival instinct a little further." He kept the flame against Keal's hip, and a slight smell of burning meat crept over the cries. Even when Keal cried mercy, Gray kept it there. "My sub?" he said quietly. "Vince? The fool who's funded it all… where are they?"

"I don't know the funder," shouted Keal, sobbing.

"Hm." Gray tilted his head, then finally pulled away the lighter and slipped it in his pocket. "But by default, that says you *do* know about my sub and Vince."

"Yeah. And like fuck will I tell you, you cunt. You're fucking marking me—your signature print. One I'll see you do fucking time for. One I'll—"

"Tell me more about your son." Gray took off Keal's tie, and he sounded so… normal asking that. "How old is he? A little older than Jack?"

Keal frowned—then squealed long and hard. Gray squeezed the edges of the straighteners together, crushing Keal's dick and balls in a scalding vice. Now he slowly wound Keal's tie around the straighteners, tying the plates shut. "He into games like you too, Keal? You want me to pay him a visit? Keep it in the family, so to speak?" Such a cold smile as he slapped Keal's face to focus attention. "Jack's not into incest—but me? I'll burn my way through any piece of cattle dumb enough to step in the playing field. Because that's all this is to me, Keal. A playing field. One I'll always fucking love."

Keal's cries were horrific, like a rat in a trap, and I'd heard a fair few of those scream.

"*Pleeeeeas—*"

"*My fucking sub!*" shouted Gray. "Where is he?"

"*Main Street, number twelve. Vince.... There.*"

"Password?"

"What?"

"Fucking code you swap between each other so they know it's you. What is it?"

"*Bourbon.*"

Gray pulled the tie tighter. "You lying to me, Keal?"

"*No. For godssake—no.*"

Gray pulled the straighteners off, leaving Keal yelping and crying in the chair as skin melted away too.

"You're in serious shit, Raoul," sobbed Keal. "I'll have you slung in jail and make sure every goddamn con in there knows you're ex-cop rape fodder."

"I've already spent many a night in and out of prisons." Gray got to his feet and pulled two things out of his jacket. "Decrease the surplus overpopulation... it's our playground."

Keal went as quiet as me as Gray attached a silencer to a sidearm.

"Wait. You..." Keal's voice came as a whisper, his gaze darting between the silencer and Gray. "You don't carry a fucking gun licence. You're MI5."

The sidearm levelled smack bang in the middle of Keal's forehead. "I'd sack your intelligence department, Keal. You've got no fucking clue as to what nest you've stepped in."

Brennan came over to me, the grip on my arm more

than suggesting I leave now.

Gray's hand wasn't even shaking, and I wanted—needed to see it not lose his grip.

"Get him out now," said Gray, not looking my way.

Brennan pulled me out into the hall, then blocked my view when I tried to sidestep him, get past, maybe not shout, not cry against what Gray was threatening, maybe just to see, needing to—"Fucking see."

"Listen. You're different. I see that now, and—" Keal whimpered, sniffled as though he was crying, and the legs of the chair he was tied to tapping his need to get out—run. "I know other things."

"Yeah, no doubt you do," said Gray, softly. "But you'd tie my people up in bullshit for months to escape the inevitable. And I'm pissed off enough."

Carr brushed by me, along with other men carrying computers and CCTV equipment. Keal's other guards were also nowhere to be seen. Everyone was leaving. All evidence removed.

"No. Christ. You do this, they'll know," shouted Keal. "Whoever paid to fuck your two whores over, they'll—you kill me, they'll know it's you."

"Yeah," said Gray, and the chair stopped moving, as though Gray rested his foot on the seat between Keal's legs, keeping him still. "Guess they will."

Brennan came in close, pinning me against the wall. Not to hurt, but to shield as hands pressed to my ears, blocking out whatever came next. Didn't matter, I still jerked even though I knew no noise would come from the silencer. It was more to block out the scream that was cut short. Then as Brennan backed off and quiet hit the hall, I pushed him away, stumbling out into the light, over to the car.

Brennan came out as I doubled over behind the boot, throwing up. Gray took longer, and when he came out, he carried the rope he'd used to tie Keal down, some tinged with a heavy hint of red.

"Get in the car, Jan," he said calmly, and I stared at him as Brennan moved away from me, over to Gray.

"You've got two, maybe three hours before the director-general gets word," said Brennan, close to Gray's ear as Gray pulled open a door to one of Keal's cars.

"Keal's been on the MI5 hit list for a few months," Gray mumbled back, the gun now out of sight. "A culler contract would have been called in eventually."

"Yeah, but you know what the bastard's like for wanting to make sure your MI5 ranks are closed and watertight when a culling like this takes place. The director-general has influence."

Gray snorted. "Not over this. I'll call in housecleaning to sort any official details over Keal's death."

After a moment Brennan winced and hit his arm. "Okay. I'm back with the confiscated tech. I'll borrow Konami from you to see what secrets he can pull from them, if that's okay? Carr is with you." Brennan flicked a look over as Gray gave him the keys to the Merc. Why the fuck was he giving Brennan the Merc keys? "He should come with me," added Brennan.

"No," bit Gray as he flicked a look over at me. "Jack's his concern."

Giving a puzzled frown, Brennan nodded. "Jan, go on." He was still looking at Gray. "Please."

CHAPTER 28
12 MAIN STREET

BESIDES HAVING A fresh coat of paint on the front door, Twelve Main Street looked no different than the other terraced houses lining the road. Like Jack's neighbourhood, curtains twitched, some onlookers curious, some perhaps opportunist. Yet get a police car around here, nobody would have seen or heard a thing. Maybe that was how Gray liked it or had played it countless times in the past. He hardly seemed interested in how some people were looking, that cattle comment digging a little deeper now. The switch in cars made sense, leaving the Mercedes with Brennan and opting for one of Keal's, with Mistress Carr having done the same with her car. That included not drawing her sidearm. Mannerisms were enough to say that people here were better off hidden behind their curtains. Although having me stumbling from the car to the front door no doubt raised a few brows. Gray had already given me my order, but his gaze when I joined them was enough to say *stay back* as he slipped his hand in his jacket.

A nod at Carr, and she pressed the bell.

"Who's there?" came a voice from inside.

Eyes closed, resting my head against the rough rendering of the wall, I whispered, "The doctor." The fear was there in the man's voice. "Goes by 'Doc.'" I frowned. "A drinker."

"Doc," called Gray. "One of Keal's. Bourbon."

"Oh thank—" A few locks were drawn. "—hell. Ketamine, have you got some ket—"

Gray hit Doc in the face with his palm, sending him staggering back. There was a shout, then another thud as Gray took care of someone else behind the door, finishing by making sure his black gloves were pulled up with a creak of leather. Carr followed, and I gave them a few minutes, just staying against the wall and nearly lulled into a strange safety as silencers added thuds to the whoosh of the passing traffic. A whistle came from inside, forcing me to shake off the need to fall, and I eased inside. Carr was in the lounge, one man meeting her knee between his legs, another already on the floor. She gave a nod over to me, then indicated upstairs with a flick of her eyes, her gun levelled on the man at her feet. The two men from by the door were also in there with her. Four down.

I took the stairs slowly, feeling every pull on the muscles in my legs and arms. The stairs were a winding sort, obviously saving space, which only added to the whole-world-spinning effect. It took me into a small hall, which then led through into a front bedroom. The door was open and three men lay on the floor, one moving, gripping his shoulder, the other two... not. Gray had Doc up against the wall, his silencer up under his chin, making the man look up for divine intervention.

"Vince? Henry?" said Gray, that calmness still in his voice, and I knew he was talking to me even though he never took his gaze off Doc.

"None of these," I said, distracted by another door that led into what must have been a back bedroom. I didn't look at Gray as I made my way over.

I should have jolted when Doc was slammed face-first into the door, stopping me from entering, but it was scary how little feeling came, especially hearing Doc's pleas to be set free, how he had a family, wife, kids.... Gray threw me a hard glance. It took me a while to realise it was for thinking of opening a door without it being cleared. Grabbing the doctor by the collar, using him as a shield, Gray gave me the nod to stand out of the way. He pulled the door open, pushed Doc in front of him, to which Doc instantly gave a yelp, covered his face, and cried a warning of, "Vince, it's me."

The bastard was in here.

But hearing no scuffles as Gray went in, I followed a few seconds later. A look around the dingy backroom said Vince wasn't there, but with how still Gray stood—somebody else was.

Arms bound out wide on the bed, black blindfold on, sheet down to a very bruised waist, Jack lay naked on the mattress, not moving, but his chest—his fucking chest.

"Move...." After pushing past Gray, I clambered onto the bed and tugged the ties from Jack's wrists. Blood dampened the sheet between Jack's legs, and I ignored the stains as I pulled him onto my lap, taking care to remove his blindfold. An oxygen tank and mask stood watch close by, some tubes to suggest Jack had been given fluids, drugs, maybe antibiotics. He was bleeding, bruised, battered... but breathing—he was still fucking breathing.

"Got you, Jack." I hugged him close. "Fucking got you now, baby." Head, face, cheek, I kissed it all, then brushed away the hair from his eyes, hating how limp his body was, how cold and clammy he felt as I rocked him there on the bed—how blood stained around his nose. But, breathing— a soft rise and fall of his chest filtered through, even though it ended in this long, drawn-out rattle. He was still fucking breathing.

A huff, Doc was pushed down by the bed, knocking us slightly as Gray's brief aim of firearm was enough to make sure Doc stayed exactly where he'd been dropped. Gun lowered, kept held in both hands, Gray glanced down at me. At Jack. His business face never fell. I was ready to call enough, running away with what I had and not looking back, but Gray....

Now over by what must be the bathroom, Gray opened the door—and instantly swept back, out of the path of a bloodied baseball bat that Vince swung at him. As it crashed into the door, Gray took aim and shot Vince in the shoulder at point-blank range. A sharp kick at the back of his knees helped Vince slump down, and in the next moment, Gray had given six or seven bone-cracking kicks to the man's ribs, then two to his head that left Vince moaning on the floor as he curled into the door for cover.

Easing off, Gray aimed his gun at Vince's head.

"You won't kill me," Vince let rush from his mouth, trying to hide as he offered a faltering and very blood-filled smile. "I know... know what you need." He tried a laugh, some attempt at a brave front, but as Vince got my full attention now, it slipped. "Deal. I'll do a deal... I'll give you a name, you give me a cell with as much access to... to—" That brave tint in his eyes flickered back into life for a moment, escaping his agony, "—access to pretty boys like your slut over there—we're both happy."

Vince groaned. "I'll do the rehab classes: make you look good." Again the need to try and keep some of the control filtered in the look he gave over to us. "Ask me nice, I might even let what I've done to your slag over there carry me through the lonely nights." Another laugh, looking more pained by the minute as though nervous of how quiet Gray was. "Christ knows he'll be remembering me for a few thousand nights to come, right?" He coughed, choked up some blood.

"But such a sweet, sexy kid beneath all that roughness." A pause, Vince looked up at Gray. "But you know that, don't you, tough guy? It's why you keep him close." Vince started to shiver under Gray's scrutiny. "Mine now, though, sez so on his skin. Mine in every possible w—"

A thud, Vince hit the floor. Hard. Then everything was quiet but for Jack's rattled breathing.

After resting Jack gently down on the bed, I managed to ease over to Gray. He cuffed Vince's hands behind his back now while Vince was out of it. A look up at me, the blueness to his eyes swallowed by black, Gray got to his feet, then dragged Vince back into the bathroom, maybe to cuff him to some pipes.

"Information, Jan," he said, coming out of the bathroom. "You have all you need over there. You don't watch me now."

I heard him say it, heard his footsteps as they headed for the door, then Gray grabbed Doc and took him to search for whatever tools Gray no doubt needed.

Vince started to stir, just the soft shuffle of shoe on bathroom tile.

"Hmph. Really bloody hated my come on him, remember, pet?" Vince choked out, and I could picture him smirking, hidden away in the bathroom. "Even with how fucking good he is to have… to have underneath you, he's such a fucking headcase with things like that, right?"

The red smear lines from Gray dragging Vince into the bathroom looked so vivid, so vicious.

"I mean." Vince's voice was slurred, like blood ran into his mouth and all that came out was that thick, slicked up sound. "How does a slag like that, whose probably been fucked more times than even I could get it up, how does he survive in life with those problems?" Quiet, almost as though he'd passed out, then—"Just buh-buh-begs for fucking it out of his system, if you ask me. Like you on Christmas night, eh?" A snort of laughter came. "You remember Christmas night, Jan? How real men get dirty?"

The baseball bat slept just a few inches from my feet.

"His ass is gonna be sore for a while, though. Right along with yours," chuckled Vince as I picked the bat up. "Woke up all hard 'n' horny after you ran away and left him with me, but blushing and crying frustration with how he needed something extra. Have to give him what he wants to ease the need sometimes, right? So I asked him real… real sweet to let me tie him up and play at rape again. Well." Vince gave a blood-filled chuckle. "You should have been here for that last time, pansy boy. You missed one hell of a fuck session. Bitch really fucking cried when I raped his ass hard, then tried to fuck that bat up him in there to stop him wanting it rough ever again. An—"

I was there, in the bathroom, baseball bat in hand and hitting, just hitting. Jaw first, sending out a sickening crack I wanted to carry on hearing, then missing and catching the toilet. White bone and blood mixed on the end of the bat, and I swung it again, needing more blood and bone on the walls, dirtying the walls, showing how real men, they really can get dirty now.

"*No, dammit.*" Someone swept in behind me, pulling me

out of the bathroom, hands wrapping around mine with enough persuasion to stop hitting anything else. Behind, Vince gurgled something on the floor, the sound of blood bubbling from his mouth, and I wanted to make it bubble some more, drain every last ounce out of his fucking body, use it to wash the floor, roll around in it, let it cover me, get dirty, let real men get dirty and—

"You bring every ounce of normality to our table, Jan," Gray whispered quietly. "That's what holds Jack, and as jealous as I am that you can give him that, I can't thank you enough for it. His head needs grounding in normality sometimes."

"He raped him," I said quietly.

Gray pulled his hold a little tighter. "I know."

"So loving, Gray," I mumbled. "Jack just wanted to hide, to stay close. Not tough, not so fucking tough." I suddenly cried out. *"And Vince said he answered all of that tenderness by raping him with a fucking bat."*

"Easy. Take into account that he could just be winding things up, Jan. You need to let it go. Focus on Jack." Gray's head rested against mine. "Please…" Quiet. "I need you to focus on Jack for me."

The bat slipped from my hands, into Gray's, and looking briefly back at him, I went over to the bed. Blood spotting the sheets around Jack's thighs suggested more than just words, and I choked down sickness.

Carr was there now too, checking Jack's pulse, mine, as I clambered back by Jack, again pulling his head onto my lap, letting life play out around us as I kept sweeping the hair from his eyes. He stirred at one point, just briefly, and made things worse by mumbling "Dad," before the bliss of a drug-induced sleep pulled him back under.

"Yeah," I whispered, "get you home, martial arts guy. Let you sleep. You need to—"

Vince's chuckle hit the air, and I glanced up to see Gray head into the bathroom. Gray hadn't looked back at Jack since, not once. Maybe there was a reason for that, that he was okay so long as—

Please... I need you to focus on Jack for me.

"Oh, pansy boy there will get Jack back in body." Vince was back to choking blood, his voice barely audible. Sounded like the bastard was hiding. I needed him to be hiding. "As for where his fucking head will be... right here. His pretty ass and head will always be right fucking here, taking my cock."

"You've been left a little in the lurch, haven't you, Vince?" That... normalness to Gray's voice sounded so wrong in the context of all this mess and hurt.

I went to look back, but a finger under my chin from Carr and her shake of head stopped me.

"See, I noticed a few things. It's why I haven't bothered finding any toys to play with," said Gray, and I had enough time to pick up how the baseball bat wasn't anywhere to be seen. "There's no cameras here," Gray added quietly, and again another touch under my chin stopped me from looking around to check.

"On Jack," said Carr quietly, her gaze going to the bathroom. "You focus on Jack for him, okay, honey?"

"The doc was a little too eager to open up the door and get some ketamine in here." Gray again. "Has Jack been stirring a little lately, hmmm?"

"So fucking what?" snapped Vince.

"Where's your audience gone? And you, are you too stupid to ask why?"

Everything went quiet in the bathroom.

"You've been on your own since you got here, right?" Vince answered that with a strangled cry. "They paid all of that money out to set this up, then cut and ran when it started falling apart?" Gray went quiet, then—"You really should have asked why, Vince. I'd have liked you a little more, then."

I jerked, forcing my eyes shut hearing the sound of a bat hitting... something: hopefully the bastard's jaw. The need to look was there, to see if teeth slept with the blood on the floor, if the angle of Vince's neck was twisted to an impossible angle as bones snapped, then the sound came again, and—

"For them, you fuck," said Gray, flatly.

Carr smiled at me, hinting with her eyes that paramedics were here. I stood, watching them call Jack's name as lines were put in his veins, and blankets were wrapped over him and one around me. An oxygen mask came next, then Jack was being lifted onto a stretcher. Some other things were on the bedside unit: mine and Jack's mobiles, and after picking them up, I slipped them in my pocket.

Carr was busy with Jack, and this time she wasn't there to stop me looking back into the bathroom, at Gray, how he turned to look at me with the bloodied bat in his hands. I didn't look away. I made damn sure I didn't look away, now needing to see him—imprint everything about who he was and what he'd done to Vince in my mind. No secrets, no layers, just exactly what Gray was, what he'd done— what he'd... love *doing* to the rest of these bastards.

And yeah, I liked how Vince looked there at his feet, hair matted with blood, skin missing on part of his skull. It was a good look. A damn good fucking look. One I never wanted to forget, because I needed to know Vince was gone and wouldn't be coming back.

CHAPTER 29
AFTERCARE

IT HAD TAKEN a lifetime to get back to the Masters' Circle. Part of me wanted to question why they hadn't taken Jack to hospital, but then this was the MC, with all the best in private healthcare that life could offer. Perhaps it was the better choice.

The room we were taken to was full of bodies, but I couldn't really see who: most faces just white blurs, voices just as obscure. Brennan was there with Mistress Carr, both quiet as they stood in the shadow of the doorway. I sat in a chair by Jack, stroking repeatedly through his hair. He felt hot to the touch, his body coated in a thin sheen of perspiration, something I hadn't noticed earlier. He lay on his side, facing me, a ruffled sheet offering him a little modesty around his groin as doctors busied themselves.

The startling whiteness of the observation room only made the reality of what had happened worse. In amongst the bruises, bites, and branding mark, the hell of the past two weeks was on full display. There was no dirt, Jack looked surprisingly clean, yet among more recent bloodstains on his inner thighs, finger bruises and thumb imprints marked paths of indecency all over him, showing he'd been held down. Whip marks from what looked more like a cable covered one side of his body, more defensive marks on the back of his right hand where it appeared he'd curled to his side and tried to shield his head. Bruising on his face from his beating was never more colourful, but the mark around his throat was new. It looked like someone had controlled his breathing in a more frightening way.

I knew what happened whilst he'd been with me of a night, but what the hell had happened in the last few days? During those times he hadn't been with me? He'd been ill. Vince wouldn't have used the bat, not....

I closed my eyes, shut it away. I could see Gray for who he was; I couldn't see Jack for what Henry and Vince had made him. What I'd made him Christmas night after Vince had spilled his come on him.

"Okay," said a doctor who stood behind Jack. "We need to get him into surgery right away."

This doctor barely looked out of med school, young, too young, and he was feeling Jack's stomach. He was *touching* Jack's stomach, and having anyone touch Jack again...?

"In the last hour, we've made every effort to stabilise his condition. Blood pressure itself is sufficient now and blood levels are balanced, and under antibiotic treatment, the inflammatory markers haven't risen any further. But he is still in a lot of pain despite high-dose analgesics. There is diffuse abdominal rigidity and also abdominal distension. Sonography revealed free fluid in the abdominal cavity, and this is really worrying." A look of concern filled the doctor's thin face as he carried on prodding. Then he shifted his touch around to between Jack's legs, and I tensed, wanting to hit him for touching Jack in such an intimate way. Images of the last man who'd touched him there surfaced, and I clenched my fist.

"Yeah," said the doctor quietly. "Based on clinical symptoms and laboratory findings, I suspect an anorectal trauma and most likely a rectal or colorectal perforation further up."

I didn't know what the hell that meant, but the bat and Vince's grin came sickeningly to mind as I eased out of my seat to allow the nurse access.

"Plus, he's running a fever," said the young doctor, now checking the reading taken from Jack's ear. "All of this hints at peritonitis." He nodded thoughtfully. "How serious the internal injuries are can only be clarified by surgery, though. It's planned we keep the procedure minimal invasive. That means endoscopy and laparoscopy. But you should know, it can only be decided intraoperatively whether he can be spared an open surgery. We want to avoid that if possible. Time is working against us in this case, and that's why we should get mov—"

Movement back by the door caught my attention. Gently pushing past Brennan and Carr, Gray came through, hands now clean, clothes changed or burned, one of the two. His gaze found mine, then either through natural default or the inability not to look away anymore, Gray's gaze rested on Jack.

"Ah." He seemed transfixed on Jack. His hip. "You." He came a little closer, his lips thinning, a hand running through his hair. "Get... get that the fuck *off* him."

The branding initial on Jack's hip was exposed, the V all open and scabbing. I didn't know much about branding; neither had Vince by the look of things. That looked more serious than the burn most brandings left. More like a third-degree than anything else. Vince had hit Jack's hip twice, and in the same place, maybe thinking it would mark him faster. There was no infection, suggesting Vince had at least taken care of that. Said it all really: that he'd take care of the ownership mark and not Jack.

The doctor started to say something to Gray, looking more ready to wheel Jack into surgery, but Gray, that aggressive look back on his face that said the doctor had moved when he should have stayed at a safe distance, he shifted a hell of a lot quicker, grabbing the young man and pinning him down on the bed.

"It'll fuck with his head. Get that cunt's fucking ownership mark off him, or I swear to God I'll—"

I was over, grabbing at Gray, not making any difference until Brennan stepped in and we managed to drag him out into the hall. Brennan pushed him away from the room, saying nothing. Gray regained his footing, only to glare at me, Brennan—then the coffee machine he spotted took all of Gray's anger and rage as he started to kick the shit out of it.

"Fucker," he cried. *"Thought the bastard was winding things up saying he'd brand—"* Gray cut himself off with a cry, and this time Brennan seemed unwilling to intervene a second time as Gray pulled the coffee machine to the floor, sending bits flying over to us. *"Fucking mine. Nobody's ever but fucking mine."*

I watched, waited, let the chaos run as he kicked at the machine. Yet giving a look over at me, something seemed to drain out of Gray, and he slumped back against the wall, crying out. As Jack was wheeled from the room, I stepped through the debris of the coffee machine and went over to Gray. He went to push away, but I pulled him into a hold. There was a fight for a second to get me off, then he rested into silence against me, his head on my shoulder.

"That night he walked," I said quietly, "Jack, he held onto me saying he'd see you in the morning. Said he knew better than anyone how Cutter fucked with someone's head." I kissed Gray's cheek. "Jack said he loved you too much to let Cutter take you down too, that he should have taken his own head out of his ass, kissed the hell out of you, and just told you again how much he loved you." I knew I held Gray, but I didn't *feel* Gray. "The only thing that stopped him was those bastards, Gray."

Gray gripped at me for the briefest of seconds, and I returned it.

"Whoever paid to watch that?" I said to him. "They were the only thing that stopped him coming back." I closed my eyes. "Fucking loves you so much, Gray. Saw it every time they put your photo by him, how he'd risk rape and torture just to brush his cheek against yours, how they twisted that. So for his sake, for mine, please remember that. You focus on that: you find the bastards—" I gripped his hair, hard, and meant every word that I breathed next. "—and you make it stop."

Gray's breathing deepened, that long inhale, exhale, and he pulled away to run a hand through his hair. A look back down at Brennan, at me, he gave a nod. Just the one.

"Anything from where we were held?" I asked quietly, and Gray shook his head, his hand going on the back of my neck, pulling me back in close.

"Prints showed that the obs room only had Vince and his bastards in there." He dropped his head a touch, resting against mine. "It's too early for anything else, but I get the feeling whoever funded this never went near the warehouse itself, or they were careful enough to cover their tracks."

I returned the touch resting on the back of my neck, digging a little harder into Gray's. Then things started to come back, the grey areas as talking back down the corridor filtered over. "There was a voice that came over the speaker system. Someone Vince listened to."

Gray looked up. "It's possible that the computers were hooked up to an external live webcam feed."

"The funder could have been watching from home?"

"If they wanted to lie low, yes. You say he spoke?"

I nodded. "Sounded strange, though."

"How?"

I shrugged. "Doctored," I said to him. "Like the voice was being distorted."

"Good," said Gray.

"Good?" I couldn't understand that. "How?"

"Because it suggests they didn't want their voice recognised, so...." Gray pulled back slightly.

"What?"

He shook it off, but still seemed a little distracted. "How angry was Lisa with you, Jan? Rob's wife?"

It hit me why he'd gone quiet. "You..." I swallowed hard. "You think this is down to me? That Lisa wanted revenge and—" I stopped talking when I tugged two familiar items out. A frown crept in, and I turned away only to have Gray pull at my arm and take the mobile phones off me.

"You shouldn't have taken these." He was already nodding over to Brennan, who dipped into the medical room Jack had just been in. He came out a moment later with two plastic bags.

"I need Jack's phone, Gray," I said quietly. "I..." I

shrugged. "I don't know his mom's and dad's numbers. They need to know."

"I know," Gray said quietly, but he still slipped one mobile in one bag, another in the other. Sealing one after the other, he then handed me Jack's mobile. "Keep it in that." A wipe of hand over his face, Gray tapped at the mobile I held. "I need that back when you're done."

I nodded and sorted through for Gregory's number.

The dialling tone kicked in, then a voice the other end said, "Jack?" Gregory didn't sound happy. "For God's sake, boy. I just hope your time with lover boy was worth me being a manager down over the Christmas period. I had to get Paul to cover your ass, and you know how much your ass riles him. You—"

"Mr Harrison?" I stopped him mid-flow. "Gregory, it's Jan Richards here—"

"Jan?" A pause. "Oh, I'm sorry, son. I'm just a little pissed with Jack. Can you put him on?"

A hand went to my mouth. Then I kept it brief, not going over any details, just giving Greg the directions to the base as Gray nodded, let him know that Jack was in surgery, then told him to drive carefully. For all of the minute it lasted, it was the hardest phone call I'd had to make.

Two security men were wrestling the coffee machine back to its feet when I looked back, although it wouldn't work again from the amount of water that bled on the floor. Giving Gray a thin smile, I handed Jack's phone over, looking down at mine and burying the need to smash it to pieces and leave it bleeding with the coffee machine.

"You two, in here," said Brennan, indicating to a side room opposite Jack's. I slumped down next to Gray as he sat on a comfortable-looking settee, my hands falling on my knees. Nobody spoke, which was strange considering I thought that was why Brennan had pulled us out of the corridor, maybe to talk about anything he gained from Keal's computers even though his team and this Konami had only had them for a few hours. But quiet. Everything was so quiet, Brennan and Gray sharing that quietness, a glance.

The image was there, choosing a Christmas tree with Jack, dragging the giant thing into Gray's, and Gray trying to look so bloody pissed as Jack hung that spanner after such a sheepish shrug.

Not so tough. Not so fucking tough at all.

A sob choked free.

"Jan." There was a touch to my knee, and I opened my eyes to find Brennan crouched by me. "I need to get you checked over by the doctor now." He took my hand, turned it over, and ran his thumb over the bruises ringing my wrist.

"I'm okay." I pulled away from the touch. A shake of head, Brennan held my hand up and watched how badly it shook.

"No. You're not," he said gently. "You need—"

"Jack," I said quietly. "Just need Jack…." I shrugged. "So badly now. Just, just leave me alone, yeah? I'm good. They barely did anything to me."

An arm slipped around my shoulders, and I jerked away only to find Gray pull a little harder before my head found his shoulder. "Fucking sleep. You're both in a place with enough surgeons, MI5, CID, MOD ops, and MC security to make the Queen sleep soundly."

Too little too late. That nearly pulled me away from

Gray, but he held on a little tighter, his silence maybe suspecting it. After that, nothing mattered. My body didn't care, started to shut down without my consent. Even my own body denied me control now, and it pulled me into a darkness that brought pain between my thighs and a heavy body that weighed me down, threatening to drown....

CHAPTER 30
BROKEN PIECES

I WOKE TO darkness and the shuffling of feet outside. Breathing came to a stop, caught in the fear that any noise would open doors and Henry would come in for force-feeding time. Then other senses kicked into gear, soft sheets against my cheek, against my shoulder as I lay curled to my side. Disinfectant too. There was also that thin pencil of light through the rim of the door, and it ran over a smooth, polished floor. MC's infirmary. I was in the MC's infirmary, and I'd been shifted from the leather settee onto a bed. From the corridor came shouting, and someone sounded aggravated—

I eased up, looking towards the door. Several voices drifted over the quiet of the hospital room, and I tilted my ear to try and catch what was said, but the mix was too much, tones too angry. Wincing at the aches in my body, I went to ease off the bed, the fact I was wearing a hospital gown hitting me a little more seeing my bare legs. A catheter jutted out of my hand, and I blindly found the IV stand next to the bed. Electrolyte solution in the IV bag shifted from side to side as I made it over to the voices in the corridor. Managing to pull the door open, I blinked against the onslaught of light.

Gray was just off to the right, not far from the reception desk, where the coffee machine had lain broken. Brennan was close by, and I recognised Elena immediately, looking irate and pale not far from them, but still so business-like in her suit. And the other older man next to her, he must have been Gregory. Jack's dad. Yeah. He looked like Jack's dad.

I coughed. Nothing deliberate, just an ache from my ribs and sore throat, everything feeling a little hot, chesty. Conversation stopped and people looked over. I offered a small smile, but Gray's eyes darkened, then he was by me, calling a nurse over. "It's okay," I mumbled, but Gray was already back with the nurse as she stopped by us.

"Mr Richards should be sedated. Why the fuck is no one watching his obs—"

"Jan?" Greg pulled Gray away from me as Elena came over. "Jan Richards? My God...." Hands mapped my face as he looked me over. "Jan.... Just what the hell's gone on, son? You, you look—" He looked at Gray. "Just what the hell is going on?"

"Mr Harrison—"

"Don't you fucking Mr anything me, Gray," shouted Greg, and I saw all of Jack's inherited ability to go from calm to chaos right there. Greg was suddenly very calm again as he glanced briefly at me, then back at Gray. "The only time people get hurt is when you're around. So you, you tell me what... you tell me just what the hell's going on here. Where's my son?"

The doctor who had helped wheel Jack away came over, looking very tired. "Mr Richards, Mr Raoul—"

I stopped him there, knowing Greg and Elena needed to

hear this too. "This..." I looked at them both, "... these are Jack's parents. Gregory and Elena Harrison."

The young doctor nodded, paused long enough to shake their hands, then said, "Come on through, please." He indicated back into my room. Not that I minded. I stepped aside to let Greg and Elena enter, waited for Gray and Brennan to go through, too, but when they didn't move, more waited for me, I slipped in after the doctor, who was wiping the sleep from his eyes. Greg and Elena had taken the two chairs next to my bed, the young surgeon sat opposite, Brennan stayed back by the door after he came in last.

I opted for resting right there against the wall. Gray didn't move from by my side, the tension hidden in his face but apparent in his body as he stayed resting back against the wall with me.

"Okay," said the doctor with a sigh. "We've given Jack a strong sedative that will be topped up over the next twenty-four hours. He sustained a number of serious injuries, and tied in with the ketamine overdoses, I took the decision to keep him sedated to allow his body extra time to heal." The young doctor glanced briefly at Gray before focusing on Greg and Elena. He looked uncomfortable, more so towards Gray than anyone else. "Among several deep anal fissures, which were sewn, the rectum a little further up was perforated. That caused internal bleeding and local peritonitis. We had already suspected that much before surgery because of the fever and the abdominal distension. Fortunately, the injured area was covered so that no diffuse peritonitis has developed. The perforation could be completely repaired and will heal easily without further complications. The abdomen was lavaged after that, and antibiotics will work against the infection. On the positive side, the laboratory findings have mostly normalised by now. But he's still very sick from the infection. Besides the contusions to his body, the burning to his hip, there was also penile trauma. We had to do a retrograde urethrogram to rule out urethral injury—"

"I'm sorry?" Greg was looking around us. "How...." He shrugged. "Just what kind of accident causes those kinds of injuries?"

The young doctor looked down at his hands. "Mr Harrison," he said quietly, "Jack is showing every sign of being drugged, repeatedly brutally raped, and tortured over a sustained period of time."

Greg got slowly to his feet, shooting a glance at me, the doctor—back at Gray. "You."

"Mr Harrison—" said the doctor.

"*No*," Greg shouted at him, then he looked at Gray. "You." Anger battled just plain confusion. "You tell me how—why—why someone would rape my boy. He, he...."

Gray pushed away from the wall, and Greg sank back down into his chair, his universe seeming to crumple in on itself as Gray crouched in front of him.

"Greg, a few weeks back, someone sent me footage of Jack and Cutter together," he said quietly, and Greg snapped his head up, went to say something, but then failed to manage anything. "Whoever sent that tape," said Gray, "I'm one hundred percent sure they're responsible for everything that Jack and Jan have been through for the past two weeks—"

"Jan? Two week—"

Gray carried on, needing to get the details out quickly. "There are numerous leads we're following. You have my word that I will find them."

Greg frowned. And again so many questions flashed in his eyes. Yet it was the most basic parental request that came out. "I-I need to see my boy."

"Of course," said the doctor as Gray eased back to his feet.

I watched them leave, then found Gray staying behind to hold the door for me. I didn't realise until I pushed through that Greg had lingered too for a moment, just watching, then he was gone.

In Jack's room, something other than the IV stand stopped me from going over to the bed, the same thing that had forced me to hold back following Gray to Jack's room. Greg and Elena were there, Greg running his hands through Jack's hair in much the same way I had. Elena sat opposite, seeming unwilling to touch, to disturb and wake the sleeping to the hurt.

Jack lay on his back, an IV line set up close by, breathing, pulse, and blood pressure under close observation by machines. But he was unconscious, lips pale, cracked, his left eye sporting a bruise. No blood, and again it shocked me how clean he was. His hair had that shine to it, like he'd just washed it, that he'd taken a shower and—

All evidence removed, washed away.

A slight jostle, Gray rested next to me by the door, and the brush of his hand came against the back of mine. I couldn't return the touch; as much as I needed to feel something, to be able to feel *someone*, the fear was there with what images would surface if I allowed feeling to creep in.

"I'm...." The doctor fell into silence for a moment as he stood next to Elena. "We have run other tests." Greg looked up, startled, and the doctor seemed to slip into his role and push tiredness aside as he looked over at me. "For all cases like this, sexually transmitted diseases are a concern."

A groan hit the room, and it took Gray's brush of hand to realise it was from me. "They didn't wear any protection."

"They?" Greg frowned over. "Did you—did you see it, son?"

I looked down, grinding my teeth.

"I need to know." Greg glanced down at Jack. "Jan, please," he said back to me. "What happened?"

Vince was still far too close, Henry still climbing on my skin, Jack being forced against me, me against him. "Greg, I can't," I said quietly. "The details… they should come from Jack, and all in his own time."

"Any other time, somebody else's son," said Greg, "I'd agree with you. But I'm Jack's father, Jan. I've watched him grow up and fight with his disorders, then coped with the fallout. I need to know what I'm facing now. Basic care plan, Jan. Let me know what I'm dealing with, please. He's my son."

Christ, there was everything else to contend with surrounding the fallout. Jack's disorders. Gray knew it, he'd always known it. Everything planned in advance around Jack, reactions thought out, anticipated—catered for. How on earth could they cater for this now? How Jack's head had been so twisted?

Details were kept brief, just going over what happened to Jack. They didn't need to know about me. By the time I'd finished speaking, Greg was looking at me with this strange blankness. Elena… she refused to look away from

Jack, the speed at which she stroked his hand, how she steadily increased it, being the only indication of emotion threatening to overflow. Gray remained quiet, very fucking quiet. Maybe he knew I'd brushed over the worst.

"His disorder?" Greg didn't look as though he believed it. It was just the stuff of nightmares to me. "Some twisted fuck's idea of curing his disorder?" said Greg.

"Psychological reconditioning," said Gray quietly, and both Elena and Greg were back with him. "There are similar cases found in the likes of cults or rape-to-straight… This seems a perverted version. The issue with placing the photo away from Jack but still in sight is a known technique to psychologists to help ease OCD symptoms." I looked at Gray, wondering when he'd found that out.

"But tied in with BDSM…." Greg frowned. "Jack isn't into BDSM."

"Oh, Greg," said Elena, giving a deep sigh. "What do you think that man was doing to Jack as a boy? All the cuts… the bruises?"

"I'm not stupid, Elena. People live BDSM lives, showing something beyond a liking for sadomasochism. What Cutter did…" His fists clenched, unclenched. "How he exploited Jack's disorders, all to cut other kids up—that wasn't BDSM. This…." He pointed at Jack. "*This* isn't BDSM."

That surprised me. Step back six months, compare me to Greg, he knew more about BDSM than I had as a vanilla. But he still looked as confused as hell. "Why?" he said, looking between me and Gray. "Jack isn't into the BDSM lifestyle. Why that? Why this?"

I resisted looking at Gray, damn my soul. I resisted

looking at him and throwing this further into the land of chaos for Jack's parents. But how much did it hurt Gray knowing Jack denied who they both were when it came to Jack's family?

"Greg, Elena," said Gray, seemingly in no way wanting to make this any harder for them just yet either, "I'm going to have to ask you a few questions soon. Mostly surrounding anyone you might remember asking questions about Jack, his disorders, his home life. Also just a brief statement on your whereabouts, on—"

"Mine?" Greg took a few steps away from Jack. "*Elena's?*" That ability to go from calm to chaos rushed the room with Greg's voice and body language. He was coming around the bed, and Elena, wiping tears from her cheeks, she moved at the same time, but only to quietly step in front of Greg, her back to us, cheek gently brushing Greg's. Had Jack taken that from his parents, those quiet touches? "*You think us—we had something to do with this?*" snarled Greg. "*You—*"

"Greg," whispered Elena, eyes closed as she kissed his jaw. "Please… please. He's doing his job. Let him do his job—Let him…" She couldn't say anything else, falling quiet as she held on.

But that raised a few serious questions on my part, ones that took me exactly to the same place Greg had already reached.

CHAPTER 31
BLAME GAMES

STOOD NEXT TO Gray as Elena tried to control Greg, I looked at Gray, now questioning that quiet word that Brennan had originally given to Harry back at the warehouse. Had that been to start pulling names up on Jack's immediate family? His friends? *My* family? *My* friends? "Gray—" I started, but a touch against my hand off him stopped it.

"Okay, okay," said Greg quickly, running hands through his hair, then pushing Elena gently to the side. "We'll give every move we've made over the past two weeks and beyond, list every one of Jack's relatives, his friends—even down to the bloody milkman and how many times Jack pissed him off with pinching milk off his milk cart. Maybe that pissed him off enough to do this, eh? Then you ask your questions—but you damn well make sure you do your job and find who's hurt him. Clear?"

Elena had sat back down, her touch now on Jack, for Jack.

Gray remained distant, waiting for things to calm, maybe

used to family reactions, maybe knowing it was part of the job. Only his silence said something else too. "Can you think of anything out of the ordinary happening lately?" he said eventually. "And I'm not just talking about these past few weeks, but over the last couple of months." There was a professional bite to that, maybe recognition he'd never be viewed as anything but an outsider to Greg. Maybe rightly so with everything I'd witnessed about Gray. He wasn't exactly... normal.

Elena glanced over her shoulder, her look more understanding, more on Gray and needing him there. "Gray, we don't—"

"It's important just to take time to think," he said to her gently as Greg went back over by Jack, opposite Elena. "These people," added Gray, "they had a replica of Jack's whole house in the warehouse. They knew everything about his life and disorder. They would have found that out some way, either through friends or family, or just through getting access to his home and medical records. So anything, anything at all you can remember, no matter how minor, will help."

Greg's gaze seemed to startle. "A woman." He glanced at me, then Gray. "A woman. She asked if I was Jack's dad."

Gray eased off the wall a touch. "Woman?"

Gregory searched for the memory. "We bumped into each other. Well, when we'd stopped for a coffee." He glanced at Elena. "Back in July, the morning of the solicitor's visit. Remember?"

Elena frowned. Shrugged. "Back at Epping Forest? Butler's Retreat?"

July? I'd just met Jack around that time.

"Yes." Greg was nodding. "You'd headed into the café; I was just locking the Range Rover up. As I turned, I bumped into this woman." He didn't seem to like the memory. "I dropped my wallet, my keys."

"And she asked if you were Jack's father?"

Greg glanced over at Gray. "Yes. She helped me pick my things up, some of the solicitor letters I'd also been carrying. She seemed a bit surprised when she saw my name. She asked if I knew Jack Harrison."

"Did she mention her name?" said Gray.

"No." Greg tried to think back. "But she had a watch, one attached to her shirt. A nurse's watch." I glanced at Gray as Greg frowned. "Jack's been in contact with enough medical people. I just took it that she was one of those he'd met."

"You said items were knocked out of your hands," repeated Gray. "Was there any moment when you were facing away from her? You carry a set of Jack's house keys; did she handle them at any time?"

"She turned her back on me, but it was only to pick up some loose change, I think."

"Okay, good. Thank you." Gray sounded thoughtful. "I know it's been a while, but if I call in a forensic sketch artist, would you be able to describe her?"

Greg rubbed at his chin. "I'll damn well try. It stuck in my mind because I know plenty of men who have called after Jack. A woman is a rarity."

"You think there was a sexual undertone to her questioning?"

"Sorry?"

Gray dug a hand in his trouser pocket. "Jack has contact with plenty of women, yet you put this meeting on a par with men calling after Jack on a more personal level."

Greg thought it over. "I guess I did. Only not in a good way, like a bad memory on her part. There was a short clip to her tone when she spoke to me."

"And she said Jack's name specifically?"

"Yes. Why?"

"Doesn't matter," said Gray, then—"Anything else at all? Anything out of the ordinary. Either of you?"

Greg looked at Elena for confirmation, but she shook her head as Greg said, "There have been times when Jack's been away for Christmas over the years on business." I wondered if that business meant Masters' Circle business. "Okay, it was a little sudden," said Greg, "but Jack, he goes casual sometimes to, well, you know, to order things, to..." He trailed into quiet, looking back at Jack.

"He phoned." Elena wasn't quite with us when she spoke.

"What?" said Gray.

"A call. I spoke to him." She glanced over at us. "A few days before Christmas. He phoned. He wanted to know about the garage." She was back with Jack. "How could he have phoned? And sick..." She seemed to search for something, nodded. "He sounded so sick and tired."

I frowned. "Called?"

"I got texts," said Greg to Elena as he stroked through Jack's hair, "asking for cover for the garage, wishing me Happy Christmas, apologising that.... He said he was...." Greg stopped, looking sick. "Why didn't I even question tha—?"

"From the look of Vince's MO," said Gray, "everyone who could have asked questions received various texts at just the right time, including Steve. I received a call off

Jan—"

"No," said Elena, quietly, and it was quick enough to bury my strangled cry over calling Gray. "I didn't get texts…. Phone call. I got a call." She looked at me and nodded. "A few days after I thought you two had gone away, he phoned."

Elena looked at Jack. "He sounded exhausted," she mumbled. "Like he'd just woken up, yet…." She went to say something else but stopped again.

"What?" said Greg.

Elena looked up. "He wanted you, luv."

Greg's hand seemed to lock in Jack's hair.

"And the garage." Elena distractedly reached over and rested a touch on Greg's. "He mumbled something about cover…."

Greg was struggling, I could see it on his face as he looked over at us. "Why? Why would he call? Why would he call and not say anything?"

"Do you remember what Jan said about the ketamine and psychological reconditioning?" Gray said quietly, and Greg nodded a little. "To make it more real for Jack, they could have given him access to a phone, and with the ketamine in his system, a drug that allows suggestive stimulation, planted both idea and topic to make the scene more real for him." Quiet. "As they did with Jan."

Elena's face creased. "They… they used me to… to…" Greg was suddenly by her, crouching and grabbing her in close. "Greg, Jack. He was…." Elena was crying. "Tired. He sounded exhausted, and quiet, like when he'd come out of his blackouts. Sleep, like he just wanted to sleep. Should have, I should have—"

"He's sleeping now, luv. He's—" Greg was about to

repeat himself, he saw it, I saw it, and he fell quiet, Elena pulled close as he stroked her hair.

"I'll find who's behind this," said Gray, more to me than to anyone, and just then Greg looked back at him.

"Gray, I know you're damn good at your job. Christ knows you got Jack to not only testify, but also change his dark outlook on life, and get away from Cutter's head games," he said flatly. "I have no doubt at all that you'll find whoever's responsible before they do this to someone else." Greg looked down at Jack. "But again, as far as Jack's concerned, it's too late." He looked back at Gray. "Damage already done, boy cut to pieces." He fought back tears. "So forgive me for hating the fuck out of you all of these years, but you go do what you've always done: you save the world for somebody else's son. I'll pick up and try and hold what's left of mine."

Gray's jaw tightened, then he opened the door and left. After a look at Greg, I followed Gray out and managed to catch up with him, IV stand still in tow but seeming harder to push with each passing moment. "Gray." Grabbing the cuff of his shirt, I backed him against the wall. "You focus," I said coldly, hands running through his hair, body tight against his. "You put whatever you're feeling aside, and you find the people who watched that. You make them hurt. No OCD, no worry over paperwork slotting into the right holes: you find them and you make them fucking hurt."

Gray's gaze never left mine.

"They were determined," I kept that flat and focused. "They would have taken him at any available opportunity, so don't think pushing him away caused this." I wiped hair from his eyes. "Jack, that night we were at his, he mentioned something about someone called Martin."

Gray suddenly stiffened.

"He mentioned he slept with women when he'd meet this Martin. But he was talking about himself, wasn't he? He doesn't know what he's doing in the blackouts, but this Martin does. He's Jack."

"No. Martin's a world a-fucking-way from Jack." That was said through such gritted teeth, but he knew exactly who I spoke about.

"But Martin... when Jack said he'd walk, then wake in someone else's bed, he was in mostly women's beds, mostly nurses." I frowned as Gray narrowed his eyes. "And the woman that Greg mentioned, she was a—"

"Yeah," said Gray, his look cold. "I heard."

"So she could be someone from Jack's past who this Martin knew? Who... who he—" Hurt? Jack's blackouts... mindless, more an animal with as much remorse as Gray...? Just who had he hurt back in his past before Gray stepped in?

Gray nodded, just once. He was already there, and I let him go before glancing back down the hall. Greg stood watching us. "My mother and family," I said back to Gray. "You're going to question them too."

Gray's gaze searched mine. "Yes."

"Can I talk to them first? Please?" Sickness coiled in my stomach. "Any detail... it should come from me, in my own time."

He shook his head after a moment. "I can't allow that, Jan. You—"

I pulled away a little more, seeing what was going on in his eyes. "You—you think I could have worked with my own family to do this? Be a part of whatever this nurse is up to?" I took more than a few paces back now. "I'd do *this* to both of us? You—"

Greg was there, pulling me back, as I went to push Gray the fuck away.

"Easy, son, Gray's just leaving. Aren't you?" said Greg. "He's got a job to do, right?"

My look stayed on Gray's—refused to move from Gray's. "And Jack," I mumbled quietly. "Will you treat him like a suspect too? Or is that just reserved for me?" I wanted to cry out as a tear escaped. "*And you—who the hell's going to fucking question you, Gray? You know him too: you hit him, made him bleed, walk out that fucking door and—*"

Gray came in close, not in the slightest bothered by my anger or Greg, who went to stop him with a hand to his chest. "I know how damn hard this is for you, but I need to get this done, nothing more, kid, okay?" The gentleness surprised me; he looked black-eyed enough to cull someone else, but then he whispered quietly, "You're new on the scene. So is your family. I'll always be frank and honest with where you stand around us, especially now, and I won't discuss any personal detail that went down with them, not unless you give me your permission. But you, you have my word the only people who need to be worried now are the people who hurt him. Who hurt you. You do anything now, you let me do my job and wipe out the background noise as fast as possible."

After a moment, I eased back, giving a nod seeing that honesty on display. A last look at me, Gray moved off.

"Jack," I said quietly, and Gray looked over his shoulder. "He's my priority. Everything else? That's yours." Quiet. "Okay? You focus on one thing only."

Grief, anger, relief… it was all there, then not there in the same moment. He gave a small nod, then was gone.

After a moment, I gave Greg a glance, then eased back up the corridor and into Jack's room. Elena offered a sad smile at me as I went to the opposite side and pulled up a big chair. I slumped down, close enough to rest my arm next to Jack, and closed my eyes.

"Have you called your parents at all, son?" Greg crouched in front of me. "Do they know about any of this?" Such a sad look in his eyes. "About you?"

No. No they, my mother, didn't. But then the details…. They hid in the blackness of a drug-induced sleep I really didn't want to fall back into.

"Then me," Greg said gently, that paleness to his tanned features making him nothing more than a ghost, "I'll go get the coffee. And you?" His touch came gently at my knee. "You need anything, and I mean anything, I'm here, all right? We all are."

"Speaking of which, Jan, you need to rest again now." Brennan stood over by the door, and I hadn't noticed. He came over and paused at the foot of Jack's bed, looking down. "I've made sure your room isn't far from Jack's," he said over to me, "but I'm going to more than insist that you go, rest, and wait for your results. Gray's asked that you receive them when he's back here, if that's okay." The softest smile. "You're not to hear them alone."

Results…. I stiffened. "I need a shower, sleep, then to stay here. Nothing more," I said, almost losing my temper.

Brennan gave a deep sigh. "You can shower anytime you need now," he said quietly, and so much was passed over in that look, understanding I didn't want to see in anyone's look.

His gaze not leaving mine, Greg eased up to his feet.

"Just how much have you fucking checked whilst I've

been asleep?" I tried to ease up, but Greg's hand on my shoulder kept me down. "What gives you the right to goddamn touch me whilst I was asleep?"

Brennan came over and crouched down. "Whilst you were asleep because talking is hard right now…." He didn't offer any kind of touch, and that seemed to say so much more. "We look after our own, and we'll do it until you tell us otherwise." His look was so gentle. "Tell me what you need, Jan."

A serious frown, I could only offer a shrug, nothing more. There were things I didn't want to know. To remember.

Brennan nodded. "Until you can voice it, will you trust my people with your peace of mind until you can?"

Greg's rub came at my shoulder. Talking was hard, but reliving… living… that was so damn harder.

I nodded, just once.

"Thank you," said Brennan, and he eased to his feet.

"What about Jack?" I didn't look up at him. "He hated everything in the end. Recognised no one but…." The anger was still there. I refused to face Jack now. Vince. He'd only seen Vince in the end.

Brennan stroked once at the back of Jack's hand. "From what the doctors have said, he's going to be kept out of it for a few days because of the heavy infection he has." He found me again. "Use those days to rest, please. When Jack wakes, we'll evaluate what damage has been done."

Greg seemed to shrink where he stood. "Who?"

Who what? I frowned at him, then Brennan.

"A call's been made to Halliday," Brennan said gently, and tension seemed to drain out of Greg. Brennan looked down at me. "We have the finest psychiatric facility.

Halliday has been with Jack through the years since he first met Gray. Depending on the extent of the psychological reconditioning, he'll try and help." His look was a little deep. "Both of you."

CHAPTER 32
STATE OF MIND

Jack Harrison

WHISPERING.

The whispering had stopped, but wind flittered through a blind, tapping it against the windowpane. The room was warm enough to only need a light sheet pulled up to the shoulders, but it still seemed fucked-up and cold. An empty comfy-looking chair slept close to the bed, angled slightly so it looked like the bed and chair were in some silent conspiracy. I'd seen it a few times over the past few days, had known someone sat there, tossing and turning, eating, talking—whispering—but it was easier just to ease the stinging in my eyes, keep them shut, and give in to the heat and headache that had clouded life. It had taken every ounce of self-control not to curl up as someone pulled a catheter free of my prick this morning, although from how they kept stopping and starting, occasionally stroking my fucking thigh, I didn't play dead as well as I thought. Now life was clearer, all headache, heat, and the need to fall back to sleep eased away into the quiet of the room. The need to piss was there, and it came with this burning in my groin. But it seemed safer, softer to stay down for a while. Movement before had caused whispers to stir in the silence, and social…. I didn't do fucking social and—

Don't…

… look at him, Jack.

I shifted, easing up onto my side. All dizziness had gone, but aches and twinges worked with my body, forcing me to go ape and tentatively ease back on my knuckles and sit back against a raised portion of the bed. The movement seemed to make things a little worse, and I let my heart slow only to find my hand hurt. Rubbing at the IV line jutting out of a vein, I followed the tube as it dropped off the bed, nearly touching the chair, to run back up into whatever shit was being pumped into me. Looking any further beyond that hurt my neck, so I eased back, rubbing at my forehead.

"How are you feeling, Jack?"

Jerking slightly, I didn't expect anyone to be sitting to my left. But a man with a book resting in his lap sat there blinking at me. Late fifties, yet his full head of hair kept its colour, all sandy-blond and young-looking. His smile was easy, creating more of an aged look his hair seemed unwilling to share. Lines creased at his eyes, the corners of his mouth, shifting the mole that weighed down his lips a touch. He looked comfortable in jeans and jumper, the sleeves drawn up to show tanned and very hairy arms.

"Do you remember me?"

Something came through, but it seemed to shift a whole crap-bucket load of other memories.

"Philip Halliday," he said, even offered over his hand.

"We've met each other a few times through the Masters' Circle's psychology unit."

Don't....

I stared at his hand.

... look at him, Jack.

I shook it quickly, leaving Halliday frowning, then he picked the book off his lap. He held it up. "James Herbert's *Moon*," he said with a wry smile. "It's a weakness, one I usually keep for the privacy of home. My son tried to get me into Steampunk, but I can't quite understand that genre. Is it non-fiction that you still prefer?"

I stayed with him, his goddamn fucked-up book, then let the room take my gaze.

"We're in a hospital room at Regent Manor," said Philip as certain smells kicked in. "The facilities here are second-to-none. But then it's the MC." He sounded like he was smiling, and I briefly looked back at him. "Do you remember being here about six months back? Taking a hit to the head that left you mildly concussed?"

I pulled the needle in my hand out, causing a little blood to spill, and pushed the covers back. "Out. I remember needing to be out," I mumbled as the door came open and someone pushed through.

"Mr Harrison—" Whoever it was, they didn't sound impressed. "—it's best you keep that catheter in place until the doctor's done his rounds."

I winced as I eased my legs off the bed and glanced up to see a nurse head over.

"I insist—"

"It's okay," said Philip, now on his feet as I got to mine and steadied myself, a hand blindly searching for the bed so I could stop the world and all its screams from screwing with my balance. "Can you give us some time alone, please?" he added, now more a whisper, and I gritted my teeth.

"He needs to stay in bed," she whispered back. "He needs—"

"Space. Give him it." More whispering. "Just—"

"*Shut the fuck up.*" I managed to lift my head and look at the nurse. Whispers. I hated fucking whispers. All of my fucking life, even in my fucking dreams, whispering. "What shit have you given me?"

"I beg your pardon?" said the nurse, giving that drop of her chin to look over her glasses.

"What meds?"

"Just some antibiotics, some fluid—"

"Get the forms I need to sign myself out." I started looking around for some clothes. I had pyjamas on at the moment, but I needed jeans, a shirt. "Anything I need can go on prescription."

"I'm sorry," said the nurse, glancing back at the door, then going over and closing it. "You've recently had an operation that requires certain aftercare before I can allow you to leave."

"Yeah?" I glanced at her. "Get me the forms or the legal shit is on MC fucking hands if I leave without signing them."

"Do you need these?" Philip came over and laid some clothes on the bed. I hadn't gotten a clue when he'd moved or taken the clothes out of the cupboard.

"Thanks," I said as jeans played dog-pile with a clean T-shirt and a zip-neck jumper. Tossing the shirt aside, I tugged on the jumper, and the nurse disappeared when Philip gave the nod. More aches came into focus; my abs, back, thighs, groin, ass, now all no longer a dull ache, more forcing me to bite back a cry as I gave up trying to take my pyjama bottoms off, just slipped my jeans on over them, barely noticing how loose they both were.

But as the socks came off the bed, I went still seeing what lay isolated on the covers.

"Jack," said Philip quietly. "Can you pick that photo up, let it drop casually? You remember the MC. That's good, but can you go casual with the photo?"

Covers were all wrinkled on the bed, and there, just caught in the ruffled crease that ran the whole length sat a photo.

It was strange, but the sun had been bright that day, forcing Gray to wear his sunglasses. The black of his suit matched the black of the Merc, and stones... I'd counted over a hundred or so stones surrounding one tyre, the same with the ones closest to Gray, and why....

"Come on." Vince pulled the covers back. "Get in bed before you catch your death..." Don't give the bastard a name....

"Jack?" whispered Halliday.

"Hmmmm?"

The door eased open and part of me registered the nurse coming back over to the bed. She held a bag of medication, some forms, and how she moved and thinned her lips said she wasn't happy. A hand against my elbow made me flinch, and I looked back to find Philip shoulder to shoulder with me. He picked the photo up, flipped it over his fingers like a magician playing with a coin, and tucked it in his pocket before looking at his watch.

"Do you know how long you've just stood staring at that photo?" Halliday's voice was clear, but his facial features were blurred at the edges. "It's taken the nurse thirty minutes to go and get the information you've asked for," he said quietly.

I looked back at the bed, now photo-free.

"Do you remember the term Dissociative Identity Disorder? It was something that was attached to your conduct disorder as a teen? Rare for that age. This particular one is known as an absence, a dream-like state to the onlooker," Philip said quietly. "You've had different variants in the past, is that right? Sometimes seems like people are time-lapsed around you, moving fast one moment, slow the next. Or you black out completely. Do you remember? Leaves those who experience it disorientated as people flitter in and out of focus. And usually after a great trauma, you wake up in strange places with women calling you Martin?"

I was back with him, watching as he searched my eyes.

"Do you remember your minor blackout a few months ago?" He gave another soft smile. "You were in a hotel room from what Gray said back then. You couldn't find the lid to the toothpaste. You didn't have your photo on you and you were trying to use it to go casual, but you couldn't put the toothpaste back together and drop it on the surface; the hotel bathroom in Essex ended up in need of refurbishment, from what I hear."

Remembering the socks were in my hand, I eased one on, ignoring the need to get back on the bed, just go to sleep now. "Gray wasn't there."

"Sorry?"

I eased my other sock on, no longer just staring at the bruising circling my ankle. I grabbed the trainers off the bed. "Steve…." I winced, for a moment gripping onto the bed. I'd dropped the shoes and bent too quickly, setting off every muscle in a heated row. "Steve and Sam knew... they were, were there." I slipped a trainer on, and an image flashed into view....

Leaning against a door... slipping trainers on... a long coat, no shirt, just suit trousers that night. It had been cold by the door, snow-cold, and it had covered the grounds by a pool and road as I'd started to walk home.

I'd made it home that night. I'd been at home that night, but after that...?

I straightened, fingers still digging into the mattress. "Gray wasn't there."

Philip offered a smile. "That's good, Jack, that's very good. Core memories are partially intact away from the scene." He sounded so calm, and I looked at him. "Do you remember anything about the past two weeks?" he said, more stated directly. "Do you know why you're here? Who—"

Vince stood over by the unit, taking off his watch and glancing over. Naked, side panels of muscle beaten into place, dwarfed mine. My cock should have gotten a kick out of the offering, but there was only a deep, rooted fear; that need to bolt, not just walk—just bolt for life and not stop running, and that was something I wasn't used to. Only dreams... they kept me here, or the promise of a dream. Who was held captive within them....

"Come on." Vince pulled back the covers. "Get in bed before you catch your death. You earned it after that blowjob on Boxing Day."

I made a point of easing Halliday away, then I reached over and grabbed the chart that the discharge papers were attached to. A pen was fastened to the top, and I pulled it free only to find the words kept blurring on the backdrop of startling whiteness. It took someone calling my name and tugging the board from out of my hands for me to focus again.

"I'll sign this." My old man's hand shook as he took out his own pen and started to scribble on the form. "Get you home to mine, yeah, son?" He mumbled something else, then, "Need to get you home."

"I'm fine." He'd picked up the medication, but I took it off him. He stared, mouth open slightly. Unable to look at him for too long, I sidestepped him to go for the door—but two other people stood in my way now.

"You need to listen to your father, Jack." Gray kept closest guard by the door, Jan just to his left, looking more ready to bolt.

Jan.

You earned it after that blowjob Boxing Day...

Head down for a moment, I calmed every ounce of shaking and looked back at my old man. "Dad, as ever, it's really good that you take time out for my shit. I love you for it, you need to know that, because fuck knows I've never said it enough, right? But I'm going back to the manor." I needed the manor: lots of rooms, lots of doors, too many to try and open before...

Kisses came at my neck. "Don't... look at him, Jack."

"Dad. I'll give you a call later, okay?"

That knocked him sideways in all the wrong ways, but I needed to get out now. Gray got my attention as I held a hand to the wall to steady me. "I'm in no state to drive. Will you call Ed, please?"

"You remember? Then I'll dri—"

"No," I said through Jan's words, not taking my gaze off Gray. The need to get out and breathe crushed my insides. "Ed. Please?"

Not saying anything, Gray nodded. Giving Jan a glance, he left. That left my need to go to the bathroom, and I pushed on through, shutting the door and breathing in the space as I leaned back against the door. That need to piss was there, but the toilet held me still. The ache in my groin had grown to cock-grabbing annoyance, and it was a choice between standing here and pissing myself or dropping my jeans and facing the toilet. A rub at my head, I went over, naturally finding my clasp, my zip, yet my gaze finding sole focus on anything, anything but lower than the waistline. It burned, in ways that had me frowning and fighting back tears, the stream of water I pissed felt like heated wine, with just as distinct a smell.

I scratched at my right hip before I realised it, grateful I didn't need anything more than a piss. Especially nothing that meant I'd have to sit on this and....

I tucked everything away; the fuck did I shut everything down quickly and wash up.

Fifteen minutes later, I was in the back of the Rolls, the world passing by outside. Fresh snow still touched the ground, deep enough to force the Rolls to a slow crawl. The brightness of the afternoon matched the whiteness of the medical facilities, yet it left behind that startling blank sheet.

A good place to leave things, forget the piss stains that were out there, hidden under bushes that buckled from the weight of the snow. Hiding. Something always hid beneath fucked-up surfaces, willing to throw life into unordered chaos.

By the time we pulled up outside Gray's manor, a black Merc sat in the drive, indicating Gray, and no doubt Jan, had made it home first. They both waited by the fountain, and as I got out, whispering stopped and glances took over.

Fucked-up whispers and bastard watching. The meds came off the back seat, and I rested against the rim of the open door, briefly closing my eyes, using the excuse that it was against the hurt in my body. After a push away, I headed into the manor.

The cold from outside followed me in and I took a moment, staring over at the stairs as I inched off my trainers. Bending down brought up too many aches, stirred itching, echoes of—everything that was best left outside on plain white backgrounds.

Somebody spoke, Ed, maybe, and I looked back at him. He'd asked something, but I couldn't really give a fuck what even though his mouth was still moving. The stairs took all of my attention again, breathing seeming to ease, to calm, and I followed them up to where the stairs branched in two, then just followed my feet, heading right, more stairs, through corridors that took me deep into the west wing.

The familiar came up, and I pushed on through to the bedroom Ed always ensured I took when Gray needed space. Covers hadn't been changed, curtains opened, my assortment of work boots I kept in here nowhere to be seen. I went over to the bed, meds still in hand, just looking around before noise back by the door caught my attention.

"Let me arrange for Mrs Booth to set the bed with fresh sheets," said Ed, coming over, hands running over the duvet cover almost as if to check for creases.

"Why?"

Ed looked at me. "Because they've been on since your last stay here and…." He glanced at the sheets, then back over by the door. I knew Gray and Jan were just in the doorway. "I know how you…" Ed started to say, but I looked at him and he seemed to falter. "But if they're okay?"

"They're fine." I briefly stroked at the bottom of the bed. Yeah. Fine. Just fucking peach—Just fine.

"Jack, you don't have to stay in here." Jan came a few steps closer; I could feel it, space reducing. "I mean…." He frowned, stopped, threw his hands out. "Gray and me…."

"It's okay, Jan." Gray stayed over by the door, watching. I watched him back. "Jack knows we're here. All in his own time, yeah? Same with you."

"Maybe?" Jan was in front of me, seeming to cover those last few steps in record time. "Me, talk? We need…." He stumbled with his words, but the softness in his eyes said so much: it offered so fucking much. He needed to talk. He needed to not be alone, maybe needed to hide, to forget how—

Covers kept us warm as kisses came at my neck again. "Please. Just tell me that you love me, Jack, not that bastard that's in your dreams." More kisses tenderised my throat. "Fucking say it—you love me."

Amongst all the grey cloud, echoes, and screw-ups, that instinct was there to grab hold of Jan, hold on, say sorry, not let him be alone, to let him know it was okay, block out the tumbling images. I think I even started to, but the breeze from the doorway shifted at the same time, catching his cologne, something else… how—

Real men get dirty now, Jack. You know that now.

"Fuck, no." The rejection was soft, not meaning to hurt, and I wanted to swear all the fucking sorries in the world for all the hurt that tore through his gaze then, that had haunted nightmares back then, but I was already in the bathroom, stomach hurting, paying homage with the acrid taste of meds in my throat, and nearly crying hate and hurt with it.

CHAPTER 33
OCD

Jan Richards

AS JACK'S RETCHING went on in the bathroom, I ran my hands through my hair, gripping tight, watching that closed door, the silence breaking in the bedroom choking me.

"Hmph." It was all I had.

A look at Ed, nothing but a shrug at Gray, I turned and ran. By the time I'd reached Gray's bedroom, passed his bed, clothes were already torn off as I headed into the bathroom. For the sixth time in five days, steam instantly clouded the cold air, leaving the bathroom in near-clouded darkness, and I stumbled under the steam, water instantly hitting skin, soaking—drowning out all noise as I gripped onto the showerhead above my head and held on. Just fucking held on.

Hands traced around my stomach and a body shaped me from behind. Kisses came in quick and the hold tightened, forcing me to cry out.

"Easy, easy."

For a moment I thought Jack; the care and love behind the touch said everything about him, the tenderness so fucking much the same, and Gray only made everything hurt more when I realised it wasn't Jack. Crying out again, I let my hands and head fall to the wall, fingers digging, desperate to keep a grip on something. Anything now.

One hand on my stomach, the other around my neck, nearly strangling me, Gray pulled me back, held tight, so bloody tight. "Time," he whispered quietly, "you both need time."

After the second day of watching Jack in hospital, I knew, we all knew that he'd woken up over the days that followed, just listening, drifting in and out of sleep over the New Year, twisting the covers as he'd dreamed. I'd let him, knowing he'd speak in his own time, if he was ready. Christ knows I still couldn't to staff. Yet when he had, it had been to say he needed to run, to throw up at the thought of being near me. Why wouldn't he? Nightmare. I was just his fucking nightmare. I'd fucking lain down next to him as he was raped; they'd made him hide in me as he was fucking raped, then....

Images swam in and out of focus, just whispers, cries... echoes of screams. But something new. Something I'd forgotten, or blocked out—and it caught me out so badly. I elbowed the tile behind, forcing it back down as—

"*Should have stopped it.*" I cried out, digging my grip hard into Gray's arms. "Should have fucking fought and stopped it." I tried to get Gray off, hating him being anywhere near me. "You didn't, you fuck," I growled. "He fucking cried out for you to stop it, crawled up close to me, nudging my neck up as if I was you, asking me to stop it and—he needed it stopped, we both needed it to just... fucking...

stop—"

Gray shifted, turning me around. Hands came to my face, forcing me to look at him, gaze so angry. "I didn't," he snarled, brushing my cheek with his thumb, each swipe hard enough to hurt. "When it really mattered, I wasn't there for him, for you..." A kiss at my cheek, he pulled me in close. "Fucking kills me, Jan," he said into my ear. "But that's not my priority. Jack is." He gripped my hair. "You are. And you, you've done nothing but hide in Jack's hurt these past five days, watching, fucking waiting. You've got your own wounds."

"I'm fucking fine—"

"Don't." He shouted that. "You're never more far from it. There's something else here. Something you're fighting. So same question again, Jan," he said quietly, keeping me close. "Nobody else here, just you, me. Vince and his bastards, what did they do to you?"

Cries... screams. How real men get...

Head resting down on his shoulder, I screwed my eyes shut and cried out.

"I don't want to remember it."

"I know. I know. But you cry out in your sleep over something, about how real men, they.... What happened? No one else here, Jan. I need to know who, I need to know how. But I also think you need to face it. To tell someone what happened when real men, they....."

"You took bloods whilst I was asleep. You know what they did back there."

"I know what they didn't pass on when they raped, nothing more. But what's got you hitting the tile now? Why is that making you cry out more than anything else?"

"Jack—"

"Not Jack. You."

"Don't…" I gripped onto his back. "I don't want to see it, Gray. I don't, not that how, how—"

≈

"This cleaning yourself shit is really starting to piss me off now, Jack." Vince wiped the come on Jack's cheek for a second time as Jack sat on the bed. Christmas dinner was long since thrown up, Vince making the mistake of giving Jack a full Christmas dinner when he'd been pumping nothing but drugs and fluids into Jack since he'd touched him. Now all that was left of Vince's Christmas fun was Jack, sat there on the bed, a thin sheath of sweat covering his body after he'd let Vince fuck him again.

He'd enjoyed it. How the fuck could he have enjoyed it? Bound there in the corner of the bedroom, I'd died from it.

"S-sorry," mumbled Jack, hand still gripping onto the mattress, body all rigid, breath barely drawn as he looked down at the come staining his thighs.

"We'll sort you out, kid," said Vince, folding his arms. "Don't… worry."

Henry seemed to come out of nowhere, two other men licking close at his heels. Jack's startled snarl was as hurt-filled as mine as I struggled on the floor. He tried to fight, but a look came at me, followed by a cry that said fighting would make it worse, then fear hit hard, feeding his flight reaction instead. They caught his scramble off the bed, his intent to get to the door, maybe just remove one half of the problem, and a needle was pushed into his arm as he was held down in the sheets. Struggles eased on the bed, watering down until soft groans and half-hearted attempts disturbed the covers, but not much more.

Vince slipped his black leather gas mask over his face, and Henry and another man grabbed hold of Jack and dragged him onto the floor not far from me. I tried to shuffle over, but my hands were still bound behind my back. Henry had loved dragging me in and out of the lounge and dining room, playing with my head as much as Jack's. Although the way Jack had looked at me, how he sat there with no ropes, barely any drugs—not doing anything but eat… talk….

Fight. Why the hell hadn't he fought—*"Why the fuck don't you fight? You're trained to fucking fight."*

He was on the floor, quiet, lost to the drugs that only brought on a worse nightmare. I curled up, whispering all the sorries in the world, just needing to get close as the bed was upended, clearing a space, and leaving Jack amongst the dirt on the floor. A black necklace with a black cross sleeping on a silver cross rested around his neck. It looked familiar, only I couldn't remember why, didn't really care as Jack was tugged onto his back and bound in a standard X position on the floor. Arm and leg spreaders with black leather cuffs came into play, each fastened to two hooks in the floor, one above his head, one between his ankles, keeping him down, but coming with a bit of slack to leave Jack trying to pull his legs up.

Vince crouched by Jack, slipping a bit gag into his mouth and tying it in place. "Don't…" he said quietly, and I tried to shield my ears, hiding in my suit jacket, not wanting to hear it anymore, "… clean yourself, boy."

Along with Jack's half-hearted struggles came groggy grumbles into the bit gag.

"Not talking, boy?" A tut was given into the low light. "All that dirt on the floor, and you don't… clean yourself up." A heavy sigh. "You really ask for this, don't you?"

The two faceless men disappeared from the bedroom, and that left Henry undressing in the light of the doorway, his slim gold watch jangling about his thin bones. A wink over at me, he took a narrow black case off a man who came back into the bedroom, then Henry handed it over to Vince. As Vince knelt between Jack's legs, Henry put his black gas mask on.

"Noticed how hard you get around Jan," Vince whispered up at Jack as he opened the case. "If you can't control yourself let alone clean yourself up, then as your Dom, I do that for you."

Alcohol swabs were pulled from the case and Jack tried to close his legs as his groin was cleaned. Through the drugs, he seemed to recognise the action, what it would lead to. Next came lube, and Jack's dick was slicked up to gratuitous lengths, with special attention paid to his tip.

Vince pulled on gloves. Then I cried out as a cock cage came out of the case. Echoes were there of seeing Jack kneeling by my door, head bowed, wearing a silver cock cage that bulged at the silver seams with how it had tried to cull his heat. This one looked different. Just a round circle that slipped under the hood of the penis, with a very sharp strip of silver metal, hooked over and down in the middle as if to—plug. Jesus, a penis plug, one that pushed into Jack's tip to stop him getting hard.

"*Don't*," I cried.

The fine point of the penis plug touched Jack's tip. At least Vince seemed to know what he was doing, angling Jack's tip to a certain angle, then allowing gravity... Jack had said the Dom needed to allow gravity to help pull the plug in. To him, it was like being fucked from the inside out. That wasn't the case here. Jack cried out, forcing his head back, stretching neck muscles as he tried to writhe from under the touch. The plug pushed into his tip, squeezing out some lube, and the straps took the whole tension of his body as the plug was inserted fully into his urethra.

"Sore, boy?" whispered Vince, slipping the ring over the head of Jack's cock and locking everything in place. He rubbed Jack's balls. "It'll stop you coming on yourself at least. Making a mess of yourself on your skin."

Sweat coated Jack's body, one droplet taking the chance to escape and running over Jack's hip to the floor. Groans mumbled through the blackness, Jack's, as he tried to close his legs.

"Focus." A slap went to Jack's face, then a thin needle was pulled from the case and wiped with the sterile swabs. The fine point touched Jack's left nipple, fingers pinching either side to make sure the nipple stood on end, and Jack dug his feet into the dust, arching his body, knowing the pain before it even kicked in.

The piercing came slowly, slower than the urethra insertion, the needle pushed back and forth a few times as if it were a vibrator trying out a few deep strokes.

"Oh yeah, fucking good," mumbled Vince through Jack's cries. With the needle kept in place, a small trickle of blood ran from the pierced nipple as it was squeezed between fingers. Another hand stroked roughly between Jack's thighs, slicking them up with the lube, slipping past his balls, over his taint. Massaging the pierced nipple, making it bleed some more, two fingers then pushed into Jack's ass and he was forced to jerk under each brutal push into him.

"Hmm," purred Vince, muscles defined in his arm as he watched himself finger Jack. "Like coming home, boy." He chuckled. "Or coming somewhere." A kiss graced Jack's hip. "You need my marking. Fuck me off enough, I just might." A lick of tongue left a long, wet trail on Jack's hips, Vince's fingering and blood-play making Jack choke and gag. "Warmed up enough in here for me?" After undoing the clasp to his jeans, Vince pulled out his cock and started laying a hand along it. "Yeah." He shifted slightly to look at Jack's ass. "Looks ready for me, all right." Slipping the tip around Jack's ass, he pushed in, making sure he won an extra cry out of Jack as he leaned down and bit at his pierced nipple, needle now caught between his teeth. The chain keeping the leg-spreader in place had allowed for slack, for Vince to get exactly the angle he needed to rape and—

Giving a strangled groan, I hit my head off the wall a few times, trying to force blackness over what I was witnessing, how Jack cried out to each hard taste between his thighs, how Vince would arch his own body up, pulling at the nipple almost as if to tear skin as he pulled the needle free, then let it go at the last moment, but only to swamp it with his lips, sucking, licking, nipping the blood—

"No you don't, pet," whispered a voice, and a rattle of chain came from overhead. Forced over by Jack, I stumbled to my knees. Henry came down behind me, his grip to the back of my head, forcing me to look at Vince pounding into Jack.

"C'mon, you've seen Vince fuck him after the Queen's speech, you're used to it now," said Henry. "And we really need this bastard to get dirty now."

"Fuck you."

A thump went to my ribs. "Fucking watch."

Jack cried out too, and it jerked my eyes open.

"Hurts him as well if you don't do what you're told, pet," whispered Henry. "Doesn't like you hurting, even now. Vince'll soon fuck that out of him."

Vince was up on his knees slightly, leaving enough room to look down and watch his dick sliding into Jack. "Fuck, yes." He groaned, hips slamming home hard.

"Looks real sweet taking that, don't he?" whispered Henry, and I stiffened as his hand fell onto my dick. "Bet you're missing that body, huh? Having that tight ass there take all this?" He massaged me through my trousers. "Show me how much you miss him, pet."

"Fuck... *you.*"

Clasp undone, Henry forced his hand into my boxers. "Yeah, fucking good-sized cock here. Gotta be why Jack likes you." Henry's hard-on pushed against my ass. "Bet you make him writhe and cry out taking this?"

"Fuck... you." I tried to shake him off, but he carried on stroking at my dick.

"How about a deal?" Mask shifting slightly, he licked at my ear. "Get hard for me, pet. I'll see if I can stop Vince there, let you take over? Let you fuck him better?"

I choked a sob.

"I know you're missing him, and I don't mind, really. So c'mon. I'm giving you the opportunity to stop that roughness going on there. Let you take care of Jack, let you lick his wounds your way." He was chuckling with that. "Or lick his ass, anyway. Tastes good now that Vince slicked him up for you. Won't even give you a sore dick."

"Not like that—*never* like fucking that."

"No? Think you're better?" Every ounce of playfulness was gone as the grip tightened on my hair. "Vince's raping the fuck out of your boyfriend—again—and you, you're just watching. You like to watch, eh, Jan? Is that what gets you going? Jack being rough-fucked in front of you? Well take a good look now, you watch him get fucked hard."

Vince gave one long, hard punch into Jack, forcing Jack to stretch his neck back and cry out. The desolation of my own cry was lost to how Henry still rubbed at my cock, still gripped, played, roughed along my length.

"Oh for fuck's sake. I need his come for this—" Giving a growl, Vince leaned over, grabbed at my ass, then took my dick in his mouth.

"Oh yeah, oh yeah, baby." Henry was breathing hard, fast. "Get the bitch stiff. Let's watch the boys play."

"Stop," I cried, hating Henry, hating Vince, his touch, how my body went against my mind's need for it to stop, just—"Fucking stop."

"Oh no," said Vince, giving one long lick along my dick. "Not now, kid. Not looking like that." He grunted a smile and pulled out of Jack, leaving Jack trying to close his legs again.

Vince unlocked the leather ankle cuffs, then did the same with the arm spreader, and pulled Jack up. Forced to face me, his gaze found mine, all that frowned greyness now just for me.

"Jan?" Nothing more than a whisper.

He was shaking, slick with sweat, and with how the urethral insertion had hurt, perhaps suffering from something else entirely—

"Jack," I said just as quietly.

He flicked a look away, then up at me, then just briefly at Vince. "Don't... look," he mumbled.

Face screwing, I glanced at Vince, but automatically found Jack again. "Baby..."

He shook his head quickly, just once, then cast his eyes away, to Henry—to the floor, as Vince went in close and smiled at me over Jack's shoulder.

"Don't... love Jan, Jack."

A tear slipped over Jack's cheek. His gaze briefly found mine again, but something else tortured his eyes, something his torn body brought so easily to the surface—a deeper need to risk everything, to hide, to get close, even if it was only a few minutes in one fucked-up nightmare that would see him hurt for it and—

"Don't, Jack." I groaned.

Head dropping slightly, shivering, he still came in, hands creeping up to the lapels of my jacket, so close now, seeming to want to hide, needing care, love—tenderness. Not so tough—not so fucking tough.

I cried out feeling him against me, mostly how familiar everything was, mostly how I needed him, but knew what came with it. "Hurt...." I tried to push him away for his sake, for mine. "Don't... please, baby. Fucking hurt you. Us." But Jack only gripped tighter.

"He'll make me kill you for it," he mumbled, sounding so tired and hurt. "Dream... real... he'll keep pushing my head until I hit out, not care about cleaning the mess up, just... hurt someone. Christ... please. I can't hit you again, Jan. I can't—"

"Touching someone you shouldn't, boy?"

Jack stilled the same instant I did.

Vince tutted, then grabbed Jack by the hair, pulling Jack back into him. "You attempting to get hard down here?" he snarled quietly, his hand mauling Jack's dick, and a strange look came in Jack's eyes at the rough treatment, nearly mirroring everything about Gray's look, only not quite… cooked enough yet.

Jack said nothing as Vince bit at his neck. "Dirty. Real men get real dirty. And guess who's gonna show you how?" Vince looked over at me, still nuzzling into Jack's neck. "Needle," he said quietly.

"What?" Forced forward, I was taken close to Jack's pierced nipple.

"Get it out or we leave it in," whispered Henry. "Blood on skin. Either way: a real man, getting dirty." Henry pushed me flat against Jack's nipple, hands strained behind my back. "Pull it fucking out now or I rape your ass. His hurt or yours."

"*Jack!*"

A hand hit my head. "To me," snarled Henry quietly. "You talk to fucking me. And I'm telling you, pull that fucking needle out or you talk to my fucking cock. Got it, pet?"

With my tongue flicking under the bluntest end, I made it quick for Jack, but he only cried more when the traces of blood forced me to lose grip. Giving a snarl, I gripped at it again and tugged it free, leaving Jack yelping, me crying.

"Aw, you chose his hurt over yours," chuckled Henry. "Way to go, pet. He won't remember anyway, right?"

As a trickle of blood ran from Jack's nipple, keeping him so oddly still, Vince messed with his cock cage, loosening the lock. "This too."

"No." I was forced level with Jack's groin.

"Out," breathed Henry. "Take the plug out of his cock with your teeth. Or you take me and Vince together. You had two cocks yet, Jan? That vanilla ass of yours up for a double stretching?"

Shaking, tears misted my vision as Jack looked down at

me, head cocked slightly. "Can't... don't... please. I'll hurt him." He looked so sore there, not just from the penis plug.

"Yeah, you being pansy vanilla, you just might." A slap came at my head again. "Better get it out of his cock quick then. Or I'll shock the penis plug and really get him the mood to handle you."

Giving a cry, I gripped the end of the plug with my teeth and made it gentle, made it slow, then spat the plug away when it came out so easily. A hand crept between my thighs and stroked at my dick. "Good boy," whispered Henry. "I like this side of an animal; hurting others over being hurt himself. Can we get you to do more to him, pet, hmmm?"

Jack was pushed down to the floor, now on his stomach, and Vince shifted, holding him facedown. Only everything in Jack's body was wrong. Not scared of the handling, listening for... me?

"Go on, pet," mumbled Henry, in my ear. "You've earned it. Climb on lover boy. Fuck him. Get him dirty."

"No," I snarled through my teeth, pushing back into him.

That hand stroked at my dick. "Do it." A chuckle. "Do it-do it. Or we'll fuck you."

"You fuck me, because I won't ever touch him like that! You can cut off my dick first." I'd scared the life out of him last time I'd forced him down to a bed. I'd never go there again.

The chuckling stopped. "It's rape, Jan. You don't get a choice."

I let out a cry as I was pushed down onto Jack. Trousers pulled over my ass, I grunted as Henry crushed his weight on me from behind and forced his tip into me, splitting me raw. Vince undid my cuffs, then in the struggle, forced my hands over Jack, so I was holding him down too.

"Feel that, boy?" taunted Vince. "Jan's into a little frottage, rubbing himself off on you."

"Yeah," grunted Henry, slamming my hips into Jack's. "Make you come on him, pet." It seemed to last a lifetime. Jack was quiet beneath me, body slick and salty, but an undertone of CK One filling every part of my senses. I cried out, lost my voice through crying out, then went as quiet as Jack as the constant push on my prostate forced my come onto him.

Henry pulled free, cooing out and wiping his dick on my ass. When he eventually moved, I suddenly scrambled up, off Jack, nearly knocking back into Henry. Vince let Jack go, and, pushing up awkwardly, looking stiff, his movements mechanical, Jack knelt there, facing me, head down, shivering.

Rape. It didn't give you a choice, but I still couldn't understand how a man's body could come despite being raped. But a sick part of me understood it now.

"Just pig meat in need of a decent basting every now and again, aren't you, boy?" said Vince from Jack's side, watching him. "And Jan, his come looks damn good between your thighs there."

There was the briefest frown as Jack looked down.

"Wasn't me, Jack. Oh Christ. Sorry," I cried. "So sorry, baby, so…"

Now Jack looked up, and the levelling of such a cold gaze made me try and crawl back over to him and wipe every trace of me away. "Not me, Jack. Not fucking me."

Jack was lost to the come between his thighs, how it stained his skin, and everything hit so hard. He snarled, shifting to wipe between his thighs, just to get the come off.

Vince cuffed him up the head. "Leave it. You're a man, not a ponce. Real men get dirty."

It seemed to stop Jack for a moment, leaving him scowling down at his body. But then he eased a look at Vince.

Shoving at him, hitting him with his shoulder, Jack knocked Vince down. Nothing in his eyes said he knew what he was doing; he was just after the nearest cloth to wipe himself clean, the nearest thing stopping him, and Vince just happened to be there.

Pushing him away, Vince grabbed Jack by the hair and forced him down into the dirt on the floor.

"Roll in it, fuck hole, because only real men get dirty. Until you can get dirty on your own, that makes you nothing but meat for fucking."

Jack tried to roll around, even if it was to wipe my come off with the dirt on the floor. Marks scuffed his body, dusty patches he'd need off his skin any other time, on his outer thighs, his ass, top of his shoulder, one on his cheek.

And then he found me again, and all anger, all hate, all drop of any recognition focused on me. The one who'd put come on him, who forced Vince to question every aspect of being a man.

Jack came at me, and Vince slipped an arm around him, then a needle in his throat. "Easy, easy, our kid." Jack relaxed completely into Vince, eyes closing, and Vince eased him down to the floor.

"Progress." A finger traced through the dirt on Jack's shoulder, then Vince came over to me. "You know something?" He smiled as he dusted his hands down.

"Next time you see him, I think our Jack might just kill you and all his fears, Jan."

I got a pat to my abs. "Well done. Really… very… well done, our kid. Couldn't have done it without you. Well, your come. Couldn't have done it without you coming here tonight."

Henry snorted a laugh from behind me.

I cried out, still tasting blood in my mouth, feeling the needle scrape teeth, dust bite into Jack's skin, and standing there in the shower, I pushed away from Gray, cleaning—scrubbing the dirt hard off of me until I felt skin tear.

"Stop." Gray covered my hands with his, stopping me from clawing at my skin, then taking over with a gentler touch, he started to cleanse my skin with soap. With it he brought a heavy tiredness that seemed to pull me down with each gentle stroke of sponge as we stood there in the shower. Words became slurred as all of the details spilled free, what I could remember anyhow, but each whisper he'd give into my ear was clear, saying I was doing good. And then he took as much care, time, and attention drying me. I'd stopped talking. I'd told him everything Henry had done, Vince, but the relief and exhaustion came with telling him how I hated Jack back there for a while, that I'd wished that they'd take it one step further and just… stopped.

The thing that hurt the most? There was no judgement in Gray's eyes, just that constant "You did good, Jan." Life didn't feel good: it felt pretty shit, and the grief that mixed with droplets of water had shown it.

"Get your head down," said Gray, going through to the bedroom and pulling back the covers. Wrapped in his housecoat, I climbed in without any protest and felt the light weight of the duvets cover my body. "I'm going to see to Jack," he said, and a touch ran through my hair. "I'll be back in a minute. Security is doubled outside, both day and night. You're safe. More than. Get some sleep."

No part of me protested at shutting life out for a few hours. In fact, I willed it on. Just a few hours without thinking, without needing, without remembering—without guilt, without missing, without being next to Jack as his body was forced into mine, without real men getting—

"Nothing you could have done, Jan." I felt a kiss to my shoulder. "Nothing at fucking all. You got out. You got out and you stopped it."

JACK L. PYKE

CHAPTER 34
LOST WITHIN

Jack Harrison

THE DOOR EASED open and I stilled, just calmed. Someone came over to the bed, and for a moment there was only silence. I added to it as I lay there facing the window, eyes closed, needing my eyes to stay closed and for the bedroom to stay quiet. But after a moment, the bed depressed and a hand dusted my hip before gently resting there.

Deep breath in, hold for one twist of screw, two twists, release—

"Yeah." The touch was gone. "I know you're struggling, stunner. But I need to make sure the details are filled in." Gray's breathing was just as calm, just as controlled, just as practised. "You've been in the hospital for five days. You and Jan were gone twelve days before that, held in a warehouse with part of it set up to mimic your own home." A very steady fall and rise of breathing. "Maybe you don't understand the why behind it all, but you knew details; your father, Jan, me… I'm hoping it's because of all the scenes you've done. With the drugs working their way out of your system, maybe something's telling you it was a bad scene, it wasn't real. And that's half the battle fought, stunner, if that's the case. You saw Jan is hurting, and despite all the build-up of anger, you were prepared to react as a lover to a lover. But their sensory games kicked in."

He waited for a reply; he waited a long time.

"Okay." A heavy sigh. "The medical side of things." There was the ruffle of a bag. "Someone didn't wear a condom; they've passed on an infection. There are meds that you will have to take daily, mostly antibiotics. HIV test was clear. The virus PCR tested negative. Twice. So too was Jan's, although he picked up a chest infection from his forced feeding. But the main concern now is the damage that was done to your rectu—"

I shifted. The movement was enough to get him to shut up—he really needed to shut the fuck up now, especially over how much hurt Jan had taken too.

"Yeah, I know. But you need to know fearing even the basics like bowel movement is normal in these circumstances."

Fingers dug into the pillow.

"The doctor has also prescribed something to soften your stools. Please take them. If you're struggling going, talk to me, or even the doctors as soon as possible. You've had significant damage, went through surgery five days ago because of it, and you need to take it easy, rest. Get your system back to normal, and then start therapy sessions with Halliday next week. One issue you don't worry over is Vince. He's been taken care of. He won't come near you again. Keal played a part in this too, but you don't worry over him either."

Gray fell quiet, and for a moment, the world went quiet too. All colours muted, just a mixture of grey and dark as sleep started to drift close.

"Jack."

Eyes came open.

"Why I've never let you top me…" Quiet. "I'm a top, nothing more. It's my sexual preference," said Gray. "Jan… Jan was my second, and I did that purely to push your buttons, to see you heated. After eleven years together, I thought you'd recognise me as a top. It's nothing to do with your disorders, nothing at all." He sighed. "What happened afterwards? I've only ever been used to pushing you into the black when it came to crossing the line, when it came to feeling for you." His hand was back on my hip again. "That shit over Cutter, over collaring?" Breathing came a little shorter. "That was all my fuck-up." Forced control came into play. "Professional distance." He snorted. "Christ, distance is so much easier than dealing with the emotional bollocks that comes with loving you. You make being forced to feel such a fucking dangerous place to be. Part of why I Dom for the MC is because of the formality behind the Dom/sub relationships. It's not just about sex, but it is about business and keeping it as such."

Gray stroked at my hip.

"The only feelings I have anymore centre around every single move you make, and I fuck up constantly because of it. Trace, back over in America… he learned that the hard way too." Gray fell quiet for a moment. "He was already at the MC when I was first initiated as a Master, another Master sub at that, one I was told I couldn't touch." He snorted coldly. "I understand your kick against authority, Jack, but few people in my life have ever had balls enough to tell me no. That one Master did, and I partly took Trace knowing that it was purely because I was told no. Then I learned that if you go against one Master, you go against all.

"It should have taught me all the lessons I needed to learn over trust, respect, over learning to recognise another Master's compassion, but even after that, I made damn sure Trace stayed in my bed, right up until I was taken to one side by Trace's Master and told what Trace had come from. I saw more of myself in that moment than I had through all of my military and MI5 training." That quiet again. "I was no better than the pimps he'd been with, taking him from another Master just for the thrill of doing it, even though after a few weeks I knew I was in far deeper with Trace than any MC Master and sub relationship. So I walked away. At a time in his life when he needed so much better, I walked away, and pretty much killed everything inside of me in the process. I loved him, but those few weeks had seen it earned on the back of youth and corruption. Mine. I swore I wouldn't get involved and play suicidal run with anyone's feelings like that again, not without getting into their heads.

"Then you... Christ. Jack. It wasn't embarrassment I felt over you and those videos. It was much worse than that." Breathing became hard and heavy. "How Cutter looked at you, you were his, body and soul, and I was back to seeing someone else hold what was mine, what I loved, and being told in a whole new way that I couldn't, and wouldn't, have you fully. I wanted to tear Cutter to fucking pieces for it, like I had with Trace's Master, only Cutter wasn't there, you were. I wanted to hurt him even if it meant going through you to do it...." A sigh. "I'm a bastard, Jack; I get paid damn good money away from MI5 to be the worst of them, I know that, and I could feel myself slipping. It was safer for me to push you away. I thought you'd be safer away from me."

A kiss graced the back of my head. "Head fuck." Gray's head rested against the back of mine for a moment. "I should have taken my own head out of my ass and just told you how much it kills me not to have you here." He paused. "I should have stopped you leaving that night, should have kept you close, should have—Christ, Jack, just not enough bollocks to say what matters, when it matters with you...." He sounded angry and let that fade into nothing. "I'm sorry. So fucking sorry for hurting you in ways I'd kill anyone else for, stunner. You fuck up my world in so many ways, but only ever in every right way that matters anymore."

He was gone, the bed taking its natural shape as Gray went over to the door. It opened but didn't shut.

"I'll take care of Jan until you're ready to; he needs looking after. You made me promise to do that a few months back, just after Rob's funeral. It still stands, especially now. He's a damn good man, Jack, but he's scared, hurt, and so bloody confused in this fallout."

The room fell quiet and I relaxed into the silence, heart now slowing as I breathed, shifting only slightly to ease the itching in my groin, my side. Sleep. I was so fucking tired. That and I just wanted to black the world out.... Not dream.... Never dream again if possible.

≈

"Tell me you love me, Jack. Not that bastard in your dreams. I'm sick of sharing now." Vince came down, kissing at my neck. "Please. Just tell me that you love me."

More kisses tenderised my throat, and I swallowed hard, really fucking hard.

"Fucking say it—you love me."

"Yeah... love you."

"Yeah?" Vince tilted my head back, kissing at my neck, and Jan? He was back in the room. Boxing Day had gone, but he was still there, brown eyes blinking at me as I blinked back at him. Vince was on top of me, tilting my head back with a grip in my hair, eyes almost forced on Jan. "Prove it, baby." Vince was hard, so fucking hard, now pulling back and looking down on me. "Open your legs."

I breathed, very fucking deeply.

"For fuckssake, Jack." I winced as a fist slammed into the covers, inches from my head. A grip went into my hair. "Open your fucking legs. Love me."

Yeah, such a fucking easy whore.

"Fuck," mumbled Vince, coming down into my neck, biting, his body rubbing against mine now I'd allowed him in. Reaching down, he slipped his hand around my outer thigh and lifted my leg so the heel rested on the bed, then he reached between us, his cock brushing mine, before he shifted his hips back and rubbed his head against my ass.

"Come on, Jack. Touch yourself. Get this fear of Jan and the other bastard out of your body; stroke your cock against me. Let me feel you on my abs, because men: we're both fucking men here, not ponces, and real men love getting fucking dirty."

~

My breathing came to a standstill.

The light had gone from Gray's spare room and everywhere was in that almost-dead silence when I woke. A soft scratching came, and it took a while to register it came from my own fingers on skin as I eased itching at my side. Darkness was broken by moonlight, silver light that cast shadows over the room. Trees moved, stirred by a breeze, sending out shadows that danced the latest rave over the walls, the unsettlement gnawing in my stomach with how quiet the dancing scene was lately.

Social. I didn't do so—

"Just tell me you love me, Jack. Not that bastard in your dreams."

I eased the covers off me and pushed out of bed. Before Gray had come into the room earlier, I'd changed jeans and hospital clothes for jogging bottoms, the harder material of the jeans pressing the hospital gear into my groin and hips, only adding to the goddamn irritation spreading over my lower half. Giving a scowl, I looked at the bottom of the bed. The meds had been kicked out of the bag and lay tossed in the blankets, almost seeming to sigh as they settled down for the night. The bathroom was back to my right, and I glanced over my shoulder, echoes of Gray's earlier conversation kicking in.

Shivering, I left the meds there and pushed on through to the corridor outside. Eyes closed, letting the walls run under my touch for guidance, I forced calmness into the feel of the familiar. I knew the west wing, had spent many a night as a teen wandering them like this, just ghosting the night. Even back then, life was better with as few people around as possible. And over the eleven years I'd been here, nothing had changed. The walls still felt as smooth, the run of wood with red carpet striping the middle, just as known under my feet. Everything was so fucking familiar, I'd made it downstairs, through the hall, into the main lounge before I'd had the sense to open my eyes.

The giant panelled windows were covered by curtains, and I went over, using the cord to open them both so I could see outside. Gray's black Merc slept outside on the gravel, his Rolls-Royce just beyond that. From the fountain, the lights now timed to off, the sound of water was barely audible, but seemed too content to share a conversation with the forest just off in the distance. Water ran, trees waved, life went on. Fuckin' peach—

Fine. Just fucking fine.

Fucking peachy hadn't been liked here....

Feeling things calm a little more, I made it over to the white leather lounger and brought my feet up as I sat with my back against the armrest. The moon was cut into sections by the window frame, the uppermost panels lengthening the silver light, almost stretching to get farther into the room. Some fell on my feet, giving them a grey colour. Arms wrapped around knees, I listened, looked, just letting the still of the night quiet everything else. The monitor I'd broken had been replaced, so too had some of the mechanic manuals I'd left on his bookshelf. The jogging bottoms I wore were new, not ones I'd chosen, but then, I hadn't had much time to do much shopping over Christmas, Vince—

∾

"Hey, easy—easy, our kid. You need something more, don't you?" mumbled Vince.

"Huh?"

Thumbs stroked at my temples, body weighing mine down and pushing me into the bed. Breathing hurt even without Vince's weight on top of me. The deep ache and rattle with each breath felt like I'd been coughing and throwing up as tubing clogged up my throat. Dreams had been cloudy, heated: fighting Jan one moment, then scared and missing holding onto him another. But he'd not haunted my nightmares for a few days, and it confused my world. I'd woken hard and swollen between my thighs, a whole new ache playing havoc with my body. Eyes were closed, body curled away from Vince. Jan and playing with my body seemed to go hand in hand together, and with Vince sleeping, it didn't feel so wrong to explore and play nightmares off against a slow touch between my thighs.

Then Vince woke, turned over, stretched behind me, and let a hand rest around my waist.

Wrong. The bastard's touch felt so fucking wrong. On me... Jan. Which only threw my head into dark places a little more. Angry... I was supposed to be pissed at nightmares, fight them. It's what real blokes did, right?

"Oh, in the mood for playing, boy?"

He took over stroking along my dick. That displaced feeling kicked in. Nothing felt familiar. Not the bed, not the unit by my side of the bed, nor the stand that had tubes dangling down. Never the touch on my cock. Only Jan... and he was, what? Missing even from my nightmares now?

But Jan... I angrily gripped around Vince's hand, screwing my eyes closed and making him stroke harder, faster.

"Look at you there, our kid. Fucking work it for me."

But I twisted my head into the pillow, missing something, missing someone. Heavy pants of breath turned to frustrated twists of body and grunts as my orgasm hid away from me, laughing somewhere in the distance as I tried to catch up.

"Hey, easy—easy, our kid. You need something more, don't you?"

I stilled, not wanting to look at Vince, even after he'd pulled me onto my back and climbed on top.

"Those rough dreams." Thumbs stroked at my temples. "They leaving you horny now, baby?"

I twisted my head away. His voice grated on every nerve, and I wanted, needed to shut the cunt up now.

"Hey, it's okay," said Vince. He pulled me back and asked for a kiss. Needing release, any kind of release, I kissed him back, heating up in his mouth. Vince pulled back after a moment and rested his forehead against mine. "Fuck, that was good, kid." His breathing was heavy, so was mine. I guided his hand down my body. "Oh yeah, baby. You need something more. Jack, I don't like doing it, but… just to ease this ache between your legs… you want me to tie you up? I'll… I'll rough sex up enough to give you what you need this once."

Huh? That jolted me out of lust land for a moment. Why the offer of that? Without Jan, the nightmares, the familiar feel of my bedroom, Vince seemed… different. But… I groaned, body arching up into his. I needed… needed— "Christ, yes, please, Vince."

The name came with no feeling attached to it, but it came nonetheless.

"Oh yeah, baby." Hands drawn above my head, Vince reached into a drawer by the bed and tied them there with a leather belt. "Let's you and me play for a bit. Swear I won't be too rough, our kid…." A grip snaked around my throat. "It's not as if thinking about Jan has got you hard, right? This is all because of me?"

Life went pretty still.

"Oh." Vince chuckled as he reached beneath the bed and pulled out some lube. "Caught you out, Jack, our lad. You're going soft on me here."

He pulled out a baseball bat next, then started rubbing lube over the thick end.

"Give you some early morning wood in the truest form, then, eh? Then we'll see if we can get something in your cock to help with your little problem there."

Changed... something was definitely wrong with the undertones here. Vince. He came with the same voices from my nightmares.

Thick legs parting mine as I started to snarl, he came down and kissed at my cheek. "Fucking hate that you make me do this, Jack," he said with a touch of sadness, the bat rubbing along my balls, sometimes tilting and slicking my ass. "But anything to help you. You did ask for this, right? You—"

~

"Jack?"

Sat there in Gray's lounge and giving a frown, I shut out the blood-filled screams and glanced right to see a mug of coffee steamed the air from the coffee table. A bacon sandwich sat next to that, lashings of brown sauce easing out of the sides.

Who the hell eats breakfast at this shit hour of night?

But then other things started to kick in, how I wasn't on the settee anymore, but over on the chair, legs pulled up, with the telephone pulled from its usual place on the wall and sitting close to my feet. Light wasn't sliced into individual panes, but lit up the whole lounge, willing life to stir with it. Back over by the windows, moonlight had given way to a crisp winter morning. Trees looked too tired and burdened with fresh snowfall to wave anymore, and the water was lost to the morning chorus of birds. At least those bastards didn't whisper. But it did highlight how the Christmas tree was gone too, along with all of the decorations. Everything back to normal, put in its place, or replaced.

"You okay?"

I looked back to see who'd spoken. Ed crouched in front of me, eyes narrowed with worry as he blinked back. He had pure blue eyes, making him almost alien with his lack of hair and high forehead. He was close to Gray emotionally, always had been, even in blue-eyed look, although Gray carried the colour so much better.

"How long have you been down here, Jack? You look half-frozen, son."

The cold kicked in a little more, but I resisted rubbing at my arms, but couldn't stop my bastard shivering as I tried to shake myself into gear. Not long. I hadn't been down here that long.

"Take this." Ed shifted and reached back for the coffee. "Maybe have something to eat too, then go get some sleep. I think…" He glanced at the phone. "I think we need to talk to Gray, see if Martin's starting to stretch his feet more an—"

"What—what time is it?"

Ed frowned, the coffee only halfway to me. "It's getting on for six thirty. Gray will be up soon, and I'll do us all some…."

I pushed off the chair, forcing Ed to move as I headed for the door.

"Jack, where are you going?"

"Work," I mumbled, heading out into the hall for the main entrance.

"Jack, you still have your pyjama bottoms on."

I glanced down, frowning. Yeah, change. I had to get to work, but change first. Something else was said from behind, but I was already heading up the stairs. I made it back to my room ten minutes later and peeled off my clothes. I showered quick, other memories coming into play, but I shouldered them off, buried them firmly in getting dressed. Jeans on, T-shirt over my head, coveralls. Routine. Routine was—

... worry, Jack.

I stopped, just easing the itching going on with my side before finishing pulling on my coveralls.

The meds caught my attention, then the bathroom again. Giving a huff, I went over and picked up the three bottles. After dry-swallowing what I needed to take, I was downstairs, picking my car keys off the table where I'd left them a few weeks ago, and heading out for my Merc.

Gray was at the door by that time, mobile already in use as I shifted into gear. But work... I'd shirked work for long enough, and routine. No, fuck routine, this was just work. The gates to Gray's manor opened up, and I pulled onto the main road, conscious of a black Merc that followed me out.

≈

Aid was already sorting through the client list when I headed on in. I got a smile up at me as I stopped by his desk, then just a real strange, longer gaze. "Christ," said Aid. "I mean, well, are you, hmmm, okay to be in work, boss? You look…" He seemed to struggle for the words.

"Fight with an engine," I said. "I lost."

"Ouch." He grinned. "Not a good Christmas holiday, then?"

I smiled. Almost. "How have things been?"

"Good," said Aid, slipping the book over to me. "The guy your dad sent over is a bit of an arsehole, but—" Aid shrugged. "—he got the job done." Aid seemed to stiffen as the door came open behind me and I looked back to see a man in his fifties wearing a suit come in. "Speaking of which," mumbled Aid under his breath.

"Jack."

I took the man's hand. "Paul." He'd worked with my old man long since before I was born, but other than his name, I knew nothing about him. "Thanks for looking after the place. I'll see you right to the end of the week for the inconvenience, but I'll take things from here."

He seemed to stiffen a little. "Are you sure? Yesterday your father said I'd be needed for a few more weeks here yet. After your op—"

"I'm sure," I said, cutting him off and picking up the client book. "Thank you." I gave Aid a smile, dismissing Paul. "Anything in particular you want me to handle today?" The door went, and I knew we'd been left to it.

"Sure," said Aid, already sorting through the list. "We've been really busy on the run-up to Christmas. Sam was working on a job that came in late last night. It's already set up in your station."

"Christ, give him half an inch...."

Aid chuckled, and I gave him the book back before heading for the main workshop. Before I reached the door, I stopped and looked back at Aid. "Sorry for leaving you in the lurch with no warning."

Aid was waving me off. "Your dad handled the business side; I just got on with the usual. Steve came over and sorted the wages and Christmas bonuses. Moaned something about having enough on his plate, then was back over at Strachan's."

Always someone around to clear up the shit. Yeah, real man here.... "I'll give him a call later; smooth things out."

Aid nodded, then winked. "Only don't tell him I said anything about it. He's already sore about me not going with him."

"Okay. Thanks for the heads-up. Can't have Steve pissed off, now can we?" I let my smile fade as I headed on through to the main garage. The Rover took my attention, and I barely noticed as mechanics started to slip into work around me. But as someone tapped me on the shoulder, I bit back a curse and buried the need to hit something.

"What the hell are you doing, Jack?"

Giving a glance to my left, I saw my old man peering down at me as I worked by the front wheel.

CHAPTER 35
WHERE I WANT TO BE

I CARRIED ON tightening up a bolt, but another tap on my shoulder stopped me.

"Jack," said my old man. "Answer me."

"It's a garage, Dad, and I own it. What the fuck do you think I'm doing?" I didn't look up, and the torque wrench I held was pulled from my hands.

"Get home," said my old man, and I eased up. "You can't be doing this now." He leaned against a side panel.

"You have your own business to run. Leave me to mine, yeah?"

"No." He suddenly came in close, forcing me to back off a few paces. "I have a son, one I didn't even know I nearly lost." He reached to touch my neck, but he let his hand fall dejectedly to his side. "Please, Jack. Go home, even if it is to Gray's. Rest. Get better. I mean, have you even eaten anything yet, because, Christ, you, you look so fucking ill."

Pulling the cloth from my back pocket, I wiped my hands. "I'm fine."

"Yeah?" said my old man. He went over to my work table and picked up a pair of gloves. They were put in my hand a moment later. "Why aren't you wearing them, Jack? Forget your OCD, they're standard for all mechanics, or have you forgotten health and safety now?" he said, looking at me. "Now tell me you're fucking fine."

I pulled the gloves from his hands. "I forgot," I said, slipping them on. "I—" The ringing of a phone came from reception and—

∾

The phone was picked up the other end as I stood there in the lounge, pressing the receiver close to my ear.

"Dad?"

"Jack?" A pause. "Jack, honey. I hope you're enjoying that man of yours over Christmas."

"Mom… Is… Is Dad there?"

"No, honey. He's at work; I'm just picking up some solicitor's letters. What's wrong? You sound funny?"

"Tired…." Christ, it was bloody hard to talk. "Garage… is the garage okay?"

"Garage? Oh, yes. Your dad arranged someone to stand in for you when he got your text. It was short notice, though, honey—"

"—Sorry—"

"But he's got it covered. Just don't worry about it, okay? I'll see you two after the Christmas holiday, honey."

"Mom—"

"There's someone at the door, Jack. Talk soon."

The line went dead before I'd finished, and I closed my

eyes. I still held my coffee, so I let the receiver rest back in the cradle, then went over to the sofa. I sat, the coffee going in my lap, my head dropping onto the back of the sofa, and the heavy rise and fall of my chest forced me to close my eyes. Hot coffee soaking through my jogging bottoms jerked me awake, and I put the cup down.

Tired. Curling my legs up onto the sofa, I lay down and gave up the will to stay awake. Sleep... I just needed to sleep.

"Jack?" Vince crouched in front of me, head tilted slightly as he managed a small smile. "Hey, you made it downstairs on your own and had a coffee. Bet you didn't make it so far as to make that call to your old man, though?"

≈

"Jack?" Standing there in the garage, my old man's face had paled. "You..." A hand brushed mine, then rested down as my old man knelt next to me. "You were gone then." Hair was brushed away from my eyes. "An hour's lunch, son?" I looked at him. "Just enough to get something to eat, five minutes time out, maybe catch up with some sleep. I'll go get you something. But you... you need time out."

"I have food in the office," I said, easing to my feet and finding life waltzed with me. The lie over the food came easy, but it was needed.

"Good, good." My old man stood shoulder to shoulder with me as I downed my tools. For a moment I thought I heard something back over by reception, but Sue was busy working, her dinner hour staggered with Aid's so the office was always open.

"Jack, you can shout and curse me all you like when I'm gone, but—" My old man was looking back at me after he'd found Aid. "But I'm going to have a word with Aid. He's going to be made aware that you can't do any heavy labour."

He eased back a touch as I levelled my gaze on him.

"Yeah?" said my old man. "Like I haven't dealt with that look enough times through the years. I'll say you've had an op whilst you were away. Nothing more." He tried a diluted smile. "It's either that or I come here and supervise things. And trust me, I will."

The satisfaction that came to his eyes said it all when I looked away.

"Aid it is, then." I got a rub at my shoulder before my old man headed for reception. "Call me when you get off at five, Jack." He looked over his shoulder. "And I mean when you get off at five."

I wiped my hands again as he went on through to reception. He stood talking to Sue, and he made it pretty clear he wasn't going anywhere until I took a break. After tossing the cloth onto the work unit, I went on over to see Sue grin.

"Good break, Mr Harrison?"

I smiled, knowing she only kept the formalities for when my old man was around. "Yes, thanks. You…" I frowned a touch. "You have a good Christmas?"

"Quiet," she said, her look saying it had been a lover's quiet Christmas. There was still that light flush to her face, that hint of a new relationship in her eyes, and I ground some teeth away seeing it.

"Good, good," I said, registering somewhere that I'd just

repeated my old man's words.

"Steve's upstairs." She shifted slightly and pointed up. "Something about the accounts?"

"Right." I nodded at my old man before I headed through to the stairs. Old aches came back, sending glitches, little trickles of pain up into my groin, and I took things slowly with each step. By the time I'd made it upstairs and into my office, I needed to sit down.

"Jack." Steve hovered by my desk, or more my computer. Two long disposable cups were resting on it, close to my mail, and I headed on over, casting a glance at the cups, then Steve as he stood there, flicking through an accounts book. "Glad you're bloody back," he said, not looking up, but managing a scowl. "I think I fucked the accounts up a bit over Christmas." He gave a disgruntled sigh, shut the book, and then threw it on the table. "I've kept receipts and wage slips for you to review. The guy your old man sent said he'd handle it." Steve really didn't look happy, but he still wouldn't look at me either. "But he wanted to do it all via this computer program your old man uses. I tried to explain that you had a system that didn't rely so much on computers, and it took your old man stepping in to stop him screwing things up."

He stepped aside as I went over to the window. A flick of the blind saw my old man heading for his car.

"Got you this."

Letting the blind fall back into place, I saw a cup offered to me as Steve rested against the window sill. After taking the cup off him, I opened the lid. He had coffee. I had soup.

"Good break?" said Steve.

I smiled down at my soup and put the lid back on. "You

know I've been on no fucking holiday, Steve."

Things fell pretty quiet very quickly, and I looked at him. "Get a nice call off Gray this morning, did we? Just like my old man did? Everybody's suddenly best buddies lately, wanting to clean up my shit."

"Jack—"

The soup went on the window sill—and I pinned him up against the blinds. "How long have you been playing eye-spy for Gray?"

"Jack—"

"See." I pushed his head back against the window. "I never actually mentioned anything to Gray or Jan about what happened in that hotel in Essex, not outside of Sam. Yet Halliday knew." I breathed: deep, long, slow. "Surveillance… surveillance was outside of my dojo when all the shit hit the fan afterwards with Mark Shaw." I ran a thumb along his jaw. "You make that call to Gray to let him know I was at yours too?"

Steve didn't let his gaze drop. "Let me go, Jack."

"What else have you told him over the past eleven years, hmmm?" The thumb tracing his jaw dug into his throat, making it hard for him to swallow. "Because you know that surveillance crew? They were slaughtered."

Steve's face creased.

"Hmmm," I said. "Usually if I choose to disappear, it's for a good reason." I shrugged. "Either I've fucked things up for people I care about, or I need to get away from people I care about. Tell me…" I gave a small smile. "What would have happened if I'd gone back to my old man's? My mother's? Would you have seen them fucked up just to keep your nose up Gray's arse? Did you—"

An arm slipped around my throat, and I was torn off

Steve, spun back towards my office desk. Breath caught, I felt every jolt hit my body. My hip caught the corner of the table, and I stumbled away, doubling over and glaring up at Sam as he stood in front of Steve.

"Leave him alone, Jack." The scrawny bastard was shaking, yet there was something there to say he'd defend what was his. "You'll no doubt kick my ass, but I'll damn well make sure you break your neck slipping on my blood if you touch him again."

"Sam." Steve tried to push him aside, but Sam shook himself like a dog, keeping Steve behind him.

"This have anything to do with the guys that chased me away from your house all those months ago?" Sam looked ready to jump at the slightest move, mostly away from me. "With the black Mercs I keep seeing around you?" He wiped at his nose, not exactly wiping at his nose, more to stop the tears that were threatening to fall. I fucking hated those tears that threatened to fall because he mirrored Jan so much. "I don't know what you're into, what's gone on to get you all beaten up, but, Jack, stop, okay? You—just leave Steve alone. Please."

"Sam, Sam it's okay." Steve pushed him to one side. "Jack, for Christ's sake." He came over, but I shrugged him off as he went to grab my shoulder.

"Okay, okay," he said, easing off, hands up. Then he took hold of my soup and put it on the table by me. "Yeah, I called Gray over the Essex shit. And, yeah, he called me this morning and told me you'd been kidnapped and fucked over." Seeing I made no move to grab the soup, he forced me to lift my hand and take it. "Fucking sue me, Jack. Gray worships the ground you walk on. Me? I'm your fucking best friend."

I went close, nose-to-nose close. Sam was there again,

but I caught him by the hair and kept him still. "You go behind my back again, I'll forget any history we have together. We clear?" I pushed Sam between us, at Steve. "And I'll go through everyone you care about first."

Giving a sigh, Steve rested back against the window, pulling Sam away to the side, away from me. "Nice to see the thug again, Jack," he said coldly. "You know, there are a fair few people from our past who'd say you got everything you fucking deserved the past few weeks. Tell me, do you even remember the likes of Mase, what you did to him and his old man?" His lips thinned. "And now you threaten Sam? Another kid? All we need now is for Martin to make a full appearance, eh, Jack? Really get the shit-party started."

There was a lot of knowledge there in that gaze, and I eased my cup back onto the table, not letting Steve's hard-ass glance fall from mine in that moment.

CHAPTER 36
WATCHERS

STANDING THERE IN my office, Steve didn't seem fazed in the slightest about my reaction to what he'd just said. "But," he added quietly, "those people you fucked with back then, they don't know how daft and downright soft you can be around the people who you care about. Gray, your dad, now this Jan bloke: they've helped you get there." Sam started to say something, but Steve shut him up with a shake of head. "So will I phone Gray again at the risk of getting a beating off you?" Steve came in close. "Every fucking time, Jack." He eased back, tugging Sam away from me. "Now, I'm not here to make sure you drink that." Steve glanced at the soup. "I need to get the accounts sorted. Whether you believe that or not is up to you. Either way, I need to get some work done, and I need your input over *your* business I've been running, unless you still think managers are ten-a-penny, like me. Or are you gonna help?"

"I can get coffee." Sam looked between us, then settled on me. "You need a coffee, right? You always need coffee." He looked down at his hands. "Sit down for God's sake, boss, you look like you need a coffee." He was on me again. "And if this is all because of those black Mercs... please, keep them away from Liam, yeah?"

"Jack. Please," said Steve.

Whatever anger had been there was lost to nothing, just a need to get through the day, not think. Thinking led to dangerous places, ones I didn't want to open the lid on. Flicking a look at the desk, I eased the chair out and sat down, all to hear Steve rustling in his jacket pocket for something.

"Got you this," he said, placing a square-boxed present on the table. "Saw it a few weeks back and thought of you."

It took me a while to reach over and pick it up. For such a small package, it felt so fucking heavy. Picking off the ribbon, then easing the edges of the paper open, I opened the lid and pulled out a mug.

Like, worst boss e-ver was printed on it, over and over again.

I snorted a laugh, then chuckled a little more. "You twat," I said, looking at him. Steve was smiling too.

"Oh here." Sam started sorting around in my desk, hands all everywhere. "I got you this." He offered something over, and I took it off him. "Socks," I said without opening it. "Sam, socks?"

"Special ones," said Sam, letting a grin take away some of the ghosting on his face as he took the gift back and opened it himself. "Here."

They were good quality: soft, smooth. And all sorts of spanners were printed like skull and crossbones all over them.

"Y'know, for those times when you're, y'know, a little

nuts."

"Fuckssake," I choked, rolling my gaze. "Didn't exactly have the chance to get you pair anything," I said, and Steve's smile instantly dropped as Sam waved it off.

Burying it, Steve gave a shrug. "I did the Christmas bonuses, Jack. Why do you think the books aren't balancing?"

"I'm not generous enough?"

"When I'm pulling strings, yeah, you are," he said, and offered this smug grin.

"Forewarned is forearmed and all that bollocks," I said quietly, rubbing at my head. "At least I know where I stand, who to trust." A little hurt crept into his eyes. "Accounts, yeah?"

Sam seemed to relax a little. "Coffee, I'll go get you two some coffee."

"Thanks, Sam," said Steve. As he set out the books, I took a sip of the soup, then another, then it was finished as I set about sorting the books and Sam brought us up our coffees. Yeah, a few times I got a look from Steve, from me, to my soup, but I ignored it, that and the need to take a breath and not feel so fucking claustrophobic.

We were finished for three, and I was back on the garage floor for ten past. Aid had assigned Sam to give me a hand doing any heavy work. He came in handy. With Sam doing most of the moving, I kept my head on someone else's problems. Problems that were easily fixed with a spanner and torque wrench.

By five I made a call to the old man, but by half past five, I was back on the main floor. Jobs came in that needed to be done, shit always needed to be done, and after that, I couldn't give a fuck about time.

~

It was going on for twelve midnight as I threw my keys on Gray's table, then started unbuttoning my coat. Lights were still on all over the place, and it had that warm feel to it, bodies moving and having kept the old place company. Ed came out first, and nothing pissed me off more than to have him take my coat off my shoulders as I shrugged it free.

"I've got this, Jack."

I let him take it, watching as he hung it in the closet, then came back out. "I have homemade soup ready to serve, maybe some coffee? The soup, just some lovely caramelised onions, wild mushrooms, carrots. One of your favourites."

I looked at him, thinning my lips. "Thanks. I'll take some up to my room."

His eyes lit up. "Excellent. You go and get comfortable. I'll bring some up to you." He was already heading off towards the kitchen. Giving a scowl, I headed on over to the stairs, but a glance back into the open lounge had me pausing.

Jan lay curled up on the sofa, fingers curled around the edge of the blanket that was draped over him, up until it covered almost half of his face, leaving only closed eyes to the elements. He had this deep frown etched on his brow, barely visible under hair long enough to touch his eyes, and despite the warmth, he still looked as though he'd spent most of the day outside in the snow. His face was pale, the skin pulled tight over his fingers, looking more arthritic, painful to move.

Sad. He just looked so fucking sad. And alone. He shouldn't be alone now. I couldn't stand him being alone now. Wasn't us back there. Wasn't him. Although it stung: part of that had been me back there.

"He's missing you, kid. Badly."

Breathing became very calm. Gray stood behind me, and it took everything in me to look at him. There was a good few feet between us, and distance. I needed fucking distance.

"Steve call you after lunch to say whether I'd eaten?" I said, and Gray nodded. No pause, no apology for the whole spying bollocks, just a nod.

I gave a small smile.

Gray didn't. "Jack, you need to know that you can't do what you've done today again," he said calmly. "If you're going out, I need to know where and be given time to arrange surveillance."

I wiped a hand over my mouth. There was a need to run, to hit out, throw up, I just couldn't decide which. Gray came close, and I buried a groan, maybe opting more for hitting out now.

"I know you need to work, to get back to normal and see your family, but you need to know you will be under surveillance once you're outside of this property, at least until I find who's behind this. You—"

"Whatever the fuck you want," I said, looking away. "Your way or four feet under the motorway, right?"

Gray eased back. "Safety's way," he said gently, then, "What I'd *like* is for us to try and take some time out, maybe talk over the next few days. Get a statement and find out if you remember a woman named April Leamore, a nurse. Your father said a lady had bumped into him in a café in Epping Forest. CCTV picked the exchange up, and photo ID tagged her identity." Gray paused. "Miss Leamore hasn't been at work or her home address for a few weeks. Do you remember meeting her at all?"

There was a need to chuckle. "This 'talk,'" I said. "Is it something I need to dress all formal for, or will just jeans and T-shirt do? While we're on, shall we arrange a location? Your office, perhaps? Or have you gotten over being seen out in public with me yet, maybe enough to wander out in the yard, hmm? As for Martin and Leamore? How the fuck do I know? Maybe he did, maybe he didn't, maybe he just wasn't soft around the edges to allow April to put him in a box and hide him under the bed, like the more recent, and slightly more fucked-up owner—you. Have—" Time slipped. Strange thing being, I felt it coming, but couldn't stop the fall of images as—

≈

"Come on, Jack, stroke your cock against me. Come on," whispered Vince. "Touch yourself for me." I groaned, nearly clawing backwards on the bed, into Jan in the corner.

"Just me, Jack." More kisses along my throat. "There's only me now."

Jan was there, he was right fucking there in the corner.

"Chase away those bad dreams."

Bad dreams….

I let my hand find my soft cock and tried everything I could to get some life down there. I needed life down there to show him I didn't dream, that I could let him touch without worrying about dirt, but I needed quiet sometimes, just a brush of head against hip, a gentle nudge of nose to jaw, to get him to allow me to kiss, to touch, to fucking come alive, to—

"Fuck, yeah, Jack, just—just like that, beautiful. So fucking hard."

I had life down there, the fuck did I have life in my hand, in my cock. There was something—everything about feeling my cock brush hip—and as I played against Vince, he watched. I loved that he just watched.

"Yeah, fucking love that." A hand swallowed my balls, massaging, tugging. "Harder. Let me see this fucking hot body of yours shoot."

Strokes came harder, faster, and an arch of body, dig of my cock into his hips, I fucking loved it. Just that touch of cock against tanned hip, feeling all that control above me.

"C'mon, kid. Fucking work that body." I cried out feeling my cock brush his hip, every ounce of my come covering my abs as he flattened my cock against them.

"Fuck." Hands ran over my ass. "Fucking gorgeous watching you shoot like that."

I eased up as he headed into the bathroom, now sounding happier as he whistled his way through.

Come. Come stained my abs, and men—real men got dirty—let the come stay, only—

∾

"Jack?" Gray frowned at me in his hall. "You weren't here for a—"

I grabbed him close, pulling him in, stifling a cry in the curve of his throat, needing the right control, the right

413

scent, the right feeling—Gray. "Off, get the fucker off my skin."

He jolted for a moment, then I had all of Gray as— "Easy…." Hands instantly came up, stroking gently at my back, head resting against mine as he shut the world out with his hold. "Easy, stunner."

"Images… fucking fragmented—they keep tumbling around in my head, catching me out. And bastard… the bastard got the piercing wrong," I mumbled, screwing my eyes shut and gripping hard at the nape of Gray's neck— not even knowing where that last image came from. Jan's terror with being pushed down level to my chest— everything, it tried to force its way up at once. "With nipple piercing. Left's for a fucking Dom. Didn't know, he didn't fucking know subs take right," I said quickly, scared with how fast it rushed out. "Just couldn't stop it, couldn't stop them hurting us, killed me knowing Jan was hurting, that he might just be some fucked-up dream I needed to punch through, that you and Jah—"

"Jack?"

I glanced back by the lounge at the same time Gray did. Blanket wrapped around his shoulders, Jan was all barefooted with his head resting against the doorframe. Eyes seeming to ask a thousand and one questions as he frowned over at us.

It was there, that instinct to shift, to grab him into me, just hold on, and let him know it was okay. But… worry. Giving a groan as he took a step closer, I pushed away from Gray. Burying the need to throw up, I headed upstairs. Turning left to take more stairs into the west wing, I rounded a column, out of sight. Breathing a little easier, I let my head rest against the cool of the column and closed my eyes. Voices drifted up from downstairs, Jan's, Gray's.

Quiet, soft—whispers, maybe the soft sound of gentle sobs…. But more fucking whispers that only disturbed shouts and cries in my head. Then scratching, itching. It took a while to realise that last one came from me, and I frowned down at my side, the scratching at my right hip, just fucking itching. Always itching.

Burying a cry, I pushed away and headed on through the halls to my bedroom. By the time I'd showered, got into some pyjama bottoms, and climbed in bed, Ed was pushing through with a tray and coming over.

"I've added some homemade bread, just a few slices," he said, laying the tray on the bed. The fresh smell of coffee hit the bedroom too. "If you need anything else, you just give me a call, okay."

Hairs prickled on my neck, and I buried that rush to snarl every expletive under the sun at him to get things back to normal. I needed fucking normal. "This is fine, thanks," I said, pulling the tray closer. Ed gave a smile, then headed for the door.

"Actually, Ed?"

"Yes?" He looked back.

"Could you do me a flask of this for morning, for work? Maybe for the next few days too?"

"It's Sunday, you don't open on—oh." He stopped himself. "Okay. Only not a flask. I know your break times, so I'll arrange for one of the staff to bring some fresh soup to work for you throughout the day."

"That's really not necessary," I said, looking up, and slipping the cloth over the butter knife.

"Jack, it's homemade soup, my finest. It doesn't go in a flask." He left me to it at that, and I looked down at the soup. I wasn't hungry, didn't need coffee, but I ate and drank it all anyway. Then I got up and took my meds, avoiding looking at the toilet as I downed them with a glass of water. The knife was gone from the tray. Where? I couldn't really give a fuck.

I'd been in extreme scenes that left me dreading getting things back to normal, but the hurt going on in my body made me now want to crawl up into a corner and stay there. But normal. I needed normal as soon as fucking possible, not photo-casual, not routine, just fucking normal. No talking, no memories, no mentioning anything about Jack shit, no worries over getting dirty at work.

CHAPTER 37
DO YOU MISS ME?

Jan Richards

I WAS GETTING into a bad place, I knew that. Unlike Jack going to work for the past week, I hadn't left Gray's manor, not really noticing it until Gray had asked me to get dressed and go for a ride. There was security here at Gray's, and not just in the physical sense with Gray's guards patrolling the perimeter. The manor itself had that comfort to it, one I didn't think I'd come to rely on too much until I stood there in Gray's room, trying to dress. It was getting on for lunch, and Gray was waiting downstairs to head on over to Jack's garage and give him his lunch.

Just a trip to Jack's garage, ease up the pressure on Ed and Mrs Booth, and take Jack's soup to him, maybe sit in his office for a while, not talk if he didn't want to. Seeing him would be enough. And hopefully the smell of grease and oil would be enough to just let him be close to me without his face paling and looking like he needed to be sick.

Half-an-hour. Just half-an-hour there, half-an-hour back.

"Usually Ed's soup is hot enough to melt the icecaps."

I looked at Gray as I got in his Mercedes. He was acting chauffeur, so I took the passenger side next to him. "Huh?"

He nodded at the tub of soup in my hands. "It's not a life preserver," he said quietly. "You can loosen your grip before you get second-degree burns."

The heat from the soup kicked in a little then, and I put the tub between my feet on the floor. "At least he's eating," I said, easing back and rubbing at my hands as he pulled away. I sneaked a look at Gray. "And taking his meds." I wondered if Jack knew Gray was keeping close tabs. "Just wish he was talking a little," I said more moodily than I'd intended.

Gray glanced over as he shifted gear. "He's not been in touch with Halliday since the hospital. Neither have you," he said, eyes now focused on the road. "That's a concern."

"Yeah..." The soup took my attention. "I know. You spoke to Halliday?"

"Only to find out that Jack didn't attend yesterday's appointment, that you missed it the day before. Halliday won't discuss Jack or you with anyone but Jack or you."

I snorted. "Even though he knows what you do for a living with MI5 and whatever this... culler thing is? Brave man." I rubbed tiredly at my eyes. "Wouldn't surprise me if you have a copy of Jack's file sitting on your study desk at home. Or mine."

Gray just snorted a smile as we pulled into Jack's garage. Another black Mercedes sat discreetly in the corner. No acknowledgement was given between Gray and the occupants of the other car. I knew who they were, well one:

Gray's head of security, Ray, and they sure as hell knew who Gray was.

"You've spoken to your mother?" said Gray quietly.

I gave him a nod. The formal questions he'd asked me had been done at his, along with a formal statement. Whatever checks he'd done with my family had been kept away from me, although the rush of calls that came through off my mother and sisters, a scramble of tag-team unite to try and find out what was going on, had assaulted the usual quiet of Gray's. They'd quieted down over the past few days. Gray hadn't given them any details, I knew that much, but I was far from ready to talk too. There had been a quiet understanding from the other end of the phone from my mother, that sense that something was more than just wrong, but that it needed time and patience. She had plenty of that and seemed to calm my sisters down without saying much else either. Time. Everything needed time.

"Any further leads with the Leamore woman?" I said eventually. Gray seemed to be the only one constantly in work mode, whether tracing leads or just being aware of movement around me or Jack, especially movement around the manor and Jack's work.

"No traces yet, but her bank account held a few surprises."

"Surprises?"

"Large deposits of cash from an untraceable source that started six months ago. It's timed with large withdrawals and work colleagues stating Leamore had started spending more extravagantly. New car, clothes, meals out.

"All money was also withdrawn from her account the day we got you two back; ID cards have been recovered from her home, also some recent photos and observations of Jack's movement to and from his home."

"So she did know Jack."

"From preliminary investigations, yes. Interviews with her ex-husband said he'd caught Martin and Leamore in bed together."

He wasn't mentioned often, but every time Martin was, that coldness crept in with Gray. Surely Jack was still Jack at the end of the day? This... Martin wasn't that... destructive?

"Martin played serious head games with April's family," added Gray, "and their marriage disintegrated from that point on." He fell quiet for a little too long, and I watched him.

"What's wrong with that?"

"Hmm?" Gray glanced at me. "Greg mentioned that April asked if Greg was Jack's dad."

"And?" But I frowned, maybe seeing what the issue was. "How did she know Greg was Jack's dad, especially if she'd only seen this Martin?"

Gray gave a thin smile.

"But Jack said he woke in other women's beds... so they must have seen Jack at some point?"

"He woke in their beds. No one stays and closes their eyes around Martin."

The more he was mentioned, the more I didn't like the sound of this Martin. Jack had never shown any interest in women: why the hell would Martin? And what kind of head games had he been involved with back then? "Jack had been what, eighteen, nineteen during those states. How old was this woman when he slept with her?"

"Records put her at thirty-five when she met Jack,

seventeen years older than him."

I fell quiet. Jack was drawn to older men, Gray being the main point of discussion here. But Cutter had been older too, a good ten years. Seemed he preferred the older female too. I'd been the exception. Or maybe I was just Jack going casual, throwing something out of order? Would he feel the need to push everything back into place eventually? Where would that leave me? "And her husband, he doesn't know April's whereabouts?"

Gray shook his head and shifted to grab something out of his jacket. From his wallet, he pulled out a picture. "Do you recognise her at all?"

I stared for long moments, then eventually took the photo. Hair was long and straight, greying at the temples. The woman in the photo hugged an Old English Sheepdog, forcing her to tilt her head slightly to dodge a huge tongue that was trying to get her cheek. Although slightly overweight, there was something about her that said she'd been a looker in her youth. She carried the weight well now. But mostly she looked... normal. Not like she'd want to see two men raped for the fun of filming it.

"Jan?"

I shook my head. "No."

"Okay." Gray slipped the photo back in his wallet and tucked it back in his pocket.

"Suppose I better get this to Jack." I gave a shaky sigh. "Won't be long." I was about to reach down and take hold of the soup when Gray's hard look towards the open garage roller doors caught my attention. Jack had just come outside, followed a moment later by a man and an older-looking woman, both wearing suits. Jack had stopped by Sam's Corsa, now leaning back against it with folded arms.

The two strangers stood close, seeming intent and focused on whatever Jack was saying.

A text came through for Gray, and he was already shifting to get at it. He didn't look impressed as he read, switching his gaze between the mobile and the two people hovering around Jack. He sorted through his contacts, then he typed in a message and pressed send.

"Foe?" I said, wise enough to recognise the change in Gray.

Gray watched Jack say goodbye to the man and the woman. Then he waited for Jack to head on back into the garage. As the two strangers rounded Jack's garage and started to head off towards a few cars parked along the side of Jack's place, Gray kept a close watch on them.

"Usually friend." Gray pushed out of his Merc.

Giving a frown, I finally found the will to get out and follow Gray as he headed off after them. I caught up just as the woman pulled open the driver side door of a Lexus. She looked a little startled as Gray pushed it shut and leaned against the panel, arms folded.

"Detective Chief Inspector Sanders." He didn't look at her. "What business do you have with Mr Harrison?"

The woman frowned for an instant, then gave a nod over to the man who stared at Gray. "Detective Sergeant, can you give us a minute, please?" A look over at me as I waited on the other side of the road, the DS eased down into the car.

"Is Mr Harrison under investigation by MI5?" the DCI asked, looking at me too. If she was the police, then she'd just got me wrong. I was nothing to do with MI5, but Gray didn't correct her.

"That's none of your business," said Gray flatly, and

Sanders sorted around in her jacket. She'd had her keys a moment ago and had slipped them into her left pocket.

"Likewise, sir," she said to Gray, not even looking at him as she cursed under her breath. She found her keys and tugged the car door open. Gray shut it again, this time leaning against it.

"I asked a question." Gray eased back, folding his arms as Sanders sighed heavily.

"Move please, Mr Raoul."

Gray smiled down to the floor. "Not what I asked you. Answer the fucking question I did ask."

Sanders snorted, causing a strand of hair to fall from her bound hair. "Don't you just love the Secret Service arseholes," she added, reaching for the handle of her car. "We're investigating Mr Harrison's kidnap and rape," she said flatly, and that won all of Gray's attention.

"Not anymore."

Sanders only narrowed her eyes. "This is police business. It interests MI5 because?"

"Regional instability," he said flatly. "The case is already under investigation."

"And Mr Harrison?"

"Witness protection."

"Yours?"

"Cullers."

She stiffened. "Then we'll assist in any way we can. I'm not your enemy here, Mr Raoul." Why was there a hint of fear now? Just who the hell were these cullers? Who called them in?

A mobile text alert beeped, and Sanders pulled out her phone. "Excuse me a moment, sir," she said. "Oh, right."

She looked at her mobile. "We won't be assisting, it seems." She focused on Gray. "Have a nice day, Mr Raoul. Give my boss, Mr Brennan, my regards."

Gray had sent a text in the car. Was that who he'd spoken to?

"One more thing," said Gray, stopping her. "Did he give you a statement?"

"Mr Harrison? Not formally, no." She eased back. "With the drugs they put in his system, it makes him a pretty unreliable witness."

"Did you tell him that?" Gray didn't look happy.

"Of course not," Sanders said stiffly. "We were going to check out the details he could remember, see if we could draw something from that."

"What details?"

Sanders reached in the car and took something off the DS. A notepad. Easing back up, she started thumbing through it. "The name 'Vince' was mentioned. No surname. Also that Mr Harrison was at home during the kidnapping. He spoke to his mother, saw her, but wasn't too sure on the second one there."

"On seeing his mother. Why?"

Sanders turned a page. "Said she just looked and smelled different."

"But there was a woman?"

Sanders shrugged. "Harrison knows his system was pumped full of drugs. Even he said there was a possibility the 'she' could have been a 'he in drag.'"

Gray nodded. "Anything else?"

Sanders went to slip the notepad in her pocket, but Gray took it off her. "He just wants to know who," she said quietly. "He didn't go into graphic detail, just some of the sights and smells he remembered." She glanced over at me. "I think he's lucky to have been given those drugs. It doesn't sound a good place to be."

Gray nodded, then opened the door for Sanders to get in. She eyed him suspiciously for a moment, then took the hint, even though Gray had taken her notepad.

"If Mr Harrison phones and asks for an update," he said, leaning down to talk, "tell him you're investigating a few leads surrounding Corsica and a woman named April Leamore."

"April Leamore?"

"Leamore," said Gray before shutting the door. Waiting for a car to pass, Gray came over and we waited for Sanders and her DS to pull away, Sanders's gaze staying on us.

"Why involve the police?" I frowned. "Jack knows you're MI5 now."

"I don't know. But Sanders mentioned Jack thought it happened at his home."

"I thought you'd told him about the warehouse—that Vince was out of the picture?"

"I did." A glance down at the notepad, Gray headed back towards the garage.

～

"Excuse me, that's marked staff only."

I didn't recognise the man in the reception as I pushed on through after Gray. Gray was already heading for the stairs when the man behind the desk made the mistake of getting in his way. The look off Gray deterred him from reaching a hand up to hold him off, but the man still didn't move.

"Do you have an appointment?"

"You won't have a fucking face if you don't move," said Gray quietly, and the man gave a raised brow.

"I'm the manager here. And you just got yourself banned from going anywhere on these premises, my friend."

"Not your friend." Gray went close, but whatever threat running free there was buried as Sue came through, her eyes widening. "Gray." She noticed me last. "Mr Richards." Gray got all of her attention again. "Mr Raoul is allowed up to see Mr Harrison, Aid."

Ah, so that was Aid there.

"Okay, Sue." Aid moved out of Gray's way and headed over to the main doors through to the garage floor. He cast a wary glance back. "Be good to know these things."

"Apologies," said Sue, and Aid gave her a practised smile. "Would you like for me to take you through?"

"No thank you, Sue. Jack's expecting us," said Gray, and he took some of the stairs. I offered a smile over, which only made Sue frown, then I went up after Gray.

"You okay?" mouthed Gray, waiting, and I nodded, conscious of the soup. A tap on the door, Gray didn't wait for an answer before he entered.

Jack sat behind his desk, hair a little wilder than normal, as though he'd been dozing with his head buried in arms folded on the desk. He eased back into his chair and wiped a hand over his face, and it was only as his hand fell that his body stiffened seeing Gray.

Seeing me.

Trying to judge how many windows were open to counterbalance the draught from the door, how it might have caught and pushed my scent on him, I took the soup over to his desk. Jack started to stand, still looking so sodding pale, half-looking like he'd bolt out of the window if he could. Then he seemed to go grey, even colour draining from his lips, and he gave up, sitting back down heavily.

"Hungry?" I offered the soup over.

Because real men get dirty...

The falter was there, nearly pulling back with the soup to stop him shrinking away.

Jack didn't look at me, just glared at the soup. I wished to God he'd just look at me.

"I told Ed not to bother sending anyone if it was a problem," he said, that bite there in his voice as he half-heartedly looked around me to Gray.

"It's not a problem." Gray came over, made a point of flicking a look at me, then Jack. "I just thought you might like some company."

Jack never touched his soup as I left it there. "Not particularly," he said. "I'm wanted on the garage floor in ten minutes."

Lying fuck. Everything about him said so.

"Then this will only take five," said Gray.

A grunt, Jack pulled the soup to him and opened it up. It came in one of those special bowls that had room for a spoon, and he peered in at it. Christmas day, he'd barely touched Vince's food before throwing up. Had they been force-feeding him too? It had taken me a while to think about picking up a spoon and try eating without gagging.

"Whilst we're here," said Gray, moving over to a comfy

sofa. That was new. It even had the tag on it to say so. Jack wasn't going home to his house at all. "I want to ask you a few things," he said, taking a seat. Gray glanced at me, but I didn't move, partly because of aches and pains, partly because I couldn't.

"Not in the mood, Gray," said Jack. He'd taken a few spoonfuls of soup, but he was looking a little uncomfortable.

"Why the police involvement?" That couldn't have been put any more bluntly from Gray, but then he wasn't one for beating the proverbial bush, not without a living target in there he could leave bloodied for the effort.

Jack eased back, rubbing at his head. "Police?"

"They were just here, Jack." Gray seemed to physically push away any confrontation hearing it. "Who have you been talking to?"

"*I sort my own shit,*" snapped Jack, still not looking at me, but then he screwed his face and shrugged. "They turned up today saying I'd called them Monday morning—"

"Jack," warned Gray, looking a little on edge. "Mart—"

"*And why the fuck would he call them?*" he shouted. "*I just don't fucking remember when… why I spoke to them.*"

Thoughts drifted back to Ed, to when he'd found Jack downstairs that morning after coming out of the hospital. He'd mentioned that Jack had been sitting on a chair with the phone pulled onto the floor. Just who the fuck *was* Martin, and why the hell did he still have Gray on edge every time he was mentioned? Why would Gray be pissed at him calling the police in?

"I don't know what the fuck happened," snapped Jack. "Couldn't have been such a bad idea, though. The sooner Vinc—" He stopped, not saying anything, fingers running over the soup bowl.

"Vince?" said Gray. "Jack, do you remember me saying Vince had been taken care of? That Keal was involved as well, and he's been taken out of the picture?" Jack narrowed his gaze at the soup as Gray sat forward, elbows now on his knees. "Doesn't matter," he added, watching Jack closely. "What is good is that you remembered some more detail, like with the piercing?"

I stiffened; Jack looked at the door—made a point of staring at the door.

"Jack," said Gray. "I'm going over these details now and I'm going to repeat them every couple of days. Do you remember the cameras in the bedroom at all? When you were with Vince?"

Jack tapped his spoon on the soup bowl, knee bouncing under the desk.

"Everything was being filmed," I added quietly. A frown, nothing more. I thought he knew this. "The cameras were hooked to an observation room, one that filmed everything that happened."

"Internet?" That was rushed out, panicked, but a question. Questions were so fucking good to hear. But I glanced at Gray quickly, not knowing the answer to that myself—but needing to know the answer.

"We think there were only a few watchers," said Gray quietly. "Nothing has been found on the web, but somebody was watching."

Jack seemed to shiver.

"Do you remember that I mentioned April Leamore?"

Faster tapping came now on the bowl, enough to nearly knock the soup into a rowdy protest that would see it revolt and burn the way it was going.

"We think she's the one who hired Vince to kidnap us and hold us in the warehouse," I said. "Do you remember Gray saying it didn't happen at your home?" The new settee here suggested that he didn't remember. "The warehouse was set up to look just like your hom—"

That was it—he lost whatever patience he had as he stood and headed for the office door.

"Jack," said Gray, making him stop as he grabbed the handle. "Bad scene," he said quietly. "You were strong enough to see it."

"But not fucking fast enough." Jack glanced over at me for the first time. There was something there in his eyes; I'd seen it briefly Saturday night when he'd come back from that first day's work, that need to close the distance, say fuck to the hurt, cuddle up—hold—hide. He went to say something, there was hurt and shame in his look, but he stepped back from me in almost the same instant. A glance at Gray, a long look that seemed to cling onto him for a few minutes more, he left.

The door closed, and I went back over to his desk and put the lid back on his soup. It was something to focus on other than Jack running away again.

"Hardest part," whispered Gray, and I glanced up to find him right beside me. "Filling the blackness," he said quietly. "Time." Gray rubbed a thumb over my hand. "He just needs time. You both do. You've got a lot of anger left over."

"He's fucking hurting, Gray."

"I know." Gray frowned. "We'll watch, wait. We do this his way, at his pace, but at yours too."

CHAPTER 38
THE DEVIL YOU DON'T KNOW

OUR WAY STARTED to take a long time, and another four weeks of it led to the inevitable: Jack's home.

Arms traced my waist, pulling me back slightly into a hold, and a kiss went to my neck as a gentle whisper was given, just a simple "You okay?" I let it push down the snap of anger, the need to scurry into the corner of Jack's master bedroom and hide. Sense told me the rape and torture hadn't happened here, but all the smells, sights, just the familiarity of everything belonging to Jack was twisted and touched by Vince, even though he probably hadn't risked touching anything here at all.

Gray's men had taken prints, checking whatever else it was that they checked, but this was the first time that I'd stood here. We were close to where I'd sent the text to Gray, just before Vince had slipped in behind me, and it had that same night-hour quietness to it now. Bedsheets were gone, so too was the mattress. It was unclear whether Vince had taken Jack to the warehouse straight away, and I dreaded what tests were being done. But other than that, everything just seemed so normal; no hooks in walls, no chains, no torn-out piercings, penis plugs.

"Jan?" said Gray, quietly.

"'M okay." I'd maybe needed Jack here to face this with me, but Gray offered calmness that didn't come with nightmares. I nodded, let my arms rest across his as he held me from behind, his grip a lot gentler than Vince's.

Staff had been sent daily to my home to pick up my mail; then I found my letters appearing at the manor with the post through Gray. No doubt he'd had it redirected. Not quite sure how he got around the red tape there to do that, but then I hadn't really cared. He'd done the same with Jack, redirecting his mail, taking care of his bills, mine. But where I now showed a need to get a foothold in reality, Jack hadn't.

In fact, Jack hadn't acknowledged life away from Gray's, his garage, and his parents. All he'd done for the past four weeks was work, eat, and sleep. He looked better. A damn sight better than when he'd come out of hospital. He'd lost weight during his time with Vince, we both had, and the week that followed had only seen him lose more. His clothes had looked loose around his body, all the toned muscle that had been complemented with supple skin had just defined bone. Eventually soup had altered to light sandwiches a few days later, followed by a warm two-course meal a week or so after that. Ed always made sure Jack had the same when he got home, sometimes as late as one in the morning, although the offer of bacon in the morning was always turned down for some reason. So too were the offers from me to sit with him at lunch.

Jack had steadily gained weight, losing that pale and drawn look, looking more his old self. From the checks that Gray still did on Jack's meds, Jack had kept religiously to them, which hopefully meant that his system was coping with the basics. Christ knows I knew how that felt. My antibiotics had finished, although Gray had been the one to point that out and arrange a follow-up visit back into the MC to double-check my chest infection was gone. But with Jack, Gray didn't ask, Jack didn't say, neither did I. Some things were too private. This wasn't a lack of communication, just the need to give Jack his space, let him come around and talk under his own steam over what had happened back there. But apart from Saturday mornings where the working week seemed to catch up with him, and he stayed in bed a few times, occasionally running late for work, there was no pain in Jack's eyes when he moved. From what Gray heard off DCI Sanders, Jack hadn't been in touch with her at all, his life centring around work and the people who mattered.

That left me… where?

Other than that, he showered, changed, brushed his teeth, and shaved, all the normal routine. But I hadn't once seen him go casual with a photo or magazine. He hadn't once washed his hands more than necessary. Ed would deliberately use the mats Jack hated on the dining table, and Jack hadn't complained. Just ate his dinner and left the mess for Ed to clear up. Something Jack had never done before either.

We all looked for the signs that he was fighting not doing it, but there was none. No inner battle about him, just getting on with life.

Taking away the rape and torture, Gray said Vince had used a known technique by psychologists to help OCD sufferers come to terms with their disorder. In some sick way, it seemed to have worked.

In an even sicker way, Vince had just gotten to keep another part of Jack. And as the threat of Jack's blackouts and absences seemed to have settled, maybe it was a part we'd never get back.

"I'll have to ask Jack if he wants me to sell this place," said Gray, focusing my attention again. I looked around the bedroom, to the bed, to where Jack and I had slept that night, how he'd hid in me.

"No," I said quietly, resting back onto Gray's shoulder. "He's still here," I mumbled. "Keep the good, fucking annihilate the bad."

Another kiss graced my cheek. "Just have to get his ass back in here," said Gray, and I turned to face him.

"Maybe we can tickle him into submission? It would be good to hear him cry again how his giggles are 'manly, not fucking girly giggles.'"

Gray dropped his gaze so quickly then, maybe for different times, different memories.

"No fingerprints were pulled from here?" I looked at the DVD player in particular. I couldn't even remember if they'd been wearing gloves.

"Nothing." Gray shifted over to the window and looked out. "Same went for the fibres on your clothes, the ones they took over to the warehouse."

"This Leamore woman, the psychological aspect, she knew what she was doing."

"Certainly had the background knowledge, or access to it at least." Gray leaned back against the window frame as the blind fell back into place. "Organised. Everything timed until it fell apart with the overdose."

I looked at him. "You still don't sound happy, like with April saying 'Jack's' dad, not Martin's."

He stayed quiet, maybe not ready to say anything.

"What about the mock-up of Jack's home? Anything there?"

"No prints except yours and Jack's."

Had they been wearing gloves? "Nothing to tie Leamore to it?"

Gray thinned his lips in answer. "We know Leamore took a trip to Corsica just a few weeks after Mark Shaw died, and the warehouse changed hands via a company over there roughly at the same time, also when those links were downloaded."

"But you're still not happy?"

"Something stinks about this whole setup. Some things fall too easily into place, others… Then there's how April knew Jack, and the money deposited in her account."

"Where it came from?"

"Hmmmm. Money went to her from an untraceable source. A lot of it."

"So someone with enough financial backing for all of this is hiding her? And in the meantime—"

Gray's phone cut me off, and he pulled it free from his pocket.

"Here." Nothing else was given, just Gray listening, then he slipped his mobile back into his pocket. He looked at me, and he seemed to look for a very long time. "We're going out tonight." There was a ghost of a smile. "And this time you're wearing a suit."

Giving a frown as Gray headed out of the bedroom, I forced myself to stay in here a little longer, claim some of the space back as my own.

Because real men got dirty now.

I didn't stay for long.

~

Gray never gave an indication as to what the call was about, or where we were going later tonight, but I noticed his change in mood as I'd climbed in the Mercedes next to him. Something behind that call had his… black-eyed side going. We reached home, and Gray left me there in the reception hall and drove away without a word. He came back a few hours later carrying a few things. We waited in the lounge, not talking, just watching the clock. Gray stayed like that until Jack came home at ten. Not much was said, Jack doing his usual grunt, eating, then going off to bed; Gray watching, just waiting as he did so, giving it another hour for Jack to settle. Then I was told to go and have a shower and get changed into the clothes laid out on the bed.

The black tuxedo with matching black tie and white shirt came with a brand name my wages would never see, and I got paid damn well. Part of me questioned why Gray was allowing me to tag along, but then he'd been gently pushing me back out into normality, building confidence, everything I needed to do for Jack. Boxers, socks, and new shoes were also laid out, along with cufflinks and new cologne. It didn't take long getting ready: quick shower, dress, arrange the cufflinks, add the cologne, and I was done.

Going out of the door on a Saturday night was another matter, and I nearly jumped a mile finding Gray standing there watching, at the bedroom door, waiting.

"Sorry," he said quietly. He'd dressed elsewhere, the same classic design, but a light grey suit that made his look and eyes come alive. "We won't be out long, I promise."

I stopped by him, and we stayed there for a moment, just watching. I didn't realise I was running a touch down his jacket, missing the look—his look—until he stroked at my cheek.

"You're damn tougher than you look, Jan." Gray frowned, shifting from my cheek to my jaw. "Hurt being with him, I know. But I'm damn glad he wasn't alone." A gentle stroke at my neck now. "Glad you weren't alone."

Again that moment of watching, then my lips found his, surprising and scaring the hell out of me. Gray's reaction, his intensity, was breathtaking, but terrifying at the same time. Pushed back against the door, everything about him threatened to swallow me up, and I nearly pushed him away, crying out. We were opposite ends of the continuum, Gray crying out to dominate, me just to find comfort after the hurt. As a triad, the intensity was balanced, but take Jack away, things felt odd—too much for me, too little for Gray, and all of Gray's passion was suddenly tempered, my look going back towards the west wing, Gray's following, and no doubt hating how empty love had been as of late.

"Miss him, hmmm?" I said quietly.

Gray's gaze never quite met mine. "So fucking badly, lad."

"Come on," I said, giving a gentle tug at his jacket. "Let's go see what's got you going enough to let Jack out of your sights for an hour."

∾

Just opposite Regent Language Training School on Villers Street, Heaven Nightclub was one of London's top nightclubs, catering to mostly the gay community and with a reputation for attracting some of the sexiest clubbers going. Three floors offered rave and live entertainment, a first-class laser-light display on the ground floor, people crammed in there from all over the United Kingdom, its reputation for setting the scene for a damn good night putting it on top of the gay tourist hit list. I'd been here on the rare occasion with a few friends, mostly on Friday night, though, not Saturday, and queuing outside amongst the rows of people, like those lining the street tonight, praying a long working day wasn't showing. It was rumoured that the bouncers in any London club turned guys away for looking tired. So smartly dressed and lively was the order for most nights, which if you intended to work your way through the throng of partygoers to get to the bar, you especially needed the lively part.

Tonight it was different. Ed pulled the Rolls-Royce to a stop outside the main doors and two beefy-looking bouncers dressed in suits and wearing sunglasses instantly cleared the door. A moment later, one was over by the Rolls, allowing Gray to get out. It was strange: I'd never seen this side of the rope barrier, and as I got out, I thought there'd be that wonder, that starry-eyed, playing-with-the-big-boys bullshit I saw playing here from the other side of the rope. That barrier had offered a lot of safety, some of which I regretted losing, some of which I didn't. Faces were a blur, the bouncers an echo of a past obstacle, but who oddly only stepped out of our way now.

The club acoustics kicked in as soon as we entered, so did the crowd, heavily framed by the laser-lit darkness. Each breath drew in a thin film of dry ice, frosting the lungs slightly and almost making me cough. Men laughed, danced, got a little more heated off on the sidelines, the bouncers keeping a watch just in case it became too heated.

Some guys here looked like their jeans were spray-painted on, shirts tight, skin slightly damp from the heat—like a fine roast, basted, cooked, and more than ready to taste. Gray had pinned me as a watcher. Maybe I had been but—

"Vince's raping the fuck out of your boyfriend—again—and you, you're just watching. You like to watch, eh, Jan? Is that what gets you going? Jack being rough-fucked in front of you?"

Sickness hit my stomach. I wasn't a watcher anymore.

Someone bumped into me, knocking me slightly, some slip of a guy, drink in hand. By the time I jerked away, a bouncer was already there, doing the *back off* with a glare that earned me a dirty look off the guy. Then I was forgotten as a fresh wave of rave took him off dancing.

"Upstairs," one bouncer shouted in my ear from behind. Another had already taken up place in front of me. Gray was on the staircase, looking over and waiting some distance away. I followed the bouncers, Gray's look seeming enough to convince the lead bouncer to fall behind me now Gray was close and in the lead. All so bloody quietly from Gray, but each bouncer shifting, moving, complying to say they knew was needed off Gray, and when he'd need it.

Once we made it to the stairs, the bouncers took us up to the third floor. Overlooking the dance floor towards the far end was what looked like a VIP lounge. Glass partitions kept the normal partygoers separate, showing off more space inside than seemed fair to the people who had paid over fifteen pound a head to get in. I didn't mind getting the "London look" off the clubbers as I followed Gray in. From the twenty or so people in there, some seemed to know Gray. None knew me, although I wondered if they really knew Gray, if they'd really want to.

Going over to a group of leather settees set away from

any prying ears, Gray sat down, and I followed as a waitress came over carrying a whiskey on her tray. Handing it to Gray, she looked at me.

"Orange juice, please," I said, envying how easy people seemed to smile. After the waitress brought my juice over, we sat drinking for a while, mostly in silence, Gray content to keep it that way as he answered a text.

"Why are we here?" I said eventually, watching a young couple being served at the bar.

"Meeting a contact," said Gray.

"You're here to… work?" I said, somewhat distractedly. "When's he meant to show?"

"She already has." He didn't look up from his mobile. "You stereotyping again?" A slight smile. "It's not guys in overcoats, Jan." He glanced up, his look not as hard as his words. "You okay?"

I wiped at my eyes, drink held steady in the other. "Just tired. Just need this to be over and—"

"Intelligence takes time." But there was something about his eyes.

"But something's got you here. You do social worse than Jack does. What do you know? What was that call about earlier?" I kept that low, quiet, and Gray leaned forward to put his drink on the table before easing back.

"I need you to ID someone for me."

"*What?* Here?" I rubbed at my head. "Who?"

He leaned close, now all concern. "You stay up here at all times, are we clear? I just need you to give me a nod when you see him."

"You like to watch, eh, Jan? Is that what gets you going? Jack being rough-fucked in front of you?"

I stood, started to, until Gray eased me back down with a grip on my arm. Vince had been taken down; Doc. That only left Henry.

"You see him down there, you give me the nod, nothing more."

"No, Gray." Christ, no. "You can't do this to me." Sickness churned hard, and I looked down at my hands as I played with a cufflink. "Please don't fucking do this to me."

"You're safe here," said Gray quietly. "You have Mikal over by the manager's office." Sure enough, a guy in his forties, dressed casually in jeans and shirt, stood just outside the door marked off-limits to anyone but Staff. "And there's Kate and Hector sitting at the bar. They are MI5, with Andrews, my lead operative, on CCTV in a side office."

The youngish lovers I'd seen earlier were still laughing, their conversation hushed. They looked like any normal couple, even down to ignoring me as I looked over. And then I was shaking slightly. "If you know he's here, why not get him into a police line-up?" I looked at Gray, needing his reassurance that Henry wouldn't be able to get close.

"I'm not on duty tonight." Gray glanced at me. "This is for you."

I looked down at my hands, part of me needing that image of Gray standing there with a bloodied bat, part of me wanting to cry *Enough* and crawl under the covers with Jack and just hide. But Jack wouldn't let anyone hide with him, and nothing I had left could coax him out. Grinding my teeth, I eased to my feet and went over to look down onto the dance floor.

The clubbers were one living and breathing ocean, the

pull of the music acting like the moon to make them move to its will. It looked like you couldn't breathe down there, yet people danced, laughed, punched through the laser light in time to the bass, loving every minute of it.

"Just take your time." Gray leaned next to me, one hand in his pocket as he peered down.

Nothing would make me forget Henry, with all of his long arms, always touching, feeling hands, that pock-marked face, and cheap fucking gold watch, but I guessed I'd recognise his cock more, with how many times he'd stuffed it down my throat after a forced feeding. Giving an unsteady sigh, I was about to push away and go and get a stronger drink when something by the main bar caught my attention.

The bar itself was brightly lit, casting a good few feet of white neon and soft blue light onto the clubbers vying for drinking space. Yet face-on to me, in the far corner—

Jack stood talking to a couple of guys, his smile as easy as anything as one guy leaned in and said something to him.

"What the?" I automatically scanned the crowd for Henry, that was my first thought. Then Jack took my sole focus. We'd left him in bed. I'd *seen* him grunt his way to bed over two hours ago. How the hell—

He wore black suit trousers, crisp white shirt, tucked in, then folded up at the sleeves just to give a tantalising glimpse of what lay beneath, and the two men by him seemed to be sniffing around to find a way in. The bigger of the two, a guy packing enough muscle to push a few trucks about, said something to Jack, and Jack shook his head. A moment later he was tugged onto the dance floor by the big guy, the other, slimmer man following now he'd taken Jack's drink and left it on the side.

On the dance floor, the music shifted, some fast-pulsed, deep-bass where a guy sang about life always being sexed-up, and the clubbers sang along, the two men now moving in close by Jack, the big guy behind, the slimmer one in front, Jack caught between them both. Jack smiled shyly, not really moving as the two guys rubbed against him. But as the music hit the chorus, the pulse and shout of the crowd instantly infected Jack—he danced, and things suddenly heated up down there. Jack had that same ability to make the most simplistic shift of body against body suggest a thousand and one wicked ways to play between the sheets, and the big guy behind him slipped his hands around Jack's waist to show just how much he damn well appreciated the invitation. I could almost see his dick punch the air to the heavy beat from here.

I was about to tell Gray, then noticed somebody (Mikal?) was already by us and whispering something in his ear.

Gray looked back down on the dance floor, for a moment scanning the crowd. Then he obviously caught on as to who was here. After a slow ease away from the glass, he was moving for the doors. Giving a last glance down, I followed. People behind suddenly shifted as if to stop me, but I was already through the door and taking the stairs two at a time.

By the time I made it to the first floor, over to the bar where Jack had been dancing, he was nowhere to be seen.

Panic tore through me. If Henry was here, if he'd seen Jack—if he'd fucking *touched* Jack—

Gray leaned over the bar to have a word with the bartender, and he was pointed over to the door marked *Private*. It led on through to a comfortable hall with thick carpet, soft lighting, and mahogany picture frames. Tasteful. All that left was a door at the end that Gray didn't let sleep for long. After making it slam against the wall and the occupants jerk their heads in our direction, things went very quiet, very fucking quickly as Gray went in.

Jack was up against a wall, the big guy pressed in close, hands having tugged Jack's shirt out and messing with the skin beneath. Up close, the man was even bigger, and he was the one who got all of Gray's attention as his smaller ferret of a friend tugged a condom out of a wrapper.

Going nose to nose with the big guy, even though Gray fell short in every department going, Gray backed the man away from Jack without a single word uttered.

"What—?"

Gray levelled a *shut-it* finger in Jack's direction, yet stayed completely with the big man as something fell from the man's hand. It hadn't been visible under Jack's shirt, but now it caught the light as it hit the floor.

"Get him upstairs, Ray," said Gray, not even looking back, but I did, and just in time to see a man dressed in plain clothes standing by the door. Gray's head of security. Had he followed Jack from home? As he came over, Jack backed away, looking scared as hell, enough for me to nearly hit Ray for getting close. But there was something about Jack's look that cut short any cry. Locking Jack's arms behind his back, nearly lifting Jack onto his tiptoes, Ray started to drag him out of the backroom. There was no aggression, no fight, and Jack was usually all fight. And his eyes… what the fuck was wrong with his eyes? Maybe he'd had a little too much to drink; at times he just seemed to stare, attention occasionally broken as Ray dragged him past me, through the door. None of his mouth, none of Jack's martial arts.

And that just left big guy and his real "fucking peachy" mate.

"What's your problem?" said the weasel by me, finally finding a voice. "We're all adults in here, he—"

"*Neil,*" hissed the big man quickly, shaking his head and adding a low, "shut the fuck up." Then to Gray— "Apologies," said the man, now backed up to the settee, Gray still in his face. "The guy didn't say he was MC, certainly not a Master's. I…" He let out a shaky huff. "I'm Kris from Hester's circle. And I, I wouldn't have touched otherwise. I'd have backed off that first night—"

"First night?" I went close. "What the fuck do you mean 'first night'? He's been here before?"

Kris frowned past Gray at me. "Didn't expect to see him on a Saturday, but, yeah, the past two Frida—"

Gray's hand met Kris's throat. "You touched him? He let you fucking touch him?"

"Look, I'm sorry." Kris tried to get free, to breathe. "Like I said, we didn't know he was Masters' Circle. I'm really sorry, Master Raoul. I stated clearly enough who I was. So did Neil. He never repaid that courtesy. I just thought he was this frustrated straight who wanted in on the scene."

Neil seemed to lose all colour. But Gray pulled back, a slight frown on his face, then picked something up off the floor that had fallen at his feet. He gave Kris a nod, and Kris moved, avoiding any contact with Gray as he came over, pushing at Neil's shoulder until both men were out of the room.

That just left Jack and what the *hell* he thought he was playing at. With a look at Gray, I left.

CHAPTER 39
THE DEVIL YOU ALWAYS DO

THE VIP ROOM had been cleared upstairs, but Jack was nowhere to be seen. As we made it to the bar, Gray was met by Mikal. Something was whispered in his ear, then Gray led me through the bar, through a stock room, and into a corridor with a door marked *Manager* at the end. A man in a suit stood outside (the manager?), talking to Ray, and Gray gave him a nod and a soft apology before twisting the handle and going inside.

Jack sat on the floor, back against the wall, head buried in the arms across his knees.

"Hey," I mumbled, starting for him, but a rough grip off Gray pulled me back.

"You. Talk," said Gray, the anger evident in his voice possibly for the first time as he shut the door behind me. "You find that fucking mouth of yours and you talk very... fucking... quickly."

Jack covered his head, soft sobs shaking his shoulders, and that was enough for me. "Hey." I crashed down by him, trying to get him to lift his head, grab hold of the

447

grief, but he pushed away, jerking his head to the side. Then I frowned as chuckling took over. He glanced up, wiping his nose on his sleeve, tears falling, but mostly because he couldn't stop laughing.

"Fuck, you're getting slow." Jack nodded in Gray's direction. "Go you on the profiling, eh? It's taken you how many weeks to find out who's still coming here?"

I eased to my feet.

"Christ." He buried his head again, trying to stop the laughter, then pushed to his feet. Going over to the manager's desk, Jack sorted around in the drawers, pulled out cigarettes, some complementary matches, then lit up a smoke as he sat on the corner of the desk. "Could've at least let me get laid first," he said before taking a long pull, then pointing at Gray. "Always did know how to spoil the fun, didn't you, Welsh?"

I backed away a touch as Gray took hold of the chair, put it in front of Jack, then sat down facing him. "Hey, there, Martin," he said quietly, almost tiredly. "Jack been leaving a few names around the place and you picked them up? That how you know about Henry?"

"More the notebook you took from Sanders." Martin smiled. "But you need to revise your security setup over how I got into your office. Ray and the likes.... not the sharpest pups in the pen, are they? Why the fuck haven't you fired Ray anyway? That bastard's as old as God's cock and been stinking up your joint for just as many years."

"You got out."

Martin finished glancing around the office and offered Gray a cocky smile. "Hmm. You noticed that?" A flash of eye. "And you, you're looking old too. Jack been riding you hard all these years?"

Gray snorted and drew a leg up onto his knee, looking relaxed and tense at the same time as Martin took another long pull on his smoke and flicked a look at me.

"Jan...." Martin narrowed his eyes, and they seemed so much... darker than Jack's. "Known for your love of numbers, right?"

How...? I went to ask that, but Gray shook his head sharply.

Martin waved him off. "Pen and paper left next to Gray's bed, when Gray's never been one for leaving behind any linguistic print. Jack's always an option on that score, but an accountancy business quote next to a query over getting a... very expensive reprint rebound is, well, *not* Jack." A smirk. "You really don't learn when it comes to not giving away personal detail, do you?"

I tried to find a reply, but couldn't, not with... this, and Martin dismissed me.

"Fuck me, two lovers. And I thought I partied hard." He snorted. "Jack's gone soft over the years and learned to spread his legs without hitting someone, I see?"

"Not your concern. Talk to me about April Leamore, Martin."

Martin gave a raised brow. "Play fuck and tell with you?" He gave another pull on the smoke, threw the cigarette packet on the table, but kept a hold on the matches as he smiled. "Even after all these years, are you still trying to dig deep for all of Jack's little secrets, hmm? You know you could save yourself some time and just ask him. You learned to ask him yet, Welsh?"

"April," Gray said flatly. "I have a few ideas on just how she knew you. What I want to know is, how does she know Jack?"

"Tell me more about those ideas over... *me*." The smirk in Martin's eyes had every ounce of Jack's cock-teasing look, but something in there tainted it. "Where do they take you, Welsh?" His gaze travelled up and down Gray's body. "Hmmm. When those hands roam, heading for a little self-exploration, who do you think about? Jack? Me? Do you ever hide your face in guilt from Jack because you've missed fucking about with... me?"

"After April's husband found you two in bed, you forced him between the sheets with you at knifepoint and made him fuck her in front of you. Beats Jack hitting his father when his father walked in on him and the first man Jack took to bed."

"Knifepoint?" Martin shifted back a touch, getting more comfortable. "April's husband tell you that? That I used a weapon?" He stubbed out the smoke, still watching Gray. "Suppose he'd have to make something up to justify getting in bed with us and letting an eighteen-year-old fuck him as he fucked his missus." That smile. "If I was there, of course."

With the naked aggression Jack had shown when he blacked out, all the fear surrounding mention of Martin, I'd expected... an animal. I'd seen the emerging animal in Jack. But this...? There was intelligence there. Sharp, brutal, blunt intelligence. I mean, goddamn it: Jack... Martin had pieced together that Henry would be here, even if he wouldn't have a clue what he looked like. Why did that intelligence have Gray so nervous and on edge? Was it because Gray was used to culling aggression, but Martin himself had that *sharpness* to play the aggression with reason? Martin *played* the game with Gray?

Jesus Christ.

But why... why would Martin then need to fuck those

other men here?"

"And April? How much did that play on her mind, knowing you'd fucked her husband too?"

"Well, if I had been there, if it had been me," said Martin, and he winked over at me, "I can honestly say I wouldn't have let April's whining ruin a perfectly good threesome."

"But something did?"

Martin shrugged. "I suppose I might have gotten bored. April probably had a killer mouth, but being, what? A nurse working for the NHS, what came out of her mouth can't have been none too bright. If I'd been there, of course."

Gray gave a little smile. "Of course. Fuck off now, Martin, let me talk to Jack."

Martin cocked a brow. "Fuck you. He doesn't let me out too often these days. Besides…" Matches in hand, Martin slipped off the table, then went and straddled Gray's legs, draping his arms over Gray's shoulders. "You took my ride off me." He bit at Gray's lip. "Fancy being mine? You can pretend I'm Jack." He traced Gray's jacket, opening it up so he could get at Gray's shirt. "Like his mouth, don't you, Welsh?" He was grinning as he kissed at Gray's neck. "How he fights to sub." Martin groaned as he let his hand fall to the clasp of his own trousers, flicked them open, and slipped inside to start touching himself. "Fuck," he mumbled, biting at Gray's throat again. "I might play sub for you someday, let you collar me, Christ, even call me bitch. One condition," he added quietly. "You collar me—I collar you, we chain them together and see who really manages to fuck who first—"

Gray suddenly shifted, shoving Martin off, then up against the wall, knocking the wind out of him.

"You let those bastards fucking touch him? You——"

"Oh yeah, there he is." Martin went cold and traced a touch along Gray's jacket. "I feel you fucking him each time, do you know that?" He sighed and traced his touch down to Gray's ass, pulling him in, hips against hips, lips now ghosting his jaw, and there was a slight smile there as he played. "Pity he doesn't know what gets you going" was whispered in the wake of his kisses. "I remember. From how pissed you are even after all these years, I know you remember showing me, Welsh."

Giving a frown, Gray eased back a touch, his hands coming up more onto Martin's waist, putting a little space between them. Martin pulled a match free with his teeth, flicking it over his tongue and tossing the match box aside. Then reaching high above his head, he struck the match on the wall. Lifting his shirt slightly, he bit back a cry, body arching into all of the hurt as he ran the match just below his ribs. "Fuck… me," he breathed, head thrown back, eyes closed. Dropping the match as I cried out in disgust, he slipped a touch down his own body and found the heat going on between his thighs, his dick hard and topping his trousers as he stroked along it. "You like playing with bastards," he mumbled, pulling Gray back in by the ass as he played. "You told Jack about us yet, Welsh? How we've played in the past?" Grey eyes flashed playfully. "Want me to?"

A snarl, Gray wiped at his mouth, looked distractedly around, then grabbing Martin's wrist, Gray pushed him back against the wall again. Body pressed against body, everything was so much calmer with Gray as he ran his nose along Martin's jawline, forcing Martin's head up slightly when he didn't react, and he gave such a gentle kiss to his throat as he traced a hand down Martin's side.

"Give me Jack back, please, Martin."

"Doesn't want to come and play," he mumbled quietly. "Sent me instead to handle Henry." There was that slow smile again. "But he needs fucking so badly, that kid. Something else you're failing so fucking miserably with, Welsh. He wants to be tied down, fucked, forced to feel you, get Vince off his skin. But he's too scared to ask for it."

"Yeah, I know," said Gray. "If he's craving BDSM, if he's craving this, and can't ask for it yet—" Gray's free hand caught Martin's, guiding it up the wall, and a knife was slipped into Martin's hand. "—then it's mine to give it to him when he's ready, not you."

Martin groaned. "Now that's playing dirty." He took the knife and let it slip down his own body, arching into Gray. "He fucking loves a blade. Can feel it, how he likes it." He let it brush his exposed shaft. "Always did know how to play him, didn't you, Welsh?"

A snarl, Gray shifted, taking Martin with him, forcing him over the manager's desk, onto his back. A tug at Martin's shirt, exposing just a slice of tanned side, he pushed the flat of the knife against Martin's skin.

"You think he needs this now?" Gray brought his body down, the knife caught between them, a grip in Martin's hair, lips now so close. "Think you know him better than me?"

Exposing Martin's throat, Gray licked a long trail, collarbone to jaw, then nipped at the skin. There was something in Martin's eyes: fear belonging more to Jack, but something so much more. A need. A playful arch of body that said *yeah, fucking like that, baby.*

"Yeah," whispered Gray heatedly, adding a little grind of

hip. "Got all of Jack's gorgeous reactions going on there, Mart. So fucking hard."

"Like it, Welsh? Fucking hurt it, then. Let's go play with fire and really burn it out of him. The culler's signature mark… to fucking burn. It's what you really want for him, right?"

Gray kissed more heatedly at Martin's neck. "Yeah, you still know how to play someone, find their kink. But the knife's been on the floor, Martin. Did you know that, hmmm?"

Martin went very still.

Gray followed that stillness, his look now as cold as Martin's as he eased back and looked down on him. "One fleck of dust carries a multitude of germs." He held the knife against Martin's throat. "But that doesn't matter, does it? Vince cured Jack, right?"

"*Th'fuck* off me!" Martin tried to pull away from the knife, anything to shift and stop the blade touching. Giving a frown, Gray put the blade on the table, out of harm's way.

"Been feeling a little strange the past few Fridays? Enjoying the knife in your hand against a Dom's skin, then finding little things start to annoy you? Whether the blade is clean as it touches skin? Because I know you. You'd push for control, even over Doms."

Martin seemed to shiver, frown, and Gray rested his head down, forehead to forehead with him. "Unusual for you to call the police in, Mart. Why'd you do that? Were you after details on Vince? Or has Jack given you some strange limits that are fucking with even your head?" He sighed heavily. "Caught between seeking out the BDSM Jack's missing and crying out something's wrong with you?"

"Cunt's fucking poisoning me."

Gray stroked at Martin's face, eyes screwed shut. "Yeah. I know. Christ, I thought you were coping, Jack." He shook his head. "I know you're trying to help him, Martin, that he's asking for your help. But you need to let go, let him stop hiding. Please. He needs to face this and know there are people whom he can hide with again."

"Gray?" I got a look back at me and it was very distant off Gray.

"Jan, tell Ray he's to let Ed bring his car around to the back."

Giving a frown, I relayed the message to the man outside, then shut the door to see Gray ease off Martin and pull him to his feet. Martin stood there, looking down at the knife he'd picked off the table, his pupils fully dilated as though he were in desperate need of sleep. He had such a strange fucking stare.

"Jack?"

"Hmm?" he mumbled over to me, and heart pounding a little faster, I went over to find Jack looking at me, everything else, *everyone* else hidden behind such a lost look. There was little recognition in his eyes, and he gave the same glance to Gray, then something shifted, a touch, a slight flare of panic as he looked around the staffroom again.

"Easy," said Gray, taking off his jacket and slipping it on Jack's shoulders. The movement from Gray looked slow, weighted, troubled. He'd drained any feeling from his face, slipping back into whatever business face he kept calling on, but something was slipping, starting to take longer for things to slip into place, because as Jack flinched, looking at

Gray like he was Vince, all blood and bone to boot, Gray seemed to deflate, pull back. "You're at a nightclub, stunner, Heaven—"

"Heaven?" Jack seemed to shake more life into himself hearing that. "I..." Again he looked around, frowned. "Clubs." He shivered. "Don't... don't do social too good...."

"No," said Gray, "you haven't done social for a long time, not like this."

A knock on the door saw Ray poke his head in and give a nod.

"Jan, can you get him home?"

"Just what the fuck's going on, Gray?" I said. Although of course I'd get him back.

"No." Jack was rubbing at his head, his voice sounding so slurred. "I'm..." A look at Gray, me, he seemed to focus a little more. "Just need to go get some sleep," he said. "Stay here, Jan." He came over and the world stopped turning for a touch as a hand slipped around my neck and pulled me so Jack's lips pressed gently against mine. "Mmmmm," he said, pulling away. "'S good that you're spending time together, things." He smiled, kissed me again, and it seemed to last a lifetime. I needed it to last a fucking lifetime. "Old mukka here." Jack was with us a little more. "He's not such a tough bastard, needs looking after too."

Jack was gone then, Gray's words to Ray lost as I stood there. Just stood there.

CHAPTER 40
MISSED OPPORTUNITY

"JAN?" IN THE unfamiliar surroundings of the manager's office, it took a while to realise someone had called my name. "You okay?" Gray stood in front of me, his hand on the back of my neck, mimicking how Jack had touched me, forcing a shiver.

"Gray..." All I had was Jack's fading taste. "That.... That wasn't Jack." I shrugged, looked at the door and how it had closed behind him a few minutes ago. "What the fuck was—"

"I first met Martin a few times as we tried to get Cutter sent down," said Gray, and he took my attention now. "Martin usually, but not always, makes an appearance in the aftermath, when Jack thinks he has no one to turn to. Stress would build to a point where he'd drop all identity, sometimes for a few hours, sometimes days, and just... walk. Only his walking would lead him into Martin, into the likes of April Leamore, and the whole reason behind why Jack doesn't do social. Period."

"But you said Martin slept with women back then, that

he was into women. Why men now?"

"Sexual orientation doesn't come into play with Martin; it didn't back then. Jack's perception of his past, he has difficulty remembering, and events become warped or shrouded. Martin will find whatever Jack needs: male... female, Dom... sub, and find a way to cope, no matter how brutal he is with that person and the people around them. One of the worst times, he'd just gone nineteen; he'd had a bad day of OCD and CD playing with his head and mouth. I'd caught him just before he slipped. Jack had stood at mine, looking out at the forest, that dead-man-*walking* look in his eyes."

"The night you painted in the loft?"

Gray frowned a ghost of a smile. "He told you?"

I nodded. "Some." All of that just touching the tip of the Martin iceberg. "He never mentioned—"

"He's known you for what? Seven months, Jan? If he told you everything that's happened, and I mean over events surrounding the Jack I met, even you would take several steps away from him. Martin seeks to find a way to ease the stress that Jack can't fix in his own life, and he's... brutal with it. Disassociate Identity Disorder," said Gray. "He drops everything he knows. Main causes are stress, trauma, abuse...." Gray looked back by the door. "His absences had eased," he mumbled quietly. "After that shit over a month ago, they'd damn well eased."

"And he's been here, with them, and they've—" Anger battled confusion, then went straight into grief, only to throw me back into anger again. "You couldn't have tightened fucking security?"

"And done *what*, Jan? Lock him in a room and drug him when he's already still locked away in his head, back with

Vince—his drugs? Nobody has seen this in years," said Gray, looking just as pissed. "And with Jack being rape—" He stopped again. Gray couldn't finish it. He couldn't acknowledge verbally what had happened to Jack. "I've had people watching him and you twenty-four seven for any danger signs, Jan. You needed your own space and—" Gray looked at his watch. "Fucking bollocks," he spat, then spun away to the door.

"What?"

He didn't answer, just left. And like a dummy, I stood there staring at the door. After a few minutes, I shook it off and went after him. Gray stood outside talking to a bouncer, the big man who had shown us in, and whatever he said back to Gray didn't go down well.

"Not your fault," said Gray as I joined them. The bouncer gave me a look, then turned away as a black Mercedes pulled up. "Get in," said Gray. "This night's been one huge fuck-up after another."

I was about to when I caught sight of a car passing ours. Heat flushed my cheeks, practically welding me to the spot, and it took Gray saying something to snap me out of it.

"Henry?" said Gray. I could barely nod. Henry drove a red sports car, one hand resting casually over the wheel, the same cheap and nasty gold watch around his wrist. A young kid was in the car next to him, barely looking legal, and as much as I wanted to shout a warning to the kid, I couldn't move.

"Good. Not such a waste after all," Gray muttered as he waited for me to get into the Mercedes.

❧

I couldn't get over how quiet things were when we got back to Gray's. The Rolls-Royce waited out front, suggesting Ray wasn't relaxing his watch over Jack until given the all clear. True to form, we found him standing a little back from Jack as Jack sat at the kitchen table. A half-eaten sandwich was pushed out in front of him, which allowed Jack to fold his arms out and rest his head down. Ed was there too, looking just as confused as Gray sat opposite Jack.

I rested next to Ray, and it was only then that Gray seemed happy enough to let Ray go and gave him a quiet thanks before the man left.

Then only one man took Gray's attention. "Look at me, Jack," he said quietly.

"Gray…" A heavy sigh, Jack gave a slight twist of head, no willingness to lift it, just settle into sleep. "I'm fucking knackered." And he sounded it, voice all muffled, thick, and heavy.

"Do you even know why you're so tired?"

Jack pushed up and wiped both hands over his face. "Jesus." He let his hand fall on the table, and his pupils still had that dilated state to them. "What the fuck's your problem with me now, eh?"

"Things swimming a little?" said Gray. "Limbs feel heavy, like you've just pulled yourself out of a swimming pool, and all you want to do is go to sleep?"

Jack half-heartedly twisted his wrist to look at the time. "Well, it's getting on for one in the morning."

"What's the last thing you remember before Ray brought you home tonight?" said Gray, and Jack looked around the kitchen, bypassed me, then sighed.

"Taking a shower upstairs." He shrugged. "Getting into

bed."

"What time?"

Jack let his gaze fall on Gray, and it looked a little angered now. "About fucking ten fifteen, why?"

Gray's lips thinned. "Because you just said it was getting on for one."

"And?"

"And you went to bed at ten fifteen," said Gray. "Where are the missing hours, Jack?"

Jack went to snap something but stopped himself.

Giving a nod, Gray eased his elbows onto the table, one hand brushing at his lips, the other gently tapping at the table. He looked ready to hit out. "Martin's back on the scene and going social—"

Jack never even gave Gray time to finish before he was pushing his chair back, then heading for the exit by me, trying to get out. Gray stood, caught hold of his arm, to which Jack only pulled away and snarled, "Fucking back off."

"Jack." Gray went in close. "You're on lockdown here until I can call Doctor Halliday in. And this time you damn well stay in the room with him."

"Like *fuck* you're putting me on lockdown," snarled Jack in his face. "I do social once—"

"*Three times*," shouted Gray, twisting Jack around and forcing him to sit down, physically pushing him down into a chair. "Three fucking times you've gone social, and twice you've gone threesome with two other men."

Jack paled very quickly, enough to force Gray to a crouch and pull Jack's head to his. "I'm sorry. Christ, Jack. It shouldn't have come out like that. It's just—" Gray ran a hand repeatedly through Jack's hair, his hand shaking a little more each time. "—I need you to be safe. I need, I really need you to stay fucking safe now, stunner, I—"

Jack pushed away and stood. "This shit's always about what you fucking want, what you fucking need. I—"

"*What?*" snarled Gray, now up in Jack's face, hands either side of his head. "You tell me, Jack. You fucking tell me what you want, because this silence is fucking killing me. Tell me what you want, what you need—and I'll sit and re-order every sodding piece at your fucking feet just to see this fucking head of yours calm."

Jack tore Gray's touch off, backed away, stumbled into the unit behind, and then turned as he knocked the crockery and plates into a tremble. Seeing the threat of broken plates, he grabbed onto the display unit, giving a cry, just trying to stop things from falling. Only it didn't work: he couldn't stop the fall, and a few plates slipped and broke on the floor.

"*Bastard.*" He headbutted the unit with another cry. "*Control of my fucking head, Gray. You give me that.*"

Gray was already there, trying to turn him around—see the damage done, but Jack pushed him off. Blood ran down his nose from a cut on his forehead, trickling like a tear down the corner of his eye, over his cheek. "Did you fucking bother to stop and ask whoever it was if they used protection, because, fuck—" He let out a laugh. "—seems I forgot. Or at least I think I did. And Christ knows I can't catch anything else and bring down the MC any fucking further, right?"

"They would have used protection," said Gray, trying to get close and wipe at Jack's cut. "They were Doms for—"

"*Doms?*" Jack's eyes were wide as he pushed Gray's

hands away. "Fucking Doms?" Another laugh, hand now running through his hair. "Good old Martin… At least he got the sex right this time around, eh?" He gave a groan. "I bet he pushed the fucks, pissed them off enough to really go for fucking me hard."

Jack grabbed onto the unit and tipped it up, sending wood and crashed-up crockery all over the kitchen floor. Ed cried out, but it was lost to Jack's. *"Fucking bastards,"* he shouted, now kicking the shit out of the unit. *"Explains why I've been waking up as sore as fuck on a Saturday, that's for fucking sure. Fucking cunts, fucking—"*

Shifting from the unit, I grabbed Jack by the waist and dragged him out of the kitchen. Pinning him against the wall, I kept him there, hands either side of his head, my body against his, making sure his gaze focused purely on mine.

"Calm it *down*."

For a moment he stilled, completely calmed; frowned.

"Love the bones off you, Jack," I breathed against him. "Things are so fucking tough right now, you can't stand being by me, but you remember." I gave him a gentle kiss. "Remember I love the bones off you: mind, body, soul, every fucking inch, martial arts guy. I always will."

He responded to my kiss, just a gentle move of lips, slight play of tongue, and I heard him catch his breath as his semi dug into my hip, automatically stirring mine.

"Fuck." Jack's struggle with his senses slammed headlong into him, and I felt him try to push me off.

"No, just a few seconds, please." I covered his nose, blocking his reaction. "Please, just a few seconds more, please, baby."

But he struggled, first against the sickness making him

choke, then the struggle to breathe as I held on too long. Pushing me away, shaking, he looked down, not seeming to look at anything but past events. "Fucking turned you on."

A grey gaze met mine.

"You watched, he fucking *raped*, and you, *you* fucking came." Such fucking fire caught his eyes, then the wind was punched free of my lungs as Jack pushed me back against the opposite wall. "You were fucking hard when you had me pinned to your bed, when you tried rape out then. Then after you pulled the sound free, on the floor you fucking came and—"

"*What, Jack?*" I snarled, pushing him off. "Henry raped me—and you sat drinking fucking beer downstairs on Boxing Day. You, Christmas day, you wouldn't even fucking look at me. They tied me up in the corner after they forced a tube down my throat, followed by Henry's dick—and you, you were free, no ropes, you didn't run, you didn't help—you wouldn't even fucking look at me, you bastard. *Why didn't you run?*" A tear fell. "You denied every fucking part of me. Yet Vince—you said you *loved* Vin—"

Gray was there, snaking an arm around Jack's throat, pulling him off, away, then sending him skidding down the hall as Jack came in at me. "You," snarled Gray, pointing at me, "calm it." Then he was with Jack, who had fallen instantly quiet, hand on his mouth, eyes looking as though they were on continuous playback and chasing images and words and matching them with what I said.

"*My fucking head,*" he suddenly shouted. "It never matched what I said. *I heard him, felt him… but love? I love nothing but you and Gray.* But you… you got fucking hard. You—"

"Stop." Gray grabbed Jack under the jaw, forcing him against the wall and stopping him inching closer and closer to me. "Not the fucking same," he snarled. "You've done enough rape-fantasy to know how the body counter-reacts what's going through the mind. You—"

Jack cried out, such fucking hurt as he looked at me and tried to break the grip at his throat. "Masks… saw nothing but masks and you, and you… you wouldn't look away and just leave me the fuck alone. Couldn't fight and think straight with you there… you shouldn't have been there— couldn't just leave me the fuck alone; *leave me the fuck alone,* and off—" He was struggling with Gray. "*—just get the fuck off, you—*"

Gray instantly raised his hands in surrender at the heat, backed off, but Jack barely seemed to notice as he cried out and tried to make a break for the kitchen. Gray pushed him back, then stepped in his way. "Where the hell do you think you're going?"

"*Work.*" Jack pushed at his shoulders. "I need to get to—"

"*One o'clock on a fucking Sunday morning,*" shouted Gray, and Jack seemed to jolt, fall quiet. "Yeah," said Gray in an even tone. "You get to bed, calm that fucking head. You need—"

"*Fuck all from you.*" Jack had already spun away, heading for the stairs, and the next thing I knew, Gray was wrapping his arm around me, pulling me in close.

"Easy," he said quietly. "Jack doesn't know where he is at the moment, you know that."

Strange thing was, I didn't need the comfort.

When the hell had I stopped needing Jack's comfort?

JACK L. PYKE

CHAPTER 41
WRITTEN IN THE DARKNESS

GRAY WAS UNUSUALLY quiet as he undressed for bed. Occasionally I'd catch his glance towards the bedroom door, and I'd stop the mundane act of washing just to listen, try and see if I'd catch anything unusual in the night. He'd left the door open; he always had since Jack had slept in the west wing, both of us seeming to live by the constant tension of listening and waiting. Gray had made the call to pull in extra security for tonight after taking a walk outside to see that muddy footprints had led him through the trees, over to the huge wall running his property. He'd given his night staff a serious dressing down over Jack, but then had needed to apologise. Jack was re-setting the alarms, taking out a patio window, putting it back in, then going an hour's walk through the woods, scaling the wall, then either hitching a lift or calling a taxi. There was nothing security could have done. Instead he'd called in extra staff for the night: two guards at the back of the mansion, two more sitting in a car beyond the wall Jack had scaled.

Now it was touching three in the morning and Gray looked close to exhaustion.

After folding the hand towel onto the rail in the bathroom, I went on through in just pyjama bottoms and pulled back the covers. Undoing his watch, Gray looked over as I got in and pulled his side of the covers back. Neither of us spoke, both too wrung out and unwilling to disturb the silence in case we missed something. Waiting for me to settle, Gray switched the light out, allowing just a little light from the hall to creep over the bottom of the bed, then he slipped in by me, all black silk pyjamas coming in close. He pulled the covers over both of us, and I found him watching me as I watched him. His gentle touch to my cheek didn't startle. We'd slept like this for the past few weeks, at first Gray coming in behind me as I refused to face him, but at some point I'd turned around, faced some of my demons. Not all, but some.

Gray's hand slipped from my cheek, and he pulled me in close, kissing my head. From the way he held me then, it wasn't just for my comfort.

No dreams tonight, please. Just this. Just us. Just quiet.

Someone laughed in the darkness. Then a hand touched my mouth, fingers digging into the corner to force entry. I gagged, choked—tried to fight. Only my hands were bound above my head, legs spread wide with a doggie-stock. Henry had fastened himself by the ankles so that they were in between mine, keeping us locked together, his hips forced into mine, his dick rubbing into my groin, trying to find a reaction as I was bound there in Jack's spare room. And laughing. The bastard was laughing against my throat as his hands wandered up and down my sides.

"*Jack*," I cried, needing him here, but it only increased the laughter against my throat.

"Jack's mine," a voice whispered from deep in the shadows as Henry's dick left a trail of wetness down to my ass. "Yeah," whispered Vince, "slut's right here with me, always right here, Jan." And he grabbed his crotch: despite the blackness—I knew he grabbed his cock.

Henry teased his tip against me, trying to gain entry, I could feel it—but who the shadows hid and who they wouldn't let go? I could feel that more.

"*Jack*."

A hand brushed my cheek, just gently, and it felt so familiar, so tender against everything else that was happening, I cried out at Henry's new-found cruelty. Jack. He felt so much like Jack, all his tenderness, his love in that one touch. Tears were wiped away, each trail caught and shared in that single touch. But Henry was laughing; he was always fucking laughing as he nudged his dick into me.

"*Stop*."

∾

I jolted, shaken out of my dream by my own cry. Gray's arm instinctively came around my waist, the weight heavy, but his own exhaustion kept him deadlocked in sleep. In a way I was grateful as I lay there, eyes screwed shut. Some grief was private, some grief needed to be kept private. I swore I could smell Jack, everything that was Jack, him, it was here, and that only made the grief harder to bear. Opening my eyes would force all that away, so I tried to hide in my pillow instead. Keep him close with the scent I found there. Only the touch to my cheek, it wouldn't let me be, just gave another gentle stroke, wiping away tears. I eased my eyes open, not really wanting reality to creep back in, but knowing it couldn't last forever, no matter how much I cried for it.

In the darkness of the bedroom, Jack's light grey eyes looked so bright as he knelt there by the side of me. His head was tilted slightly, as if watching the trail of a tear, his face screwed lightly, and a tear slipped over his cheek as he watched me.

"Hurt you real bad, didn't he, Richards?"

"Jack," I breathed, but as I lifted my head, he shook his, eyes widening a touch. He seemed to struggle with the need to run, but then he came in hard and fast, head going against mine.

"Head fuck," he said so quickly, voice hushed, "so fucking bad, Jan." He screwed his eyes shut. "Love you both so much. But it hurts. Everything fucking hurts. You know. You're hiding in here from it too."

I whimpered as he kissed my cheek.

"*Stupid*," he whispered heatedly. "*I say stupid fucking things*. Wasn't you back there, wasn't us, never fucking us except when I kissed you on the floor, when it hurt more being pulled away from you. Just… my head. It's everywhere and I can't ground it long enough to stay with you. I want to so fucking badly, baby. Just… just please hang on in there. Stay with me."

There was movement from behind me, a gentle shuffling, then, "Jack?" That came from Gray, and Jack suddenly jerked back, away, nearly falling onto his ass. Maybe it was the darkness that jolted him, maybe the threat of a black gas mask easing up from behind me that scared the hell out of him. Didn't matter which; I lost him to wherever his head had kept him hostage. Gray was already up and out of bed, scrambling over me, then reaching to try and help pull Jack up as Gray hit the floor.

"Fucking don't," hissed Jack, scuttling back.

"Jack," said Gray again, this time easing back as I rushed to join them in the darkness of the room. Jack had pushed up to his feet, back pressed firmly against the wall, trying to look for a way out, then Gray was up against him, body pressed in close.

"Easy, stunner," he said quietly. "Easy." He played his hands around Jack's face, just gentle swipes with thumbs against jaw, and Jack calmed.

"Nobody touches you again," Gray said, his body shifting against Jack's. Both wore just pyjama bottoms, Gray's black silk on Jack's white. Jack hadn't taken his gaze off Gray, and when Gray ran his nose along Jack's jaw, Jack let out such an unsteady breath before shifting slightly and allowing Gray access to his throat, even though he was shaking like hell.

The kisses from Gray were just brief brushes of lip against throat. No marking, claiming, just tender nuzzling, and Jack's uneasy sigh gave way to a soft murmur, his shivering easing into calm, deep breaths.

"Miss you, stunner," breathed Gray, and the hurt was there in his voice. "Miss you so fucking much."

Maybe he forgot himself for a moment, but Gray let his hands slip down to Jack's ass and gave a gentle pull in against his groin.

"*Cunt.*" Jack suddenly pushed him off, then in one movement shifted so he pinned Gray up against the wall, his elbow digging into Gray's throat. That anger was there, that need to tear heads off before sex became a conscious thought. Jack even added a growl to say he needed to rip a few heads off, but he faltered, maybe confused with how his body naturally reacted to having Gray by him.

"Jack." Gray tried to reach for him, but Jack growled, shaking off Gray's touch, then slammed Gray's hands up against the wall before moving in close. Jack bit at Gray's throat, heated, full of every need going, and something changed in Gray's eyes, I saw it as he suddenly looked away, let life drain into nothing as the open door caught his attention. Then I realised Jack had tugged down Gray's pyjamas, just at his hip, and was rubbing his tip against Gray's exposed skin.

Jack's breathing was heavy to begin with, then grunts and frustrated growls took over. He was so hard, and any other time seeing him play himself against Gray was my number one thing to see, but Jack was using Gray with one hand, wiping away tears with the other, trying to find some comfort in old habits, in Gray, but getting nowhere fast.

"Oh Christ, Christ." I groaned, hands going on my head.

"*Us...*" cried Jack, giving one last attempt to melt into Gray, but his cock was softening, losing all life. "*Not Vince, not Cutter, just you. Just fucking you... me... Jan.*" Crying out, Jack thumped the wall. "*Fucking put me back together again, Gray. Please. Trust.... respect—fucking control.*"

Giving a snarl, Gray suddenly shifted, slamming Jack up against the wall. "Put you back together?" he snarled against his ear. "Like this?" Gray pinned Jack's arms above his head, body now crushing in close. "Through BDSM?" He made sure Jack couldn't move. "Let's see how ready you really are for it, then, Jack. Let's see how much your head really fucking needs a Dom's control in any way." Reaching over to the unit, Gray pulled something out of the drawers. "Take a good look around you, Jack," he snarled in his face, and he flicked one of the handcuffs around Jack's wrist, "you fucking remember what it looks like. Then when we're done, don't ever ask for my control like this again, not to ease a disorder."

As soon as the metal slipped around Jack's wrist, I started to back away. Jack had started to struggle just seeing them pulled from the drawer, but as the cool metal touched his wrist, clicked into place, something switched in his eyes.

Jack became very, very still.

"Now you're scaring him, Welsh." Even the change in his voice was different, slower, each syllable given a hard bite, but the switch had been so quick. "And I think we really need to fucking play now."

Gray stumbled back, already defending against another smack in the face off Martin, then with all the shouts, cries, crashing of furniture, I scrambled back by the bed, sinking to the floor and covering my head, not wanting to see the fallout anymore, see all of Jack's complications on final display.

~

I looked into the darkness of the bedroom now everything had been quiet for a while. Jack sat in one corner, looking like he was waking from one nightmare into another, so subdued, tired, tear marks at his wrists where the handcuffs had once been. Gray sat in another, breathing heavy, blood pouring from his nose and split lip as he watched Jack, arms rested on his knees. The bedroom was wrecked, units and glass-fitted wardrobes were kicked, beaten, and broken into pieces, leaving huge splinters of glass running up the walls, and the contents pulled out and spilled around us. The bed had been pushed a few feet out of place, the covers now on the floor. It looked like Gray had pinned Jack still on there for a few minutes, only to lose his hold, his grip on Jack, before he'd been tipped off. Although it was dark, the spinning of a lampshade on the polished floor could still be heard as heavy breaths fought to gain control.

"Jack," Gray said quietly, and something seemed to clear in Jack's eyes hearing Gray say his name. He looked up, focusing for a few moments. "I remember Martin from the fallout over Cutter," Gray mumbled quietly. "You don't. Not properly. I didn't touch you for two years because I loved the hell out of you, because I knew how torn your head was back then. So control? Don't dare ever ask again for me to Dom you when you run and hide in Martin from me. I'll give you anything in this fucked-up world that you want, but Martin? I can't fucking stand that bastard. Okay, kid? I'm here for you, when you're ready, not him."

"Kid?" Something tore through Jack's eyes. "Fucking man."

He was up, making a break for the door, and I caught up with him, pinning his arms at his sides, coming in behind him and holding him tight, shaking right along with him. "It's okay, baby. It's—"

"*Fucked up,*" snarled Jack. "*So fucking fucked up. Dirty... only men get... Only men....*" Shaking me off with a cry, Jack was out of the door before either of us could stop him. I rounded the corner, hands on head, but the hall was already empty, with Jack having disappeared from sight.

"Fuck." Briefly closing my eyes, easing back against the wall for a moment, I headed back into the bedroom. "Gray—"

Whatever I was going to say was lost as I saw him.

Kneeling down, I tried to lift his head now he'd buried it in the arms across his knees. "Not you, for fuckssake." I gave up and just wrapped my arms around him, holding him there. "Please, Gray. Bloody look at me."

Gray gave a wipe at his nose, at a tear, then I was forced to steady myself, just stop falling on my ass as Gray shoved me gently away. Now to his feet, he headed for the door.

"Where the hell are you going?"

He never even looked back. *"To find someone to fucking* hurt."

And that was it, Gray was gone. I knelt there on the floor for a few minutes, the cold creeping into my knees finally making me conscious of how I was still staring. As doors slammed in the distance, I scrambled to my feet and followed the corridors down to Jack's room. Without Gray here, that fear that Jack would bolt again made me slam the door open to Jack's bedroom. Moonlight shaped the bed and I saw Jack jolt under the covers. Again just fine black strands to his hair were visible on the pillow, everything else firmly beneath the white covers. Everything hidden, out of sight.

Not tough—not so fucking tough.

Letting the panels scrape my back, I sat on the floor. "Still here, Harrison." I wiped a few tears on my arm. "It gets better and—" Head resting back against the door, I closed my eyes. "And I'm here for when it isn't, okay? Even if it means sleeping here by the door so you can't catch my scent."

∾

Morning came, and I sat there staring into my bowl of

cornflakes, the silence of the manor a deadweight that wouldn't allow me to lift my head. The golden flakes had long since soaked up the milk, almost offering the perfect adhesive if left for much longer. Or so my mother had always joked as my sisters and I had sat with legs swinging, sometimes kicking each other under the table. I snorted. Maybe I could use this stuff to glue our lives back together, the perfect paste to accompany the morning paper that offered no respite from how hard life was lately.

Almost—almost a hard life. I'd seen some of Jack last night. I'd seen *our* Jack last night. What followed?

Only real men get dirty...

Elbows on table, I let my head fall into my hands, refusing to go over the details again. Gray hadn't returned; Jack was still up in his room; Ed... Christ knows what had happened to him this morning. Grunting away my loneliness, I pushed the cornflakes away, only to have something land on the table in its place.

"For you" came a voice. "You look at it, remember it, then Ed destroys it."

I couldn't find the will to look at Gray, not long enough to tear my gaze away from what had landed inches from my cornflake bowl.

Henry's gold watch still looked cheap, still just as nasty with parts of the gold plating chipped off in places around the clock face. It ticked, still counting the time, almost matching the clock on the wall with a synchronized heartbeat. Maybe it should have stopped, considering what it represented. Head down, I finally found my voice.

"For you too?" I looked up at Gray. He wore a long black overcoat, black jeans, and shoes. I just took it for granted that he wore a shirt; his black coat was fastened, no doubt against the rain outside. His hair was wet, neck damp, but a lot of the edge had gone out of his eyes, even if the bruised and battered look was still there. Now he just seemed tired, maybe a little lost, always very distant.

"No," he said quietly. "The last bastards, they're for me."

"Your people have Leamore on a wanted list?"

He nodded.

"Good." Not touching the watch, I looked back at Gray. "Can I ask how?"

Gray moved over to the coffee machine and flicked it on. "You can try," he said, then he glanced back at me. "He won't touch you again, Jan. That's all you need to know." He spooned sugar into two cups. "Jack?"

I looked up to the ceiling. "Not awake yet." It's too early. Gray had had no sleep. I hadn't fared much better. Maybe at least Jack was finding some bliss in oblivion. The scent of coffee brought my nose back down, and I saw a mug there in place of the watch. I snorted a cold smile. Here one minute, gone the next. All evidence removed.

Gray sat next to me, rubbing at his forehead as I took a sip of coffee. "Do you need anything for that?"

Gray looked at me. "Hmmm?"

"Your headache?"

He shook his head. "Just sleep," he said quietly. I toasted that with my mug of coffee and went back to quiet sips.

"Martin."

Gray looked at me.

"He knew your nationality, that you're Welsh." I frowned at him. "How can Martin know and not Jack?"

Gray sniffed and looked down at his coffee. "Because

he's a bastard."

"But it's still Jack, right?"

Gray gave me such a hard look. "Nothing like Jack at all. Jack…" His face screwed slightly. "Jack survives in his own bubble, and when that tumbles, Martin kicks in."

"Pity he didn't kick in with Vince," I said, the coffee taking on a bitter taste.

"Oh no," said Gray, snorting a flat smile. "Martin mostly likes to come out after the shit hits the fan and then just stir things up."

I went quiet for a moment. "He knew your signature mark as an interrogation's officer," I said quietly. "Gray, have you eve—"

"He's a bastard, Jan," Gray replied coldly, cutting me up. "A very fucking clever and psychotic one at that. And trust me, he's certified as such."

I nodded. Frowned. "Can you answer me something else without resorting to silence and quips?"

Gray frowned at me.

"Brennan." Giving a sigh, I rested my mug on the table. "He said his department was police, Met to be precise, back when we were in the warehouse." Gray just looked so bloody tired. "What the hell is the Masters' Circle, Gray?" I knew my own tiredness took any fight away. "You said the MC wasn't a usual Dom/sub setup. Your trained Doms are sent overseas, but you didn't just mean to BDSM clubs, did you?"

CHAPTER 42
LOST VOICES

NOT ANSWERING MY question for a while, Gray lost himself in his coffee as he turned the mug in a slow circle. "No," he said eventually. "They're not sent only to BDSM clubs. If they pass, the majority are sent on tours, some with missions with the likes of MI6."

"Tours?" I frowned. "You work with the Ministry of Defence, as well as MI5—MI6—*and* police departments?"

Gray finally looked at me. "You know yourself the physical, psychological, and emotional stresses that come from being a Dom or sub. Recognising those attributes is an advantage to be used undercover with the likes of interrogations." He snorted. "The army is a recent addition. They fucked up a few years ago by supposedly letting some recruits be filmed during naked combat training out in the woods, so Carr and her associates came on board."

"Carr?" Christ, she didn't look the type. But then, what the hell did I know? I avoided combat let alone any *naked* combat involving women. "So that makes the Circle what?"

"Fully funded," said Gray, managing a smirk. "I told you

that."

My eyes widened a touch. "As in fully *government* funded?"

"As in providing extra specialist training for most departments, ergo providing training on both extracting information and being forced to give it. Whether it be a tendency for a Dom or sub inclination, it's important to recognise both elements and temper them within a recruit."

"But not all are government personnel," I said quickly. "Ben, the trainee who was with Jack those months back… you said he was a psychology student."

Gray nodded. "We also cater to ex-military personnel, providing employment opportunities in many departments once they leave the service, the same for the MOD, CID, et cetera."

"The cullers?"

All emotion fell from Gray. "You don't mention them again, Jan."

I frowned. "Okay. But what about the Dom clubs like the one we went to see in America?"

Gray took a sip of coffee. "It's just a Dom club in America."

"And Ed? Some of the terminology Ed uses, he—"

"Ed's family."

"MI5?"

Gray choked, then tried to control it. "No. Ed's my grandfather."

Something didn't register here. "Hang on, you have your grandfather as the *butler*?"

"Have I ever introduced him as the butler?" said Gray.

"Well, no, but Jack—"

"Jack what?"

"He… hmmmmm. He takes a while to notice th—" I stared at Gray. "He's your what?"

Gray let his mug rest on the coffee table. "When Jack first came to the manor, my grandfather had been due to go to an evening fundraiser meal, so he was dressed in the required black suit and tie. He met us in the reception hall just after we'd arrived home, and Jack, well." There was a ghost of a smile there. "Jack had been sitting outside a house for a while and his jacket was soaked. He threw it at my grandfather and slipped some loose change into my grandfather's hand with the comment 'In your own time, like, mate, chop chop.'"

"Ouch." I even winced. Gray was almost laughing, but he seemed to sober up quickly as I said, "Is that what the whole hate-hate issue is from your grandfather? Because Jack hasn't stepped outside of his head long enough to see the wider picture?" Gray's hands seemed to take comfort from the warmth of the mug, and I narrowed my eyes. "Because your granddad thinks Jack needs to wake up to you too?"

Gray sighed heavily. "The fact he hasn't told Jack and put him straight, it's been a debating point over the years between us many a time."

"But you still haven't told Jack yourself? Why?"

"Because Jack gets there eventually. He just needs…"

"Time?"

Things fell a little quiet for a while. "Yeah. Time."

"So this place, is it his home?"

"Hmmm?"

"Your grandfather. Is this his place?"

Gray shook his head. "Our family home is in Wales. This is mine. My grandfather followed me from Wales, or more, he followed Mrs Booth and her backgammon skills."

"The maid?"

Gray nodded. "It's why you find him in here most of the time, and the echo of a retreating Mrs Booth." He took another sip of coffee. "He's my house manager; a title of his own choosing that he says almost keeps him out of trouble."

"It's got to be hard," I said, "for you, I mean, knowing the respect, care, and attention Jack gives his own family, yet with yours?"

Gray winced. "I'm more worried Jack will find out and give it the typical 'yeah, still fucking hate you, mate,' mouth."

I chuckled. Gray might have something there.

"And your grandfather is okay with all of the..." I shrugged. "Masters' Circle business?"

"He worked there long before I did, on the tech side, kitting out the scenes with surveillance, but I didn't know that until I became a Master."

"Ah. You didn't find that a little awkward?"

"I saw him retired from the post."

I chuckled. "That couldn't have gone down well."

"It was around the time that I noticed he was interested in our old ex-maid who'd started work in one of the London hotels."

"Mrs Booth, by any chance?"

"Hmmm."

"And Mrs Booth got a very well-paid job here at that time, I take it?"

Gray shrugged.

"Do you manipulate and control everyone you meet?"

"I keep an eye on the people I care for, and I make sure they get what they need out of life. So control and manipulate? Yes, every fucking time."

"And your parents? Where do they fit in?"

"Ex-personnel are given the option to train as a Dom and work as a Dom at the Masters' Circle," said Gray, the change in direction smooth, but noted. "They've earned it in my eyes. It's also the main reason why we have a psychology department."

"Post-traumatic stress and other conditions," I said to Gray's nod. A look down at my empty coffee, I mumbled, "It's a good cause."

"Hmmm?"

"Looking after serving and ex-serving soldiers and such."

Gray downed his coffee. "When the government's not pissing about and trying to cut funding."

I nodded, then managed to snort a smile. "Jack doesn't know, does he?"

Gray glanced at me.

"About the history of some of the people he helps train?"

"Yes, he does," said Gray. "I wouldn't put him in a situation where he didn't fully know a trainee's history. It's also why I make sure he's trained." I caught how Gray fell pretty quiet with that, but a slow burn of pride still came in, but then it wasn't hard to find it. Jack had a good soul; he'd love helping out ex-personnel.

A text came through, and I pulled my phone from my

pocket.

Work…

Mr Hammond's report past due-by date.

I snorted. Over by nearly three months. Christ, hadn't Stefan diverted my workload?

"Anything interesting?"

I shook my head. "Just work." Something filtered in just as Gray went to say something, and it took a moment to register that voices were coming from the lounge. Gray followed my gaze too. A sigh, he put his coffee down and pushed away. After giving my own sigh, I followed.

As we neared the front entrance, the heat in the voices grew louder until I rounded the corner into the reception hall and saw there were actually four people there. Two men blocked the front door, a third, Ray, was already heading over to us, and Jack, he was looking as pissed as hell, caught mid-flow ordering the two by the door to—

"… *Fucking move.*"

Glancing back, Ray said quietly as he reached us, "I've just had confirmation that Doctor Halliday is on his way over." He stopped, hands going in his pockets. "Jack's not in any mood to wait. What—"

Jack saw us—Gray. "You got any idea of how fucked up this is?" he snarled at him. "I'm a fucking adult, for fuckssake, get them the fuck out of my way, Gray." We made our way over. "I need to get to work."

Gray shook his head. "No, it's Sunday. You don't open the garage on Sundays," he said calmly. "Certainly not when there's a risk of Martin. You stay here at least until Doctor Halliday has seen you."

"No. Move them, or I'll fucking hurt them," said Jack.

"For tomorrow, Steve's been called in to look after your

side whilst your father sorts a manager—"

"*What?*" Jack was in Gray's face. "You go behind my fucking back and sort *my* business out with Steve? With my old man? Since when did you start talking to my old man?" Jack laughed, throwing his hands out. "Well ain't that just real *fucking peachy*. Ain't that—"

Taking hold of a bunch of coverall at Jack's arm, I pulled him aside, away from Gray, away from Ray. Everyone but us. He went to tug away, almost like I was the stranger getting in the middle of a street brawl, and I moved in quick, pulling him close, knowing he wouldn't hit me. "Stay here, Jack. For me, please. Be safe."

At first he fought to get away, then he was holding on almost for dear life. "Get him to let me go, Jan. Please. I need to go. I need to, to *work*. Please. Get him to let me go."

"I know," I whispered quietly, and I kissed his head, held him a little tighter. "Just please stay, just until Halliday has seen you. He's on his way. An hour, maybe two. I'll see him too. How's that? Then you can work." I groaned, nearly crushing him. "I'll go with you and name each part to stop you thinking if that's what's helping you."

Jack pulled away slightly, his hand between my throat and jaw. Tears threatened his eyes, nothing that spilled, but everything there that needed to.

"I can bring cotton wool to stick up your nose," I said quietly, trying a smile, "or worse, some of Ed's socks, because, Jack, I'm getting so fucking desperate right now, and I'll resort to stuffing anything up your nose just to get close to you."

Jack choked a chuckle, and as he did, a tear fell. "You taking the piss, Richards?"

I kissed him hard, quick. "Fuck yes—always, if it gets you to laugh like that again," I mumbled quickly before pulling back and risking losing him again to my scent. "Just give Halliday his time, please."

Rubbing at his head, looking as though it was splitting with how hurt he looked, Jack nodded. "Head fuck," he said quietly, and I stroked his face, then the bruise and small cut just above his brow from when he'd headbutted the unit. "Yeah, real bad, baby."

As Jack turned and headed back upstairs, noise from back towards the kitchen caught my attention as Ed came in, sorting through the mail. Pausing for a minute and giving Jack's retreat a school-teacher glare over the rim of his reading glasses, he then handed one particular package over to Gray. A look passed between them, and Ray and the other guards dispersed as I went over.

"I've had it run for fingerprints," said Ed. "Same MO as all the others."

I went still hearing that, and Gray looked up, trying to ease the tension. "Intercepted and a message under a UV light?" he said quietly.

Ed nodded, and this was probably the first time I saw the family resemblance, just a touch, not so much in the eyes, but the slender build, shape of nose. "No website address this time, though." He tapped the package. "That one, it's marked for you." Ed flicked a look at me. "He's still staring. What have you told him?"

Gray didn't look up from the package. "What he needs to know."

"Hmmmm." Ed eyed Gray warily, then I found I had a hand offered over. "Good to meet you properly, Jan."

"You too as well, sir."

"Ed's just fine," he said kindly. I shook his hand; his other came on top of mine, almost cupping it in his. "More than fine, okay?" He glanced at Gray. "More than."

"Thank you," I mumbled as he headed off up the stairs. Gray watched him, then asked me to follow him into his study. Once we were in his office, I saw how his hands shook as he donned plastic gloves, then took the package out of the plastic bag. As I shut the door, Jack's UV security light came out as Gray took it from his drawer.

Gray opened the package, taking every care in the world, and a black DVD case slid out into his hand. No writing was on the front, none on the back as Gray turned it over. Waiting for me to join him, he clicked it open and ran a light over the inside casing.

Don't...

... watch this, you bastard.

April.

Giving a brief look at me as I rested against his desk, Gray headed over to his inbuilt flat screen and inserted the DVD. He didn't press play until he'd sat behind his desk, where he took his remote from a drawer.

A black screen; that was all that greeted us for a moment. Then a cell came into view and air became hard to intake. Life around the flat-screen TV blurred, blanking me to everything and everyone else. I was looking down on Jack's bedroom. Wearing a suit, I'd just been dragged in by Henry. Vince was naked but for a gas mask, with Jack unchained and staring at me. The night he'd threatened to kill me, the night of the...

The groan that came wasn't from the DVD, but from me as I closed my eyes. I knew this scene already, what was going to come, and I went around the desk, knelt in front of Gray, and took the remote off him. "You can't see what happens next," I said quietly. "This, it's been sent to taunt, to hurt, nothing more." I aimed the remote at the screen. "Don't fucking watch this." But it came nonetheless.

"Not real, Jack." I sounded so odd in the video. *"What they've made you feel, it's not real, baby."* Jack was naked, but not chained in any sense, and when I'd shifted, just easing the aches in my body, he jolted as if a rabid dog had inched a few footfalls closer.

Not even looking at me, gaze fixed firmly on the screen, Gray slipped his hand over mine and took the remote back.

"Is Jan here, Jack?" The volume wasn't even up that loud, but I couldn't miss Vince's voice.

That look, it had terrified the life out of me. Gutted me in so many more ways. "Gray," I said gently. "Please—"

"Is he real to you?"

I groaned as Jack nodded in the video, just a single shift of head that never allowed his eyes to fall off mine. Because Vince didn't mask his voice now. He stepped into the nightmare, looking to ground Jack, make him... what? Face his fears? Me.

"Real men get dirty. That's the natural order of the world," Vince said gently. *"So show him how you handle men who make you inferior, forcing you into needing to wipe gorgeous come off your body."* Quiet. *"If it helps, baby, hit him. Break him apart for how he holds you down. Nobody holds you down. You like getting dirty. Get fucking dirty."*

Vince stroked at Jack's cheek. "Kill him, baby."

Giving a snarl, making me cry out, Jack was over, pulling me from the wall by the hair and forcing me down.

His body came down on mine, one hand pinning mine above my head, another gripping hard into my jaw as if he was going to headbutt me. Snarling into my face, forcing my head up and—

"What... what the fuck am I doing to you, soft lad?"

I stifled my groan. All the tension drained out of Jack at that point, and I felt it now too in my own body.

"Don't..." Jack mumbled quietly, so bloody quietly. *"Don't say my name anymore, baby."* A sob wracked his body. *"Please. Don't look at me. Don't touch me. Hurts, hurts us so fucking badly.... Don't—"*

"You touching again? Not getting dirty, boy?" Vince.

"Gray, you need to stop. Now." He wouldn't even look at me, and I sat back on my heels, blinking at Jack's cries as he was dragged into the middle of his bedroom.

"For pissing your Dom off again, boy."

Christ, the smell of the branding iron as Vince came in carrying it.... "Stop," I mumbled to Gray, but in the video—

"Mercedes... Mercedes-fucking-Benz." Jack doubled, trying to hide, to get away from the heat of the second burn pressing down on his hip.

I closed my eyes and dropped my head, knowing what was coming next from Jack.

"Gray. Gray, for God's sake—please. Mercedes. Mercedes-Benz—Mercedes-fucking-Ben...."

"*Enough*," I cried, taking the remote and pressing a button, any button. Gray stared at the blank screen, letting his thumb brush distractedly at his lip, yet everything about him still looking so fucking calm. All except for the tear that spilled over one cheek, finally denying his will to keep it contained.

Easing up, I blocked his view of the screen, gently kissing his cheek, then lips, anything to distract from the to-the-death stare. "He's here," I said quietly. "This shit, it doesn't matter. We got out, we're—"

Gray got up, and with a hand on my shoulder, he pushed me to one side. Taking the remote with him, he aimed it at the screen and pressed play to repeat the branding.

"Gray." Now I was up, in his face, trying to pull it from his hands. "*Stop.*" Cries hit the air again, and I tried to fight the need to hit Gray and get him to stop. Needing him to stop. "Needs to fucking stop now—"

Everything went quiet and the sudden silence made me jerk around as Gray went over to the flat screen. The DVD had been frozen, catching Jack as he lay on his side, head twisted into the concrete, smoke from his branding mark caught mid-air and close to his hip.

On screen, the black rope necklace with the sterling silver cross, a smaller black one sleeping on top of it, was nearly out of shot and lost under Jack's arm as he was caught mid-cry.

Gray glanced back at me. "I asked you to tell me fucking everything. Why didn't you mention *that*?"

The thing had completely slipped my mind. Put it next to everything going on in that video, it was the last fucking thing I'd thought about.

Gray was suddenly by me, grabbing me in close. "Not your fault, not your fucking fault. Sorry," he whispered heatedly in my ear before kissing at my cheek. Then he was over by his safe, sorting through it.

I needed the images to stop and went over and switched the TV off, just locking the images away in the inbuilt unit. "Necklace?" I mumbled. "It was just a replica of the one he wore in the Cutter videos. Vince was obsessed with everything that happened in those videos."

Hearing the safe shut and automatically lock, I went back over to find Gray was staring down at something in his hand. He offered it over and slipped a black rope necklace into my palm. The light caught the tiny sterling balls, then the two crosses at its centre. "What?"

"He wore that the day in the alley when I caught him beating Mark Shaw's dad."

"The policeman he put in hospital?"

Gray nodded. "It broke during the fight. Losing it had pissed him off no end."

"Because Cutter had bought it for him?"

Gray shook his head, just once. "Oh no," he said quietly, and there was something very dangerous playing in his eyes. "But I know who did." He was heading for his office door. "Come on," he said, looking back at me, and the door was open, this time Gray not even waiting for a reply.

We made it back into the reception hall as Jack made his way down the stairs, rubbing at his head. Looking at me, he held up his hands. "'S okay, I'm just going for some breakfast." He didn't sound happy about it, but then he was all for Gray. "What's going on?"

"Stay here." Gray was already heading for the door. "You don't speak to anyone until we get back."

Looking at Gray, Jack came over to us. "What th'fuck did you just say?"

"I'll explain when I get back, I promise. For now, you don't talk to anyone. *Ray.*"

Even I jumped at Gray's shout. A moment later, Ray came running into the hall.

"Sir?"

"Nobody's to talk to Jack, not until I give the all clear."

"And Halliday?" said Ray, coming over. "He's just called to say he's had to stop by Jack's dad's. He's running late."

Gray's eyes narrowed.

"What th'fuck d'you know?" Jack was reaching for his coat, but Gray took it off him and handed it to Ray. Jack pulled back. "You, you take Jan with you over me?"

Gray was suddenly by Jack, pushing him back as he cupped his face. "You listen to me. This is nothing to do with what you can and can't do, stunner. This is—"

Giving an angered snarl, Jack pushed him off, hands going to his head. "He isn't trained, I am. I'm fucking a fourth Dan in—"

"Jack," snarled Gray, but Jack started to back off.

"Sit pretty, right?" he said as he reached a display case of Gray's. "Because only real men get dirty? And Christ knows he got out where I didn't." Giving a groan, he pushed the display case over. "*Fuck you. Fuck you both an—*"

"Fucking watch him," Gray snarled to Ray, then he was pulling open the door, mobile in hand, putting a call through to someone....

CHAPTER 43
PSYCH-PLAY

I WANTED TO ask just what the hell was going on, but maybe now wasn't the time for questions, certainly not ones Gray wasn't prepared to answer just yet. He wasn't holding out on me; I could tell he was working over details in his mind, piecing things together. We pulled up outside an old Victorian house, white brick and wood panelling speaking its finery and class. From all of the hospital visits, I recognised Greg's Range Rover in the drive, but not the two others that sat beside it. Gray stopped just behind a black Mercedes, but before he got out, he tapped something into his phone, his gaze on the Mercedes touching the nose of his Mercedes.

"Halliday's?" It had to be; Halliday was MC, head of their psychology department, but still MC, driving one of the two MC signature-mark cars.

Gray nodded, his attention still on the phone.

"What's going on, Gray? What's the issue with Halliday? Is he tied to this Leamore woman?" I frowned. "Would he have known about April through past sessions with Jack when Jack was a teen? I mean, I take it Jack would have come under MC scrutiny when you first met him?"

"Halliday wasn't part of the department then."

"But he does have access to the files!" My skin started to crawl. "And the money aspect: he's MC—paid damn well. Is…" Something else started to creep in. "Is he anything to do with Ben? The psychology student who was training to be a Dom when I met Jack? Ben was murdered."

Gray looked at the house.

"Gray?"

A glance at me, he pushed out of the Mercedes. After a moment he leaned back down and looked in. "You let me deal with this, Jan. You say nothing. You *do* nothing."

"Except talk to Greg?" I suddenly saw why he'd allowed me to come now.

"No shit, Sherlock."

I pushed out of the car, then went around to meet Gray. But apparently Greg's radar had already kicked in because the front door to his home was open and Greg came out, meeting Gray halfway across the courtyard.

"You." Greg looked small, his back slightly arched, with heavy lines under his eyes that said he'd had about as much sleep as the rest of us. "Not at my home." He tried to square himself up. "You only ever bring trouble to my home. Not here. Not now. I've had enough, Gray. We've all had enough."

I slipped between them, urging Greg back towards his front door, yet Greg kept his gaze behind us, on Gray, his cracked lips as thin as Gray's.

"Doctor Halliday told you that he got a call this morning, to come and see Jack?" I said quietly.

"Yes, why?" Now Greg was back with me. "What's wrong?"

"Martin's back on the scene." That came from behind us, and Greg stopped and pulled his elbow out of my grip, all to look back at Gray.

"*Martin?*" The name was hissed through his teeth. "He... Jack's been doing fine. He's been doing *more* than fine."

I started pulling at Greg's arm again and managed to get him through the door. "Jack's been slipping out for the past three weeks," I said, hearing voices in the lounge. "We found out last night."

"Is..." Greg pulled me to a stop, panic in his gaze. "Is he okay?"

"No," said Gray, pushing through the middle of both of us, "it's why we called the good ol' doc in."

Leaving Greg there in the hall, I followed Gray into the lounge to see Gray do exactly the same as he did to Kris when he'd purred around Jack at the nightclub: he went over to Halliday, nose to nose with him, and backed him away from Jack's mother.

"Hey, hey-hey," snarled Greg, pushing past me and grabbing at Gray's jacket sleeve. "You don't come into my house and threaten my gues—"

Gray looked at him, and the look going on in his eyes shut Greg up. Halliday had already fallen dumb, Gray leaving him pale and shaking despite Halliday being a foot taller. Christ, that look shut me up and I'd said nothing.

"Take a seat, Doc," said Gray, not even looking back, and Halliday did just that. Forget the fact there was nothing there for him to sit on *but* the floor, he sat, hands searching blindly behind him.

Giving a glance down, happy that Halliday seemed to be staying put, Gray moved away to the mantelpiece and picked something up that had caught his eye. After a wipe at his face, he traced a finger over the photo frame he held, then smiled in my direction and showed me the photo.

"Stunning-looking kid," said Gray to Greg. "How old is Jack here? Five, six?"

"Six." Greg moved a little closer, but something caused him to stop, and he glanced back at me with that same questioning innocence of Jack's. Gray was running his thumb over the frame. The picture had been a mass of black hair and big grey eyes, this huge cheeky smile as Jack stood posing in trousers, white shirt, and blue jumper with a school logo on the front. Only his tie had been pulled down, the first button undone, and the cap he wore looked fit for the lead guitarist of AC/DC.

"First day at school?" said Gray.

Greg nodded, but it was Elena who answered with a quiet, "First year. That was his first school photo." Her smile reflected the little boy in the photo.

Gray put the picture frame back on the mantelpiece and looked around. "No others?" he said over to Greg.

Greg shrugged as Elena said, "I have them."

Gray nodded. "Must have been a good place to be for you," he said over to Greg, then Elena, "Jack with no troubles." He indicated to the photo. "Back then."

Greg only shrugged again. "Jack's... Jack," he said quietly. "Past, present... all of it makes up who he is."

A wipe at his face, Gray nodded, then looked down at Halliday. His look was questioning, almost mimicking Halliday's, only Gray's was a lot harder.

"Do you remember buying Jack this?" He was back with

Greg, and he pulled the necklace out of his pocket.

"Oh my lord." Greg came over and took it from him. "Where?" Greg turned the necklace over in his hands. "Where did you get this?"

Gray took it back off him, wrapping his fist around it, enough for the silver and black cross to dig into the skin. "The night I met him," said Gray. "In the alley, when we fought, it came off in the scuffle."

Greg snorted. "When you beat the sh—"

"*Don't*," shouted Gray, enough to make Greg jolt and back off. Gray laughed, gave a slight shake of his head, then a small smile. "Jack was so pissed at me for breaking it," he said, his body having lost all of its calmness, its ability to relax. "He spent days looking for it afterwards. Always back at the same place, that dumbass intensity on his face." Gray seemed lost in the memory. "To be honest, I never even realised I had it until I'd had my suit dry-cleaned a few days later."

He looked down at the necklace. "I wanted to keep it until after the trial, get it fixed for him as a thank you." A slight frown. "His head was in such a bad place, yet he still stood up to that fuck." Gray's voice was a little quieter. "See, he mentioned his 'old man' had bought it for him, and, well..." Gray smiled at me, Greg. "We all know how much he loves his old man, right?"

"Gray..." Greg stepped a little closer, almost reached out to him, and then drew back a touch. "This... all this, it's been hard on everyone. Hard on... on you. But..." He shrugged. "I don't know what this is; I don't know what you're doing here."

Gray looked over at Elena. "I never really hear him talk much about you, though."

She frowned. First at Greg, then me. "Have you ever asked him?" she said, looking just as confused.

Gray chuckled. "All movements and alibis checked out, and—" Gray glanced down at Halliday, "—psych evaluations too." He was back with Elena. "And yet still I'm left asking: what the hell have you done with April Leamore, Elena? What the fuck have you done, period?"

Greg frowned.

"See, Greg here, he said that April asked if he was Jack Harrison's dad, only problem being, April only knew Martin." There was a cold smile. "And Martin himself said he got bored with April being less of a challenge on the intelligence score. So... the question is: how did she find out that Jack was Martin?"

Elena still didn't seem to understand. "Both national and international papers covered Cutter being sent down—"

"Jack was under witness protection; there was a media blackout on pictures and his name," said Gray. "Try again."

"Try what again?" said Elena.

"Greg himself mentioned April." The necklace in Gray's hand looked ready to cut into skin. "And after that? Everything fell into place really easily. The CCTV footage from the meeting in Epping Forest catching the exchange, tracing her ID, her home, her history with Jack...." Elena still didn't seem to understand, and Gray nodded. "Even the porn links, now I think about it."

Gray slipped the necklace in his pocket. "They took me to America," he said. "They took all three of us there. Jack and Jan, they met some very special people. That visit led to finding out that the porn links were actually uploaded from Corsica, then to April herself being there."

"Huh?" said Greg, but Gray was purely with Elena.

"Exact locations are always hard to pin down, but Gabe, clever little sod that he is, he located country, city, then even a local internet café. But like everything else, he was meant to."

"And?" said Elena, coming close, her face creasing.

"The only thing you couldn't plan," Gray said quietly, "was this." He showed her the necklace again. He gave a small smile. "So carefully planned, Elena, but enough to leave a real bad taste with how it all connected together. You weren't lying when you said you spoke to Jack on the phone. I checked the phone records."

He offered her the necklace.

"But on the other hand, as drugged up as Jack was, he wasn't lying when he said he saw you there with Vince, was he? You'd just tried to make sure you kept your identity slightly screwed so he would question himself later."

I eased off the doorframe just as Greg looked at Elena. Elena stared at the necklace as she turned it over in her hand.

"You shouldn't have taunted me with that last video of him," said Gray quietly, his hand going into his black overcoat. "See, those porn uploads were done by April herself in Corsica." Gray smiled. "But guess who was just a short trip away in Italy, the same place where you bought a necklace that looked very similar to this one, and for Vince to use in the warehouse."

Gray looked over to me, then nodded at the necklace. "That's Italian design, and only made on home soil. It's why Jack was going so nuts with trying to find it as a teen. He'd chosen it on his first trip to Italy with his parents when he was, what, fifteen? Sixteen?"

"Sixteen," mumbled Greg.

Gray nodded. "It was the last holiday you'd all spent together before the real shit over the fights and troubles over the courts really kicked in." Gray took the necklace back, then slipped it into his pocket. "Did Mark Shaw send you those video tapes of Jack and Cutter together when you were in Italy a few months back? Just before he died? A backup plan? And you started buying a few things there for your mind fuck with Vince?" he said quietly. "Mark would have known you: he was the cameraman behind those videos with Cutter, so he knew both Jack and possibly Martin. Take all of that away, though, there's a lot of planning behind this; had you already put the feelers out for guys to 'help sort Jack out' long before Mark got in touch? Is that why April came to know both Greg and Jack? You'd tracked her down, talked to her? And then Keal... he caught wind of it and got in touch with you to 'help out'?"

Nothing came from Elena.

"You would have known about Jack's fugues. Part of his therapy as a teen was getting Jack to recognise Martin, and vice versa with Martin recognising Jack via notes on Jack's part. Of course Martin would never play the game and leave Jack any, but he knew to look for notes; it's why he picked up on Jan's on the bedside table, even now, years later. But you saw the notes over the years too, especially with Jack encouraged to tell Greg and you about Martin, what he knew, what he'd found out in therapy from Martin himself. Although Jack's lost some of that detail over time." He looked at Greg. "Basic care plan, right?" Then he was back with Elena. "Did you get in contact with April just before you asked Greg to meet you at the café, then have him meet April, all so it would be in the CCTV when I looked? That's a hell of a lot of hate there over such a long period of time, not just for Jack, but April, Greg, Jan…. And tell me, what was your occupation before you took over control of one of Greg's garages, and what was the one concern you had when you told me Jack had been sent that message in your DVD of *War of the Worlds*, Elena?"

Something seemed to shrink Greg where he stood. Elena didn't seem fazed in the slightest as she said, "Computer engineer."

"And it really played with your head when Jack smashed the computer in his office, huh?" He snorted. "But there we have it," said Gray, quietly. "Quite the clever old tech-lady that Jack has. Certainly clever enough to set up tech equipment to watch him away from the warehouse, transfer money from one account to another." He still looked as though he was searching for one last detail.

"Funding gets me, though," he said, coolly. "No divorce payment could have given you the backing to do what you've done, April's wages, Vince's, the warehouse itself…. So that means what? You have friends in high places? Very high places, hmmm?" He smiled. "Who are they, Elena? Why is Jack on their radar?"

I'd been watching Gray so fucking closely, and I shifted the moment Gray lost that beautiful blueness to his eyes and that dead black came in. I went in front of him, stopping him going for Elena now it seemed he'd pulled together nearly everything he needed.

"*You had your own boy and his lover raped, you sick fucking cunt? I'll rip your fucking heart in two.*"

"No. Stop-stop-stop, stop," said Greg, stepping in between all of us, his hands raised uselessly against the tides sweeping through. Then his finger levelled on Gray. "You. My house. This is my fucking hou—"

"*Your son*," shouted Gray. "He's *your* fucking son."

"No," Greg said, lowering his hand in defeat. "I…" He shrugged. "I can't play these games, Gray. I can't do this anymore, please—not with Jack, not with him. You—"

"Oh, grow some balls, Greg." The hardness in Elena's tone forced even Greg to turn around. "I sorted him out; I corrected him."

Greg stood there as I let Gray go.

"That's why your voice was altered in the cells when Jan heard you," said Gray, his tone carrying this strange deadness to it. "You couldn't have Jan or Jack recognise you."

Elena snorted. "Oh for… Jack and Jan were never in any *real* danger, stop with the dramatics," she said, picking up a pillow and patting it down. I choked out a reply—just a grunt, or a snort, something to get across the absurdity of what I'd just heard.

"No *real* danger?" I said. "*Your son was fucking repeatedly raped.*" Gray grabbed at my arm. "He was tortured—held down and branded like an animal with a fucking iron." I couldn't get my head around this. "They forced him to lie next to me as they raped him—and you say we… we were in no *real* danger?"

"*My* son?" snapped Elena. "That wasn't *my* anything back there." She looked at the mantelpiece. "*That's* my son." Her lips turned up in a disgusted sneer. "The bastard you know? He's just a thing, a stained and mindless, spoilt *thug.*"

Gray snorted, pulling me out of the way. "You said no real danger." Eyes narrowed. "You knew we'd find Keal, that he'd lead us to Vince," he said. Greg was still staring, not at me or Elena, not Gray, just staring out of the window, lost.

"You found nothing, not until I deemed it necessary," she said. "I switched the bottles to make sure the doctor would overdose the bastard," she said calmly. "I knew once Jack and Jan were split up, attention would fall off Jan. Again, just a switch of bottles. Doc was a buffoon, most men are; it's why I hired him. He was too drunk to tell the difference, and I just helped things along to ensure just that."

Bourbon. The doc had always stunk of bourbon. Jesus fucking Christ.

"Usually I'm paid for contract work," Gray said icily. "Like setting April up, you put out a contract on Vince, Henry, and Keal well before they were all even on the scene."

"It's your job to slaughter dirt like that, or do you need reminding every now and again about the finer details like Jack does? You did your job, well done." She even applauded. "Pick up your certificate on the way out."

"And April Leamore?" said Gray. "Where's her certificate? Where's she?"

"She's corrected." There was coldness there. "Fool her for her and her husband being weak enough to give Jack what he wanted."

Martin. He came on the scene afterwards, to take over and face what was wrong in his waking life. A nurse for his cuts, a nurse for his disorders—but a female nurse? "What the fuck did you do to him, you fuck?" I muttered quietly. "Why the hell would Martin look to find a female fucking nurse?"

"Jack? Nothing. I loved him."

"Yeah?" I grunted. "And when you stopped loving him,

what happened then?"

CHAPTER 44
HEAD GAMES

"THE DIVORCE COULDN'T have been easy." That came from Halliday, disturbing even Gray from staring Elena down. "And before that, Jack—all the fights, seeing him bruised, having him arrange your house in the early hours?" added Halliday.

Elena frowned for the first time.

"His condition only worsened when he met Cutter, correct?" continued Halliday, and it earned a grunt off Elena.

"It's not right, a boy, *my* boy, lying on his back to get hurt, spreading his legs like a slut, all to play a pathetic sub to another."

"You raised Jack tough," said Halliday, and he went to stand, but a signal off Gray told him to stay down. "All that rigid structure with karate, I can see your toughening influence there."

Elena nodded, even smiled. "He was the best in the county for a while, won loads of awards. Nobody would come near him. Not the neighbours. Anyone." No awards lined the wall either, no trophies in bookcases. This had been Jack's home, but, and I think Greg noticed it now too, it wasn't the home of Elena's Jack. Had she taken all of those photos and awards to hers? Greg perhaps agreeing because he knew, maybe he knew deep down Jack was closer to him? "That was when he should have been spoilt, not with, with—"

"Then it started going wrong?" said Halliday, and Elena's smile fell. "Appearances in court," added Halliday. "Battles with the police, the neighbours? Where did the respect go in their eyes? Was it replaced, maybe, with what they now knew about Jack? Where he went night after night, that he liked rough sex, that he would hurt other people just to lie still for Cutter?"

"*He craved one and fed the other,*" she snapped, curling her lips in disgust. "Take away the craving, starve the mental weakness. His disorders overtook our lives."

"Mental *weakness?*" Greg groaned. "You... you think my boy's weak for what goes on in his head?"

"This." She tapped hers. "This is weak, and it's weak because of his craving to be ordered, to be hurt-fucked by other men. It's not right, not normal." Her eyes were hard. "It's *nothing* my quiet boy had when he was growing up."

"And when it did tear him up as a teen?" shouted Greg. "*What did I miss? What did you do to him, Elena?*"

"*I* loved *him.*"

"*Loved* him?" A tear spilled from Greg. "How? Enough to *straighten* his kinks out when he got older? You... you were always there whispering to him it was okay." A tear spilled. "I *heard* you say it was okay."

"He was just a boy," she said flatly. "Of course it was all right—he was supposed to grow out of it."

"And... and when he was lying in hospital," Greg said quietly. "When we got him back, you, you said it then, when he was all battered and burned. You..." He shrugged, gave up. "You whispered everything was okay, that he was going to be okay. Why?"

Elena went over, her gaze never more puzzled. "Because I saw him, I watched him with Vince, all polite, well-mannered, and able to have sex without wanting to be hurt." She lifted one shoulder in half a shrug. "Okay, he looked uncomfortable to start with, but when he called out Vince's name, not Gray's, I knew—I knew he was looking at life normally. Like my boy: waiting nicely, wanting nicely."

Greg looked at her. "You... you *watched* it?" It wasn't a question, just stated; an acknowledgement.

"I *controlled* it," she said flatly. "Men like that needed watching, needed controlling. But Jack... he cried and fought like a thug most of the time, when Vince hurt him, but during the day..." She was smiling again despite a tear. "So sweet, so normal, so quiet." She reached for Greg, but he pushed her hands away. "I controlled him, nothing more," she said quietly. "He needed controlling, Greg. His disorders, they needed correcting properly. Jack, he just needed to know his place in the family." She straightened and her smile was so beautiful, showing everyone here where Jack got his looks from. "We got our boy back. Look how he's been around us lately. So polite at the dinner table, so, so—"

"Hurt," said Greg quietly, almost defeated. "And Jan. Oh my God—Jan." He looked at me. "You..." He was back with Elena. "Just what the hell have you done?"

"Him? Jan's okay." She even waved me off. "Henry barely touched him, just a little roughing up. In fact, I made sure he stayed by Jack as much as possible—"

"We were fucking raped next to each other in what we thought was the safety of Jack's own bed."

Elena raised a brow at me. "Jack's slept in so many beds he barely knows the safety of his own. Don't throw that at me, boy," she said stiffly. "And you, what's all of that done but made sure you won't let Jack be touched in a BDSM scene again? You can help keep his disorders in line."

"And, and Gray?" said Greg, looking at her.

I stiffened slightly and even Elena narrowed her eyes.

"Those tapes were sent to people Jack cared for," Greg snarled through his teeth. "I'm not as stupid as you're making out, Elena. You've known for a long time that Jack's been seeing Gray too—I saw how Gray was in the hospital. Jack went home with him."

"Two boyfriends," snapped Elena. "And you tell me Jack isn't the thug who always gets what he wants, especially because of those disorders?" Elena flicked a look at Gray. "I've been in Jack's home. Through his bedroom drawers. He has BDSM gear in there. I know they're not Jan's, especially when I saw Gray's photo. He's like Cutter; he's a Dom. He's Jack's Dom."

"You've known that for a while, haven't you?" I mumbled. "You found out what Mark Shaw failed to find out. You found out about Gray? What he is to Jack?"

"Keal told me," said Elena. "And where Gray lived. Although I'd have found that out anyway." She couldn't have said that any colder. "You carried on where Cutter left off." Her face creased as she looked at Gray. "You take spoilt little shits and twist them into toys, ones that only want more." She looked so smug. "Well he doesn't want more now, does he?"

Greg looked back at Gray, maybe seeing him for the first time.

Elena gently tapped at her chest. "I stopped it. I made him bett—"

"*He wasn't sick.*" Greg suddenly grabbed her by the hair and pulled her close. "He made wrong choices, got himself involved with the wrong people, but…" Greg looked at Gray for a brief moment, tears streaking his face. "That stopped," he said in Elena's face. "That stopped when he met Gray. And no matter how Gray did it, he stopped Jack from ruining his life."

"*He ties your boy up,*" she shouted just as heatedly, just as much in Greg's face as she pulled him closer. "Keal, he told me. He said Jack opened his legs for a Dom, that he let himself be tied up like an animal, whipped, and fucked. That Jack trained other Doms to do it to other people: men, women—boys like Jack had been, screw with their heads and bodies…"

Greg was shaking his head. "You know nothing about Jack, Elena. How can you not know a thing about our own boy?" Greg pushed her away and wiped at his face. "Cutter twisted his reasoning, poisoned his reactions, and if you tell me he works with Gray to stop other men and women taking advantage of people who show enough trust to allow someone else to tie them up—*then I'm damn fucking proud of him for i—*" Greg choked, automatically smothering his mouth to try and stop it. "He faced it," he said to her, "he faced what Cutter did and gave Cutter the fucking V in doing so, and that—that's Jack. That's *my* Jack. Spoilt thug?" He suddenly sobered up. "*You.*" His fist clenched. "You stand there—nothing but fucking jealous of a boy's disorders and the attention he needed. So you corrected him—by watching him and gentle Jan being *raped and tortured?"*

Gray moved quicker than I did, sweeping in behind Greg and pulling him out of the way, more or less spinning him away as he shifted for Elena. "Don't...." he said, levelling a finger on Greg as Greg glared at him. "How did you intercept the packages? Jan's book was ordered via a private collector, the DVD from a supplier."

Elena said nothing, and Gray narrowed his eyes. "Oh. You weren't responsible for that?" A smile was given. "Who was? How?"

Elena returned his hard stare.

"Back to the people backing you, huh? And if they're powerful enough to hide their financial trail, then they're powerful enough to look inside someone else's, certainly mine, and see where I purchased items. A word in someone's ear here, there, and the parcels themselves are interfered with, maybe before they even leave their destination." Gray's whole mannerism seemed to come alive. "Oh, I really need to see your contact list now."

"You do?" said Elena. "And what the hell are you going to do with them? With me?" she said coldly, maybe even with an added touch of smugness. "I stopped Jack wanting more of you, just how do you think he'll react to you after you tell him you've taken care of me?"

Gray smiled, actually smiled, and it looked quite charming. "As if I'd hurt Jack's old lady." He pulled something out of his back pocket, and Elena jerked back, no doubt expecting a firearm. Instead, Gray stood there typing in numbers into his mobile. After a moment he nodded when the mobile declared he had a message.

"Home Secretary finally learned to text," he said, looking up at Elena. "And under the *Immigration, Asylum and*

Nationality Act 2006, your British Citizenship has now been revoked." He offered her the phone. "You'll be re-arrested on home soil. Now get the fuck out of Jack's life."

Elena, eyes wide, fists clenched, stared at the phone without taking it. "You can't deport me—on what grounds? I've done *nothing* wrong."

Gray shrugged. "Not my problem, I'm afraid. Even I have to listen to politicians at times. But to paraphrase her words: you fuck about with British Nationals, you lose your privileged right to *be* a British National. Which, in general, means that you don't get to download porn concerning underage children onto the 'net, you don't acquire a building to solicit the filming of rape, torture, and captivity, you also don't get to hire rapists, fraternize with suspected sex traders, and use a date-rape drug to psychologically recondition other British Nationals." His smile faded. "But most of all—" He stepped really close. "*You don't* ever *fuck about with what's mine. We clear on that?*"

"Yours?" She raised a brow. "A Master Dom who never collared his sub? Even you hid from his disorders and Martin. Hypocrite."

"Hypocrite?" he said flatly. "For the past eleven years, I've just made the constant mistake of prioritising Jack's disorders over Jack himself, and probably damaged him just as much in the process. But—" Gray went close. "Wearing no collar and given the choice between the bastards, Jack came home to me. And I'll use every last mile you put between us to ensure I find out why."

Elena hit the phone out of his hand. "Here, Italy," she shouted, "Jack will come after *me*."

"You've yet to reach the safety of home shores." Gray raised a brow. "And there are a variety of bastards out there, Ms Fortello. I should know: I've trained a good proportion of them." He smiled. "You keep that heads-up real close."

"You—" Whatever else she went to say was cut short as Gray pushed her back, sending her stumbling to the front door. "Greg—Greg," she shouted as she tried to look back into the lounge. "For godssake, stop this." I grabbed Greg's arm, seeing the tension in his face. "Fucking grow some," Elena added, and every ounce of feeling drained from his face. "All that weakness—*he gets it from you.*"

Someone passed in front of the window, and I guessed that call made earlier had kicked in as the front door was opened and Elena's cries bled outside. Seeing Gray talking to another man, I took hold of Greg's hand and watched how he nearly jumped back from the contact.

"Greg, I think you should sit dow—" He choked the last bit out of me as he threw an arm around my shoulder and pulled me in like nothing more than a piece of broken wood to stay afloat with.

"Jan... for godssake, son. I'm so sorry. I'm so sorry."

"'S okay," I said quietly, although everything felt far from okay. Halliday came over, straightening his jacket but frowning between us as Gray came back in and picked up his phone.

"Apologies, Philip," he said, nodding at Halliday.

Halliday just smiled thinly. "Any time you need a private session, Gray, you let me know. Any time you want sectioning, I'll get the papers signed and sealed." He fell quiet for a moment. "Everything pre-planned, Gray," he said softly. "The psychological evaluation report my department gave, she would have known how to hide any psychological instability."

"You think...?" Greg frowned, winning Halliday's

attention. "I've seen nothing," he said quietly. "I—"

"She's hidden any signs and let you see what you needed to see," said Halliday, and his eyes narrowed, "and over a sustained portion of her life, by the look of things."

Gray smiled thinly, then looked at Greg. "I'm going to have to confiscate all of your computers."

Greg stiffened. "In my home? She... she watched that here?"

"Your internet usage has been checked and watched continuously—"

"What?" said Greg, eyes wide.

"But with Elena's skill, codes could have been encrypted over many months now," said Gray, gently. "I won't know for sure until we've looked at her files. I'll call my department and make the arrangements." He was back with me. "We need to go."

I pushed Greg to arm's length. "Greg, is there anyone I can call? I don't want to leave you alone."

Greg wiped at his nose. "I'm fine."

But Gray was already making a call. "Steve," he said, looking at Greg, "I know it's your day off, but can you come over to Gregory's?" A pause. "Thank you." The mobile was slipped into Gray's pocket. "Philip, can I please ask that you stay here with Gregory until Jack's manager arrives?"

"Yes, yes of course."

Gray nodded his thanks. "Once he arrives, could you make your way to my manor?"

"Jack." That came from Greg. He looked so bloody pale. "Gray, wh-what the hell are you going to tell him?"

"The truth," said Gray, already turning away.

"You can't." Greg forced him to a stop. "For godssake, you can't tell him *this*."

I went over to them and gave Greg a small smile. "He needs the release." With how hard Greg kept shaking his head, I fell quiet.

"I know him," he said, looking at Gray. "Goddammit, Gray, I think you do too. This—this will kill him."

"He's struggled enough—"

"And you think *this*—" Greg swept a hand around his room. "—you think telling him this is going to help right at this moment?" Greg was suddenly very close to Gray. "I love my boy; I love him so fucking much, even though every time he leaves me battered and bruised from the inside out. I've watched him grow up, knowing the pressures and stresses that make him fugue. Telling him this, he won't cope—not family, not this—you know it. You damn well know it. So please, please don't tell him. For me. One thing, just give me this one thing."

Watching Greg, Gray tensed the muscles in his jaw.

"Please," said Greg. "Give me the space to talk to him as my son, when I know he'll cope."

A look at me, Gray turned away, heading for the door and leaving Greg there looking at his feet. I rubbed Greg's arm as I passed and let him know I'd get Jack to give him a call as soon as Halliday had finished talking to him.

CHAPTER 45
MERCEDES,
MERCEDES-FUCKING-BENZ

I CAUGHT UP with Gray as he got in his Mercedes-Benz and slumped in my own seat, just about managing to fasten my belt before I felt the pull of the car. Eyes closing, I rested my head back, no longer able to think beyond the basics of breathing.

"Operatives are heading over to Elena's to check for leads on the whereabouts of April Leamore," mumbled Gray. "I've handed Elena over to one of my team for questioning regarding April too."

"You won't question her?"

"No," he said flatly.

"Because of the personal connection?"

"Because I wouldn't give a fuck about what she has to say, and that won't give any release to April's family."

Clarity over understanding that left me quiet. I wouldn't give a fuck either. "Do you think she's dead?"

"Gut instinct says yes. She's been out of the picture for far too long."

I nodded. "And the people behind the financing of all this?"

"They're my priority."

The tone to that kept me quiet for a while. "Why didn't you get the necklace fixed?" I asked eventually.

There was quiet. "Jack asked me not to," he said. "After I showed it to him, he said he wanted me to have it. That things shouldn't be fixed to hide the screw-ups. And that I should let him have it back if he was ever close to losing himself again."

"And you kept it," I said quietly. The fact that Gray had kept a broken necklace in his safe all these years with more acclaimed possessions on display outside of it said everything.

"You okay?"

Cracking an eye open, I glanced at Gray. "No." I wiped at my eyes. "You?"

Gray shook his head, and I rested down. Life was fucked, fucked up and beyond the point of listening to the shouts for a final time out.

On the ride up to Gray's manor, I noticed the state of the Rolls-Royce before Gray did. Gray's security team were either around it or over by the main manor entrance, where the door stood wide open. Just to the left of that, an office chair lay on the gravel, surrounded by broken glass. The office window lay broken, with cool air gratefully clambering inside. Ray stood cradling his wrist as blood dripped onto the floor, and he stood by the Rolls, his head turned in our direction as Gray pulled the Mercedes to a stop.

"Jesus. What the fuck now?" breathed Gray, already unbuckling his seatbelt. I'd beaten him to it, opening the door and pushing out. The alarm to the Rolls cried hurt into the afternoon, yellow hazard light blinking and more than showing its distress.

Gray headed for his Rolls. "Just what the *fuck's* gone on—?" A touch ran over a broken indicator light.

"Gray." Ray was already over by us, and he held on to a nasty gash on the back of his hand. "You need to get in there," he said quickly.

"What?" said Gray, looking ready to bypass slaughtering someone and just go for burying alive.

"Everything was quiet with Jack for a while. He had some breakfast, then he disappeared into your office—"

"No," breathed Gray, and he was suddenly moving for the manor. "*Where is he now?*"

"*Your new gallery*," shouted Ray as I ran after Gray. We followed the thuds of music and breaking glass and found more security guards closer to the gallery we had set up. Ed stood outside, looking wide-eyed and pale. My first thought must have been the same as Gray's as he instantly stopped by Ed, checking him out for wounds.

"*I'm fine*," shouted Ed. Iron Maiden's "Number of the Beast" drowned out most of what he'd said, but so too did more breaking glass from in the gallery. "*But Jack. Careful, Gray. He's armed. He's got a baseball bat....*"

Gray nodded and looked back at me. I made it to the door as Gray pushed it open and let me pass. The musky smell of sweat hit me first as Iron Maiden threatened my eardrums. Then as Gray came in, heading for the stereo, the wreckage of photo frames, art, torn banners, and broken glass held me still.

Gray cut the music, seemed to stare around at the broken debris of art, then moved for Jack with such bloody speed. Jack was mid-swing of the bat, all aimed at a piece of art that had already taken one hit. Gray slipped his arms around Jack's, almost forcing them behind his back, but Jack seemed to jolt, swear, shrug free—then turned and slammed his elbow into Gray. Gray pulled away at the last minute, but it still caught his jaw.

Nearly losing his footing, Jack laughed, then threw his arms out, baseball bat in hand now he faced Gray.

"Hey, boss. Missed me? Thought I'd help out with the new private exhibition here." He indicated the broken pictures and frames littering the hall. Most had been splintered by the bat—only one lay untouched, and it seemed to steal all of Jack's attention. I remembered when I'd unwrapped that a few months ago. Christ, I'd been stunned by it, how the ropes around Jack's body held him in such a beautifully submissive pose, all his disorders brought to the surface and captured in soft light, me just there in the background, watching.

Giving a cry and burying mine as it nearly choked free, Jack took a swing at the picture and hit dead centre before hardly seeming to take breath—and hit it again.

This time when Gray shifted for him, Jack never saw him coming.

Going with the swing of the bat after it whirled past him, Gray set Jack off-centre with a push at his shoulder, sending him stumbling back into the swing, then grabbed him by the wrist. He moved in close as he forced Jack up against the wall and made sure he dropped the bat. It looked and sounded violent, but Gray had his head resting against Jack's, eyes screwed shut, whispering repeatedly in

Jack's ear.

"I didn't mean for you to see that. Not the branding. Hurts... I know it fucking hurts, stunner," he said to Jack.

Shouting out, Jack bucked under Gray, pushing him back, and glass crunched under Gray's foot as he was forced away.

"Saw the kind of things you've taken to watching lately, mukka."

Jack pulled out the DVD and a notepad. He threw them at Gray's feet. "You get the police to back off too, hmmm? That's DCI Sanders's notebook. I mean, leaves me wondering a few things here, Gray. See Vince? He would have needed a hell of a lot of financial backing for that shit. Not to mention behind-the-scenes knowledge over CCTV setup and *then* the tech people needed to maintain it," said Jack, suddenly looking very calm. "And the only person with that kind of money, with the contacts to set up a scene like that—not to mention being the only one who had issues with me and Cutter—" He smiled. "—is *you*."

"Jack, what?" I took a step closer as Gray frowned.

Head tilting slightly, Jack narrowed his eyes, the grey in them seeming to sparkle in the sunlight that split the broken gallery, throwing everything into abstract... realism. "What was it you said to me when I got out of hospital; you were twisted enough to take me down to get at Cutter?" Jack's voice was a whisper. "I should be fucking flattered really, that you'd go to such extremes. I mean, hiring someone to rape the fuck out of me. Fuck knows, I cried no often enough even Cutter would cover his ears an—"

Gray was up against Jack, making him flinch as he slammed a fist inches from his head. *"You think I did that?"*

Gray grabbed Jack by the throat. "You think I'd fucking hurt *you*—like *that?*"

"*Twice. You beat the shit out of me twice for my screw-ups as a kid,*" Jack shouted back. "*A little too convenient all the shit that came after, don't you fucking think—boss?*"

Gray laughed, then wiped a hand over his mouth. "And you, you think I'm behind it all?"

Jack went very calm. "You never once asked for a witness statement, Gray. Why was that?"

I tried to stop Gray as he pulled his fist back, but I was too slow, and he slammed it into the wall inches from Jack again.

"*I fucking did. But you know what?*" he let rush out. "*It wouldn't have stood up in court. Wanna know why? Because of the drugs you had in your system, because of how they twisted your head—because you're such a fucking headcase with a longer history of being a fucking headcase, you fucker.*"

Something seemed to slip in Jack's eyes, and he lost all the colour heating his cheeks. Gray groaned instantly and went to grab Jack, say a thousand and one sorries, but Jack shoved him away.

Gray nearly lost his footing, crunching glass and broken frame into the wood floor—then cried out.

"Easy," I said quickly, coming between them, my back to Jack, head resting against Gray's. "Mind games." I took hold of Gray's hand, ignoring how slippery it was. Blood stained his knuckles. Christ, that hurt was nothing compared to what was tearing through his eyes. "One serious fucking mind game, Gray; hers," I said warningly in a low voice. "Please. You need to step back, think." But my head and heart were with the debris on the floor with Gray's. Christ, Jack. Not Gray.

I shuddered, then realised Jack had gone quiet. He stood itching at his side and something caught my eye.

"Jack?" I went over and hit his touch away.

Blood covered the tips of his fingers and stained the waistline of his trousers on his right side.

Frowning, I inched his joggers down a touch. The whole area where he'd been branded on his hip was either open wound or scab, the V now lost to a perfect square of a wound, all lined up and angled to perfection with Jack's body.

That couldn't have been scratched out; Jack would have had to have cut it, maybe with a knife, like the butter one that Ed said had gone missing and—

"Oh my God. Jack?" I breathed. Knife... played.

He seemed to shiver, then looked at me, eyes a little distant. "Straightened it," he mumbled quietly. "Needed... wouldn't straighten." A tear slipped free as he looked down and frowned. "Yeah... headcase."

Gray groaned out loud, managing to make a sound where I couldn't, and Jack looked over at him, almost instantly dismissing the wound, or willingly forgetting about it as he let his shirt fall back over it.

"One thing," Jack said as another tear fell. "You said you'd give me one thing, mukka, all I had to do was ask." He shivered. "Why? *Please*, Gray. Why didn't you just let me walk if you hate me that much?"

"I...." Gray frowned, caught somewhere between a promise to a father and keeping the failing love of the son. "You, you need to get the fuck out now, Jack," he said quietly. "You... you need to go, and you..." He sighed heavily, frustration, fear—grief. "I'd never hurt you: you need to know I'd never…." He gave up then; I saw it in his eyes. "You and your old man, you need each other now. You don't need me. You don't need this."

As Jack frowned, Gray came in and ran a light touch over Jack's hip. "Fuck. You're so lost, stunner." Gray shifted slightly, screwing his eyes shut. "Please. Leave me alone. It hurts too much, so fucking much now, Jack. Mercedes. Mercedes-fucking-Benz. *Please.*" He took a step back after he'd slipped something into Jack's hand, put some distance between them. "*Ed.*"

Ed came through a minute later as Jack looked down.

"Phone Gregory, please. Tell him…" Gray frowned. "Tell him Jack needs looking after." And he glanced at me. "You have to decide for yourself, Jan. I'm not going to tell you what to do here, but if you walk too, it'll put so much strain on you with what you've been through. Jack needs professional help; I can't give him that." He snorted a smile, gave a half-hearted shrug—let a tear finally slip free. "I… I don't even know where to start with all this."

I went in close to Gray, gripping his jaw, kissing his lips. "I'm here for all of us, because it's so goddamn hard on all of us now. If you need time away, take it. But don't shut the door. That will hurt more. I'm here with him for as long you need."

Closing his eyes, Gray nodded, head now resting against mine, but his eyes had said it all. He was out. "For God's sake look after him, please." A hand came to my neck, stroking gently. "I can't do this anymore."

"Yeah," I whispered heatedly, wiping at his cheek. "I know. I know."

"Slow and gentle," Gray whispered quietly, and I could feel him breaking, the shaking going on under his touch.

"Hold him tight; keep him close, even when he's pushing against it and crying he can't take it—you hold him fucking close. You're damn tougher than you realise." He shifted his stance slightly, coming in so close. "I wouldn't let anyone else get fucking close to him but you, you know that. I wouldn't trust anyone else but you with him. You fucking know that, Jan."

I took a step back, wiped a hand over my mouth to strangle the grief into silence, then nodded.

Jack was looking down at what he held. The necklace, all its black cross atop of a silver one. He was lost, so bloody lost, and that was Gray letting him know it and calling enough where words could be, and were, easily forgotten in Jack's world.

When Jack looked up, it was at me. "Somewhere along the line you fell in love with him, didn't you?" he said quietly, barely glancing at Gray. Then back at me—"*What the fuck is wrong with you?*"

I ignored all of Jack's fire. "Yeah," I mumbled quietly. For all of his Jack-related faults and flaws—"I love him." Thing is, I didn't realise I did until that moment.

"Right." The necklace briefly took Jack's attention, and his look was so fucking confused as he looked up. Life didn't seem any clearer for him. "My things. Yeah? I'll…" Jack glanced at me, shrugging a touch, not knowing where this would take him or what to do about it. "I'll just go and get changed." Giving a rub at his head, a look at me as a tear fell, Jack didn't move, just shrugged again.

After going over, I rested cheek to cheek, hating that he jerked away. I pulled him back, holding him, half wanting to hit the life out of him for what he was doing to Gray, the other half needing to inject life back into him to stop what he was doing to us all. Ease his head, his heart, those goddamn fists. "Changed," I mumbled. "Get you some fresh clothes, yeah, baby?"

He didn't respond at first, and I knew his look was on Gray over my shoulder. He mirrored Gray's shaking, all the history that splintered between them. Maybe something was trying to shake free, those first few cold breaths without Gray by his side sparking the need to find warmth, to find reason in why his body wasn't capable of reacting and stopping this fallout. There just wasn't enough of the spark to go around, and he stopped shivering, flat-lining out. I could almost feel him scurrying back into whatever broken reality he'd built up around himself.

"Clothes," he said flatly. "Need to get changed. Out." And he made a point of picking up DCI Sanders's notepad and the DVD of the branding, the wariness in his eyes saying exactly where "out" would take him and his "evidence".

Letting him go, I watched him leave, just head out of the gallery, never more aware of the people who moved out of his way and gave him a wide berth.

"You understand what Halliday will do with him?"

I looked back at Gray, hearing him speak. Ed had edged a little closer to him, but Gray himself looked unable to move.

I nodded. Halliday was MC, and all of this… I knew where it had landed Jack. I didn't think Jack did, not yet.

"Whatever help he needs…" Gray shrugged. "I'll pay for everything. And safety… you'll be under full surveillance protection from the MC. You don't worry about safety, not yours, not his. Ever."

I went to speak, but Ed shook his head. "Jan," he said quietly, "I need you to leave us alone now, okay?" He smiled back, but it couldn't have been more haunted. "I'll phone Gregory and ask him and Doctor Halliday to come over and get you two, just please give me time with mine now." And there it was: the wish of a grandfather protecting his grandson. Lines drawn, but sometimes they needed to be when it got too much.

I gave him a nod, then looked at Gray. "It doesn't heal," I said gently. "It just gets better." I glanced behind at Jack's fading footsteps, then Gray had every part of me. "When the hurt starts to ease," I said to him, "you come and find me. If you don't, when Jack's hurt starts to fade, I'll make damn sure he comes and finds you. This isn't over."

I turned away as Ed went over to Gray and eased an arm around him, drawing him in close. There didn't seem any fight there, and that was one thing I couldn't look back and see for too long.

Gray had always had the fight. That had been the one constant. Elena had won. Damn her to hell. She'd won.

JACK L. PYKE

CHAPTER 46
AFTER GRAY

Jan Richards
Five months later

FRAMED BY THE shadow of the doorway, Gray waited with his keys in hand, head turned slightly towards the exit, towards his black Mercedes-Benz. The manor was packed up, the removal trucks having taken all of his private possessions. He hadn't called me. Being here was pure luck on my part. A visit from Trace from over in America this morning at Jack's new apartment had made sure that I'd caught the morning paper today, how a manor had been put for sale. Going by the location, the mention of Welsh family heritage, it hadn't been hard to figure out the rest. On my way over, I'd called to start off with, leaving a message for Gray to pick up, but it had gone unanswered. I hadn't been the only one calling him over the last few months: Jack had too, but like mine, his calls, from what Jack had told me, went unanswered as well.

I'd come here more than a little fired up with how final

Gray had made the break. No contact, nothing to see how Jack was doing under Halliday's care. It had been the hardest time of our lives, worse than facing Vince. Jack had hidden away from life, but mostly from himself with what Halliday had made him face. He'd called Gray a few times from the MC psychiatric unit, just to talk, but each call had been met with silence, Gray more than standing firm and hard behind his decision.

It had hurt Jack like hell, and he'd eventually stopped calling both of us for a while, going back into hiding with Halliday. I'd hated how Gray was prepared to let him.

Yet when Ed had let me into the manor a few hours ago and I'd bypassed the mail, seeing Jack's letter of resignation from the MC, but also the list of messages, most of the fire had disappeared. I knew Jack had resigned as Master sub and it must have cut so deep with Gray. But his blackouts over BDSM equipment were something that wasn't going to go away anytime soon. Ed had bypassed the letter, instead pressing play on the answering machine, and Jack's voice had come over, the first few calls marking just how bad life had been for him for a while. Gray had kept them all. And for the past five months, when Jack's calls had come in, I knew he'd stood exactly where I had, listening to each one, maybe playing the calls back, just listening. My call was the last, still stored, but like the others, unanswered. The one before had let Gray know that Jack was out of the unit, and as though he'd been waiting to hear life was a little easier for us both, he'd started to finish packing his life away.

Up until a few hours ago, I would have had the will to ask Gray to stay, used all the will in the world I had to keep him close, maybe show some of my own weakness and run with how I needed his comfort now, not just Jack's, because I missed them both so bloody much and I hated how I'd been left out in the cold. Left to deal with it all on my own.

That was only partly true, I knew that. Gray had kept to his word of providing security. I hadn't been able to go anywhere without feeling the presence of a black Merc or catching the familiar sleek design slip around the corner and park up as I pulled on to my drive. Cameras had been re-installed, Mike taking me through all of the security, making sure the designs weren't similar to Vince's, that there were no red lights, but plenty of panic buttons. Jack hadn't needed them, not with where he'd been, and the only time I'd felt like hitting them myself was when Gregory had come over. He'd been doing that more frequently towards the end, sometimes asking after Jack, most times just sitting, just staring. That had been hard to see, that same drug-induced stare of Jack's there in his father's eyes.

I'd hid from everything for a while myself despite Halliday's care, not wanting to see, not wanting to live and flow with humanity. Most appointments had been missed, but I doubted most noticed. I hadn't wanted them to. Not being seen... I'd just wanted to not be seen for the longest time.

Yet the hardest had come today.

If anyone had suggested that a year after meeting Jack I'd be in Gray's hall, Gray close to one exit, looking desperately for a way out even if that meant packing up his whole life and pushing feeling away, I'd have broken my council-bred skill of running away and smacked them one for thinking the three of us wouldn't last the year, let alone the distance. All that feeling, that passion, hell, just the ease in smiles between us was gone.

I looked down at the keys in my hand.

Gray had done what he always did with anything that hurt him emotionally: packaged everything up, taped it firmly out of sight, and pushed it to such a distance moving had been the last and final option for him. There were too many memories for him here, too many thoughts, too many nights of holding Jack. And no matter his feelings as a formal MC Master Dom, it didn't take away the hurt of being a lover, of losing a lover and being left with nothing but an empty bed and home.

Everybody had their own ways with coping, both Gray and Jack. I was still struggling to find mine. Or maybe lingering here around Gray, needing him to stay, to see me, *was* mine.

The jingle of keys came, and I looked up as Gray glanced around his hall with a smile. We'd stood here a few months back, discussing *The Bard* painting, and it seemed like different people, easier times. Now all the paintings were gone, taking with them all life. Turning the clock back wasn't an option anymore; it was there, written in Gray's soft smile.

"I hope the new owners have better luck with her."

Something in that made me smile sadly. "You call all your homes a 'she'?"

Gray looked over at me, then smiled down at his keys. Yeah, it was still close how Jack had preferred to call an inanimate "this fuckable" a "he". When Gray looked back, I started to say something. It was there, the need to make him unpack all of his paintings, just sit, talk about the last Welsh Bard as he jumped to his suicide, but it would only be a bad reminder for him. A worse reminder for me and my secrets lately. Love was there, but we were nothing more than representations of different periodic ghosts:

bodies unable to react together because we came from different walks of life, different times, ones that needed a living, loving host to make us drop the haunting and allow us to love. He saw that too, which is why he let his gaze fall from mine, and no talk filtered into the hall on either part.

A disgruntled sigh, Gray held the hall door open, and I went over, pausing by him for a second just to brush his hand with mine. He caught my finger, and we stayed like that, locked.

After a moment he let go and brushed a hand against my cheek. "Thank you for not forcing this, Jan. It was good just to be seen for a while. Nothing more. But it was good to see you too."

I nodded, still wanting to cry no against the injustice of it all. Any future relationships would be tainted now. Nothing would come close to this. But then again, I also never wanted to allow a relationship to be this intense again. It was right to call a stop. Gray was right to *call* a stop, my head told me that. But my head wasn't the problem here.

I kissed gently at his cheek and Gray turned into it, brushing against my lips.

No, heads weren't the problem here.

He was the first to pull away, and I nodded, moving past him and heading through to where Jack had thrown his car keys at Gray all those months back. They were still there on the table too, something else Jack hadn't needed lately. Ed stood at the bottom of the stairs, looking lost in the emptiness of the old manor. He stood holding on to the banister, maybe knowing if he let go, that would be it: the final move. Yet his eyes were still all for Gray, and he let go the moment he saw him.

"All furniture has either been moved back to Wales or

stored at the MC base until needed," said Ed, and Gray nodded a small smile as he made his way to the door. A final goodbye to me, a nod that seemed to ask quietly if I could change Gray's mind, Ed wandered back into the mansion, no doubt to do final checks of his own with the removal van still waiting out the back.

Gray held the door open, and I smiled down as I made my way past. Jack had taken a lot from Gray, including his manners: the simple gesture of holding a door open for someone saying so much. Yet Gray had taken his aggressive protection of family from Ed. That was never clearer now either.

"Can you make sure he gets his keys?" he said as we made our way over the courtyard. My Mercedes huddled next to Gray's, Jack's stored away over at the MC, and I was about to nod when a soft noise made me look back over my shoulder.

Music played in the distance, just gentle in the heat of the summer night, disturbing the darkness at the back of the manor.

Now catching on to it, Gray frowned, Jack's keys already going in his back pocket as he took his gun out from under his jacket and made his way over. I followed, but if there was a thief trying to steal his way in back there, they were doing a lousy job of being stealthy. As we rounded the back of the mansion, past the swimming pool, through the tennis courts, a string of lights led the way into Gray's maze, the trail of music doing a lousy job of giving away position.

We followed both through the twists and turns, Gray knowing the shortcuts, his gun now at his side, showing how much tolerance he had even for a lousy thief. But as we found the centre and stepped through, the music now a little louder, sending a soft pulse deep into my chest, Gray went still seeing who danced barefoot in the soft light.

~

Jack Harrison

I didn't expect Gray to be happy seeing me here. Fuck knows, give me a mirror, and I'd nut the bastard for showing me my unhappy ass. But this place, these two men...

I fucking loved it here.

Everything it represented, what it meant, all the history it covered. My head walked a path of its own at times, leaving me with blurred edges trying to figure out the route it took without me, and I'd lost just how special this place was, how special these two people were. Somewhere along the line, that had all been fucked up.

"Jack?"

As Jan spoke and came closer, I went over, cupped the back of his neck, and pulled him in, tonguing him deep, keeping an eye on Gray as he stood over by the exit.

Jan went to say something, but I shook my head, glancing at him briefly. "I know you're going nowhere, soft lad, and I owe you so much for that. But now, I'm here for him." Taking Jan by the cuff of the shirt, I pulled him behind me, then went over to Gray. I couldn't meet his eyes, the fuck I couldn't meet his eyes. Talking to him would be the hardest, I'd known that, and I was hoping this place.... I looked around us. I hoped that this place would translate something, most of the words I always had difficulty speaking around him.

He'd tucked his gun out of sight, but I'd caught that he'd held it: nothing more to him than a thief caught trespassing in the night. Giving a gentle stroke with the back of my hand to his, I caught a finger. The single touch triggered a barrage of emotion, and I moved in so fucking quickly to rest cheek to cheek with him, needing to feel him on me instead of just *remembering* how good he felt against my skin. Giving a slight shift, just a gentle nudge at his jaw with my nose, I needed to see if he'd respond, shift, allow me access to his throat—to him—even if it was just as an MI5 operative to a teenage thug asking for his protection.

He never moved.

I hadn't done emotion, not even with Doc Halliday—okay, slight lie there, I knew, but I hated how Gray's denial of me stirred it. But then Gray being pissed with me always had knocked the life out of me. I stepped back, wiping a hand over my face.

"I lied," I whispered quietly, heart falling as I looked around. "I said I'd do the bastard, always." I finally looked at him. "When all that really mattered was the man."

Still nothing, and I shrugged. "Gray, I'm not here to apologise for fucking up your world. I know I have; I probably always will." A smile touched my lips. "But do you remember this place? We stood here, that first night I met Brennan ten years ago?"

He didn't answer; I didn't expect him to.

"Friday night," I said quietly. "You were hosting some charity event, and I'd hated how the manor was so fucking full of stiffs in penguin suits. So I stole a portable stereo, that one over there, in fact." I pointed behind me. "Also some champagne, and left some cheese dotted about the place so I wouldn't get lost when I came here." I looked around the centre of the maze. "Brennan found me first, just watching as I made a prat of myself dancing; then you, you came in through there." The exit stood behind him. "Dark grey suit, one hand casually in your pocket." I let a smile ghost my lips. "I remember thinking then, 'Fuck me, I could do casual for the rest of my life.'"

I took something from my pocket and smiled down at it. The photo of Gray. I'd only been able to pick it up recently. Easing out a long breath, I let it fall casual on the floor. "I never even made the connection until Halliday asked me to remember: between you looking casual and me using casual to calm life all these years." Frowning, I looked up at him. Back locked away in the MC psychiatric unit, there was so much more to that, but nothing that needed mentioning here. "Pack all of your things away, it won't take away how much you've calmed my whole fucking existence through these years. How you will continue to calm it whether you're here or miles away in Wales, because I know that's where you're heading, mukka. It's where you always head when life hits hard."

Gray stayed quiet, his gaze on me, not looking at the photo. "What has your dad told you, Jack?"

I shrugged. "I know it wasn't you, is that enough?" I found that blueness in his eyes. "Please?"

"You still can't open up to me," he said flatly.

"No: I can't climb into my head and order thoughts as easily as I do my sock drawer. It's not about talking to you, not yet, it's about pace." I gave that shrug again. "I wanted normal so fucking badly after what happened, Gray. I worked at the garage, fixing engines, thinking each one I did was one more step away from what happened, one more step closer to normality, one more—" I gave a hard sigh. "One more step closer to Ed being pissed with me again, not haunting my shadow with that sad-ass look in his eyes. But it was all just another compulsion, another way to force order in the chaos, and I didn't fucking see it. I should have fucking seen it, I—" I stopped the anger there.

"And now?"

"Slow and gentle," I said quietly, and I offered a shy smile. "You, Jan… Halliday, you have a lot in common. But it's not about keeping anything from anyone. And that's something I need to explain to Jan, because Christ knows I've put him through hell the past five months too." I gave a sad smile. "But I think he understands; I think it's why you left him with me: you knew we needed each other despite how much I fuck up relationships along the way."

"And your hip?" Gray reached for me, but I instantly backed off, hiding it with my hand. Gray eased off almost in the same instant.

"Slower, easier," I warned quietly. "There's no magic cure. You know that more than anyone, Gray."

"So you resigned from the MC," he said angrily, followed by a hard sigh, as if trying to stop all that hurt showing.

He needed it to hurt, and it forced me in close—I grabbed around his neck, pulling him in hard, just fucking held on as I roughed his cheek with a kiss.

"*Not from you. Never from fucking you,*" I whispered heatedly in his ear. "I got it wrong, so fucking wrong, Gray. I know I hurt you—but like fuck will I ever apologise for it." I gripped his hair, forcing him to wince. "This? It's such a good fucking hurt: it's us. It's the most fucking intense I've ever known: no kink, no chains, no restraint—just every goddamn ounce of right that comes with touching you. We both fuck up so badly because of it, but we're at our best lost in it too."

Yeah, that hurt was on full display in Gray's eyes, but he resisted falling into the touch. "Go back to the night we stood here with Brennan," he said in such a hard tone. "I wish to God I'd just admitted how much I loved the ghost I brought home. You'd haunt my home of a night. Tracing the walls by moonlight, you made everything of mine familiar under such a light touch." More anger ruled his eyes now. "I fucking loved how you mapped out every single part of my life as yours. Marking... claiming...."

Frowning, that rough grip still in his hair, I stroked at his cheek.

"I wanted you to wear my collar so fucking badly, Jack. My simple thank you, but also the need to show that you'd allowed me to map and mark my presence in your life, keep you there for when I came home. You've got no idea how fucking much I've needed you there every time I came home, stunner."

"I'm here now," I said quietly. "Might take me a while, but I get there eventually." I nudged his cheek, asking him to look at me, but he still wouldn't respond. "Might take me a while longer, but I'll get there eventually."

"Fucking hurts, Jack."

"Yeah." After taking something else from my pocket, I slipped it into his hand. "You're lost now, mukka. Let me take the walk back with you. Christ knows I know the way blindfolded and better than anyone."

And there it was: hurt broke as my necklace sat in his hand.

A nudge came against my jaw: a quiet ask for permission to touch. I let him, shaking like fuck knowing this was Gray's touch. His hold came with so much more beyond the Dom, beyond MI5 that had most subs knowing this

Dom wasn't right, and he could and would hurt beyond any safety guidelines found in the lifestyle. But I wasn't exactly… right as a sub either. We both had a dark side to life we didn't show often, so we slotted perfectly together: mind, soul, but mostly in fear and hurt over losing each other. I hadn't done touch yet, not even with Jan, and Gray seemed to sense it, keeping his touch light, but his ask for our touch offered to lick wounds together, as Dom and sub, where fuck-ups were dealt with, then let go in order to move forward.

But forward… we *would* move forward now. Maybe.

"Jan…" I said gently, kissing Gray's cheek, "smart bastard that he is, he had it right all along, huh?"

Gray looked so confused as I let my lips hover close to his.

"Just take what you hold and run the fuck away from any trouble." A tear slipped free. My own. "If it means me getting one leg, Jan the other, I'll damn well make sure I take you with us this time, run the fuck into the woods until we're ready to get back into life. And if anyone tries to get close to either of you along the way, I'll break a few fingers and post them back to each member of their family for it."

"Slightly twisted there, Jack," mumbled Gray.

"Yeah?" I whispered, gently kissing his cheek at the tear that slipped free, wanting to soak up his hurt. "It's been known, baby. But the Master reins him in when it matters." I closed my eyes, held on a little tighter. "And if you see that Master along the way, help me pin him down, kiss the fuck out of him, and just let him know how much I fucking love him."

His hold came, a slip of hands to waist, soaking up hurt

as it coated me, but also wanting to hide in his own. "And if he still says no?"

I gave a sad smile and kissed at his jaw. "Then just remind him I know where he keeps the key to his chloroform cupboard at the MC, and I come with friends."

Jan came over and I pulled him close. "Of course I mean Steve, because Jan here, well—" I tried a smile. "—you know he's not one for manual labour. Although the way his head is, he'd make a fantastic psychologist."

"I am here, you know, and I'm taking note of everything you say," said Jan, smiling a little, hurt more evident in his eyes as he kissed at Gray's cheek. Yeah, he'd fallen in love with him somewhere along the way, and I'd missed all the signals. That somehow hurt more than what Vince had done.

"Great. Add more to my shit list there, things, why don't you?" I said.

Jan came in hard, fast, his kiss nearly cutting my lips. "If it gets you to call me that again, fuck yes," he said heatedly. "Always, baby."

I returned it for a moment, breaking off when Halliday's tricks of the psychotic trade kicked in with Jan's cologne, even though I knew Jan had changed it. "That just leaves big badass Dom here." I looked at Gray. "You?"

Looking around the maze, he gave a sniff. "Ed—"

"Fuck no." I groaned. "Three in a bed is enough for me. The butler gets the dog basket in the kitchen."

"He's my grandfather, Jack."

Jan's smile faded, and it matched my own. "You're not bullshitting, are you?"

Gray shook his head slowly. "No secrets, Jack. We do this, we do it slow, gentle, but most scars open."

Most? Frowning, I gave a sniff. "Your granddad, huh?"

Gray raised a brow, nodded.

"Most scars open?

Narrowing his eyes, Gray nodded again.

"A twelve-year one that you could have told me at any time and not let me make a fuck out of myself?"

"One you could have asked about at any time."

Looking around the maze, I shrugged. "Yeah, well, still hate the old bas—"

"*Jack*," said Jan, pulling me in close. "Digging your grave with two shovels. Shut the fuck up and kiss Gray. He needs it."

Looking at Gray, I cupped his neck and pulled him in. "Needs it, huh? But will he allow it?"

Gray's brush of lips against mine was gentle. No conversation needed when words were still tough to voice. "Your pace, Jan's—"

I rested my head against his, Jan still caught somewhere in between us. "Ours," I said quietly, closing my eyes for a brief moment. "All the fuck-ups that might come with it." Jan's dampness was on my throat as we kept him close. He'd been so damn quiet over the past five months, and just what had gone on with him kept Gray's hold as quiet too. "Still hate Ed, though," I mumbled to Gray, and he screwed his eyes shut and let a wry smile creep up.

"Yeah. Somehow thought you might, stunner."

FINAL THOUGHTS &
ABOUT THE AUTHOR

THANK YOU! If after all of that you're still with me: thank you!! This really isn't an easy series to read, but then it wouldn't be a psychological thriller if it wasn't. The next in the series is *Breakdown* (Don't... Book 3), and we get to see the missing months of Jack's life in the psychiatric unit, but more than that—we get to see how Martin emerges and just what happened when he first met Gray!

And Martin and Jack. Wow. They're one hell of a wild mix of personalities!

I love hearing from readers and appreciate any thoughts you have. Authors also survive on reviews, so if you'd like to leave a review at your favourite sites, that would be... stunning!! If you'd like to check out any of my other novels, please follow the link to my website. Visit Jack at: http://jacklpyke.com.

Love always,
Jack

Jack L. Pyke blames her dark writing influences on living close to one of England's finest forests. Having grown up hearing a history of kidnappings, murders, strange sightings, and sexual exploits her neck of the woods is renowned for, Jack takes that into her writing, having also learned that human coping strategies for intense situations can sometimes make the best of people have disastrously bad moments. Redeeming those flaws is Jack's drive, and if that drive just happens to lead to sexual tension between two or more guys, Jack's the first to let nature take its course.

ALSO BY JACK L. PYKE

DON'T... SERIES
Don't... (Book 1)
Antidote (Don't... book 2)
Breakdown (Don't... book 3)
Backlash (Don't... book 4)
Ash (Don't... book 4.5)
Psychopaths & Sinners (Don't... book 5)
Fractured (Don't... book 6)

NOVELS
Broken Ink

NOVELLAS
Lost in the Echo
Shaded Chains

ANTHOLOGIES
Being Me
Love is Love

Made in United States
Troutdale, OR
07/14/2023